THE CREST OF THE BROKEN WAVE

THE CREST OF THE BROKEN WAVE

*A Novel of
the Life and Loves
of
Robert Burns*

by

JAMES BARKE

COLLINS ST. JAMES'S PLACE LONDON
1953

PRINTED IN GREAT BRITAIN
COLLINS CLEAR-TYPE PRESS: LONDON AND GLASGOW
1953

THE WIND THAT SHAKES THE BARLEY
THE SONG IN THE GREEN THORN TREE
THE WONDER OF ALL THE GAY WORLD
THE CREST OF THE BROKEN WAVE

In preparation
THE WELL OF THE SILENT HARP

*These novels when completed will
form a work to be entitled*

IMMORTAL MEMORY

NOTE

THE ELLISLAND period, 1788-1791, has been of conflicting interest to Burns biographers. But it was here that Burns reached the crest of his wave and here that the wave broke under him. The biographers, however, have been unanimous in admitting the fact that they know little or nothing about Helen Anne Park. But the poisoned-pen gossip-mongers of Burns literature have been assiduous in libelling Burns (the characteristic of their unsavoury commerce) by inventing in her place a barmaid who was vulgar and blowsy and if not a common public-house whore at least an accommodating light-o'-skirts who was generous and indiscriminate with her favours. That such a gentlemanly version of feminine frailty bears any resemblance to the Anna Park of history hardly merits correction but for the fact that, by implication, it makes Jean Armour Burns a dim-witted dupe and Robert Burns something very much worse. With the morality of the Anna Park affair I can, as novelist, have no personal concern. But I welcome the privilege of restoring Anna to the lineaments so decisively specified by her lover.

In connection with *Tam o' Shanter* (the "pretty tale" of Captain Grose's *Antiquities*) it would be unpardonable, at this late date, to condone the deletions made at the behest of Edinburgh gentility. The Grose version has, therefore, been treated with the respect it demands.

It is a pleasant duty to acknowledge the kindness of Professor Robert T. Fitzhugh for providing the transcript

7

of Ainslie's letter to Mrs. MacLehose; nor is it less pleasant to acknowledge with gratitude the unfailing kindness and efficiency of Mrs. M. D. McLean of the Ewart Library, Dumfries.

J.B.,

Daljarrock, Ayrshire,

1st May, 1952.

CONTENTS

Part One

THE ELBOW OF EXISTENCE

Part Two

THE YEAR THE BASTILLE FELL

Part Three

THE TAVERN IN THE TOWN

CHARACTERS

in their order of appearance

(Fictional characters are printed in *Italics*)

ROBERT BURNS.
ROBERT RIDDELL, Squire of Friars Carse.
MRS. ELIZABETH KENNEDY, wife to Robert Riddell.
JEAN ARMOUR BURNS.
GILBERT BURNS, brother of Robert, Mossgiel.
DAVID NEWALL, lawyer, the Isle and Dumfries.
MRS. AGNES MacLEHOSE, Edinburgh.
WILLIAM BURNS, brother of Robert.
ALEXANDER (Lang Sandy) WOOD, surgeon, Edinburgh.
WILLIAM NICOL, teacher, Edinburgh.
ALEXANDER CUNNINGHAM, lawyer, Edinburgh.
ALLAN MASTERTON, writing master, Edinburgh.
WILLIAM CRUIKSHANK, teacher, Edinburgh.
ROBERT AINSLIE, lawyer, Edinburgh.
WILLIAM SMELLIE, printer, Edinburgh.
WILLIAM CREECH, bookseller, Edinburgh.
JENNY CLOW, maid-servant, Edinburgh.
LANDLADY, The George Inn, Haddington.
AGNES (Nancy) BURNS, sister of Robert.
THOMAS BOYD, architect, Dumfries.
MRS. WILLIAM MUIR, The Mill, Tarbolton.
FANNY BURNES, cousin of Robert, Ellisland.
JAMES ARMOUR, mason, Machlin and Dalswinton.
ADAM ARMOUR, mason, Machlin and Dalswinton.
FRANCIS GROSE, author-antiquarian, London.
FRANCIS WALLACE BURNS, second son of Robert.
MRS. AGNES BURNS, mother of Robert.
ROBERT BURNS, first son of Robert.

DR. JAMES MUNDELL, physician and mill-owner, Dumfries.

JOHN MITCHELL, Collector of Excise, Dumfries.

GEORGE S. SUTHERLAND, actor-manager, Dumfries.

PATRICK MILLER, Dalswinton and Edinburgh.

JEAN LINDSAY, wife to Patrick Miller.

JOHN SYME, laird of Barncailzie.

WILLIAM and ELIZABETH HYSLOP, the Globe Inn, Dumfries.

ANNA PARK, niece of Elizabeth Hyslop.

MEG HALLIDAY, the Jerusalem Tavern, Dumfries.

WALTER AULD, saddler, Dumfries.

NELLY ARMOUR, sister of Jean.

JANET LITTLE, Mrs. Dunlop's milkmaid, Dunlop.

WILLIAM NICOL BURNS, third son of Robert.

ELIZABETH, daughter of Anna Park.

WILLIAM LORIMER, farmer-merchant, Kemys Hall.

MARY CARSON, wife to William Lorimer.

JEAN LORIMER, daughter, Kemys Hall.

JEAN BRECKENRIDGE, wife to Gilbert Burns.

WILLIAM AULD, Machlin Parish minister.

ANNABELLA, sister of Robert.

ISABELLA, sister of Robert.

JAMES ARMOUR, mason and wright, Machlin.

MARY SMITH, wife to James Armour.

JOHN RANKINE, farmer of Adamhill.

ANNIE RANKINE, wife to John Merry, New Cumnock.

WILLIAM STEWART, factor, Closeburn.

' *Searching auld wives' barrels,*
   Ochon, the day
That clarty barm should stain my laurels;
   But—what'll ye say?
These movin' things ca'd wives an' weans
Wad move the very heart o' stanes.'

"An Extemporaneous Effusion
on Being Appointed to the Excise."
ROBERT BURNS

Part One

THE ELBOW OF EXISTENCE

IN LONELY BOUNDS

THE roads were deeply rutted and pot-holed. The two carts juddered and creaked and lumbered on their journey. The light Galloway ponies sweated and snorted. The carter, holding the bridle of the leading horse, encouraged it with soft reassuring words. He too sweated; and sometimes he groaned, for it was his third rake that day and he had tramped close on twenty miles. It was four miles from his farm at Ellisland to the Closeburn lime kilns.

His throat was raw and dry. His eyes were red from shovelling the lime into the carts—especially in the high wind.

He had crossed the bridge spanning the river Nith at Auldgirth and was on his last mile home when a carriage approached. He drew the beasts into the side of the road and halted them. The road was too narrow to do otherwise; and the carriage had the right of way.

He took the opportunity to wipe the sweat from his face: he was too tired to bother about the occupants of the carriage.

But Captain Robert Riddell, the owner and occupant of the carriage, had more leisure to be observant. When he had slowly passed the stationary carts he turned to his wife and said: "That—or I be mistaken—was Robert Burns."

"Carting lime?"

"He's building a new farm-house—as he told us."

"Must he do his own carting?"

"Must—or he wouldna be doing it."

Mrs. Riddell shrugged the subject into dismissal and pressed the back of one kid-gloved hand into the palm of the other. Morning and night her husband's breath smelled abominably of alcohol.

The Friars Carse carriage gathered some speed once it had

passed the lime carts. The Bard jogged his leading horse forward with a grunt of irritation. Carriages . . . The gentry. . .

His irritation was momentary. He was driving on with his farm work. He had need to drive. He must urge the builders to finish his new Ellisland home before the rigours of winter set in. He must get Jean down from Machlin. . .

Rain came blustering across from the bare Dunscore hills. It was a cold drenching autumnal rain. It squalled over them. . .

Soon the wind died; but the rain descended mercilessly, soaking man and beast. The roads were running gutters and the pot-holes became dirty dubs of rain and glaur.

The Galloway ponies plodded forward stoically and maybe with a sense of relief. Maybe there was some relief in the rain running down their steaming sweaty hides. The Bard was as stoical as his horses. It was his last journey for the day. Against the morrow his sodden clothes would have to be dried before the fire. This meant more reek filling David Cullie's spence where he lodged. But he had been reared to stoicism. Many a hundred days and a hundred again, year in and year out, he had laboured and trachled in bog and mire.

Aye; and if but lately he had trodden the plainstanes and the causeways of Auld Reekie as the wonder of all the gay world—that had been but an aside from the tenor of his rustic ways.

After two years of enforced idleness in Edinburgh he was back where he had first come to adolescent consciousness: in Mount Oliphant. The scene had changed; but the routine was the same. He was thirled to beasts and ploughs, carts and harrows; to sowing and reaping and all the endless drudgery of barn and byre, crops and weather, infield and outfield.

Less than at any time in his life did he feel like the tasks that lay before him. Less than at any time in his young life was he fitted for his heavy manual labour. His hands had blistered and burst and healed and blistered again. His fine white hands and immaculate nails from his Edinburgh days were calloused and the nails were broken. . .

More than his nails were broken. But he did not at the moment allow himself the luxury of indulgent introspection. Maybe to-night, when he would be lying down in the smoke-spewn spence of David Cullie, damp and draughty, he might allow himself some measure of introspection. But at the moment he was stoical. There was a job to be done. Rain, however incessant, had to be accepted. The lime had to be unloaded near the site of his farm-house-to-be. Then he might hand over the Galloway ponies to be groomed down with a bunch of straw and given their bite. Or maybe he would be better to do the job himself. Hired labour was not always to be trusted; and he did not want to run the risk of his ponies going down with a chill.

Afterwards he could see about his own miserable bite. Then he would throw off his wet seeping lime-impregnated clothes. Then he might, if he had any energy left, write an odd letter or two or read some of his correspondence or even peruse a passage from a favourite author. . .

Maybe. . . But the carts had to be brought round by the Isle and up the rough-cobbled road by the banks of the river Nith. . .

As he turned left from the Dumfries-Kilmarnock road into the Isle, he found the wind (which had risen again) in his back and was able to raise his head from the muddy road and look forward. But there was nothing to see but the waves of grey rain sweeping ahead of him and ever the wet boggy road filled with ruts and holes and wretched puddles. Visibility was little more than twenty grey yards. . .

Against the stoicism with which he faced the daily task was a deep-seated, deep-rooted melancholy.

Robert Burns had known fear and despair from his earliest youth. Often enough, when his growing body was sadly under-nourished and overtaxed, he had been a prey to deepest melancholy, amounting at times to the nervous disease of melancholia.

Now in his twenty-eighth year and alone on his farm of Ellisland—at the elbow of existence—he experienced deeper fears than he had ever known; and his melancholy became more all-engulfing.

Sometimes his loneliness and isolation were hardly to be endured; and sometimes, when endurance was beyond him, he saddled Jenny Geddes and rode the four miles to John Bacon's inn near Closeburn, where he endeavoured to banish the gloom of his mind and mitigate the terrible cancer-gnawing worry that writhed within his belly.

He drank; and for the first time in his life not for social mirth and fun but from want of them.

The farm of Ellisland lay on the Nith boundary of the Parish of Dunscore. It was a parish of many small hills, some titbits of romantic scenery (of which Ellisland was one), much dreary boggy and barren hill grazings, bad and infrequent roads, miserable road-houses, wretched whisky and a rough, uncultured, unlettered and inhospitable Nithsdale peasantry . . . and farmers.

There was little to choose between the parish of Dunscore and the adjoining parish of Glencairn—or any other adjoining parish.

But lately he had been the toast of Edinburgh and had known the acclaim of many shires as Scotland's Bard. Little more than a year ago he had been fêted by the Dumfries magistrates and made an honoured freeman. Dumfries was but six miles away; and yet here he was an utter stranger and regarded as something of an alien, an unwelcome interloper.

Not that he was entirely friendless. Willie Stewart, the factor of Closeburn estate, had gone out of his way to help him and to press on him the friendship of his table and the comfort of his fire-side. Willie's sister, Mary, who was wife to landlord John Bacon, had ever a friendly word for him when he visited the Brownhill inn. John MacMurdo, chamberlain to the Duke of Queensberry's many acres at Drumlanrig, had not stinted his friendship either. But Closeburn was almost five miles away; and Drumlanrig lay some three miles beyond Closeburn. . .

The western boundary of Ellisland marched with the estate of Captain Robert Riddell of Glenriddell. First and last Riddell, who was still in his sunny thirties, was a gentleman and a country squire. After that he was many things: an amateur musician and composer; an antiquary who had contributed antiquarian papers to learned antiquarian journals; a great trencherman and a heavy and boastful drinker. A massive man with the voice of a bull and fists like hams.

Robert Riddell had held out a hand of gentlemanly friendship towards the Bard. True, Robert Burns was but a tenant-farmer of neighbouring Patrick Miller, Esquire, of Dalswinton. But was he not also Scotland's Bard? Had he not been taken up by the titled nobility of Scotland and shaken by the hand; had not my lords and ladies of Gordon, Glencairn and Atholl given him an honoured place at their tables?

Elizabeth Kennedy, English wife to Robert Riddell, did not think she should be asked to sit beside a working tenant-farmer who did his own carting and ploughing—especially when he was a neighbour. But certainly if the Duchess of Gordon could have him to dinner. . .

So the Bard had been invited to Friars Carse; and Mrs. Riddell and her mother-in-law had to agree that his conversation and his manners were beyond reproach. Obviously his contacts with the great had put considerable polish to his rusticity. It was agreed that though he might not drop in at the Carse he might, on occasion, be invited to do so.

Riddell, in a gust of generosity, gave him a key to the damp rectangular hutlet which he had named the Hermitage, that the Bard might have access to this secluded corner of the estate. There, in an inspired moment, the squire hoped that either a ballad or a song might be forthcoming extolling the virtues of the Riddells and the beauties of the Carse. The Bard of Scotland could hardly be expected to do less in repayment of the patronage of Squire Riddell.

Yet he was a cut above most country squires. He did have interests apart from over-eating, over-drinking and over-wenching. The man did have a love for his country, its history, its songs and ballads and folk-lore. And he did have some music in his soul and on the tips of his fiddle-fingers. But such were his social prejudices that he could not offer the Bard one of his many spare bedrooms, but allowed him to return, from a late visit, to the damp spence of David Cullie at the Isle.

The Bard had no illusions about Robert Riddell—or John Bacon. Bacon was an illiterate landlord greedy for the money his customers placed in his grasping paw: Riddell was a gentleman and in no way to be blamed for his inability to step outside the convention of his gentlemanly code. Far from spurning his patronage, the Bard was grateful for the measure of company it gave him, and indeed was developing something of affection and regard for the man.

But fear still gnawed at his vitals. He feared that Ellisland might not prove successful; he feared that he had neither the strength of body nor the energy of will to make it a success.

Yet he toiled early and late and did not spare himself. He ploughed, he bigged dykes, he dug drains . . . he showed every possible example of good and energetic husbandry to his workers. But fear remained with him and his nights were becoming unbearably lonely. It was late autumn and the mists of autumn and of melancholy gathered about him.

He knew that his melancholy was inevitable. Ellisland *was* a doubtful bargain. Apart from his generous loan to Gilbert he had sunk all the money from his Edinburgh edition into it. By the time he had brought it into such a state of productivity as would enable it to pay its rent, what would he be left with?

Ah, but with Jean by his side what was to prevent him from succeeding? Why shouldn't he fulfil the vision of himself as a contented farmer surrounded by prosperous acres, a growing family of bounding healthy bairns and the fire-side companionship of as fine a guidwife as ever blessed man?

The vision tugged sorely at his heart-strings. With Jean at his side he felt there was little or nothing he could not accomplish. His family would grow up . . . Jean and he would grow old together. But by then his sons would be able to relieve him of the farm drudgery. He would be able to devote more of his time to Coila, his Muse. . . He might even be able to write poetic drama; he might even essay guid prose plays dealing with Scottish life and character. But there was really no end to what he might not do—provided. . .

Ever and always there was this eternal question of the ways and means of life, the damned petty cash of daily existence. Nothing in life could be secured without cash. The very gift of life itself was cankered at the core because of it.

Aye: it was stupid, senseless, meaningless and monstrous; but there was no overcoming it, no getting round it or past it. It seemed that just as his father had died for lack of cash; just as his mother and Gilbert and his sisters were all harassed to death for want of it; just as all his young life had been blighted for want of it, so now that he was embarked on a wife and family and a farm he was to be persecuted and enslaved for want of it.

If that damned scoundrel Creech had settled his money with him when it had been due; if he hadn't had to kick his heels for that last winter in Edinburgh. . .

But even honest anger could not disperse the fogs of melancholy. Only company and drink could do that.

Had he reached the crest of the wave in Edinburgh—in his first winter? But he'd known even then that the wave would break under him; that he would be cast into the trough. And, by certes, he was in the trough now. Bogged. Not even a glow-worm glimmer to guide him out of his dismal despond.

God's curse on the weary drink and Bacon's ingle-neuk! He had neither stomach nor head for it so that its after-effects were as draughts of hell. . .

And yet the ingle-neuk drew him. There was fire and warmth and comfort, the smell of honest food cooking and ever the chance of company. John MacMurdo or Willie Stewart; and travellers, men passing north or south with news of the outside world. News of Glasgow or Edinburgh, London or Carlisle. Sometimes there were womenfolks travelling in company. It was fine to see a new feminine face and to hear feminine conversation. . .

Yet not every autumn day in the year of 1788 was melancholy or wet with grey rain. There came a fine autumn evening and Robert Burns, tired with his day's heavy labour, rested on the high bank of the river Nith and gazed with dreamy far-away eyes across the grain-golden holms of Dalswinton estate to the faint blue hills of Kirkmichael parish lying beyond the foreground parish of Kirkmahoe.

A letter from his Ayrshire patroness, Mrs. Dunlop of Dunlop, was clasped loosely in his hand. He wasn't worrying much about his kind-hearted elderly patroness. She had written him from Moreham Mains, near Haddington, where she was staying with her son and awaiting the lying-in of his wife. She hadn't been too well of late but was now recovered (the letter informed him) since she had "drunk two pounds of hempseed boiled in small beer." Mrs. Dunlop was of noble family.

He had been reckoning his harvest and had used the back of her letter to note down the number of thraves he had gathered from his fields. In all, five hundred and forty-five thraves: Stookhill yielding a hundred and ten and the Corner Rig but seventeen.

It was a depressing account. But here he was but reaping what old Cullie had sown. At worst he was certain he could do much better than David Cullie.

And he had plans against the future. Two days ago he had written to Robert Graham of Fintry and had put his case before him. It had been a plain straightforward appeal to

Fintry, in his capacity of Commissioner of the Excise, to use his influence with his fellow-commissioners on the Board to secure him the Excise Division in which Ellisland stood. Leonard Smith, the present Exciseman, had lately come into a considerable fortune; and the Bard saw no reason why Fintry shouldn't arrange to have Smith transferred to some other division. Had Smith been a poor man, or had he been burdened in any way with local responsibilities, he would never have suggested that Smith be removed to make way for him. But he knew that Smith neither needed the job nor had much interest in it. Smith indeed longed for a change.

Though born of fear, it had taken courage to write to Graham of Fintry; and it would be some time yet before he could discuss the matter with Jean.

At the thought of her he put away Mrs. Dunlop's letter and sought out his wife's. He had read it a dozen times already. It was a plain honest letter; but it was the touching artless honesty of her love for him that moved him so deeply.

He took a blank sheet of paper from his pocket and in the evening light wrote :

My dear Love—I received your kind letter with a pleasure which no letter but one from you could have given me. I dreamed of you the whole night last; but alas! I fear it will be three weeks yet, ere I can hope for the happiness of seeing you. My harvest is going on. I have some to cut down still, but I put in two stacks to-day, so I am as tired as a dog. . .

I expect your new gowns will be very forward, or ready to make, against I be home to get the Baiveridge.

I have written my long-thought-on letter to Mr. Graham, the Commissioner of Excise; and have sent him a sheetful of poetry besides. . .

The westering sun was warm on his back and the clear cool waters of the Nith wimpled, splashed and gurgled over and among and about the smooth boulders and the shingle beds below him. The river, with its water music, was his greatest solace and his deepest joy at Ellisland. . .

If only he could have brought Jean down; if only he hadn't to divide his time between Ellisland and Machlin. . . The prospect that he would be able to set-up house with Jean this winter was becoming every day more remote. Thomas Boyd, the Dumfries architect and building contractor, was proving provokingly dilatory. Yet he had carted lime and stones for the masons and done everything he could to speed the work.

There was so much more he could do if only Jean were with him. More and more he drew strength and inspiration from her. Here for once the fates had been kind to him—had blessed him indeed beyond his deserts. There wasn't another woman he had ever known (and he had known many) who could hold a farthing taper to her. And now, more than at any other time in his life, he needed her—needed the warmth and comfort and strength of her love and companionship.

This harvest time had been the longest period of separation from her since he had officially declared his marriage; since Daddy Auld and the Machlin Session had formally recognised the marriage that had been consummated under the green thorn tree. The fact that the Session had been forced to recognise his first and only declaration of marriage had been a sweet victory for him.

It had been a victory, a supreme victory over his Machlin enemies—and the Kirk of Scotland. It had been a not—unwelcome triumph over the pride and insolence of the narrow-minded Armours. It had humbled creatures like Holy Willie and James Lamie into the dust. But best of all it had brought joy to his friends and consolation to Mossgiel. Viewed from any or every angle it had been a master-move. And it had been a move his heart had dictated.

He had been a married man since March. But his married life was far from satisfactory. For weeks on end he was separated from Jean; and some forty-six long dreary miles lay between them. From this very bank on the Nith he had written her that glorious honeymoon song *Of a' the Airts the Wind can blaw*. But sweet beyond prose or verse or immortal harmony though these monthly reunions were, the partings were almost unbearably cruel; and his days and nights at Ellisland the more intensely lonely.

He was alone on the banks of the Nith as he had never before been alone. There were times when he had been lonely in Edinburgh. But whatever the loneliness or the despair in Auld Reekie there had always been Jock Richmond or Willie Cruikshank or Willie Nicol to come home to in the evening.

It was now that he missed Edinburgh; now that he knew its worth; now that he missed his friends there and the happy hours he had known with them.

Gone, doubtless forever, were those happy Crochallan nights in Dawney Douglas's with such sterling good fellows as Willie Nicol, Willie Smellie and Willie Dunbar; Nasmyth and Beugo; Sandy Cunningham and good kind-hearted Bob Cleghorn, the farmer from Saughton Mills.

Gone were his long talks with men like Lord Monboddo, Dean of the Faculty Henry Erskine, Bishop John Geddes, Professor Dugald Stewart, Professor James Gregory, the younger Tytler of Woodhouselea, and men like the Reverend William Greenfield.

Gone too, and that forever, the nights at the Theatre Royal and a bite and a drink afterwards with the ever-lamented Fergusson's friend, Willie Woods, the actor. . .

Often enough he had discounted his Edinburgh acquaintances. Now he could think of them by the score and scarce a one but would have gladdened his heart to meet on a Nithsdale road. Lang Sandy Wood, the surgeon, who had saved his knee (or almost, since it still troubled him. . .); Louis Cauvin, his French teacher, stout and cheery and benevolently kind; old Schetky from Saint Cecilia's Hall . . . and a dozen more.

The lassies! Maybe he hadn't fared so well with them.

Clarinda? Ah, the sweet-curved Nancy had given him many a happy moment—and many a sore headache. She was bringing down the wrath of heaven and conjuring up the black curses of hell to blast him—if all that Ainslie wrote were true.

Hell knows no fury. . . And he couldn't blame her, couldn't think in any way unkindly of her. He was glad to have managed to escape from her devious toils. And now here was Jenny Clow, her servant, pregnant and serving out a writ against him, even as Peggy Cameron had done, in order to secure provision for her child yet to be born. He had sent her some money by Ainslie; but he would need to visit Auld Reekie sometime early in the coming winter and settle her claim in due legal form.

He could not feel any anger for Jenny Clow even as he had felt no lasting anger for Peggy Cameron. But neither could he feel, in any deep sense, emotionally involved in them or their future. What was done was done—and their eyes had never been shut to the possible consequences of their physical capitulations. Yet they had served their turn in their day and had never expressed any regrets. In their day and in their way they had given and received happiness and had known, as they might never have known otherwise, an intense measure of physical ecstasy. . .

How different it had been, how different it was even now, with Peggy Chalmers. . . Peggy could still catch at his heart for what might have been. He would never as long as he lived be able to forget those walks in the Edinburgh Meadows and through the evening shadows that lay across George Square; those days of singing and piano-playing at Doctor Blacklock's and his dear guidwife, Sarah Johnston, once of Dumfries. . .

Most memorable of all, those autumn days and evenings—but a year past—on the banks of the winding Devon . . . and the fire-side circle at Harviestoun House and always Peggy Chalmers or her cousin Charlotte Hamilton, the ministering angels. . .

And maybe he would never meet them in this world again. . .

The sun had gone down; and the suffused sky above the deep-purpling hills told of the dying day. A chill wind had sprung up; and in the gloaming the Nith's song seemed to take on a deeper and more melancholy tone since the dancing light had vanished from the waters and they had turned cold and grey and black.

Something had died in Robert Burns. The past had died. What remained of his Edinburgh days and his Edinburgh friendships? He had but the words they wrote to him on a sheet of paper; and he had but words to write on a sheet of paper in reply. It was death compared to the days when they had rioted together in honest friendship.

There was only Jean now. And if Jean weighed them down in the scales of worth and attachment, her absence and his longing for her made the isolation, the melancholy and the loneliness, the more cruel.

The dew was falling; and now that the sun had gone from the sky a white autumnal mist began to gather about the river and the hollows of the land.

He rose from the bank stiff and sore and sad at heart. Tomorrow, if the weather held, he would bind all day behind his inadequate reapers. To-night he would dream of Jean. . .

THE SOUL OF EVERY BLESSING

In Machlin, Jean was too busy to have time to give way to despair. Not that there was any natural tendency in Jean towards melancholy. Her nature, gay and light-hearted, was balanced by her quiet fatalism—her uncomplaining acceptance of her lot. She had got Rab and Rab had got his farm—what was there to worry about? Every day she attended at Mossgiel and worked hard under the direction of Rab's mother and sisters: worked hard and learned quickly.

They were so pleased with her at Mossgiel that even Gilbert had a kind word. Indeed Gilbert had changed his opinion about her, though he would still give a canny Presbyterian side-nod with his head as if not admitting to himself that his opinion had changed.

There did not seem to be anything to worry about. But Jean knew that Rab was worried. She worried too about this writing to Graham of Fintry about an Exciseman's job.

When he did manage back to Machlin for a few days she questioned him.

"What's worrying you, Rab?"

"Nothing, Jean—at least nothing that canna be mended. It's just—well, Jean, we maun face it. Ellisland may never be a success—at least no' wi' my money and my work. It'll tak' years to put the place in guid heart. And we canna wait years, lass—that's all there's to it. We'll need to find an alternative somehow and somewhere. That's why I wrote to Graham o' Fintry. I'll need to get into the Excise. I think I can manage that *and* the farm. Back and forward I may need to hire a bit o' extra labour; but the expense o' a week or twa's hired labour'll never be missed out o' the Excise money. This way we'll be able to weather in a year or twa—and then Ellisland will be able to maintain us in comfort."

"If you think you can manage the twa jobs, Rab. You ken I'll dae a' I can and whatever mair."

"Fine I ken that, lass. Now, you're no' to be worrying."

"I'm no' worrying, Rab, for I've nae fear o' you. Only—I dinna like to see you sae worried and upset. And it's long past time I was doon at this Ellisland and got attending to you—saw that you got a richt bite o' guid meat."

"Aye. . . And God Almighty, Jean lass, I could be doing wi' you. What? But dinna worry: I'm no' for putting in the winter mysel'. I've been speiring in a' directions to see what there micht be by way o' a hoose—ony dry warm corner would do us the now——"

"Gey near ony place would do, Rab."

"Nearly. . . Ony place but Cullie's. I'll no' be able to stand that much longer mysel'. But patience, lass, patience. We'll win through. This winter'll be the worst. . . I'll need to gang through to Edinburgh ane o' thae days: I've some affairs to settle wi' that arch-scoundrel Creech. . ."

True enough: he had accounts to settle with Creech. But he had also accounts to settle with Jenny Clow.

Jenny had borne him a son. There might be some difficulty about that. Hell: but he had had to pay a heavy price for his bye-loves. But God be thanked: he was finished with all that nonsense now. Aye; and had things been right with Jean from the start there would never have been a Peggy Cameron or a Jenny Clow—or anyone else.

Not that he really regretted anything. He'd had many a happy hour with Peggy and Jenny and an odd one here and there forbye. What was the odds—now? His love for Jean hadn't suffered in any way. Rather had it been enriched. Maybe it was only when a man had twa-three lassies through his hands that he appreciated the right lass when he got her.

And, Lord, it was good to get home to Baldy Muckle's room in the Backcauseway and get straiked down in warmth and comfort and blessed satiation beside Jean.

This meant more to him than anything else life had to offer. Neither fame nor fortune could be half so sweet or so unutterably satisfying. . .

Clarinda! He dismissed her from his mind before her sweet sophisticated curves had an opportunity of hoving into consciousness. . .

The trouble with Mrs. MacLehose, as with Peggy Chalmers, was that their curves (their femininity, their personality) were sophisticated; were not wholly and truly aligned to their essential and natural bonework.

Gilbert said to him: "What's like the trouble at Ellisland —is it another Mossgiel?"

"Aye—and it could be a bit o' Lochlea and Mount Oliphant."

"But I thought Auld Glen advised——"

"I thought so too, Gibby."

"I'm sorry to hear this, Robin."

"Of course if I'd enough money——"

"You're no' grudging what you loaned me?"

"I'm no' grudging onything. I could do fine wi' what I loaned you—but it would only be a drop in the bucket. No: it's the future, Gibby, that worries me. I was a bit soft to begin wi'——" He spread out his toil-calloused hands. "But I'm hardened to hard work now."

"It canna do your farm much good wasting time coming up here to Machlin every twa-three weeks."

"Wasting time!"

"Well . . . I ken how you feel about Jean."

"No you don't, Gibby. You ken nocht about it."

"Maybe no': I'm beginning to appreciate Jean's parts——"

"So you appreciate that she's worth mair nor bedding?"

Gilbert turned away his face: "I don't suppose you'll ever change, Robin."

"I don't suppose I will. But make nae mistake: Jean means everything to me."

"Aye—in some ways a better wife nor you deserve."

"Granted! Aye, Jean's a better wife nor I deserve. But— in another way—I deserved her fully enough. I suffered plenty for her."

"So did she for you!"

"You're beginning to see that, are you? There's hope for you, Gilbert my boy. You'll be a philosopher yet if you watch your step. For just as much as Jean and me's suffered for each other the mair we mean to each other. . . Your come-easy loves go just as easily. I never held to the theory of one man one lass. You can only love as long as you can. But I never held to the theory of libertinism either——"

"No. . . ?"

"I ken you think otherwise, Gibby. Your platonic ideal relationship with your Lavinia has been your undoing. Oh,

I don't blame you. . . I don't blame onybody. If you've nocht but stagnant blood in your veins then you can hae nocht but stagnant thoughts in your head. I get a bit tired sometimes trying to argue wi' folk. Man—and woman too—should live according to their natures, according to the instincts, desires, capacities that have been implanted in them—or maybe inherited from their forebears. What raises the very devil in me is when folk try to threap down my throat that *their* way o' life should be mine. Folk have ceased to be human beings— they have become moralists. That's *your* besetting sin, Gibby: you're a moralist—and your morals are no' a' o' your ain making."

"So you do deny the truths of revealed religion?"

"Religion—revealed or unrevealed. Revealed by whom, Gibby?"

"By God—in the ultimate."

"By God in the ultimate. A comforting thought if you like comfortable ways o' thinking about things. When I study the kind o' folk that are familiar wi' God I ken what to think. And when I hear them putting their petty moral strictures into the mouth o' God, then I ken there's no such God. If there was He would strike them dead for their blasphemy. You've read my verses: few hae read them with more application. But I micht as weel hae been writing in Greek for a' the guid they've done you."

"Should they have done me good?"

"Well, maybe no' when you put it that way. But at least you might have understood what I've been driving at almost since ever I started writing."

"You canna say I havena enjoyed them."

"Uhuh! Enjoyed! Well . . . they were meant to be enjoyed and plenty hae enjoyed. But damn few hae kent what they were about—though the meaning's wrote plain for a' to see."

"Is this you coming back to Love and Liberty again?"

"Coming back to it? I was never away from it."

"Oh—— So why did you get married? Why didn't you tell Mr. Auld to. . . ?"

"To go to hell? You don't understand Daddy Auld either."

"I understand enough, Robin. If you want to wriggle out of your own argument you can do so. I'll no' hold it up against you."

"When did ever I wriggle out o' onything? I too can pay to Caesar that which is Caesar's and unto God that which is God's."

"Edinburgh learned you well in sophistry."

"Did it? I'll put it plainer to you, Gilbert. Plain enough for even you to see. I render to the Excise that which will satisfy the Excise into giving me a job. I see nae wisdom nor courage in *starving* myself to death or those that love me to death. So what do I do? I marry Jean to start wi'—and how do I marry Jean? By forcing you and Machlin and Father Auld and the Kirk o' Scotland into recognising *my* marriage. And if I render them a guinea to solder their conscience and get a receipt—well, that's a guinea weel rendered to Caesar.

"And the Excise accepts the receipts—and by the laws o' the Kirk God'll need to accept the receipt too—or pack the whole bluidy Kirk and the General Assembly aff to hell for dealing in contraband commandments. Though between you and me, Gibby, I'm mair nor content to leave my sins, so-called, for God to deal wi' at His ain time. Aye, I maun hae some bits o' scraps o' receipts so as to prove to the world that I'm respectable—that I'm fit to be allowed to earn a bite for myself, and my bairns. *You* think this makes me a hypocrite? Na, na: the world's the hypocrite."

"And you alone are right?"

"No: that would be too simple. Maybe I'm speaking ower big when I talk about the world. Well . . . we'll confine ourselves to Scotland. Scotland, the Scotland o' saints and scholars and country squires is nothing but hypocrisy. Not one o' them can square their beliefs wi' their practice. But, as far as ever I have been able to read in history—and that at least takes me back to the Bible—morality has ever been a snare and a delusion——"

"All right, Robin; but what has this to do wi' you settling down in Ellisland as a farmer?"

"I'll go ower it again wi' you. I've got to live. Oh, I suppose I could beg my way frae door to door—I may be forced to come to that yet. But—not yet. I've work to do. And I dinna mean ploughing and sowing and reaping. That's just my bread and brose work. I've sangs to write: hundreds o' sangs. Aye: so that our auld glorious melodies will be preserved. My reward? I'd be a bluidy gowk to look for ony reward! What reward d'ye think James Johnson's getting? Can you value a sang the way you could a wedder ewe. . . ? You think I've changed since I cam' back frae Auld Reekie. But I havena. I'm more experienced in the ways o' the world, Gibby. But my attitude to life, my ideas, havena changed either—only deepened. The philosophy that I hammered out for mysel' in Lochlea and Mossgiel here has become more intense wi' the experience o' the last two years. True enough, Gibby, at the moment I'm a bit in the depths and when I get into the trough o' melancholy it's no' easy to climb out. You see: things are still going against me. Oh . . . I havena given up hope yet. There's plenty o' fight and hard work in me still. I'm forgetting what started this discourse, am I? Dinna be surprised at the things you see me doing—and never mak' the mistake o' taking me for a hypocrite. I ken the world, Gilbert; and I'll fight the world and if necessary deceive the world wi' my own weapons."

"A' I can say, Robin, is that you'd talk your way out o' ony argument. I could have nae other desire than to see you settled down as farmer, happy and prosperous. Naebody deserves that mair nor you. I've aey felt that and I've aey said that. I've stood up for you through thick and thin. I can thole the fact that there's nothing for me but hard work and endless poverty. Even as a farmer I'm no' half the farmer you are. I suppose I'm a dull clod and will need to suffer for that."

"D'you really think you're a dull clod, Gilbert?"

"Well . . . I've little to show for the trifle o' education I've laboured to acquire. No: I'm no' a dull clod, Robin. I can read and I can reason—and I hae my principles——"

"Your morality."

"All right, my morality. I'm no' apologising for it. I'm no saint; but I've never done harm to onybody deliberately. And I ken I'm fit for better than slaving out my guts on Mossgiel for the rest o' my days. . . But still and on, Robin: you canna escape predestination; and if it's the Lord's will——"

"You'll bend your neck to the yoke?"

"Aye: I'll bend my neck to the yoke—and I'll do my best no' to complain."

"Or revolt?"

"Or revolt. Ye ken fine, Robin—and here I would fain plead wi' you—those that are stiff-necked before the Lord and refuse to bend their necks to the yoke get their necks broken in the Lord's ain time."

"Amen, amen. . . It's strange too, Gilbert, that here we stand brothers, flesh o' the same flesh, and you were born a preacher wi' the message o' submission and I was born a poet wi' the message o' revolt. You're right in a way, Gilbert. We canna escape our destiny. What's for us'll no' go by us. The thing is to acknowledge your destiny—if your destiny's strong enough or important enough to be acknowledged. The bulk o' mankind hae damn-all destiny worth bothering about. And they must be led, coaxed, cajoled, inspired to fulfil a greater and fuller life than they themselves know. And in the end, Gilbert, I'm satisfied o' this: the poet will win ower the preacher. For the preacher maun ever preach denial and the poet maun ever proclaim acceptance. In the end, Gibby, as in the beginning, a sweet sang'll triumph ower a sour sermon. My experience o' life teaches me that at the heart o' a' religion is sourness—sourness at God and man, beast and devil. Aye, and the sun, moon and stars. A sourness at life, Gibby. And by heaven! I see that sourness biting into you, biting deep into you. . . Ah, for Godsake, get yourself a wife and commence father. . ."

It was a long time since Robert and Gilbert had had a long talk together. Mostly when they met nowadays it was to exchange mundane information in lean words linked in lean sentences. But a thin dry sourness was general at Mossgiel. Only his youngest brother, William, seemed to be free from it. And William was desperately anxious to get quit of Mossgiel. Time and again Robert had promised to help him and always William had been disappointed. Yet he worshipped Robert and still anchored all his hopes in him. Robert never eluded him— not even with his eyes. Gilbert had a poor opinion of his parts and considered him feckless—if not worthless.

But Robert's relation to his family was good. They accepted him as married and if not exactly settled down, then making shift to do so. Nancy promised that as soon as his new house was ready she would come down to Ellisland and help Jean.

But, apart from Jean and their room in the Backcauseway, there was nothing to hold him in Machlin. He didn't visit Gavin Hamilton now. Hamilton had not forgiven him for not sinking his Edinburgh money into Mossgiel. He still enjoyed a crack with Dr. John MacKenzie and sometimes he had a warm gossip with Johnnie Dow. But he had few real friends in Machlin now and he would be glad when he didn't need to come back to Baldy Muckle's room.

As for the Machlin belles, he was glad enough to stop and have a word with them; but his passion for Jean was too all-absorbing for him to have either time or inclination to dally in their company.

Strange what a couple of years could do! Machlin was dead to him now. Yet he had spent some of the happiest days of his life in and about it. He would always have pleasant memories of the Machlin he had known when first he came to Mossgiel—just as he would have pleasant memories of Tarbolton when he had first come to Lochlea.

But nothing remained the same. Time gathered the waters of memory into an ever swifter stream moving relentlessly towards oblivion's shoreless sea.

No man was ever more truly poet than Robert Burns; but no poet was ever more sane, more balanced, more practical. Always he had known poverty and starvation and a toil that amounted to slavery. When the fear of actual physical starvation did not rat-gnaw at his resolve, it whip-lashed him into frenzied activity.

His feverish bouts of physical activity at Ellisland often exhausted him. Then an old tune would come into his mind and he would be threshing out words to the melody. Often he would sit far into the night cobbling an old half-broken refrain into a passable lyric. Sometimes he hammered out on a golden anvil a harmony of new words and old notes with an artistry as fresh and exquisite as the first dawn over Eden when the Lord had rested from His labours and had found them good.

And he would come back to Machlin with a packet of songs; and Jean would sing them over. He would swing on the back legs of his elbow chair and experience a deep enchantment. Jean had the perfect voice for his folk-songs. She sang effortlessly.

Often enough the Bard had to coach her patiently in the rhythm. But Jean's ready ear was quick in response. She gave him what he wanted with sometimes a subtle shade or two added for good measure.

And so the first summer at Ellisland passed into the first autumn and then chill November's surly blasts blew bleak and bitter winter across the Dunscore hills; and the Nith, swollen and red, swept in endless spates to the Solway.

Now he dreaded the winter as he had never dreaded winter— and Cullie's spence. . .

Maybe he would not have survived that winter—and maybe he had already endured more than his rheumatic-vitiated body could withstand. But just when he was about to give in, salvation came in the shape of a house.

David Newall, the Dalswinton estate factor, was a Dumfries lawyer who occupied the mansion-house at the Isle (behind and a little beyond David Cullie's wretched hovel). He usually resided in Dumfries during the winter.

One day the Bard had complained to him of the misery of Cullie's spence and the intolerable delay of the Dumfries masons over his new house and steading.

"You needna endure the winter in Cullie's cow-shed, Mr. Burns. We canna hae Scotland's Bard treated like that. And to tell the truth, Mr. Burns, my house at the Isle would be none the waur o' a guid firing through thae wat winter days—and we get a damnable rain here. I've kent it wat for four months without ony remission—day and nicht and nicht and day. You could occupy the kitchen and a room. . . You'll need to see to your ain firing; but—eh—I'll no' charge you by way o' rent provided, of course, that you're oot by the time I'll want in. If we hae ocht like a good April I'll want in by then—the first o' May by the latest onywey. Na, na, Mr. Burns: nae thanks—I'll only be too glad to get the place fired and the dampness kept at bay. An' maybe you could spare a bit look at the gairden and an odd cairt o' manure or lime, you ken . . . whatever you can spare and what you'll ken best yoursel' it needs. . . Aye . . . I'm surprised at Thomas Boyd no' making better way wi' the bigging o' your steading and dwellin' hoose. The fault wi' a' thae builders and contractor-bodies is the same. Far ower greedy. They tak' on wark here, there an a' ower the countraside. They gie a day or twa to you and a day or twa to me and in trying to please everybody please naebody. I dinna pass much o' Dalswinton work their way—unless on Mr. Miller's direct orders. Keep pressing on Boyd. Keep on his door-step, as it were: I'll hae a word wi' him too. . .

"Mr. Miller o' Dalswinton? Yes: he's a clever man. Imphm . . . made twa-three fortunes twa-three ways. Ah

well, Mr. Burns, I can see you're ettlin' to mak' a braw place o'
Ellisland. Coorse, I'm nae proper farmer—but nae doubt
you'll see your way to get back what you're putting intillt?
Well . . . I was thinking that too, Mr. Burns. I didna like to
say. Aye, aye! Just what I thocht, a cauld wat dirty dour
bitch o' a place. A grand place i' the summer days for lying
about the banks o' the Nith and fishing a salmon or maybe
writing a verse or twa. Couldna get better. But for farming!
Oh, I like a stroll alang the banks o' the Nith, Mr. Burns.
I've seen you at work and I've seen the work you've been doing.
To be frank: I was surprised. You farm weel, Mr. Burns, I'll
say that for you; and I've told Mr. Miller that. Somehow even
if I did think o' you as a ploughman-poet—the agricultural
side o' your genius I restricted to the mere act o' ploughing.
I'll allow you that methods o' farming differ frae place to
place. Quite true, quite true: sometimes from parish to
parish. . . But damned, Mr. Burns, it can be hellish lonely
and gloomy here i' the lang winter nichts and the short bleak
winter days—especially after two winters o' dissipation in
Edinburry. True, wi' wife and weans round the ingle and you
at the board-end scribbling away with the quill . . . aye:
I confess that's a worthy enough vision. And of course you're
in love wi' a young wife. Ah, that mak's a michty difference,
Mr. Burns. Juist a' the difference i' the warld. There I envy
you, sir. I mean I don't envy you your poetry—that's juist
something I've never even thocht o' aspiring to—no! But
youthfu' domestic bliss—you're juist hitting thirty years!
Not that I'm no'—so to speak—in love wi' Mrs. Newall. No
. . . I mean rural domestic bliss, contentment—and contentment on little o' this warld's gear as it were. . . That's what
I mean, Mr. Burns—and that's something that glows through
your verses like a warm house-licht beckoning on the weary
traveller. . . Aye; but then if Ellisland doesna pay its way. . .
That's where my experience o' the warld, Mr. Burns, would
add a word o' caution. I've seen sae mony guid men come to
ruin through bad ground and ane or twa bad harvests in

succession. Nae fault o' their ain. Nae lack o' husbandry or
application to the soil. Juist a lack o' the bawbees, Mr. Burns,
to tide them ower a bad season. It comes to that in the end—
the lack o' the first and readiest. When you hae to rake doon
into the pouch to pay a debt and the siller's no' there. . . Fine
I understand your experience o' life, Mr. Burns—juist as fine
can I understand your fears. But the wonderfu' thing, Mr.
Burns, is that you've managed to write verses about it a'. That
can only mean one thing. You hae a heart aboon it a'. Undoubtedly, yes, undoubtedly: the heart is superior to the brain
where that's concerned. . .

"The thing that amazes me about you, Mr. Burns, is your
conversation. You're no' only a poet—Scotland's poet—you're
a philosopher. And that's an astonishing combination. I
confess—afore I got acquaint wi' you—that I didna expect to
find the philosopher in you at all. True—I juist didna read
deeply enough into your poetry. Grant you: the philosophy's
there. But then, in your verses you clothe it in such honest
hame-spun that you juist dinna tak' it for philosophy. Whereas
when you speak—that's when you get the real smack o' the
philosopher. But much though I like to crack wi' you into the
wee sma' hours ayont the twal I mauna detain you. Now: nae
mair thanks, Mr. Burns. It was grand to read your verses:
it's been glorious meeting and talking wi' you; and if the use
o' the kitchen and a room or twa at the Isle, here, will make a'
that difference to your first winter in Ellisland, I'm amply
repaid. . . And ony time you're in Dumfries and I can be of
ony service to you—well, you ken where to fa' in wi' me."

THE THIRD HONEYMOON

On a mild December evening, following on a day of neither frost nor rain, the Bard and Jean arrived at the Isle. They had taken the journey in easy stages, stopping at John Merry's inn in New Cumnock and at Baillie Whigham's inn at Sanquhar and at Brownhill Inn, where they had enjoyed a supper with Willie Stewart of Closeburn Castle.

Nance Cullie had been prevailed upon to light a fire at the Isle and when they arrived the kitchen was warm and inviting.

"Well, here you are in Nithsdale at long last, Jean," he said, when he came in from the stable. He kissed her again and again. "Jean, my love, you'll never ken what it means to me to hae you doon here beside me."

"Rab . . . Rab. . . You'll never ken what it means to me. Here we are at last—and naebody through the wa'."

"Just ourselves, lass—though that'll no' be for long. But you're tired! Come on: aff wi' your things and into bed. By God—and that's a grand bed, Jean. And mind: we're no' getting up in the morning. This'll be our third honeymoon. There'll be a fourth when I get the house bigged ower at Ellisland."

"Oh, I'll need to see Ellisland in the morning, Rab."

"I hear you—but it'll no' be the morn's morning. . . You're no' too tired, Jean?"

"Weel . . . but you are, Rab. An' to tell the truth, Rab, my back-side's gey sair."

"I'll cure that for you, lass, never fear. God, but I'm glad to be in the Isle the nicht and to realise that I'll never be in Cullie's spence again."

"Oh, I'll need to see that too."

"Aye: you'll see it. And you'll ken then why I wouldna bring you down to it."

They were undressed and had got into bed. The Bard

had thrown some peats and an armful of logs on to the wide glowing fireplace. Long forks of flame flicked in the great chimney. Shadows danced and writhed on the ceiling and walls and flashed on the crockery on the dresser.

They were in bed, tired physically, and yet mentally alert and emotionally vibrant.

"D'you think we're near to being settled doon now, Rab? Machlin and Mossgiel seem terribly far awa'."

"Aye . . . they're far awa', Jean. You'll maybe realise now what ' a' the airts ' meant to me when I wrote it on the banks o' the Nith?"

"I wonder, Rab, that you've put up wi' it sae lang: I couldna."

"You endured mair than enough at Machlin."

"Aye—but Machlin was hame."

"And you still feel Machlin's hame. You're no' hamesick already, are you?"

"I'll never be hamesick as long as I hae you, Rab. Wherever you are'll be hame."

"You ken, my love, I canna richt believe sometimes that you and me are man and wife till death do us part. You're ower guid, Jean: that's your only fault. Ower guid, ower true, ower leal——"

"Och, be sensible——"

"Sensible! No, I'll never be that wi' you, Jean. Sensible's too cold and prudent a word. Damnit, I love you."

"I ken you do, Rab. I dinna think that in my darkest hours I ever doubted that."

"Weel, weel, lass! We're no' going back ower the past: that's closed and by wi'. We've the future to look forward to—and uncertain though that future may be the now, we'll see the brightest o' it thegither. . . But you havena said what you think o' the house—what you've seen o' it?"

"I canna say ocht, Rab—my heart's too fu'. . ."

"Weel, when that big overflowing heart o' yours is too fu', Jean——"

"Rab . . . I'm juist gratefu' for onything that brings us thegither——"

They had been brought together often enough, brought together in the happiness of lad and lass and man and wife. Under the green thorn tree; in hay loft and straw shed; beneath the Cowgate thatch; in many a green howe and hollow; under the blankets of the mahogany bed in Baldy Muckle's room in the Backcauseway, aye, and many another sweet corner besides. But here in the Isle, in David Newall's kitchen bed, on a soft damp night in December and a great fire roaring in the ingle, was perhaps their sweetest night of all.

Perhaps—and maybe not. The Bard could never recall a night spent in Jean's arms that had not been a bliss and an ecstasy. And he had ever to admit that, of all the women he had known—and in Jean's arms he always forgot how many he had known—there was no woman who could compare with her. Other women had their charms, their particular attributes. But only with Jean could he be completely and utterly stripped-naked natural. With all the others he had acted some part or another; with none of the others had he given himself so utterly, so completely. . . God bless Jean Glover—whore that she was—and wasn't—who had first initiated him into the ways of physical love. And the Lord look kindly on Jean Gardiner and sonsy Betty Paton. . . But bless and preserve Jean Armour, the jewel o' them a', to all eternity. . .

They should have been more than tired and physically exhausted. But they were on a honeymoon and so great was the spiritual love they mutually generated that physical tire was annihilated. And because they loved so deeply spiritually, they loved so deeply physically. There was no dichotomy in their love; no fractures, abrasions, no half-truths, half-way houses; no avenues of escape; no cushions of illusion. . . There was the all-embracing unity of bare-buttocked lust and the love of the red rose of life's recurrent blooming; the holy trinity of mind, heart and body; the merging of body and

soul; of love everlasting even as it journeyed to age, decay,
decrepitude and death.

The wonder would have been otherwise had Jean not
conceived at some moment during that long, seemingly
interminable night and day. . .

CLARINDA REMEMBERS

But at General's Entry, in the Potterrow of Auld Reekie,
Clarinda wept herself to disturbed sleep.

In November Jenny Clow had brought forth a son to
Robert Burns. Only now, even as Jean Armour conceived, did
Clarinda learn the truth from her part-time maid.

Oh, the cruelty, the heart-break of it! That son of Jenny
Clow should have been hers. She had denied Robert Burns
what her servant had not denied him.

She thought of him in her agony of jealousy as a blackguard, a scoundrel, a heartless villain, a monstrous deceiver—
as everything vile and shameless under the sun. . .

And yet she couldn't. He was no deceiver. It was she who
had deceived. Her deceptions with Kemp and with Ainslie
did not matter: she had deceived them even as she had deceived
Robert Burns. No: these deceptions were but white lies on
an idle tongue compared to the depth of her deception of
Robert Burns. He had been a gentleman, a knight in the
purest of white armour. Kemp and Ainslie were afraid *for
themselves* for what they didn't do to her: Robert Burns, with
ten thousand times the sexual fire and audacity of ten thousand
Kemps and Ainslies, had saved her, in regard for love, from
herself. She had been a ten times irretrievably-damned fool
for having denied him. But this deep truth only came into
Clarinda's brain to be just as vehemently denied. What could
she have done? Jenny was but a servant-lass. A servant-lass
was expected to have children no man admitted to fathering.

But she was no servant. She had had four children in awful but legal wedlock. She still had a husband in Jamaica. And she was still in the direst of poverty.

Had she conceived to Robert Burns, cousin William Craig would have denied her; Bob Ainslie would have denied her; William Nimmo and his sister would have denied her; Mary Peacock. . . But all Edinburgh, all society, all morality would have denied her. . .

But Robert Burns was as far above morality as Jenny Clow was beneath it.

Or was she. . . ?

Oh, the heart-break, the torment of it all. . .

No, no; he was a blackguard, an unprincipled villain, a heartless scoundrel. He had fled from her arms (after the most sacred vows, after the holiest protestations); he had fled from the carnal arms of her servant into the arms of his Jean. . . Oh, that she might die of the most horrible pox! But he had married his Jean and all the time he had deluded her with the most villainous letters. . .

Surely, surely he had not been so sexually intimate with Jenny Clow as he had been with her—even if Jenny had not denied his seed. Damn the fornicating hot-blooded little bitch ! She had laid herself out for Robert—had trapped him. Had she expected marriage? But how torturing the thought that he had in any way embraced her. . . It must have been a hasty furtive hole-and-corner affair—the hasty contrivance of a flurried moment. . . Impossible to think of his lips, his hands, his words, his wine-inflaming words. . . Not to Jenny. . . Oh, the little hot-bottomed bitch! But good-looking—yes; and virginal and not fat. . .

She ran her fingers over the blue vein-ruptured, post-pregnancy corrugations of her flaccid abdominal wall. Four confinements in four years had played havoc with her once drum-smooth belly and firm-fresh contoured breasts. . .

And yet Robert had rhapsodised about the sweetness of her curves, the poetry of her plumpness. . . No, no, no: he hadn't lied. The tongue might lie; but he didn't lie with his lips, with his hands; his body hadn't lied. . .

She wept. Clarinda was but a lassie. She had been harshly treated by life. The fluttering butterflies of her youthful passion had been broken on the lust-wheel of a brutal sex-maniac. And she had been abandoned to the not even genteel poverty of an inadequate allowance and the misery of two dingy rooms in General's Entry in the Potterrow. . . Her furniture, her linen, her dresses were humiliatingly threadbare and inadequate. She had been reduced to accepting clothes-gifts from Miss Erskine Nimmo and Mary Peacock.

She had been worthy of a better fate. She should have been able to dress nearer the height of fashion; she should have been able to afford the theatre, the Assembly, the concerts at Saint Cecilia's. . . She had a right to at least one fine room in a fine house where she could have entertained like Miss Nimmo or Miss Chalmers; she deserved good china and fine wine glasses and a good carpet on the floor. . .

She wept; for she was but a love-lorn affection-starved lassie at heart. As a mask, as a shield, she had cultivated poetry, elevating conversation, affected piety and what she fondly imagined to be England's fine and refined English. . . And here was courage in the face of beetling adversity. She might have broken and sunk under the harshness of fortune into a sluttish indifference. And who would, or could, have blamed her if she had ceased to struggle, ceased to battle for her own self-respect and the respect of her friends? Maybe her battle was a foolish one and her study of fine poetry profitless; but at least it had saved her from despair and the corrosion of loneliness. . .

For Robert Burns she had risked almost everything that meant such security as she had. But the happiness had been worth more than any risk. Only now there was bitterness, loneliness, rage, despair, and endless longing. . .

Oh Robert, Robert: what had she done? She had sought him from the beginning; she had protested but protested too much; she had led him on . . . she, a married woman who could never, while her wretched husband lived, offer him anything. Oh, God, in His understanding and almighty love forgive her, guide her and protect her. She had sinned against God and against Robert Burns; she had sinned against life and love.

But the flywheel of Clarinda's thoughts was loaded at the point of morality; and ever the wheel came to rest against this point.

CONTENTED WITH LITTLE

The arrival of Jean at the Isle, the warmth and comfort of the house, the honest appetising food she prepared for him soon worked a revolution in his feelings towards Ellisland. He worked hard on his farm by day; but when he came home he was anxious to get down at the end of the table with a ream of paper.

But it had ever been so. Deeply in love with Jean, he found his creative energy surging through him, giving him a great strength. Gone for the moment was his melancholy and his melancholia. Now was the time for rejoicing in life—for recreating it in life and in song.

So he wrote and wrote. Yet his mind ever raced far ahead of his pen.

He could have done to neglect his farm and to have exhausted this creative upsurge that was on him. Maybe he should have done so. But his fear of poverty was too great. He had a responsibility to Jean and his family and to Dalswinton House, lying like a grave threat to his existence across the Nith.

So he applied himself to his farm and his poetry and his Jean. The month of December was one of the happiest he had ever known.

When he composed—or rather dashed off—his *Elegy on the*

year 1788 and read it over to Jean, she realised how the opening lines so suited his moods: "For Lords or Kings I dinna mourn, e'en let them die—for that they're born!"

Everything interested him. Even his interest in the politics of the day had never been keener. Squire Riddell was often generous with his newspapers and these the Bard digested almost at a glance. Yet so apt and penetrating were his comments in prose and verse that such sheets as the Edinburgh *Evening Courant*, *The British Chronicle* and *Lloyd's Evening Post* were only too delighted to print anything from his pen.

He relished his journalism, found deep satisfaction in his political poetry. It was grand to dash off a comment and see it in print in ten or twelve days' time.

Often he was inwardly thankful that the rain prevented him from slaving at his farm and gave him an excuse to draw up to the fire to read or write or go over a song with Jean as the mood seized him.

"You see, Jean—this is how it should hae been a' along. We could hae had a' this a year ago—aye, damn-near twa years ago, had only Creech settled up wi' me——"

"Maybe, Rab. But you enjoyed yoursel' in Embro. . . And you had your tours. That did you a lot o' guid—you mauna forget that. Maybe you wouldna hae settled doon sae weel twa year ago."

"Aye . . . maybe you're richt as usual, Jean. It was fine seeing the Borders and the Highlands. Right, my lass, I'll no grumble. Only I'm no' keen to gang to Embro for that final settlement wi' Creech——"

"And it will be final?"

"Damn the fear o' that. I ken that having Creech's word for it doesna in itself mean onything. But I think I ken whaur I hae him, even though he's now God's anointed baillie o' Edinburgh. Robert Burns'll be dealing wi' a different Creech this time—and Creech'll be dealing wi' a very different Robert Burns."

But the Bard's plans for Edinburgh were upset by the

death of his father's brother Robert in Stewarton. He had
known his uncle's end was near, for the last time he had visited
him—during one of his visits to Mrs. Dunlop—he had found
him far gone in a rheumatic complaint that made his life a
terrible pain and burden to him. It seemed significant to the
nephew that his uncle Robert and his father William, from
Clochnahill, should have both died in Ayrshire in physical
distress and direst poverty.

Robert Burnes (as was the family spelling) had told his
famous nephew that he was dying and that he feared for his
growing family. The Bard had immediately assured him that
he would take care of his cousin Fanny and one, if not two,
of the boys: John maybe, or William.

Now the time had come for him to implement his promise;
and though that time had come sooner than he had anticipated,
he did not hesitate for a moment. Unable to attend the funeral
himself—by the time he could get to Stewarton his uncle
would be buried—he despatched his farm-boy to Stewarton
with a letter. . .

"Fanny'll be a big help to you, Jean."

"What age'll she be?"

"About sixteen or seventeen. . ."

"Whatever you say, Rab. If you're bringing the twa boys
and your brother William frae Mossgiel . . . we'll hae a
housefu'."

"You dinna think I was foolish——"

"No, no, Rab—they're a' welcome and mair; and you ken
fine I'll be guid to them."

"Fine I ken. . . Oh, and they'll need to work, they'll need
to earn their bite. And if Fanny's the lass I think she is, she'll
do that and mair. I'm no' so sure about my brother William.
There's something wrong wi' him I just canna put my finger
on. The boy's got intelligence and he's got ambition o' a kind
—but there seems to be nae proper gumption about him."

"He hasna much smeddum, puir laddie. But I think he'll
dae better once he's awa' frae Mossgiel and Gilbert's influence."

"Maybe you're no' far wrong there, lass. Gilbert . . . you see the trouble wi' Gibby, Jean, is that he's always right."

"Think sae?"

"Aye: if you weigh up a' Gibby's arguments, you'll find he's richt. Logically and morally speaking. But then he's so bluidy smug wi' it a' that he gets folks' backs up."

"There's a bit of the bully in him too, Rab. But I ken what you mean—he's honest enough and likes to deal fair wi' everybody——"

"Aye. . . Weel, here we are. We thocht we were for having the Isle to oursel's—at least till I brocht my sister Nancy doon in the spring. But what the hell! The house can dae wi' plenty o' young folks about it. They'll be company for you when I'm awa' in Edinburgh."

"Aye—they'll be company. Though there's nae company could mak' up for you, Rab. But you're richt: I'll need the company for I juist couldna bide in this meikle house by my lane."

Soon the long quiet nights at the Isle were no more. Fanny, John and William, his cousins, were there; and his brother William.

Many folks thought that Robert Burns was a foolhardy over-generous man giving hospitality to so many young people —especially when his circumstances seemed so ill-suited to the burden. But his uncle's plight reminded him too closely of his father's and he couldn't shut the children out.

Fanny was as bright and lovable a girl as he had ever known. Jean took to her immediately and she to Jean. Indeed in many ways she closely resembled Jean when the Bard had first known her.

And it looked as if the parallel was developing with a startling closeness; for soon Adam Armour came to work as a mason on the new wing of Dalswinton House and soon he was at the Isle every other evening and soon he was paying Fanny every attention.

The Bard had a great softness for Adam Armour and he was Jean's favourite brother; and so fortune seemed to smile on the pair.

"This is what I've aey hankered for, Jean—a hame o' my own and plenty o' young folks about enjoying themselves. And friends too. I've never had a place where I could invite my friends. But things'll be different from now on."

"I'll dae what I can for your friends, Rab——"

"My friends, Jean, will be your friends—we'll share them thegither."

"I'm no' used to mixing wi' gentry."

"Gentry! That's another story. Dinna worry about the gentry, Jean. Ony connection I hae wi' them is of no great consequence. Take Glenriddell there, ower at the Carse—he's one o' your gentry. Guid kens Glenriddell's an honest enough fellow and I like him well enough and, indeed, it's a' to my advantage that I should pay my respects at the Carse now and then. But I'd never dream o' having Glenriddell cracking awa' at my ingle-neuk or drawing his chair into my table— not, of course, that Glenriddell or his likes would dream o' honouring my fire-side."

"Well—juist as lang as you keep the gentry as far frae me as I keep myself frae them we'll be happy enough about the arrangement. I'll never grudge you the gentry, Rab. I ken they mean a lot to you and I can understand how they dote on your company—your company maun flatter them even though they wouldna admit it. But I'm nae gentry, Rab, and I'll never aim that airt."

"Aye: they're a puir lot, Jean, for a' their drink and dripping roasts. . ."

Another wife might well have grudged him his hours spent in the company of men and women who would not have invited her to share their table and who would not have dreamed of sharing hers. But Jean was too serene in her relationship with the Bard to worry about such trifles; and with the young ones about the house she had never an idle or a lonely moment.

ADVICE TO A YOUNG BROTHER

William Burns was a lad of twenty-three years of age and was trying to improve on his apprenticeship as a saddler. . .

As Robert was friendly enough with Walter Auld, a Dumfries saddler, and as Wattie promised to give William a month's work; and as William hoped eventually to make his way to England, he eventually arrived at Ellisland.

The Bard had ever had a soft side towards William. He was a good lad, gentle-mannered, gentle-voiced and good-looking in a slightly effeminate way. But he lacked guts, drive, personality—and he found the world tough-going.

The Bard knew just how tough the world could be and he knew the qualities William lacked. He talked to him as they sauntered along the Nith's bank.

"You'll get a few weeks' work wi' Wattie Auld in Dumfries —but nae mair than that—unless you prove a byornar saddler."

"I'm a puir saddler, Robert."

"But damnit, lad, you shouldna say that as if you were content you should be so. There's nothing to hinder you being a first-class mechanic. Or is there?"

"I just dinna seem to have the application. I work hard enough too—I'm conscientious, Robert."

"Is there onything else you'd like to try your hand at?"

"Y'ken I'm nae use at farming work."

"No . . . you never tried very hard."

"I dinna see ocht else for me, then. . . I like reading and writing."

"Writing? What hae you been writing?"

"Oh—nothing, nothing really. I mean I like writing letters. . . I mean, if I'd a lot of people to write to. . ."

"Weel: that's aey something. But you see, William: the main business of life consists of securing for yourself a measure

of independent security. Once you can provide yourself with
food and clothing and shelter, put a penny by for a rainy day
and yet hae a shillin' in your pouch for a modest social
emergency—once you've made your way in the world to that
extent, *then* you can think about the refinements—as it were—
o' living. . . Oh, damn fine I ken how things are a' arse for
elbow in this world. But you've gotten a kinda arse-for-elbow
approach to life yourself, William. Before you can do a
damned thing you've got to work—and work hard. That's the
penalty o' being born into a family o' puir tenant-farmers.
You're the kind o' lad who could do wi' plenty o' schooling—
and gin you'd crammed your skull fu' o' their damned learning
you'd hae made an excellent tutor in a gentleman's family.
But here you are, my lad, at twenty-three years of age and
about to venture forth into the world and you fancy haudin'
South—into England——"

"I fancied there might be more openings that way for a
Scotch lad——"

"Weel . . . there micht be something in your fancies,
William. What did Gilbert say?"

"Gilbert thinks I lack resolution—and maybe I do, Robert.
And maybe, maybe I should be different from what I am. . ."

"Now, now, lad: you're fine. You're a credit to your
father's name and never get to thinking otherwise. Of course
you've got resolution: otherwise you wouldna think o'
making your way doon into England on your own——"

"I just had to get awa' frae Machlin, Robert. You ken
how I've pestered you this while back?"

"'Course you'd to get awa' frae Machlin. What the hell's
in Machlin for a lad o' spirit and ambition?"

"But you liked it—once?"

"Aye . . . once. Yes: I've had mony a happy nicht in
Machlin as you ken. I was about your age then. Aye: when
wee Smith and Jock Richmond and Clockie Brown and Davie
Brice. . . Yes, William, my bonnie boy, there was a time for
me when Machlin was the centre o' the world. Things were

discussed in Johnnie Dow's back room yonder that paled ocht
that was ever heard in Saint Stephen's Hall. Nichts that
you and Gibby and a wheen others never heard a cheep 'about.
Over a glass o' tippenny, William, we used to set the world to
rights and strut our bit stage like giants and heroes——"

"And you were a giant and a hero, Robert. There're plenty
still talk about it in Machlin. I've heard Johnnie Dow talk
about you mysel'. He's said to me many a time: ' You're a
wonderful family, you Burnses—but there'll never be another
like your brother Robert—the greatest man I ever served wi'
a gill o' Kilbagie.' In some ways Robert, you're a legend there
—especially to the younger generation."

"A legend. . . Aye; but I was cursed as a black-hearted
sinner about Machlin too. You wouldna hear ocht about
that?"

"Oh, plenty. . . But only from the ones who envy you
your success."

"Success! Look about you. D'you see these bare bluidy
acres o' stane and water-logged clay? Upwards o' a hundred
and seventy acres o' them at damn-near a pound an acre o'
rent. And that heap o' stanes and lime—that's my new house
a-building. . . Look well on a' that, William, and you're
looking at success. . ."

"But I thocht Mr. Tennant advised you?"

"Yes, yes, Auld Glen. . . But I'm no' hiding ahint Auld
Glen. Ellisland could be made a farm and a guid farm. And
believe me I'm the very man—poet or no' poet—who could
make it a guid farm: one o' the best in Scotland. I could hae
them flockin' frae far and near to praise my farming even as
they've praised my verses. Now: dinna think I'm boasting.
I've a' the intelligence needed for farming and plenty o'
experience o' what spells failure. Then what's holding me
back? Capital, William—a guid going cash account i' the Bank
o' Scotland in Dumfries. Gie me that and I'd double my capital
in ten years and own every bluidy acre o' it forbye. But, as it is
—well, I'll hae to struggle awa' in my ain strictly limited

fashion and try by every effort no' to run into debt. For believe me, William, once you add debt to your worries, you're finished. The hell-hounds o' Justice can be bad enough; but the hell-hounds unleashed by creditors bound straight frae the kennels o' hell. . .

"And yet, William, you ken how much I dislike the language o' complaint . . . life has its compensations. I could hae been settled in waur places and, for my money, wi' waur ground. It's a grand place this i' the lang simmer day and a glorious prospect a' round you. And when my new house is finished and spring comes round again—well, I'll win through yet. It's 'never, never to despair,' lad—that's what counts. And guidkens: gloomy December's no' a time o' year for a farmer to plod about his wet acres and view his prospects.

"Sae we'll see how you get on wi' Wattie Auld and what idea o' prospects you can gather for your next stage, which should tak' you south about Carlisle way. And mind: as long as I hae a hame o' my ain you're welcome to your bed and your bite. Dinna get it into your head that now you've left Mossgiel and your mither and Gilbert that you're awa' out into the world a hameless laddie. By God no: no' as long as I'm living. And mind that what I say goes for Jean too. Jean's on your side: she kens what the world can be like——"

"I've aey admired my new sister, Robert. You ken I've always stuck up for her."

"And weel you may. You'll no' find mony like Jean on your travels—and nane wi' a kinder heart."

And William thought that his brother was the greatest man who had ever lived. A man who strode purposefully on the earth and feared no one. A man who talked with a force and eloquence that was spell-binding. A man who knew people of every class and condition and who corresponded with anybody who mattered in Scotland. An amazing man; his own brother and yet somehow not his brother at all but utterly independent of family, of kith or kin. A man who had to be approached from the outside and never from the inside.

And yet a man who was more than a brother and somehow sustained and assured him as only an elder brother could.

William was profoundly touched by Robert's kindness; but his emotions were all tangled up. He knew he would have to quit Ellisland—and soon. For there was no doubt to William that Robert would only tolerate him provided he made every effort to succeed in life.

William was determined as never before in his life to make a place for himself, so that when he returned to Ellisland on his way to Mossgiel his success would be evident to everyone, but especially to Robert his brother who was Scotland's Bard.

Standing on the soggy bank by the river Nith on that gloomy afternoon the world did seem cold and friendless and unutterably bleak. The road to England, and to York—his first goal—seemed interminably long and milestoned with uncertainty. . . William built resolution on the quicksands of his emotions and he had to build feverishly against the imminence of collapse. He tried desperately hard not to blurt out to Robin that he was lonely and afraid; that what he longed for more than anything was to have a lass in whom he could confide, who would share his life and build with him a bield, however simple, against the cold blasts of the outside world.

But the Bard could sense all that troubled William. He suffered for the lad. He was flesh of his flesh—but how damnably unfitted, through an excess of sensibility, for the struggle in the market-place of life.

AULD REEKIE AGAIN

On the 15th of February, 1789, the Bard saddled Pegasus, his sturdy young horse, and rode off by way of Moffat and Biggar towards Edinburgh. . .

There was much to do in Auld Reekie . . . and Jenny Clow who had gone out to Haddington to have her baby was almost as important a worry to him as his settlement with his publisher, William Creech. . . And there was Clarinda! Not that he feared Clarinda any more. He was safely married to Jean; and Clarinda had come to no harm through him—he had taken good care that she shouldn't.

But Jenny Clow would cost him some money; and there was no saying how little he would get out of Creech.

Yet his main business must lie with the Excise—and Graham of Fintry in his capacity as Commissioner. He must press for an appointment in and around Ellisland. . .

Still: there were many friends in Auld Reekie and for the space of a few days he would be glad to renew old acquaintance-ship.

Willie Cruikshank, his host at St. James's Square, arranged a small party in his honour.

Lang Sandy Wood, the surgeon, Willie Nicol (whose house was filled with boarding scholars), Alexander Cunning-ham and Allan Masterton, the writing master and amateur musician, were there.

The men had the room to themselves for the port and the punch bowl.

"I forgot to ask you about your knee, Robert."

"It bothers me whiles, Sandy—especially after a long day in the saddle."

"You're damned lucky you can bend it at all. Yon was a

sair knee—aye, it micht bother you off and on a' your life. There's no' much you can dae barring a cauld compress at nichts."

"I see. . . And how's the influenza been in Edinburgh this winter?"

"Damned, this influenza's a bad business. It can kill you. And quick at that!"

"There was no influenza when I was a young man," said Nicol. "What the hell is it, Sandy?"

"A fever—nothing less. But it's a new fever whaurever it's hailed frae. It's a kind o' cross between a bad cold and pneumonia wi' a touch o' rheumatic fever thrown in for good measure."

"It leaves you damned low."

"It does, Robert. What did you do for it?"

"I got some potion from a Doctor Mundell in Dumfries. But actually a' I could do was lie abed till I was fit to raise my head."

But the company was too mixed and the Bard's peculiar relations with the individuals of the company too complex to admit of intimate or personal conversation. He would have to wait till he got them each to himself.

Yet it was pleasant to sit among his Edinburgh friends and note how solicitous they were for his welfare and how anxious they were for his company.

And then, as nearly always happened in a company of boon companions, the conversation turned to women and bawdry and the latest licentious gossip of the town.

"How's the Crochallan Song Book coming on, Robert?" queried Cunningham, who was the Crochallan Club's favourite tenor.

"Coming on fine, Cunningham. You can aey pick up a sang wherever you go. But we'll need to have a session at the Club—I hope I'll see Cleghorn there."

"Cleghorn's aey speirin' for you."

"Mind you—they're a coarse ignorant lot o' beggars in

Nithsdale—oh, just about as coarse and ignorant as you'd find in Scotland. Apart from one or two good fellows, life would be gey dreich for company."

Nicol said: "What the hell's wrang wi' Dumfries?"

"Damn a' wrang wi't, Willie; but I'm no' richt acquaint there yet. I've had sae much on my hands. But when things get easier——"

"They'll never get easier as lang as you're tied till a bluidy farm, Robert. Never! How's Peter Miller doing at Dalswinton?"

"Miller's doing fine, Sandy. He's been experimenting wi' a steamboat o' Symington's in the Loch yonder. They tell me it was a great success. Steam driven oars or paddles o' some kind."

"It worked then?"

"Aye, and no blame to it. I heard the noise when I was working in my fields across the Nith. The noise would have deafened you."

"The beggar's mad."

"No: I wouldna say he's mad—far from it. Miller's got ideas and ability to carry them out."

"He carried you off to Ellisland onyway."

"Not quite."

"What! You werena a month come to Town but he had his plans made for you. You told me as much yourself, Rab. Aye . . . he was in Town the other day. . . Dining in Fortune's, Harry Erskine says to him: 'How's the national Bard faring thae days, Mr. Miller?' 'You mean my tenant, Mr. Erskine!' 'As to that I wouldna ken, though I can understand that you wouldna let the greatest poet Scotland has ever had sit rent free.' Miller was blazing, so they tell me——"

"But this is nonsense. I know Harry Erskine's a warm admirer of mine. I ken now that Miller's offer to me wasn't just the luckpenny he made it out to be—but then he did offer me something when no other body did. As for paying my rent—well, I'll be damned—or gey far through—before I take charity frae any man and Harry Erskine should have minded that."

Nicol said: "That's your crowning folly, Rab—too damned independent; too stiff-necked in your pride o' independence."

"Would you have me taking charity, Willie?"

"I reason . . . I believe I would."

"What the devil has it to do wi' us what Robert takes by way o' charity or otherwise? We've nane o' us any right to discuss each other's private affairs."

"Up to a point, Sandy, up to a point. We're a' the Bard's friends here. But you maun remember that since Robert has become Scotland's Bard what he does and what he doesna do is Scotland's concern. In a sense he's the maist public man in Scotland. Robert kens that as weel as us."

"Do I?"

"By God and you should! What I do is of interest only to my immediate friends and no' always even to them; but what you do is public news—public property. And I'm no' referring only to your poetry."

"That's all of me that should concern the public."

"Aye, should—but since when is the public to be told what should and what shouldna interest it? You're like the King or the Premier—a' your actions are open to discussion and debate —whether you like it or dinna like it."

"May I interpose a word here?" asked Masterton. "There is a code of decency in these matters. Anything that touches the private lives of the great should be treated with the utmost privacy and any violation of that code—where it comes under our personal notice—should be severely frowned upon."

"Aye—code of honour! You wouldna be minded to give ony o' us here a lesson in good manners, would you, Allan?"

"Not under any circumstances—present company is aey excepted."

"Gentlemen: this is most embarrassing to me. Since we're met here to-night as friends, has the common bond of our friendship to be strained on my account? Damnit, I'll

no' be long among you—I'm only here for a few days. Fill the
bowl, Willie Cruikshank, and let us fill our cups."

"Right you are, Robert, I'll fill them up. And if Alexander
here will no' raise his voice ower high maybe he'll oblige me
and the company wi' a sang. What would you like him to sing,
Robert?"

"What about Clarinda?" said the Bard to Ainslie when
he met him the following day.

"She's in a towering rage, Robert. She's terribly angry
with you."

"I see."

"What did you expect her to be?"

"Oh, she could be thankful for past mercies; but she's a
woman and I suppose that's too much to expect."

"I ratherly think it is."

"Aye . . . so you're becoming quite an expert in understanding the vagaries o' the female mind, Bob?"

"No . . . not really, Robert. It's damnable she should be
living in such poverty! Of course, Mrs. MacLehose is a very
fine and sensitive gentlewoman."

"Aye . . . she's all that. You havena been in bed wi' her
yet?"

"I—I'd rather we didn't discuss things like that about
Mrs. MacLehose, Robert. I just canna think of Mrs. MacLehose
in that way."

"And she knows nothing about Jenny Clow?"

"Well. . ."

"Imphm. . . It's a very interesting situation, Bob. But
I find it a trifle ironic too. You see: I ken mair about Mrs.
MacLehose than ever you'll ken for a' your learning. And in
my own way—and that's no' a half-hearted way—I loved her.
And maybe a big bit o' me still loves her. She got a rough ca'
through life and she's paid a big price for it. But I've a clear
conscience for a' that. Onything she gave me I paid her double.
I could have ruined her—in her sense—easier than most women

in her cirumstances could have been ruined. I don't want you to make ony mistake about that, Bob. I don't want you to make ony mistakes about onything. You ken where I stand with regard to morality. You and me hae our points of difference there—in theory—whatever common ground we may occupy in practice."

"There're certain things I dinna think should be discussed, Robert."

"Maybe; but I'll discuss certain things that affect *me*. Clarinda's something o' the past—though what passed between us is sacred for all time as far as I'm concerned. And I've no regrets, Bob—no real regrets. Sometimes, of course, in the secret chambers of my mind I re-live certain associations, certain scenes, and do regret that our relationship has had to end this way. But moral regret—none, Bob. Absolutely none! I've married my Jean and there's not another woman in the world I'd put before her. That's one thing I'd have you to believe, Bob."

"Most certainly, Robert. She's your wife. I hasten to congratulate you on your good fortune."

"Good fortune's the word, Bob. As far as I'm concerned she's a woman above and beyond all other women. I've made mistakes in the past—committed follies if you like—Jenny Clow's one of them. It's conceivable that there might be a Jenny Clow in the future; but that's what I very much doubt."

"I'm glad to hear you say that, Robert. Every man sows his crop of wild oats——"

"Every man doesna, Bob; but we'll let that flea stick to the wa'. I just wanted to make it clear to you where Jean and I stand and where we're likely to stand in the future. And if you want to convey a hint of that to Mrs. McLehose you have my permission."

"I wouldn't think——"

"Now, now, Bob. Dinna protest too much. Mrs. MacLehose and you have had mony a heart-to-heart talk—and there's no harm but a lot of good in that. But there's another point I would like to draw your attention to, and your legal brain will be certain to appreciate it. . . I had no *need* to marry Jean as far as the world understands and as far as you lawyers understand the world. I had my Bachelor's Certificate in my pocket. Both Kirk and State were on *my* side; and it would do Mrs. MacLehose no harm to understand that."

"Yes, yes: I do appreciate that, Robert. But—eh—there were some promises—some vows—between you and Mrs. MacLehose?"

"Now are you asking as lawyer or friend?"

"As friend, Robert. Surely you could never doubt that?"

"Well, just put your lawyer's mind to this. Mrs. MacLehose is a married woman. Her husband won't divorce her and there's no reason to think he won't reach the allotted span. Mrs. MacLehose was (and remains) in no position either to give or receive vows."

"Perfectly right, Robert—I've told her so."

"But there's another sense. Oh yes, we made vows—and meant them at the time. But they were vows without validity. Of course we loved each other—after the only fashion that we could love another. But Mrs. MacLehose couldn't publicly overstep the bounds of her morality and her religion *à la* Mr. Kemp. So what permanence could be attached to the vows? Hell, man! We were in *love*! What started as a love dalliance damn near ended in tragedy—would have ended in tragedy had circumstances not taken me back to Machlin—and my Jean."

"You argue a terrific case, Robert. You'd have made a wonderful pleader on a good plea."

"By God no! I'm no pleader and no lying-tongued lawyer —nae offence to my good friends in the law. But I see you're no' convinced wi' my argument—my plea. Nevertheless, Bob, you'll have to believe me because there's no other truth to the matter. It's beyond your experience, that's all. We were talking the other night about my private affairs being public concern. But I very much doubt, if all the facts were laid before the world, that the world could understand what passed between Clarinda and me. For that understanding, one half of the world would need to be Clarinda and the other half Robert Burns. . .

"So you can tell her that she needna stay away from her window lest she see me in the street. Tell her to look into her heart and she'll see plenty.

"And by God, Bob, were I a moralist like you I could work myself up into a bonnie passion o' indignant rage. Think o' me, a puir Heaven-taught ploughman, being seduced by a married woman of the genteel variety! Invited to her chamber —and her little innocents lying through the wa'—after ten o'clock—and come as ye werena comin' for me—Oh, a bonnie picture, a fine state o' affairs. . . And now she's in a towering rage and you talk about vows and pledges. By God, sir, but your canting, legalistic moralists insist on having the best o' both worlds—so that when you shake your feathers you disappear in the dust o' respectability and your odour o' sanctity stinks waur nor a polecat. . ."

Willie Smellie and the Bard repaired with all speed to Dawney Douglas's.

"God damn you, Rab—Auld Reekie hasna been the same since you quat. Nor the Club either. Missed you? I couldna begin to tell you how I've missed you. But you've turned famous and settled doon on the river Nith wi' your Jean? Blessings on you then, you beggar! I'd like to come down and see you, Rab. But—what opportunity hae I to quat my printing and journey the length o' Dumfries? But wait till Dawney sairs us wi' the best he's gotten and let me hear your crack.

"Just that now—and you do see a change in the New Toon. You're quite right—a body on foot's in mortal danger trying to cross Princes Street nowadays. Thae young bloods on their horse or in their carriages would run you down. You're quite right, Robert. Except when I hae a bit business that takes me there, I'd never put a foot in the New Toon. There's nothing to compare wi' the High Street and the Auld Toon. And you miss us too?"

"Aye, I miss you, Willie. Mony a grand time you and me's had here in Dawney's—and in by in the Crown Room. I've seen me sitting on the bank o' the Nith yonder bluidy near breaking my heart for the nichts we've had thegither. But you ken there was nothing here for me. And now that I'm settled down wi' my Jean there's nothing could induce me to come back to Auld Reekie save on a flying visit."

"You're happy then, Rab?"

"Yes, I'm supremely happy, Willie. I've my worries and my cares and my tribulations, same as the rest o' puir folk— but aye, I've never been happier. I'm on the crest o' the wave."

"Aye: you look it. And you're jogging awa' at your muse —and your politics. I read the public prints, you ken."

"Well, I thought I'd cured myself of politics, Willie. But I just canna suppress myself completely. A wee bit o' what I feel maun out. I should lie low and mind that I was made and circumstanced to see nae higher than the midden heap. Then I just boil ower wi' rage at my lot. I mean—the poet in me boils over. There I am on the Nith, exiled as it were from the very nerve centre o' Scotland. And I'm asked to listen to the embittered unchristian ignorant mouthings and bluidy prejudices of my parish priest as if he spoke as the Lord's anointed."

"Exactly! Wha the hell's about the Nith for you to duel wi'? And I've noticed you're at your best when in a guid bluid-and-snotters argument. There's naebody in Edinburgh was ever able to stand up to you for lang. Oh, I gave you mony a fell dour battle and I'll no' say but I bested you whiles. But by God I never knew a man who could slay wi' his tongue the way you could. And then, damn you, you could get bluidy well eloquent. Yes eloquent, be damned. Oh, we've talked about you mony a nicht—and by the Lord Harry you never kent me to flatter onybody—and that goes for you."

"Well, there it is, Willie. Away down yonder in Nithsdale I've time to think—aye, an' brood—on a lot o' things. You're in the hurly-burly o' things here. It's no' possible to think clearly in a place like Edinburgh. Here you're aey making judgments on the spur o' the moment. You see, Willie, you're apt to forget that I came to Edinburgh wi' a fairly settled and tried-out philosophy. However poor my intellectual equipment, I came equipped."

"By certes and you did. You captured the Toon and a' bodies by the lug within ten days—the whilk never happened afore and never will again. And you juist an obscure ploughman poet!"

"Tuts, Willie: the fashion o' an hour."

"The fashion o' an hour—your arse and parsley. If you hadna been a greater personality than your poems indicated, you wouldna hae lasted the skirl o' the pan. Mind you: he's an ill-tongued beggar Willie Nicol when he gets started— especially wi' a load o' drink egging him on—but Nicol's said to me time after time: ' Smellie, you ugly sinner, did ye ever meet wi' mair natural genius nor Robert Burns? ' And aey I had to answer: ' I havena, Nicol: I havena.'

"And mind you, Rab, we could dae wi' you in thae kittle times—times that'll be kittler yet. The passion for reform's mounting—folk are no' for tolerating Dundas's high-handed dictatorship for ever—to say nothing about the Rotten Burghs and election trickery. . . There's a something in the air and they tell me that in France it's no' only in the air. . ."

"It's in the air about the Nith too then, Willie. And, man, it irks me often that I'm tied to my farm and a tenant o' Miller when my verses should be thundering and my tongue free to speak my real thoughts. Oh, and there're times when I canna bridle my tongue; times when I've just got to speak out and damn the consequences. A captive poet's more tortured than a caged song-bird."

"Aye: I can understand, Rab. But I maun caution you. If you're serious about takin' up with the Excise, you maun censor every word you write or speak. A government servant canna be openly agin the Government. He can hae his private thoughts——"

"But damn it, Willie, you've written enough yourself to ken that private thoughts are nae good to a poet. A poet maun speak out the deepest thoughts that are in him—or strangle."

"Or be strangled. Hae you thought o' that?"

"Aye: sweated blood thinking o' that. And now that I'm a married man wi' a load o' responsibilities I sweat more than ever. Oh, I can write a lyric verse or twa about a lad and a lass and them in love; a pastoral stanza is no' beyond my pen or my enjoyment. But Pope hit the nail a resounding clap on the head when he stated that the proper study o' mankind is man. God kens I'm as sensitive to the fair face o' nature as ony poet—but the natural scene is but the background or the foreground against or upon which man must act—must have his being. So politics and poetry gang hand in hand—if no' hand on heart. . ."

Shrewd Willie Smellie could see that beneath the Bard's fervour there was also something of a fever. He looked healthier than when he had last left Edinburgh. But there was more than a trace of jumpiness, of irritability in his speech, though he spoke fluently and eloquently enough. It was difficult to say just what it was. But Smellie was aware of the difference and it caused him to ponder for a moment.

"Maybe you've gotten ower much worry on your hands, Rab? I'd ease up gin I were you. Damnit, I work hard mysel' and I've got my worries—mair than maist maybe—but I tak' my ease too. Aye, certes: I ken how to ease my shanks *and* my mind. . . What you're missing is guid social company. Aye, a wife's a' richt, so are your bairns and your ain fireside— aye, and a lass in the by-gane is a man's privilege gin he feels like ane—but a man whiles needs the company o' his ain kind. Boon companions, if you like: like our Crochallan boys: that's whaur Auld Reekie, for a' its habble and stinks, scores ower your rural shades, Rab."

"For a wee while, Willie. No . . . I couldna bide in the Toon now. Fine for a holiday—maybe a month at the dead end o' the year. But for a man like me and for a poet like me, it's guid for nae mair nor a visit. Oh, I miss the company— God, I've bluidy-near grat whiles for the want o' company; but there's nae choice, nae twa ways about it: a man must bide where he best makes his living—and he must just make the best o' that."

"Aye, aye! Man, Rab, for the poet you are, your feet are planted damn solid on the ground. . . But we're needin' Dawney to lash doon some mair bluidy drink."

Baillie William Creech, more prim and proper than ever, smiled the false-sweet smile of a Lord's anointed baillie of Edinburgh.

"Ah, Robert: how glad I am to see you again. You needna tell me you are prospering: I can see that."

"You're well yourself, Mr. Creech—or should I address you as Baillie?"

"Well, my friends all address me as Baillie now, Robert; and since it's an unsought honour that the Toon has conferred on me——"

The velvet purr in the Baillie's smug voice almost turned the Bard's stomach. Creech must have seen the unsympathetic glint in his eye.

He shuffled among some papers.

"I think we can settle all the outstanding differences anent your Edinburgh edition, Robert. I've drawn up a statement here, and if you agree there's only the formality of signing."

"If you don't mind, Baillie, I'll cast an eye over the papers."

"Certainly, Robert. Would you care to be left alone for a while?"

"Well. . . I've travelled a sair road to get this length, Baillie—and we've been a while in settling. . . I'd just like to be clear in my own mind; and there's a wheen o' things I'll need to refresh my memory on——"

"Well, I've got some business out front, Robert—if you want me you'll not hesitate to call me ben?"

Left alone, he began to study the statement of affairs as drawn up by Creech. But the longer he studied it the less satisfied did he become. He beckoned Creech back to the inner sanctum.

"Here's a remarkable entry, Baillie. I see you have Sir John Whitefoord's subscription down twice for 53 copies."

Creech looked at the entries. He felt uncomfortable.

"Yes . . . let me see. . . Twice! I'm afraid you're quite right, Robert. Clerks are so careless nowadays."

"Just so. Well, that's another thirteen pounds and five shillings due me."

"Yes, yes: I agree to that."

"Aye. . . How about this matter of forty copies given away as presents——?"

"Advertising as you might say, Robert. I often give away many more copies—in the author's interest, of course. To influential people—promoting sales. I know you will under-stand——"

"That's just what I don't, Baillie——"

"But you must——"

"Now, now, Baillie: there's no must about the matter."

"Are you going to question my conduct, sir?"

"Damn you, Baillie, if you're going to ' sir ' me, then I'll ' sir ' you back wi' vengeance. I'm not questioning your conduct. But your clerks have made at least one mistake: they could have made another."

"Well, yes—since you put it that way. But, but . . . I gave away those copies myself: I don't leave such work to my clerks."

"That makes it easier then. Who got free copies?"

"I—I . . . just canna tell you off-hand, Robert. Besides——"

"Besides forty is a lot o' copies to give away, Baillie—especially when my subscription sheets were well filled up wi' names. I much doubt if there was need to give away any copies."

"Why! There are folks of the Toon who would be mortally offended if they werena given free copies of such books as I handle—conforming to established custom."

"Exactly! Not in the author's interest but in yours, Baillie. I might even myself be mortally offended if I knew some of these worthy burghers who think they are entitled to free copies of my poems."

"When I agreed to act as your agent in this matter, Robert —and, if I recall rightly you were very glad to have me——"

"Not glad, Baillie—deeply grateful."

"Well, why raise a trifle like this now—at this late date?"

"Ten pounds doesn't happen to be a trifle to me, Baillie. As for the lateness of the date: considering you kept me hanging on from August '87 till April '88; considering this is February '89——"

"Very well, Robert. Must we quarrel anent this?"

"I'm in no quarrelling mood, Baillie. The date's ower late for that. But I'm leaving the Town in a few days and when I leave this time you and me will have had a final settlement. I canna run up and down frae Nithsdale——"

"I fully understand your position: I'm not a dunderpate."

"'He wha could brush them down to mools. . .' Aye, aye: Willie, naebody'll ever accuse you o' dunderpatedness."

Creech was in a fix and he didn't know how to extricate himself with any credit. The Bard's eyes had him transfixed. The tone of his voice was deadly. He knew well he hadn't given away anything like forty copies. If he'd given away four. . . But he must never admit this.

Creech racked his brain for an excuse.

"Let me think this business over, Robert. Maybe my clerk——"

"I can come back in an hour's time."

"I would rather have a day or two."

"No days, Willie: no days. A busy man o' affairs, public

and private, doesn't need days to deal with a trifle. Name the recipients o' the copies and I'll jot down their names."

"Listen, Robert: I'll make a bargain with you. We've always been friends really, and there's no reason why we shouldna remain friends. Nobody admires your genius more than I do; nobody values your friendship more than I do. We've had many happy conversations in this room. I remember when my Lord Glencairn. . ."

Creech noted the expression in the Bard's eyes and faltered. But it was too late now to falter. He coughed nervously. Creech had never been more uncomfortable.

"So, Robert—so for old time's sake I'll—yes, I'll go halves with you over the presentation copies: twenty copies to you: twenty copies to me. In full and final settlement."

The Bard couldn't help admiring William Creech. He was fighting for his dignity as a man more than he was fighting for his money. He could call his thin nervous bluff; he could press him till he wiped out the forty copies. All he had to do was to keep silent and look Creech full in the eye. But he couldn't bear the sight of the Lord's anointed squirming in his own chair. The Bard jumped to his feet and held out his hand.

"Right then, Willie, we'll settle on that—and no ill feelings!"

"Thank you, Robert. No, no: no ill feelings. Maybe you would join me in a drink?"

"Yes: I'll sample a glass o' wine wi' you wi' pleasure. After all, we're no' farmers haggling at a cattle mart."

"Exactly, Robert. How well—if forcibly—you express yourself. Certainly we are no' horse-dealers. In this room the greatest wits and scholars of the age have met and discoursed—and done business wi' me. This wine I may say, Robert, I keep only for my most cherished acquaintances——"

"Well . . . your good health, Willie. And I'll be round in a day or two with my receipt."

"Your very good health, Robert. And—eh—I'll have the

money waiting for you. Now I hope you're not neglecting your Muse entirely now that. . ."

Stephen Clarke, the organist (and musical editor of the *Scots Musical Museum*), stretched out his long legs and thrust his hands deep into his pockets. James Johnson looked up from his drink and his honest face held a look of childhood innocence and benign pleasure. The Bard had just finished crooning over a song, the rhythm of which had hitherto eluded them.

"Damnit, Jamie, I sometimes wonder at you and Stephen. How could you mistake the lilt o' that—the words just melt into it."

"Aye—when you croon it ower. But it's no' an easy measure: is it, Stephen?"

Clarke unstretched himself. "It's an impossible measure with an impossible range. It'll tak' a highly trained singer to do it justice. I admit, Robert, that you make sense of it. The turns are maist difficult."

"Must I bring my Jean to Auld Reekie to teach the lot o' you?"

"Does Jean sing it?"

"Effortlessly."

"Without falsetto?"

"Without a scraich."

"Even on the final ' come try me'?"

"Effortlessly—from first note to last."

"Did she need much coaching?"

"I crooned it ower once and she had it."

"Well . . . the next time I'm down at Ellisland that's number one on the list."

"I admit that without the melody the words are the damnedest trash—but once you wed them to the tune every word becomes a jewel—a gem of meaning and of sensibility."

Johnson said: "I'm convinced, Robert—mair nor convinced. I wish you could bring your Jean to Reekie. I'd gie a year o' my life to hear her sing Jamie, come try me."

"Mrs. Burns has mair sense than come hereabouts. Right then: Jamie, come try me goes in. . ."

They went through the remaining tunes and Clarke noted all the Bard's amendments. Clarke was quite happy to work as musical scribe to the Bard. He was passionately fond of folk tunes: they were as a tonic of country air to him after the stuffiness of his classical and religious musical labours. Sometimes they even roused him from his natural lethargy.

"Well, Robert, thanks to you again; but I think we've gotten a grand collection for our third volume. D'you think we'll ever manage a fourth?"

"We'll manage a fourth, my friend. And a fifth and maybe a sixth."

"I doubt we'll no' manage a fifth, Robert. What do you think, Stephen?"

"If Robert thinks we'll manage a fifth and a sixth, then I think we will. But it'll depend on the Bard."

"There was a time—and that not so long ago—when I would have said there were no more than a hundred good songs in Scotland. Now I know there must be hundreds of odd scraps of old songs—often no more than a title—lying about Scotland. Often enough the melodies are lost beyond recall or have been given new names as they passed from mouth to mouth down the years. But I'm certain that the big feck o' our dance measures were once songs and can be songs again. I've proved that to you and I hope to prove it again to you many times before we think of issuing the last volume. Dinna think o' the last volume, Jamie—let's just keep on collecting till we can collect no more——"

"Or the public tire o' our efforts."

"Ah—dinna worry too much about the public and dinna hope for too much either. We're only, as it were, sowing seed. And here and there the ground's no' ready for the seed—and that's a gey pity but we canna help it. And it's true we may none o' us live to reap the harvest. But that harvest will come:

hae nae fear o' that. It'll be a rich harvest when it does come; and that will be our reward."

"Amen!" said Stephen Clarke, not irreverently.

"Aye, weel:" said Johnson, "we hae done a thundering guid nicht's work, so we could hae a drink to that."

The plainstanes and the causeways of Auld Reekie had not altered: they were as wet and raw and damp as they had ever been of a winter's day. But once—and that but a year or so ago—there had been romance and wonder and anticipation about them. Aye, the bare rain-washed streets of the Town had held an unknown but beckoning promise then.

Now there was neither promise nor anticipation. The streets were hard and yielded nothing. Any promise they held was the promise of certain penury. In isolated caves among the gaunt tenement crags lurked this friend and that. In this tavern and that was the clatter of pewter pots and occasionally the clink of a glass; and ever a bawd's pale face leered behind the fringe of her shawl and a lean dog growled over a meatless bone. . .

But there was no abiding neuk or crannie in Auld Reekie for Robert Burns. And Clarinda absented herself from her window. . .

The Bard rode up and out of Edinburgh in a raw east wind and mounted slowly towards Haddington. He wasn't looking forward to his meeting there and his mood was gloomy. The short winter's day was drawing to its close and the bare countryside and slow hills seemed strangely spiritless. But then he had always felt alien to the east country. To him, the farms he passed were nameless and without any warmth of association. He rode into Haddington to find it ancient and cold and withdrawn.

Even in the soft-candled gloom of a tavern retreat, Jenny Clow proved obdurate.

"No, Mr. Burns: I'll tak' your settlement and richt

willingly, for I need every penny o't. But I'll no' hand ower my son to you. That's something naebody'll ever tak' frae me—and naebody, no' even you, has ony richt."

The Bard's eyes glowed on her burning pale consumptive face. She had hardened—but hardened in a way that won his grudging approval.

"All right, Jenny lass: I've left you a long while without your settlement, though Mr. Ainslie assures me that you got my token payments from time to time?"

"I havena denied that, hae I?"

"No, no: you've denied nothing. But you did take out the writ against me?"

"Did you want me to starve—and the bairn too?"

"I wouldna hae seen you starving."

"Did ye ken or care?"

"If I'd kenned I wad hae cared, lass."

"Aye: if ye'd kenned—maybe!"

"You're bitter."

"No: I'm no' bitter: I juist had to mak' sure o' things in the only way that was open to me."

"Aye . . . I'm no' blaming you."

"Blame wouldna help onyway."

"You're right."

"I've nae ill-will to you, Mr. Burns: I liked you at the time and I didna richt ken ony better—I was never a hure and never was a' the sair time I carried."

"I never thocht you were. But about the boy, Jenny. I could bring him up in my own name and give him a better chance in life than maybe you'll be able to do—you'll need to work——"

"I've aey had to work."

"You'd do better without the burden o' the bairn."

"I managed the burden o' carrying him in my womb without ony real help frae you, Mr. Burns. I think I'll manage to carry him through life till he can fend for himself. My bed's maybe no' a' it should be and maybe no' as well as you could provide; but I'm his mother and a proud mother; and he can mean nae mair to you than I mean. Dinna tell me, Mr. Burns. I was guid enough to lie wi' but I wasna guid enough to marry——"

"But——"

"I ken there was never ony possibility o' marriage atween us. The only time I ever hured was to you and I didna think it was ony huring then, for I liked you. Christ help me! I even loved you though that was beyond me when I thought things ower in the cauld grey daylicht. An' yet I was aey pleased to see you when you came back."

"As long as you ken I didna deceive you."

"Aye: you deceived me—only I was willing to be deceived: that's the difference. Oh, dinna worry—if ye are worrying: there is nae man'll get frae me what you got."

"Richt then, Jenny. . . But maybe the day'll come when you would like me to tak' the boy——"

"You'll never get him. What! Why should *your* wife get *my* boy?"

"He's my boy too."

"Aye—the start o' him was yours! But frae then on it was my blood and my flesh that nourished him. And it was me had the pain o' bringing him into the world. And if he goes oot o' the world afore me, I'll be there to close his een."

"And when he asks o' his father?"

"I'll no' disgrace you, if that's what you think. And I'll no' disgrace him either. I'll tell him his father died afore he was born—and that'll be nae richt lee either."

The Bard tapped his fingers on the scrubbed board. Physically, Jenny Clow seemed far from well. But she had developed a spiritual strength that he had not suspected was in her. Coolly and logically she had rebuffed him as no woman had ever rebuffed him. His admiration for her, though grudging, was genuine. And yet his leave-taking was cold and lame.

"Well, Jenny, I'll need to go——"

"Of course you'll need to go."

"You think I'm deserting you?"

"No. . . I'm thinking nothing."

"You havena too much ill-feeling towards me——?"

"I've nae feelings towards you, Mr. Burns, ill or otherwise."

"That's hard enough——"

"Dinna worry about your feelings—they'll no' kill you."

"I could say plenty aboot that. I've got feelings for you, Jenny, and feelings for your bairn——"

"No, Mr. Burns: I had feelings for you once—and you see where my feelings hae landed me. Nothing easier than to talk about feelings and I suppose that's a' that poets hae to trade on. But a hungry belly and a toom cupboard hurts in a way that feelings canna. It's a' richt: you needna look sae glum. You'll no' be left here five minutes till you've forgotten aboot me and the bairn too."

But Jenny Clow spoke from bitterness and disillusion and she shed bitter tears that night as she had shed many a night for the folly of her ecstatic dalliance with Robert Burns. And if the Bard did not shed tears, a corner of his heart was to be for ever leadened with the thought of Jenny and their son.

For Robert Burns was not made of the stuff that could forget. And though the pangs of remorse may not yet be equated with the pangs of childbirth, yet nature has provided that the pangs of physical pain pass from the memory while remorse grows like a cancer upon itself.

He had settled with her fully and liberally. More, indeed, than satisfied the law. Now that he was about to rise he drew a gold guinea from his pocket and slid it gently on to the board. It was a bright new coin and it flashed for a moment in the candle-light.

Jenny Clow gave it no more than a glance. But her eyes softened as she put a thin hand into her bosom and fished out the first guinea he had given her, pierced and secured by a once-blue ribbon that was now string-thin and grimy.

"You needna bother, Mr. Burns—I haena parted with *this* one yet."

The Bard reached for his hat and pulled it well down on his pock-pitted brow.

"Guid-night, Jenny—and if you ever need me ye ken where to get in touch with me."

"Aye," said Jenny, in a tone lacking inflection. She picked up the coin between her finger and thumb; but her eyes expressed neither curiosity nor gratitude. Nor did she seem to hear the Bard's steps echoing down the passage.

The landlady of The George padded up to the table and slid a dirty cloth along the surface. Her keen acquisitive eye noted the glint of the golden guinea.

"And wha wad your frien' be, Jenny?"

Jenny gave a catarrhal sniff:

"Him? Huh . . . maybe the Lord God Almighty or maybe Auld Nick—or maybe them baith gin there's nae difference atween them. Fill up my glass, wife—and I'm in nae mood for jawin' the nicht."

The landlady padded away. By certes and that was an ill-gotten mouthfu' frae a bit slip o' a clytrie-maid. . . But certes, the big black burnin' een o' her companion werena richt o' this warld either, now that she mentioned him.

His visit to Edinburgh had not been a success. On the material side he had won something. He had made Creech come to heel—and once brought to heel, Creech had turned remarkably fair and friendly. They said good-bye in warmer and more honest friendly terms than they had done since the first successful flush of the Edinburgh edition.

His interview with Graham of Fintry had been warm and promising. It seemed that Commissioner Graham was genuinely interested in his future welfare. But he could promise nothing definite for the moment.

His meetings with his old-time friends and boon companions had been warm enough. Yet he realised that there was a mutual feeling that he was but a fleeting visitor; that there was nothing to detain him; that it might be years before he saw any of them again; that he was a married man and a farmer thirled to the bareness of his rented Nithsdale acres.

Ellisland meant nothing to his Edinburgh friends. Yet it was home to him. When he had been a poet lodging in the Landmarket, things had been different, for then he had been in an intimate sense, one of them.

And there was the shadow of Nancy MacLehose, so consumed with bitter chagrin towards him that she refused to appear near her window. A silly bitch, Nancy—but he could not harbour any ill-feeling towards her. Still, it hurt. . .

Strange that the hurt from Clarinda should be deeper than the hurt from Jenny Clow. He would have given much to have talked with Clarinda and maybe to have drunk a glass of wine with her or even partaken of a modest dish of tea. There had been no longing to see Jenny Clow—except in so far as she was the mother of his unfortunate bairn. Clarinda had wounded his pride: Jenny had hurt him in his guts. Could it be that the hurt to his pride was the keener?

The damned thing was that trouble never came to him singly. The longer he lived the more caught-up did he become in associations and activities. Other farmers could husband their acres and take their ease by the ingle of an evening and rejoice in the wives of their bosoms. In the tavern they could sit down quietly to their ale, join in the chorus of a song and crack, mostly inconsequentially, about the politics of the day.

But he could take nothing simply. His imagination was ever on fire; his questing brain refused to lie dormant. If he rejoiced in Jean he rejoiced tempestuously; for his love for her was an unquenchable passionate fire. To be a husband meant being first a lover and then a father. There could be no such state as domestic doldrums. Jean was there to be loved; but she was also there to sing his songs and partake in a very practical way in his *Museum* work. For songs were for singing as well as for preserving on the printed page so that the generations yet unborn might enter into this heritage.

It was not for him to take a back-seat in the tavern and drop a casual word here and there. Circumstances dictated that he had to be in the centre of activity. He relished good talk and was invigorated with the glow of wit and words. The passion that burned within him invigorated his every activity. If the conversation was bawdy, there was no mealy-mouthed smirking bawdry about him. His bawdry was lusty and buttock-bare—and, like hand-claps on a tight bare buttock, his words rang clear and resonant, at once refreshing and stimulating. Men rejoiced in his bawdry and felt cleansed. . .

So with his politics. He disdained the staleness and the mean deceit of political clap-trap. He stated his case roundly and without equivocation. His whole being revolted against the shams and shibboleths of party politics. Men listened to him and were enthused by him—but most feared him. He was too daring, too sweeping, too courageous, too devastating.

He had not remained silent in Edinburgh. His friends were nowise in the dark as to where he stood on the political questions of the day. Even radical Willie Nicol, whom he considered his best and certainly most intimate friend, thought him too extreme when he was chiding him.

The Bard had been deeply affected by the successful revolution that had taken place in America; that the Americans (their English-speaking cousins) had achieved Independence— a word minted of the purest rationalist gold—from the Hanoverian régime; that they had repudiated the Hanoverians almost in the same terms as the Hanoverians had repudiated the "bloody and tyrannical House of Stewart" was all grist to the sentiment of his political mill.

The young America was on the side of independence. Their hero was George Washington. And the Bard was violently on the side of Washington.

He had no great love for and had less faith in the Whigs; but they seemed to him to represent the lesser evil to the Tories.

Charles James Fox was in advance of Pitt—and Washington was a tremendous advance on either.

And so, sentimentally and aesthetically, he favoured the Jacobites against the Hanoverians; preferred Charlie ower the Water to German Geordie. These were the sentimental fantasies of the day. Yet he saw through the fantasies: none clearer. For kings and queens he didn't mourn. . .

What he desired for Auld Scotland was freedom. He revolted against wealth and privilege and the corruption of the party politics of wealth and privilege.

Just as he automatically dissembled in his approach to the Big Folks—and to such patrons as Mrs. Dunlop—so he dissembled politically. He had no wish for the return of the Stewarts; for the Papacy; for the Divine Right of Kings. But he was more against the corruption of the alien Hanoverian dynasty and a Government of corruption, headed by an ignorant if not insane king.

But all the time he was searching for a political reality that would make an end to a compromise with fantasy. America gave him a lead and an inspiration.

And now there were rumblings and lightning flashes from France. . .

But mostly, in Edinburgh, he was overcome by loneliness. Especially in the hustle and bustle of the main streets was his loneliness, his apartness, driven in on him.

Princes Street was busier than he had ever known it. The carriages of the rich and the privileged dashed up and down its broad mile, scorning the humble pedestrian. He who foolishly ventured into the highway was an immediate challenge to the chariot-like wheels of wealth.

He had to leap for safety or be mown down by them. It was against the natural law that wealth should draw a rein in consideration of age or poverty. Now wealth and privilege, as never before, measured themselves against the background of the New Town and found themselves mighty as they had never been found mighty.

All this enraged the Bard and made him hate that wealth that was without worth with an almost maniacal hatred. But it made him feel lonely too. He did not belong, even in the humblest ranks, to this darling seat of Scotia. Yes: at one time he had been its wonder and its favoured poet. But that time had long ago been swallowed up into the oblivion of forgotten days. And he would not have had it otherwise.

He belonged to the land. Except as a farmer there was no future for him. As a farmer he must earn his bread and support his wife and family. He would get back to Ellisland—and Jean. He would make a success of Ellisland or die in the attempt—and he had no notion of dying.

There was only time now for a good-bye drink with Willie Nicol—and then farewell to Auld Reekie. . .

Part Two

THE YEAR THE BASTILLE FELL

WIFE AND SISTER

THE BARD returned from Edinburgh to find that Thomas Boyd, the Dumfries builder, had withdrawn his labour from Ellisland. He was angry and frustrated. He wrote to Boyd and expressed his disappointment and begged him to make progress.

"David Newall micht want his house back ony day now, Jean. The end o' the month at the latest."

"Then what are we to do, Rab?"

"That's what worries me, Jean. I don't know. Nothing seems to go right wi' me."

"You havena said much about your Embro visit——"

"Aboot the only time you and me can enjoy a talk by oursel's is in bed, lass. No . . . I didna get a' I wanted in Embro. Creech settled at the hinderend and I saw a wheen o' folk——"

"And some o' your auld Embro flames?"

"Damn the flame—and ye ken that's a' done and by wi'."

"I was juist in fun, Rab."

"Aye. . . I had hoped Graham o' Fintry would hae been able to do something immediate about Leonard Smith's Division. But it seems there're difficulties. He did think that Smith could be transferred to Dumfries. But at least he's for setting the wheels in motion."

"You're still set on the Excise?"

"I see nae other road, Jean."

"And if you get the Excise are you still for bringing Gilbert doon?"

"I ken you're no' verra keen on the idea, Jean. But Gibby could work the farm while I was out on my Excise rounds. Mind: he owes me a hundred and eighty pounds—he could work for his bite and his clothes till it was paid back. . . You've nothing against Gilbert as far as his work goes, have you?"

"No . . . I've nothing against Gilbert. And I leave everything to you, Rab. As long as you're sure you'll agree. And what about your mither and sisters . . . and d'you think now that William's on his way to England he'll no' be back. . .?"

"Hell, Jean: I dinna ken everything. We micht get my mither and sisters a cot-house about the district. . . I would need to discuss this wi' Gilbert. I hope William's on the road to get settled somewhere. But if he doesna, he'll just need to come back here: I canna turn my back on the lad."

"You ken I wouldna ask you to do onything like that, Rab."

"Aye . . . you've been good to him, Jean."

"And you've been good to *my* brithers. Adam worships the ground you stand on."

"A guid lad Adam; and a guid worker. There'll be nae fear o' Adam. And if he settles doon and marries Fanny——"

"There's plenty time for that yet."

"Aye . . . and Adam'll need to master his trade. . . It's a hell o' a world, lass. There's another point. I'll need to see if Nancy'll come down soon. You've got far too much work on your hands. Noo that you're pregnant you'll need to tak' things a bit easier."

"You needna worry about me—I'll manage fine."

"Aye; but gin I was awa' on an Excise journey and ony-thing happened? Old Nance Cullie's nae bluidy guid. And you'll be too far away in the new house. . . I could set aboot Boyd for taking away his men. He'd nae damned right——"

"Now, now, Rab: dinna get wrocht up or you'll no' sleep."

"Lie ower then, lass. I'm sae damned tired after my journey. . ."

By the first week in March, Robert Heron, a divinity student he had met at blind Doctor Blacklock's house in

Edinburgh, was passing through Dumfries; and he delivered a letter to the Bard from Clarinda.

It was a vicious letter. Clarinda was infuriated that he had not called on her. She raked up the past and assailed him as a wretch and a villain. And until he admitted as much and apologised. . .

He was angry at Clarinda; but he realised that her ill-nature and chagrin didn't reach down very deeply. Clarinda was still in love with him.

He replied with dignity and with subtle flattery; but he would not "acquiesce in the name of Villain." Indeed he retracted nothing and shifted the balance of any responsibility back to Clarinda. As an added caution he did not put either his name or address to the letter. Neither did he mention hers, but merely addressed her as "Madam."

The next move lay with Clarinda and he hoped that, though she wouldn't be in any hurry to make it, she would . . . some day . . . when it would be more convenient for him. . .

But the truth was that nothing came convenient to him nowadays. He was always overwhelmed with work. By the last week of March he was busy sowing his seed corn, for he did not spare himself in his farm work. At nights he was busy with his correspondence.

There were many letters to write, many correspondents to keep in touch with. And there was his labour of love and of much sweat and penmanship on his editorial contributory work for Johnson's *Scots Musical Museum*. And he had much reading to overtake.

On the 24th of March his sister Nancy arrived from Mossgiel.

Nancy hadn't changed much in the years: she was more woman now: more experienced. But her tongue could be as sharp and her wit as biting as ever. And she was still devoted to Robin.

"Aye," she said when she'd settled down for a crack at the fireside in the evening when the young ones were bedded,

"aye, you've a grand hoose here. A pity you couldna bide.
That new hoose o' yours is no' near ready yet, Robin!"

"We'll juist need to move by the end o' the month—the
kitchen and a bedroom'll be finished and another room shortly."

"It'll need plenty firing. The plaister's running water."

"I ken, Nancy; damnit, naebody kens better."

"Dinna get short wi' me. And I'm takin' nae orders frae
you, mind. I'm here to help Jean."

"Naebody's giving you orders, Nancy."

"Well . . . watch your tone. I hear Meg Muir o' Tarbolton
Mill's coming doon this week."

Jean said with slow reflective warmth: "There's naebody
I'd like to see mair than Meg Muir: she was a mither and mair
to me at the Mill. . ." Her thoughts drifted back to the
scene.

The Bard had his picture too and he immediately warmed
both to Jean and to Mrs. Muir.

"Aye: we'll be glad to welcome her, Jean."

"You mind she aey said she would preside at our first
house-warming?"

Nancy said: "Certes, it'll need warming."

"Aye: she promised. Guid for Mrs. Muir. I wonder how
she's coming? Who told her?"

"Oh, Gibby was at the Mill and said you'd be moving into
your new house by the end o' the month."

"Well, then: we'll need to hae a proper house-warming.
And it's only right we should. And a bit dance maybe."

"Wha are you inviting?"

"Oh, you'll be there, dinna fret. And there's a wheen
guid folk about the place."

"I'm glad to hear that."

"And there's the family. There'll be Adam and Fanny."

"Are they making a match?"

"I hope so, Nancy. Nothing would please Jean and me
more. 'Course, there's nae hurry."

"I've nothing agin Adam, Jean. And Fanny's a guid lass.

Oh . . . they'd mak' a guid couple. Are they stepping oot thegither?"

"No . . . not exactly, Nancy. We're no' throwing them thegither. They're young yet."

"You forget when you were young."

"No: I dinna forget *onything*, Nancy."

"It's nothing to me. Wha's the picture aboon the fire?"

"The Earl o' Glencairn."

"That's Glencairn is it? A fine-looking man. He was a guid friend to you, Robin."

"He is, Nancy. I owe more to him than I can say."

"And I see you've gotten a new fiddle?"

"A wedding present frae Mrs. Dunlop—at least part o' it."

"Some o' the gentry are guid to you."

"Mrs. Dunlop's been mair than generous to me—and to Jean, since she's heard o' our marriage. Maybe she's an auld blether whiles—but a heart o' gold—and a good head on her."

"I see. . ."

"Oh aye, Nancy. Mrs. Dunlop has been good to Rab. They write to each other a lot."

"She canna be ony chicken."

"She'll be aboot sixty."

"Coming into her second childhood. . ."

"Damn that tongue o' yours, Nancy. You'll need to clip it hereaboots."

"Ho—there's naebody hereaboots I'm caring for. I'll no' disgrace you, dinna worry."

"I'll away out and look the horse afore I turn in. You'll be wanting to bed early, I suppose."

"Aye . . . I could dae wi' my bed: it's a sair journey. I often heard you complain aboot it. I'm glad I had the nicht at Sanquhar wi' your friends the Whighams. You used to ride it in a day?"

"Nearly always. . . D'you want a bowl o' brose or some buttermilk afore you bed?"

"On you go, Rab: I'll see to Nancy."

When he had gone Nancy said:

"You've made a man o' him, Jean."

"No, Nancy: Rab was aey a man and nane like him."

"Oh, there's nane like him. And mind you, Jean, I was aey fond o' him. He's my favourite brother and I wouldna like onything to happen to him."

"Well, you ken I'll dae a' I can."

"I ken, Jean. But is this farm for daeing?"

"He's no' sure."

"He was telling Gibby that. And what's his idea o' wanting Gibby doon here?"

"He wants to tak' on the Excise."

"Seems to me he's aey had a hankering for a gauger. It's no' a job for him."

"It's whatever he thinks best, Nancy. I wouldna like to influence him."

"Oh, but you'll need to influence him if it's for his guid."

"Aye; but how can I be the judge o' what's for his guid—when it comes to a thing like the farm and the Excise?"

"There's nae guid o' bringing Gibby doon here. Besides, they wouldna agree. They think they would; but I ken better."

"I canna see them agreeing mysel'."

"Their natures are different. Robin's far ower easy-going——"

"He doesna spare himsel'. . ."

"I ken . . . but he hasna the same system to his work that Gibby has."

"You think Gilbert's the better farmer?"

"No: I juist wouldna gang that length, Jean. But Gibby's aey plodding awa' wi' a purpose. Robin goes by fits and starts—at least he used to."

"Maybe . . . but he's nae fool aboot a farm as far as I can judge."

"Robin kens a' there's to ken—and a lot mair: Gibby'll

tell you that. I ken it's Robin's money that's keeping Gibby in Mossgiel. But I canna see that we should break it up. Mind you, Jean, I'll work for Robin ony time; and as long as I get my bite and my claithes I'll no' worry much aboot wages."

"Oh, but Rab wouldna hae you workin' for nothing."

"Of coorse, if Gilbert was to marry. . ."

"D'you think he will?"

"I hear he's a notion o' a Jean Breckenridge aboot Kilmarnock. There's nae reason why he shouldna marry. He'd be a catch for ony woman."

"I think he should marry, Nancy."

"I think so too. Only I'd like to see him getting a guid wife. And I ken nocht aboot this Kilmarnock woman. There's maybe nothing in it. If I get Robin in the richt mood I'll hae a talk wi' him."

"You're no' feared o' Rab?"

"No' feared. But I ken his moods, Jean. He's no' the same wi' you as he is wi' me. And he's a famous man now."

"Famous? Aye, he's famous. But he's too guid for the half o' them, Nancy. You'd think the Big Folk could do mair for him. Mr. Miller, the laird, hasna done fair wi' him. He could hae let him sit rent free for a year or twa."

"Aye—for ever! I agree, Jean. The Big Folks haena done so much for him. And he doesna need to be starting as a gauger after a' he's done. 'Course, Robin's independent."

"He keeps up a brave front. But it's me kens how deep he feels things. Rab doesna hide much frae me, Nancy."

"You're man and wife."

"Aye: but in a sense we're mair nor man and wife. There's a lot o' the laddie in Rab yet. He's easy hurt and he hurts sair. I ken he wouldna admit it and neither would I—but it's me he comes to and it's me he confides in. Rab's fu' o' feeling— aye, for a' living things—even the brute beasts. . . I dae a' I can to ease his load, Nancy. I try to gie him as much peace for his reading and writing as I can. He writes a lot o' letters and then he's aey at his sangs. He would hae me singin' a' nicht whiles. . . If only he'd a' day to read and write and work on his sangs. . . And then he's sae mony folk to see. Mr. Stewart the factor at Closeburn; Mr. MacMurdo the chamberlain at Drumlanrig—that's the Earl o' Queensberry's place. And then Captain Riddell doon there at the Carse—Friars Carse."

"He's no' drinkin', is he?"

"No: he's no' drinkin', Nancy. Drink doesna agree wi' Rab. He wouldna care if he never lipped it. Of course when he's oot wi' company he has to tak' a drink back and forward. He tells me he took a heavy drink whiles when he was biding here by himsel' at the Cullies' place. Nancy: you never saw a damp hole like it. I grat when I saw it: I couldna help it. I should hae been doon here long ago. Nae wonder he took a drink whiles."

"I've aey been feared o' Robin and drink, Jean. If he was takin' to the drink he'd tak' it heavy. He's ower guid for this world, Jean—in mony ways."

"Weel he just canna stand it, Nancy. It doesna agree wi' him. My faither aey took a guid dram; but he was never up nor doon wi' it the next day. Rab's different: he's no worth a docken the next day—at least no' till the day's weel on. It's aey his stomach it goes for."

"I ken."

"How? Did you ever see Rab drunk?"

"Once. I was the only one that knew. I held his head in the byre. He was gey sick. I've never seen onybody sae sick. And he was sorry for himsel'."

"When was that?"

"Oh—aboot yon time he was going to the Indies. A letter cam' to him ae day. . . He raved to me aboot it when he was drunk that nicht. It was something to dae wi' yon Mary Campbell."

"Her! He's never mentioned her to me."

"Maybe I shouldna hae mentioned it—only Robin was mair sorry for himsel' than drunk."

"Oh I ken plenty aboot Mary Campbell. Mair nor Rab

thinks. But you see, Nancy, I never worry aboot other women as far as Rab's concerned."

"I'd worry—it's no' natural no' to worry."

"Then I canna be natural. It's no' that I'm no' jealous: dinna think that. But being jealous doesna dae ony guid. I ken Rab's had other women—and he'll maybe hae a wheen yet afore he's done."

"I'll no' listen to that talk, Jean. That's wicked talk. What kind o' attitude's that to tak' up to your marriage? That's as guid as encouraging him."

"If there should be onybody else, Rab'll no' need ony encouragement."

"I never thocht you'd sae low an opinion o' him. I'm surprised I maun say."

"You dinna ken how it is, Nancy. No' wi' a man like Rab."

"So he's no' as guid as other men, is he no'?"

"Far better. I hope there'll be nae other women and I've nae reason to think there'll ever be. But I love Rab far ower much to deny him ony other woman—gin he loved her."

"That's a love that's ower deep for me to understand, Jean. I ken Robin hasna been a' he should hae been——"

"You wrang him to judge him, Nancy. I'm his wife and I wouldna."

Nancy lowered her eyes. There was a quiet dignity, a simple unforced majesty about Jean that silenced her. Silenced her but made her wonder. There were times when Jean Armour seemed far too good for Robin; aye, and maybe far too good to be a woman and a married one. But there was no doubting her sincerity. And there was no doubting her love for Robin.

But it was a love, a nobility of love that lay outside the range of Nancy's consciousness and of her experience. It had a quality that was incommensurable with the love of such married folks as she knew; and it had a quality she knew in her heart she could never attain were she ever to be married to a man. Maybe she would never be married. She had loved; but it had never been a love like this love Jean Armour seemed to experience. It made Nancy feel humble and yet sad. Here was a something she had missed in life. Here was a something she could never hope to attain. There was nothing she could say. On this most inviolate and sacred ground Jean Armour was invulnerable. And yet somehow, outside of Jean, it was somehow indecent to think of Robin in the arms of another woman—and not after marrying Jean and settling down to beget and rear a family with her.

She knew that men's tongues were ever hanging out thirsting after women and that married men were the worst. But then she could never think of Robin—or Gilbert—as being men in this sense. And maybe there was a sublimated or inverted incestuousness in her feeling for Robin.

When he came back, Nancy bade them good-night and retired.

Robert looked at Jean for a moment with a look of quizzical interrogation.

"Something wrong?"

"No: nothing wrong, Rab. Nancy and me understand each other—nothing will ever come atween us."

"Ah weel: I'm glad to see that you get on thegither."

THE HOUSE-WARMING

Robert surveyed the rising ruin of his new house with a sad heart. It was roofed, thank God; and most of the windows were fixed; but inside was a wreck of trestles and planks and buckets of plaster. It would be a grand house—when it was finished. But when?

It was a T-shaped building. A good-sized kitchen and a bedroom comprised the lateral head, and two bedrooms and a parlour comprised the vertical body. The kitchen had two windows: one looking across the court-yard to the Nith and the Dalswinton holm beyond: the other looking into the kail-yard. The adjacent bedroom, which he was to share with Jean, had a window looking up-Nith towards Friars Carse. The parlour at the extreme end of the long passage had a window in either wall and a fireplace in the gable. There were a couple of long low attics for storage and where servants could sleep.

Yes: it would be a grand house when it was finished. The back door led from the kitchen into the court and the front door, sheltered by the wall of the head-piece, opened—just beyond the kitchen—into the long passage.

It was possible therefore for visitors to have access to the parlour without entering through the kitchen. This provision the Bard had insisted upon. He intended that the parlour would also be his study. Here he would shelve his books, have his table-desk—and here he hoped to entertain his more special guests.

That he was to write more masterpieces at the end of the deal table in the kitchen could not be foreseen.

But he could wait no longer, no matter how Tam Boyd pleaded.

"I can do no less than insist, Mr. Boyd. David Newall's waiting even now on his house; and he's been patience itself. The servants can go to the lofts. Right?"

"As long as they dinna romp about—yes."

"Now all I need is the kitchen, the bedroom and the first bedroom in the passage."

"Weel: I can give you that. But I'm warning you. The plaister's no' dried out yet and it'll be weel on in the summer—if we get onything o' a summer—afore it's dried out."

"Will firing help?"

"Aye, it'll help; but there's nae fires in the bedrooms."

"Well, we'll need more warming-pans in the beds."

"And the men'll be traiking out and in a' day."

"Damnit, I ken, Mr. Boyd, that things are no' what they should be; but that's hardly my fault—is it?"

"I've done the best I can, Mr. Burns. You've got my best

man here—Sandy MacCrombie. There're folks shouting and pleading for me for twenty parishes round. . ."

"Weel, I'm shouting loudest—now that I've got you to shout at! I've just got to move in and that's the ultimatum. So will you redd the kitchen and twa bedrooms for me—gin Friday? I'll move in on Saturday night when your men lowse. Things'll be quieter on the Sabbath: that alone would justify the Lord's Day."

"Weel: but you'll need to watch how you move your things in. And mind that the plaister's still saft. Damn it, Mr. Burns, I'm thinking o' your health as weel. Suppose you get a founderin'? And what about your wife?"

"Hell, man, d'you want us to bed ahint the stane fence? I'll keep the kitchen fire roasting day and nicht——"

"But ower quick a heat's no' for the plaister either—it's liable to crack and peel aff the wa's. A moderate heat's the best you can do."

"Once I was inside the shell o' this biggin I'll put up a prayer to the Lord as will bring guid weather and drying winds —the like Nithsdale has never known before. We understand each other, do we?"

"I understand you, Mr. Burns—but just as lang as you understand me!"

"Fine! And remember: I was born and brocht up in a clay biggin that my worthy parent built wi' his ain hands: sae I dinna think we'll die a winter yet."

Boyd shrugged his shoulders. He didn't like the idea of the poet occupying a damp house.

Mrs. Muir arrived from the Tarbolton Mill in a sore and bewildered state. When Robert got in, Jean and Nancy had brought her round with hot gruel, toddy and a dish of tea.

The salutations were no sooner over than she wept.

"God help you, laddie. What brocht you to a' the ends o' the earth here? Siccan a wilderness! And what'll Willie Muir say gin I get hame? Maybe I'll never see Tarbolton again."

They all endeavoured to reassure her.

"My God! And me thinking your place was just a wheen o' miles ayont Machlin!"

Said Jean: "Noo, you'll be a' richt when you get a nicht's sleep in a guid bed. I mind when I went to Paisley——"

"Paisley's in Scotland frae ocht that I ever heard. Will ye tell me richt whaur this place is—is there onybody kens?"

The Bard laughed heartily. "When I cam' to bide I used to wonder mysel' whiles. But hoots, Meg! you're near Dumfries —gey near a toon as big as Ayr. And you're amang friends and weel-kent faces."

"Lord God, but I'm glad to see you a'. I thocht the journey wad never end. My doup's sair daudin' up and doon. Ach! But I'm glad noo that I've got the length. That was guid toddy, Jean——"

"Could you tak' anither drap?"

"D'you ken: I think I could, Jean. Mind ye: if Willie Muir kent I was drinkin' toddy——"

"Awa' wi' you! Your man's gey fond o' a drap himsel'."

"Fine I ken. But Willie Muir's an ill man to get on wi'. What Willie does and what I maun dae's twa verra different things—thank ye, Jean: aye, juist fill it richt up."

"What did he say when you were coming away? He kens how far Dumfries lies."

"Oh, but God! I didna tell him, Rab. I couldna. D'you think he'd hae let me awa' here?"

"D'you mean he's nae idea where you are?"

"Oh, I left Granny Hay wi' him. He was dozing at the fire and she kent what to tell him when he wakened. You see, I had the chance o' a lift into Machlin. Sae I just threw some bits o' things into my kist. . . You see: I thocht I'd only be awa' for the twa nichts. . . God! he'll kill me when I get back. I dinna richt ken what made me dae it or how I plucked up the courage. But frae the minute I heard frae your brither, Rab —and I thocht o' Jean here, says I: Meg! you're for this Ellisland and for the house-warming. Mind you, Jean: you're no"

to put a step across the threshold afore the Bible and the
salt hae been carried in first. Before then I'll hae ale to brew,
the bite made and the table spread; and be there to bless ye and
welcome ye."

"It was far ower guid o' you coming a' this length to
honour us, Meg."

"Noo, ye ken what I think o' the pair o' ye—and I gied ye
my promise a lang while ago——"

"You did—and baith Jean and me are gey touched: we
couldna wish for a better house-warming."

"Havers! And of course Nancy here'll help me out."

"I'll dae onything I can, Meg: juist you tell me what to
dae when the time comes."

Meg Muir wasn't so many years older than the Bard. She
had seemed older when he had been younger. But now that
he was thirty years old, her seven years of seniority didn't seem
so important. She was a fine-looking woman too and happily
inclined to stoutness. She had a good head and was surprisingly
well read—especially in songs and ballads. Before her marriage
she had been an excellent and sprited dancer.

Her marriage had moved to disappointment and thence to
indifference. The gap between her age and her husband's
began to grow more marked. If there were no children of the
marriage, the fault did not lie with Meg.

She worshipped the Bard. She was physically very much
in love with him. She wouldn't have admitted this even to
herself; and she had always been careful to give the Bard no
hint of the physical things his presence did to her.

Yet when he took her over to inspect the new house, Meg
felt very unsure of herself. Her heart began to pound: the
blood flushed to her healthy cheeks.

Boyd's men had gone for the day and they sat on a plank
in front of the fire that was burning in the kitchen in an effort
to dry out the walls. The light was failing and the warm glow
of the fire flickered about the room.

"Aye: so this is to be your hame, Rab?"

"It is, Meg—and a guid hame it'll be yet. And wi' you doing the honours when we move in. . ."

"You used to be juist a laddie, Rab, and noo you're a grown man bringing up a family."

"Well . . . I'll be starting as father some day soon . . . maybe after Jean's brocht safely to bed."

"I should hae had bairns mysel', Rab."

The Bard moved uncomfortably and Meg was sensitive to the movement.

"Ach, I'm a silly bitch! But—I'm fond o' you, Rab, and I'd dae onything I could for Jean and you. If I hadna been fond o' you, d'you think I'd have ventured this length. . .? But Rab: I juist had to get awa' frae Willie Muir. I thocht to mysel'—Here's my chance and here's my excuse—afore it's ower late. I'll go and do the house-warming for Rab and Jean and then I'll come back and shut mysel' in the tomb again."

"But, Meg woman, I never thocht that you felt this way about Willie. I aey thocht you were a happy pair. I'll admit that latterly it whiles crossed my mind when I was at the Mill that he was a lot older than you. Damnit, he's no' bad to you, is he?"

"I've aey managed to put a face on things, Rab. I used to look forward to your visits on Mason nichts. . . He's jealous mad; and the aulder he gets the worse he gets."

"But. . . Was he aey that way?"

"Mair or less. At the start o' our marriage—oh, it was a gey disappointment to me, Rab. But why should I tell you a' this? Things, God be thankit, are sae different wi' Jean and you."

"And why did you ever marry him?"

"Och, I was young and I matured late, and I didna ken my ain mind richt; and my mither was anxious. And . . . he was a cheery, hearty body in thae days, was Willie Muir. He courted me decent-like, and, of course, I was ower green to ken why. Och, I was married and broken-hearted afore I kent."

"You astound me, Meg! Damnit: I just dinna ken what to say."

"I had to tell somebody, Rab, and I'm glad I can tell you. Granny Hay kens a bit aboot it—and I'm sure there're others aboot Tarbolton. Jean kens a lot too. Did you never wonder that I'd nae family?"

"No. . . Damnit no: I didna, Meg, to be honest wi' you."

"You never thocht o' me as a woman at a', did you?"

"In a sense—no——"

"Aye: I kent that. That's why I never showed mysel' to you as a woman."

"You mean. . .?"

"You ken fine what I mean. It's a' by wi' noo, of coorse. But I had to tell you."

"That you were fond o' me?"

"That I was in love wi' you. Aye; and I didna richt ken it mysel'—then. It's only looking back now that I begin to ken what was wrang wi' me. But I ken noo that's why I had to come doon here."

She put her hand gently on his knee.

"Dinna think ill o' me for telling you a' this, Rab—and dinna think it's been easy for me to tell you. It's only here, sitting at the fire—and in the shadow o' the firelicht. . . And dinna worry, Rab: there's nothing you can do aboot it—except to forget that I ever said what I've said."

"God, Meg . . . I kenna what to say——"

"Then dinna say ocht."

"No. . . I'm hurt that life's handed you such a pack of caertes. For, damnit, I'm fond o' you in my ain way, Meg. I like you . . . I've aey liked you. But. . ."

"Dinna mak' it worse for me, Rab."

"But damnit, Meg. . ."

"Say it and be done wi' it. I'm nae fool, Rab—and there's nae man kens mair about women than you dae."

"How d'you make that out? You're no' the first woman

that has come away wi' that. But why should you—or ony other woman—think I ken sae much aboot your sex?"

"Because you're a poet, Rab; and because you canna be as fond o' the lassies as you are without kennin' plenty aboot them. You never needed to run after the lassies: they ran after you."

"By God, I didna notice, then."

"Noo you've put a wheen through your hands, Rab: you canna deny it."

"There's been an odd lass."

"Can you no' trust me—even yet?"

"There're times, Meg, when it's damned unchancy to trust ony woman."

"I'm as far awa' frae you, Rab, as I ever was. I dinna mean ony mair to you than that fire-shool."

"I wouldna say that, Meg. I'm glad we've had this crack thegither. . . I've learned a lot and I'm grateful for the confidence you've put in me. You see: there's plenty I juist dinna understand about women. . . You feel the want o' a man?"

"Of coorse I dae. A' women need a man—some a' the time, some noo and again, and some whiles. I've talked wi' mony women and shared mony o' their confidences. That's what maddens maist women when their men start laying awa'. And yet maist women ken their men lay awa'—or would gin they got the chance."

"How do they ken?"

"Because they canna lay awa' withouten a hen to lay wi'. Women canna be deceived aboot their ain natures and instincts. What women but hasna had the thocht—aye and the wish—to be laid awa' wi'?"

"Uhuh. . . And you've laid awa' yoursel'. Meg?"

"Weel . . . I hae, Rab . . . but no' as often as I could; aye, or as I could hae wished. . . An' I've had a wheen o' stolen kisses. But you wouldna blame me for that? I was young, Rab. Hae I lost your good opinion o' me wi' my silly-bitch confessions?"

"You're nae silly bitch, Meg. No . . . I think mair o' you now than ever I did—though maybe in a different way. A happy marriage should mak' a difference to a couple. . . And yet, Meg, you can still love a woman, aye, and love her to distraction . . . and still lay awa'."

"And would you agree to the woman laying awa'—in the same circumstances?"

"It's a bit different wi' a woman——"

"Aye: that's aey the man's point."

"Well, on principle, a woman has as much right to lay awa' as a man—I'll agree to that. But . . . eh. . ."

"You wouldna like to think o' Jean laying awa'?"

"I think I'd go mad if she did. But there's nae fear o' Jean."

"I ken fine there's nae fear o' Jean. An' if you were dead the morn, I'm sure she'd never look the airt o' a man. But then Jean's the kind o' lass that loves you that much that she could live to eternity on the memory o' you."

"You're makin' me blush, Meg."

"But that's the truth."

"Hae you ony real notion how much I love Jean?"

"I've a notion, Rab."

"There's no' a lass like her, Meg. There's a something aboot Jean I've never traced in other women. In nearly every way Jean's far ower guid for me. And yet there's no' an inch o' jealousy in her."

"Dinna you believe that—or dinna work on that. Only Jean'll no' show her jealousy quickly."

"No . . . I think Jean's got an outlook on life that's a' her ain—and it's quite unique."

"You think Jean wouldna mind if you laid awa'?"

"She would mind and she'd be hurt; but she wouldna be jealous. Jean doesna look on a husband as a bit o' property."

"No . . . no' when you're the husband. Gin I'd gotten a man like you I'd maybe hae been the same as Jean."

"Weel . . . I've only your word for that, Meg."

"There's nae deceivin' you, Rab—and you're no' deceivin' me either."

"Listen: I'm serious. Either we're talking honestly or we're playing a game."

"A bit o' baith. Rab. Come noo: admit it. Nae man or woman ever admits to the whole truth—even to themselves."

"Allowing that they ken the truth about themselves."

"Aye: that's the whole business in a nutshell. Losh, I didna ken a' this aboot mysel' until we started talking. I've learned mair aboot mysel' the nicht and frae mysel' than ever I thocht possible."

"I've done a bit o' learning too, Meg. And you'd be wasted on Willie Muir whatever the way o' things."

"You've sensed that too, have you?"

"Willie's nae fool. To me, as a man—a young man— Willie Muir's just a big, hearty, honest, welcome-again miller. But compared wi' you his brains are a' in his big tae. It's hard when a woman wi' brains and sensibility marries a man wi' neither——"

"And it's a sicht harder when, in addition to a' that, she's hot-blooded. . ."

The Bard thought of Clarinda.

"Still, Meg, there's another side to that. I ken o' a young hot-blooded, romantic lass—comes o' a good family and has brains and sensibility—and the husband was like a brute beast."

"Maybe marriage is the wildest gamble a lass can mak' in life?"

"True at that—for baith sexes. Aye, as far as I can judge, a sensible happy marriage is but rarely achieved. But I'm bound to say this: folk that tolerate a partner they dislike— to say nothing o' hating—should part."

"You mean I should hae left Willie Muir?"

"Yes: if you put it that way. Why didn't you?"

"Where's a woman to go? What's to happen to her? She

becomes an outcast. Respectable folks winna associate wi'
her——"

"An' a' because o' our bluidy morality. What the hell's
respectability——"

"We'd better be getting back to Jean—that's ae kind o'
respectability! Come on! We'll hae a crack anither day. And
there's nothing misses your sister Nancy."

"You women! Can twa old friends no' sit and hae a crack,
aye, or a heart-to-heart talk, without fearing for other folk?
To hell: d'you think I'm worrying about Jean or Nancy?"

"Come on hame: think about *me* for a change. Respectability
means a lot to me. Appearances gang further than you think,
Rab. . . And gie me a wee kiss on the cheek here—and forgie
me for being a silly bitch."

The Bard put his arm tenderly round her shoulder and gave
her a circumspect but affectionate kiss on the cheek.

"There you are, my dear. You'll can aey say I kissed you.
But you're richt: we're a pair o' daft beggars. Wait till I throw
some mair coal on the fire."

The house-warming was carried out in style by Meg Muir
and Nancy.

Fanny Burnes was given the honour of carrying a bowl of
salt on the top of the Family Bible. The Bard and Jean, arm-
in-arm, followed. Behind them came some of the neighbours
and the servants . . . and James and Adam Armour.

It was a fine afternoon in April. There were birds singing,
bushes and trees were burgeoning; there was a scad of new-
green across the grasslands. There was the freshness of sap
rising and the mystery of heartening growth.

And folks were happy and light-hearted. . .

The Bard carried Jean across the threshold—and then they
were welcomed by Meg and Nancy. Drinks had been filled out
and were handed round the company.

"Come on noo, Rab," Meg whispered, " you'll need to say
something."

"Friends . . . I'm grateful—Jean and I are grateful to all of you. It's a fine thing to enter a new house and be welcomed by friends auld . . . and new. We aey hae a soft heart for our auld frien's—but we hae a welcome for the new. To my neighbours I want to say a special word. I'm glad to be among you; and I'm grateful for the hand o' friendship you've held out to Jean and me. We hope we'll prove as guid frien's to you as you have to us. To Mrs. Muir, who has come all the way from our bit o' Ayrshire—the Fail Mill at Tarbolton—we canna say a' that we would like to say in public. But this we can say and mean every word we say. Mrs. Muir is a friend from our earliest days in and about Tarbolton—and that friendship she has proved in deeds of kindness that can never be blotted from our memory. . .

". . . When I brought Jean down to the Isle I wrote a song: ' I hae a wife o' my ain,' and though my voice is no' the best for singing, I'll sing you a verse or twa, for it expresses my feelings now just as much as it expressed them when I wrote it."

And then and there the Bard sang his song in his rough but not unmelodious baritone:

"I hae a wife o' my ain,
    I'll partake wi' naebody.
I'll take cuckold frae nane,
    I'll gie cuckold to naebody.

I hae a penny to spend,
    There—thanks to naebody.
I hae naething to lend,
    I'll borrow frae naebody.

I am naebody's lord,
    I'll be slave to naebody.
I hae a guid braid sword,
    I'll tak dunts frae naebody.

I'll be merry and free,
I'll be sad for naebody.
Naebody cares for me,
I care for naebody."

There was a cheer when he ended but he went on quickly:
"Now that's for my independence—and as a warning to
you all. But should auld acquaintance be forgot and never
brocht to mind? For auld lang syne, my jo, for auld lang
syne, we'll tak' a cup o' kindness yet for auld lang syne.

"And so for friendship and for auld lang syne—from Jean
and me—that's the toast I give you!"

They drank the toast and there was renewed cheering. . .
Meg looked quite a figure as she stood by the table.

"Weel . . . friends: I'm nae speechifier. But I've been
asked as the oldest friend here—though I'm sure I'm no' that
auld—to welcome Robert and Jean to their new hoose. And I
dae that wi' richt guid will.

"I've kent Robert and Jean for a while noo. . . They are
blessed in themselves and they are blessed in ane anither—aye,
as two married folk haena been sae blessed in my experience. . .

"The road they've travelled to Ellisland here hasna been
a straight one—nor an easy one. They've already been tried
by life; and they've come through the test and the trials wi'
a certainty that their love will endure for the length o' their
sojourn here. There's been sunshine and shadow i' their lives
afore: there'll be sunshine and shadow in it for the future.
We canna wish them to be free o' the shadows a'thegither, for
none can escape that; but we can wish that the shadows will
be short and the sunshine lang and spread ower a' the years o'
the prophet's days—and mony efter that, gin it be the Lord's
will. . .

". . . Sae we ask His blessing on this roof-tree and on this
hearth-stane . . . and a' that dwell herein and may yet be
added wi' His blessing to the family circle. . ."

They sat down to a grand meal and everybody seemed

ready for it; and as soon as the first pangs of hunger were stilled, conversation began to hum about the table.

The Bard thought: But for Meg Muir there micht never have been this house-warming. Like as not he would have brought Jean and the rest here without fuss or ceremony. But that would have been wrong. Meg had the right way of things and it was a good fortune that had brought her down from the Mill. . . And Meg, puir bitch, was getting a vicarious pleasure out of it all. And maybe not quite so vicarious. . . He'd never seen her look so radiantly happy. And she'd spoken well—nae fool Meg; just a fine woman ruined or wasted by an unfortunate marriage. . .

There was young Fanny and young Adam: that was more natural. Fanny, puir lass, was enjoying herself like the lave— and maybe more so. Fanny had everything before her— marriage and bairns and a bit house o' her own. Adam was a well-doing lad . . . a bit o' a deil—and why not!—but steady for a' that and settling down well. . .

And Nancy . . . would there ever be a house-warming for her? Nancy was keeping quiet. She was letting Meg have it her way. But damn it! there was nae reason why Nancy shouldn't get a decent-like man yet. She was still the right side o' thirty and she had her attractions . . . and she'd a fine sensible head on her and could work ony two women blind. Aye: this was the best thing that could have happened her: getting away from Mossgiel. She'd been too long with the family . . . too long under Gilbert's influence and maybe their mother's. . . She'd meet new folks here and see a new way o' life and she might fall in with a likely lover. . .

After the meal the fiddle was brought out and there was singing and dancing. Everybody danced—and Jean was as light on her feet as Fanny.

The Bard discarded his jacket, rolled up his sleeves, loosened his neck-cloth and danced every step with gusto and abandon; and kissed every lass and woman he danced with.

Meg said: "God: you can step, Rab!"

"Aye . . . an' I could walk you hame to the Mill at the finish."

"As long as we walked somewhere—I'm looking for a byordinar baiveridge for this gown. . ."

Nancy said: "It's like auld times, Robin."

"No' sae auld, Nancy. You're needin' plenty o' this."

"I never thocht I'd dance again. . ."

"Life's only starting for you, Nancy—and I'll come and dance you at your ain hoose-warmin'. . ."

Nancy's eyes swam as she changed partners and the Bard swung young Fanny.

"Enjoying yoursel', Fanny?"

"I never enjoyed mysel' afore, Uncle: no' like this."

"That's my pet! Tak' a' the fun you can get."

And then Jean had to sing a song and the Bard had to render a couple of stanzas from *The Cotter's Saturday Night.*

And the night was cool and clear and gently dark; and the Nith sang to the sea. A curlew called from the rough pastures and a scared peesweep screamed from the harrowed field: across on the shingle beds a pyat piped a warning to his mate already on her eggs.

The first lights were blazing in the Ellisland windows and laughter and music vibrated in pulsating waves across the spring darkness. . .

Robert and Jean stood on the high bank and the river murmured beneath their feet.

"God, lass, o' a' the nichts we've ever kenned——"

"But you still mind the Ayr at Barskimming?"

"There's no' a nicht I havena relived a hundred times and more. But there's a something aboot this night—is there no'?"

"Aye—there's nae pairting for us noo, Rab. It's you and me till the river rins to the sea."

"I could turn that into a sang, lass! I've but one regret: this night should hae been four years ago."

"Would you hae wanted a hoose-warming then?"

"Maybe you're richt, Jean. Then a' we needed was a bit bield for our twa-selves. Juist you and me would hae been a' the hoose-warming that was needed."

"I've nae regrets, Rab. It had to be this way—and we should be thankfu' that it's this way it's turned oot."

"Aye! Thankfu'. . . Contented wi' little and cantie wi' mair. . ."

A soft cooee came to them from the steading.

"That's Meg," said Jean and cooeed back.

"Dinna go: let Meg come up. Let the young ones dance their fill."

Meg came to them on the high bank where they were silhouetted against the night.

"God: you lone lovers! I wadna hae disturbed you—but Nancy wants to ken if we'll set doon another meal and she's wondering what's keepin' the pair o' ye."

The Bard put his free arm round Meg and brought her close to him.

"Stand here wi' us for a minute or twa, Meg, and listen to the water. As Jean was saying, that's us down there, the seconds o' us hurrying to the sea. . . Meg woman, Jean and me stole up here for a moment so that we'd hae something to oorselves—a bit drap o' the water o' time that's flowing sae fast to eternity. . . But singing as it goes, Meg. Singing—that's the point: the significance we mauna miss. Listen. . . A' eternity's in that sang—and yet a' we get o' eternity's a moment o' time. . . The bank here is time: the water is eternity."

"And the sang, Rab?"

"The melting o' time into eternity."

"I'm sorry for interrupting."

"Dinna be sorry, Meg: you couldna interrupt Jean and me. But you see: without the sang we wouldna ken where time ended and eternity began."

"God, Jean: I'm beginning to hae an inkling o' what it means to be married to a poet."

"Aye: time and eternity dinna mean the same when Rab talks about them. Rab gathers a' things to him and smooths them oot."

"Come on, the pair o' you. It's my privilege to blether awa' to my heart's content—and it's your privilege to listen."

"Weel—we've been listening, Rab. But . . . I shouldna be standing here breaking into your peace."

"You've brought a blessing to us, Meg . . . and it's but fitting that you should be with us at this moment. But to hell —let's get down to the young folk and hae a parting sang; for, Lord be thankit, the young anes dinna bother their backsides aboot either time or eternity."

"The present only toucheth thee—is that it?"

Meg's breast was surprisingly firm under the pressure of his fingers. She squeezed him a response with her arm.

"Aye: lay hold to every minute—for the neist we may never see."

Meg sighed. "Och, it's maybe juist a dream—and I'll wauken in the morning wi' Willie Muir snoring and snorting and grumblin' aboot the parritch and wonderin' what like of a head's on the Mill water. . ."

"As lang as the dream's pleasant, Meg—what does it matter?"

"Fegs, it matters! I'm gaun clean gyte. . . I dinna want to gan hame; I want to bide here and dream. . . Oh, I'm sae grateful to the pair o' you for this break in my monotony —it's like a foretaste o' Heaven . . . and nae coo to milk in the morning."

The music died away and the blessings and good-nights faded across the fields. The first lights in Ellisland were snuffed. There was only the slow sad music from the river and the hooting of an owl muted from the Dalswinton holms.

Meg wept on her pillow and Nancy tossed in uneasy sleep. Oblivious of each other's arms, the guidman and the guidwife of Ellisland were beyond all care and all consciousness.

A cinder crumbled from the fire on to the hearth-stone, glowed for an uncertain moment, turned white and died.

ADOWN WINDING NITH

Apart from his farming activities which took up most of his time, the Bard had much literary work to distract his evenings and his wet days.

Always at his elbow was his work for James Johnson's *Musical Museum*. This was his main musical-literary task in life and he had to work at it steadily. It was a self-imposed task and though there were times when he cast it aside in an odd moment of tired exasperation he always came back to it with avidity and with affection.

His study at the far end of the house was a litter of books and papers. Once Nancy had tidied them up and he had spoken to her gently but without any equivocation.

Nancy was almost weeping when she told Jean about the incident.

"I didna mean ony harm, Jean——"

"Dinna worry yoursel', Nancy. Only: never touch ony o' his papers. And if you see a book lying open never be tempted to close it. Like as no' it'll be open for some purpose."

"He's got mair books and papers than Gavin Hamilton in Machlin."

"Aye . . . it's a wonder to me how he reads them a'! And the music he's got! He must hae every sang book or sheet that's in the country. He scrapes the tunes oot o' them on the fiddle—but aince he gets the tune in his head, he never forgets it."

"Robin was aey daft about a sang; but he seems clean-wud now."

C.B.W.   H

"Frae a' I can gather, it's Rab runs this Musical Museum for Mr. Johnson in Edinburry—what they would do without him I dinna ken."

"I thocht it was that Mr. Clarke that looked after the music?"

"Aye: so he does—after Rab shows him what to dae. Rab's no' so handy writing oot the music as Stephen Clarke is. He writes doon thae queer signs quicker than Rab can write words."

"I suppose he's clever—but he looks damned lazy to me."

"Rab would agree wi' you."

"That would be a change."

"Now, now, Nancy: there's naebody would doubt that you were brother and sister."

"Oh. . .? I aey thocht that our Robin was like nae ither body on this earth."

"Aye . . . and in a way you ken that's true enough. There's juist naebody like him. But in a hunner ways back and forward you're Rab ower the back."

"We're flesh and bluid, of coorse. But even if he is my brither and the greatest poet Scotland's ever had, I'm no' his hand-maiden; and I'm no' agreeing wi' a' that he says."

"Coorse no': you wouldna be a Burns gin you did."

Nancy reflected for a moment. "Maybe we are a bit thrawn——"

"Now, I didna mean onything!"

"Oh aye, Jean: you meant what you said. That's what I like aboot you. You're no' blate; you dinna beat aboot the bush like some folk I ken. But it seems to me Robin tolerates too mony kinds o' folk that canna dae him ony guid. You tell me he doesna get ony money for writing a' thae sangs and scartin' for hours on that fiddle, forbye you singing to him at a' hours when he's in the mood? D'you tell me this lazy man Clarke doesna get paid? Him wi' his 'charming melody, Robert, charming melody, Robert. . .' He'd gie you the boaks!"

"We're no' supposed to talk aboot Rab's frien's. . ."

"Ootside yoursel', Jean, I ken nothin' and hear nothin':
I'm nae gowk as far as keepin' my place is concerned. . . And
what aboot this man Johnson in Edinburry. . .?"

"I ken nothing but what Rab tells me, Nancy. He can get
annoyed whiles wi' Stephen Clarke, but I ken he's gey fond o'
this James Johnson and his sang buiks. He's a puir enough
fellow, it seems, and sair wanting in buik-learning; but a
great enthusiast and as honest as the day's lang."

"And d'you mean to tell me that the whole three o' them
are doing a' they're doing juist for the love o' the thing?"

"That's how it would appear, Nancy—ony-the-ways o' it,
Rab gets nothing."

"I suppose I'd be better to keep my mouth shut. After a':
I ken nocht aboot the makin' o' books . . . and the mair I see
o' Rab and the mair I hear, I juist marvel how he does it a'.
Coorse, frae ever I can mind, he had his nose in a book or a
sheet o' ballads; and I mind at Lochlea when Davie Sillar and
him started on the fiddle. He'd get up in the mornings and awa'
out to the byre . . . and I'm telling you he didna spare the
torture he gied that puir fiddle—and that's no' saying what he
did to the kye. . ."

"Oh, but he doesna mak' ony pretence to be a fiddler. He
fiddles to please himsel' and catch the turn o' a tune. But gie
him a sad mournfu' lilt o'a tune and he could gar ye greet wi'
the expression o' it. . ."

"I used to grudge him gaun to Machlin at nichts. I would
hae run a mile to hae heard him laying aff The Twa Dogs or
The Holy Fair. . . But Robin never juist fitted into the
fire-side at hame. . . I dinna richt ken how it was; but it
seems he had to get out and—of coorse, there's nae doot aboot
it, Jean—he was fond o' lassies' company——"

"And the lassies were gey fond o' him, Nancy. . . I heard
plenty aboot Rab Burns afore I fell in wi' him. And to tell
you the truth, I wasna that taken up wi' a' that I heard——"

"Aye—but there were brazen hizzies in Machlin *and*

Tarbolton that wad hae lain doon i' the toll road for him gin they'd heard his step coming."

"A lot o' folk thocht I was a brazen hizzie, I suppose——"

"Nothin' to the folk that thocht Robin was nae better than a hure-monger."

"Weel . . . there's nae point in our rakin' out the cauld ashes o' the past——"

"You're richt, Jean. . . It was me thinking o' the times —the odd times—when Robin used to draw in his chair aside us and gie us his company. . . I could greet whiles, lookin' back. . . And I lay awake till I heard his step in the close and listened to him creepin' up the stairs where he bedded wi' Gilbert. . . Coorse, women are no' supposed . . . weel, maybe it was that I was jealous o' them that had the best o' his company. It's hard whiles when you see the way the stranger can win into the heart o' your brither while you've got to bide on the step outside. Oh, dinna think I grudge onything o' Robin to you, Jean—I've told you afore and I'll tell you to my dying day that he couldna hae gotten a better wife. But did you notice how big Meg Muir could get wi' him?"

"I dinna heed sic things, Nancy——"

"You dinna need to, Jean. You're his wife—I'm only his sister. Now: I'm no complaining. I'm mair nor thankfu' to be here wi' you and I'll bide wi' you and work for you till you tell me to go. It's juist, Jean, that my feelings work up ower my heart and—and somehow I can speak to you, Jean, when I couldna speak to another living soul. You'll juist no' need to mind whiles, what I say."

And Jean didn't mind. She had more than a warm side to Nancy and there were times when she felt sorry for her in her withdrawnness, her isolation. For if ever a sister worshipped a brother, Nancy worshipped Robert.

But Jean was used to this form of worship. Meg Muir had wept to her about it . . . and there was poor Fanny, not seventeen yet, hanging on his every word and doting on his every wish. And there was this gentry-body, Mrs. Dunlop of

Dunlop, writing him long letters and her a grandmother forbye a gentlewoman.

All this built up an honest pride in Jean that buttressed her own deep single-purposed love against all possible assault.

But back in Machlin, Jeannie Smith and Jean Markland had taught her by example how fortunate she was to be singled out for his affection. And yet little did Nancy—or any of them—know what she had endured up and until that triumphant moment when he'd taken her to Baldy Muckle's room in the Backcauseway.

Well might they all wonder at the number and variety of his friends and of the gentry that paid court to him. She was never beyond the wonder of it all herself. . .

For many a long forenight the Bard would sit in the study-parlour writing letters, working on his songs, making an odd verse and especially trying out new forms, making himself familiar with the latest intelligence concerning affairs of state and society as contained in the Edinburgh and London prints.

Sometimes he was infuriated as when some hack published some scurrilous lines in a London print concerning the Duchess of Gordon dancing a reel—and put the name of Robert Burns to it.

Such dirty tricks made him realise that his name was of more public value than he had thought. He could write and protest, and did; but the damage had been done.

And nearly always his enemies hid themselves in anonymity. If only they would come forward and face him openly.

Walking one fine evening with Jean along the river bank he said:

"Nothing could be fairer, Jean, than the face o' nature. You canna go wrong where nature's concerned—and maybe that's one reason I could never think o' biding in Auld Reekie. . . Maybe someday we'll gang there thegither and I'll be guide to you. Aye, I ken you've nae notion o' doing any such thing.

But we're young yet, lass. There'll be plenty time yet for jaunts thegither. . . You ken: I fret whiles that I am here on the banks o' the Nith . . . and no' somewhere else. I fret for a hundred reasons, Jean. We're embarking on a family— but what's to become o' them? I'll never hae money to mak' them scholars or schoolmasters or doctors; and I dinna ken that I would like them to be onything o' the kind. No: they'd be better to be decent mechanics. Better having a guid trade and be independent o' the damned trash o' college education. . . And since our bairns can never be gentry there would be no point in giving them gentry-like notions. No: we'll feed them and clead them and bring them up to be honest men.

"I canna see that I'll mak' ony money now as a poet. I'll never fill another volume like my Kilmarnock one and I canna keep on adding to my Edinburgh volume. . . I may write a drama—but whether there would be money in it I couldna foretell. That's the devil about literary work, Jean: it's uncertain, damnably uncertain. . . Maybe you think I should make money by employing stumpie—and if the bawbees do come my way I'll no' refuse them. But I canna write to order and I canna write what the public are supposed to like. I maun write whatever pleases me—and only what pleases me. So I've got to look to the Excise as my sheet anchor. . . Suppose that I got a supervisorship: say in some good port town like Greenock. . . Then I would hae a steady guaranteed income coming in every year; then I would hae leisure to read and to write juist as I liked; then I could make arrangements for our family to pick and choose their way in life—at least to an extent I couldna think on now. . .

"There are prospects aboot the Excise, Jean, and I've got friends on the Excise Board. I'll need to commence riding officer; but there's no reason I should do that for very long— a year maybe at the best. . . Then I micht get a foot-walk about Dumfries for another year; and then as I got to master my duties thoroughly. . .

"No: there's no word of me starting yet; but I'm still

hoping for something this year. Graham o' Fintry as much as promised me that. It's just a matter o' dealing wi' Leonard Smith; and I hear he's likely to be resigning his appointment ony day. He's thinking o' retiring: that's what an independent income can do for you!

"Do you think I'd dirty my hands wi' the Excise gin there was ony other way open to me to earn a *steady* income? And we need a steady income, Jean. In the Excise, you dinna lose your income because o' a bad harvest, bad seed, bad land or bad weather. There's nae security for a poor tenant-farmer: never was and never will be. You're at the mercy o' the elements and the devil's dice-box o' fate and circumstance.

"But a steady job and a steady income—that's where the Excise scores every time! And to hell, Jean: there's decent Excisemen and you ken some o' them yourself. Jamie Findlay was a decent fellow, was he no'? I ken it looks like a gey sorry come-doon for me that was the Toast o' Edinburgh and a tenant-farmer to end up as a common riding gauger combing ten parishes for impost dodgers and orra smugglers—Scotland's Bard searching auld wives' clarty ale-barrels!

"Well . . . the shame, gin there's ony shame in it, is Scotland's shame as weel as mine. And why should I hae ony shame in the job? If the Excise is nae honour to me, then I'll be an honour to the Excise. . .

"And, as I said, you canna go wrong wi' nature. The Nith will flow just as sweetly to the sea when I'm an Exciseman as now that I'm farmer. The birds will sing the same and just as fresh will the trees bud again in the spring. . . And true enough, the bluidy rain will be pouring down; there'll be wind and sleet and frost and snow and I'll need to ride out in a' weathers. . .

"But as I'm aey telling you, Jean: we havena died a winter yet—and Excisemen live as long as other men and their wives are as happy as other men's wives and their bairns as like the world—and as thriving.

"No, lass: I'm no' trying to convince you o' something

that's against my better judgment. It's just that it's the best road out o' this damned riddling o' stanes that Miller has got me thirled to. . .

"'Course, there's nae need for me to give up the farm. Nancy's earning mair nor her keep in the dairy. Fanny and Willie are doing fine—couldna do better. And there's naebody can cook and bake and keep a hoose like you. I'll need to hire a good ploughman and I'll need seasonal labour as the work demands it—but a' that put thegither will no' eat up a tithe o' the fifty pounds that the Excise will bring me. And damn it, Jean, if the worst did come to the worst, we could live bein and snug on a pound a week wi' no farm to worry about.

"Aye: we could be a lot worse. . . And if the farm wins through and we're blessed wi' good boys and they grow up. . . Fine: you see, there's no need for ony despairing. Let's count oursel's settled here and look forward to health and happiness —and a bouncing boy every other twelvemonth and a weel-waled lassock for every three laddies!"

Jean was happy hearing him talk on in his easy confident happy way. She was conscious that there was an under-current of fear and of apprehension running deep below all his certainty and buoyant assurance. But she had faith that he would overcome all difficulties, surmount all obstacles. She felt no fear where he was concerned.

"Of a' the wark you'd like to be at, Rab, what would it be—sangs?"

"Aye: sangs. No' for the words, though I can mak' a braw set o' verses when the mood's on me. It's the tunes. Jean: there're endless tunes that we've lost or are in danger o' losing. A good tune, many of our glorious old tunes, do something to me—fire me, enthuse me, build me up to a pitch o' keenness that nothing else can do barring my love for you. There's something in me just thrives on music. I can often feel the blood leaping, bounding, racing in my veins when the lilt and lift o' a tune goes through me. . . A' the heights o' joy and the depths o' sorrow are in our Scots tunes. . . And for my ain deep satisfaction—maybe for the gratitude for my gift o' life itself—I'd like to rescue a' the auld melodies frae oblivion and put words to them that will bring them back to folks' lips.

"I'll get nae money for doing it. Who is there to put their damned gold and silver on the value o' a sang? My work here is either above judgment or below payment; but there'll never be ony huxtering commerce about it.

"In the end, lass—although I canna see the end—there'll be glory in it. Maybe our grandchildren will glory that you and me—aye, for you're in this as well as me—maybe our bairns will ken the glory we're handing down to them and to posterity.

"The day'll come, Jean, when maist o' my poems will be forgotten—there's thousands o' young folks that know nothing o' such things as Holy Fairs; and in a year or twa the fight o' the New Lichts ower the Auld Lichts will be a meaningless jumble concerning antiquated theological warfare.

"But a sang gangs doon the years and the glory o' it never fades; and even if it does lie neglected for a wheen o' years it's only till it gathers a new strength and a new freshness for another generation. . ."

Happy hours, wandering about the banks of the Nith in the lengthening nights and the sun going down in glory behind the gentle hills. Happy hours since man and wife were still lad and lass and still deeply in love. So deeply in love indeed that it didn't really matter what happened or what they talked about.

They had both known poverty and hardship and disappointment. They didn't expect things to be easy nor fate to be kind to them. They would face their destiny with toil and sweat; but they would face it—and without fear.

And when the gods were good to them—sending a fine warm evening and an hour of leisure—they would respond to the goodness.

Maybe it just wasn't Eden's bonnie yard this summer-pleasant Ellisland prospect. But it was paradise to anything they had hitherto known—and they knew something of the happiness the First Youthful Lovers had known.

THE ANTIQUARIAN

The summer of '89 was memorable for many fine things. It was their first summer together as man and wife in their own house. It was memorable too from the visit to Captain Riddell at Frairs Carse of Captain Francis Grose, the celebrated author and antiquarian.

It was at Riddell's table the Bard first met with Grose and they took to each other almost on introduction. Grose was not only a character: he was an outrageous caricature of a character.

His height when young might have been five and a half feet. It was less now, for Grose was weighed down with excessive fat. He had an enormous protuberance of abdomen which was almost balanced by what he himself loved to describe as "my huge rotundity of arse." If his build was Falstaffian, his humour was Rabelaisian. His wit was his own.

Everything about Grose was big and generous. He ate heartily, drank heartily, talked and laughed heartily, and, when in the vein, added gusto to his general heartiness. He had a resonant baritone voice and knew how to use it with effect, though he was a forceful rather than a fluent speaker. Unlike the Bard, he was unable to essay long intricate nervously-energetic periods—and, unlike the Bard, he was not always a good listener—at least, not at their first meetings.

Grose disliked pomposity, snobbery, social superiority in manners: and meanness. He warmed to a character whatever his standing; and he gloried in good robust conversation.

So he soon found his way to the Bard's fire-side. Riddell, finding himself host to two giants, had to strain himself to his utmost to dominate the conversation; and, in this, he only partly succeeded out of the respect the Bard and the Antiquarian paid him as host.

And with his huge ham fists and bull-bellowing voice, Glenriddell seldom experienced difficulty in dominating any company. It wasn't the first time he had split a table with his fist-thumping, nor the first time he had caused the glasses to tingle and tremble at his roar.

Robert apprised Jean of Grose's impending visit.

"I think ye'll like him, Jean. But dinna laugh when ye see him, for ye've never seen a fatter man."

"Is he as fat as a' that? Where'll he sit?"

"A sensible question. We'll get a cushion on that stool there and clap it agin the fire-side, for he couldna get his dowp into ony o' our chairs. . . An' you're wondering what an antiquarian is? Well now: the Captain—he's retired frae the army this wheen years and his family are grown up and doing well for themselves—the Captain collects a' things o' historical value—auld swords, weapons o' ony kind, ancient domestic utensils or furniture and the like. But mainly he's engaged in drawing and describing auld buildings o' historical importance. He's already published a wheen volumes on the antiquities o' England and Wales, and now he's doing the same for Scotland. Aye, there're few mair learned men living the day concerning antiquarian affairs. . . I mind when I was in Auld Reekie I fell in wi' his then newly-published Dictionary o' the Vulgar Tongue. . . I'll need to write Willie Smellie to lend me his copy for a day or twa: you'd enjoy bits o' it. Oh, a fell wit and keen is Francis Grose, and God, Jean, as kind-hearted and generous as you'd ever hope to meet."

"Just as you say, Rab. I'm glad you've fa'n in wi' somebody ye like as much. But dinna ask me to bide and join in your conversation."

"And why shouldn't you join in our conversation? Damn it, Jean, that's what's wrong wi' you. You're ower modest.

You can talk mair hamespun-sense than ony lass I ever kenned
—but damn me if you'll talk fornenst strangers. . . Some o'
them maun think you're deaf or dumb or brainless."

"Aye—and as far's the stranger's concerned, I'm a' three.
That way I'll no' put my feet in things—and I'll no' disgrace
you by being quoted outside for a fool. Now dinna gather
your broos: I'll meet your Captain Grose and I'll be civil to
him as I am wi' a' bodies; and at the first opportunity I'll
gang ben the hoose wi' the others and leave the pair o' ye to
enjoy your crack by the fire-side."

"Weel, weel, Jean. . . But mind you: I think you'll like
him."

Grose seated himself by the fire for the night had grown
chilly.

"You'll excuse me, Robert, but I must let out my top
buttons—if Mrs. Burns will also excuse me?"

"As lang as you keep to the tap buttons, Captain, naebody'll
object hereabouts. Mak' yoursel' at hame."

"Thank you, madam. . . Ah, the richness of your tongue,
and the richness, the breadth of your native dialect. Your
tongue is richer even than Robert's. . . Madam: if I sat long
enough at your feet, I'd be a master of the Scottish dialect."

"Meikle guid that would dae you, sir."

"Meikle guid—ah, wonderful! But, madam—everything
about you is rich and warm and hospitable. You have beauty,
abounding health, grace of figure—I apologise, madam, I
know you are carrying and I meant no offence. Madam, you
are wealthy beyond queens and duchesses for all their gold
and pearls and diamonds. You're a damned lucky husband,
Robert."

"Fine I ken that, Francis."

"But then, madam, you make a handsome and worthy
couple. You are blessed in your husband—Scotland's Bard
and a damned fine fellow to boot."

"He could be waur."

"Waur? Worse! Excellent!" Grose slapped his bulging thigh in delight. "Scotland's first poet—and his goodlady says ' Aye: he could be worse.' Ah, you Scotch can be masters of understatement. At first when I came among you, I thought you could be damned sparing in your compliments. In fact, I doubted you knew the meaning of the word. The English, you know, are the most insincere flatterers in Christendom. The English husband will address his spouse in public with flowery phrases and nauseating little endearments. This you never find among the Scotch. Damn it! I understand that Scotchmen don't even kiss their wives after they're married——"

"I wouldna believe a' you hear, sir. But a man would look a gey saft clown kissing his wife in public. There's a time and place for everything."

"Quite right, Mistress Burns: hence the innate modesty and decorum of the Scotch lassies. But come, madam: draw your chair into the fire and join us."

"You'll excuse me, sir: I've plenty to do ben the hoose. There's the young folk to see bedded——"

"The Captain will excuse you, Jean—though I ken he would like fine to have your crack. But you'll be back, Captain?"

"Thank you: yes indeed. That's if I'm not intruding in your domesticity? Ah! give me the unpretentious warmth of a farm-house kitchen—they make your drawing-rooms seem draughty, over-stuffed barns. . ."

". . . The Scotch laird is invariably a proud man, Robert. Huh? But then all you Scotch are damned proud, huh?"

"We could have good reason for that, Francis."

"Damn you: the Scotch have all the reasons for everything under the sun.

"Lord! I met a Highland clergyman—he thought himself something of an antiquarian—and, by God, he assured me that Gaelic was spoken in the Garden of Eden—huh?"

"That's a quaint idea."

"I thanked the old gentleman most profusely. I—I told

him he'd made an unparalleled contribution to our earliest
history. 'Sir,' I said: 'since Gaelic was spoken in Eden you
have accounted, more satisfactorily than the theologians have,
for our First Parents being thrown out of the Garden.' Huh?
I'm glad you see the joke, Robert: I'm afraid the reverend
gentleman took offence. Damn it, Robert, you must admit
you Scotch are touchy!"

"Aye: we're touchy—and none more so than our High-
landers. Perhaps you share Doctor Johnson's views——?"

"Johnson——? God forbid! The man was an ass—a
pompous ass! An unhealthy bear of a man growling his petty
spites to such nonentities as would give him ear."

"Such as—Boswell?"

"Yes: such as Boswell! Scotch, I'm sorry to say, Robert.
But what a loathsome toady. What a pair! Huh?"

"Boswell has his parts, Francis. Come now—be fair!"

"Parts! With the vital parts of manhood missing—yes.
And another Scotch laird, by God!"

"Were he at Auchinleck and you were passing, he'd make
you right welcome!"

"Welcome! You can't top the Scotch for hospitality—but
somehow I don't think I'll be driving up to Auchinleck."

"It's in Kyle—my own part of Ayrshire."

"And is your Kyle rich in antiquities?"

"Very rich, I should think. You must tour Carrick, Kyle
and Cunninghame. The countryside is studded wi' auld
biggins, castles, monasteries, old keeps o' the gentry o' by-gone
days—enough, I should think, to keep you busy for—well—as
long as you want to keep busy."

"You meant to say for the rest of my days? Huh? I can't
expect a long term of days now, Robert, and I'm damned if I'm
going to wear them out in Scotland. After I've done Caledonia
I've got to do Hibernia. But I'll visit your Ayrshire—I've
already heard much about it. If you could assist with my
itinerary——"

"Nothing would give me greater pleasure—and I'll give

you an itinerary that won't take you an hour off your main route."

"I like you now, Robert! No bloody wanderings into your damned bogs to see a heap of stones that might have fallen from a pig-house. People harbour the most fantastic ideas about antiquities—especially people who haven't travelled a mile outside their own parishes and who know no more history than the legends of an old ballad, huh?"

"Aye; but many an old ballad contains more sense o' history than a learned tome written by a learned historian that never travelled outside o' a college."

"Good! Defend your trade, Robert. Yes: and damn you! there you speak truth too. Otherwise there would be little need for my peregrinations. But no bogs! I will not leave the comfort of my carriage. Look at your roads! I sink in them often enough without risking your bogs."

"I know the roads o' Scotland better than most, Francis, and I can endorse everything you say—or may care to say. But it's a bluidy crime to ask ony beast to drag you about the countryside—whatever the roads."

"At least I don't ask the brute to *carry* me about."

"I read your poetry often, Robert. I do understand it, though much of your dialect defies me to put tongue on it. Except in the finer shades of meaning, dialect isn't so difficult: it's only damned perverted snobbery to say otherwise. And, by God, you've got some prize stinking snobs among your gentry."

"And are the Scots gentry worse than the English in this?"

"Well, the English at least ape nobody but themselves. But your Scotch gentry ape the worst of the English gentry. There's a bastard kind of English some of the younger gentry are trying to speak in Edinburgh——"

"I've heard some of them! It made my flesh creep. But you're hard on the Scots, Francis."

"Not as hard as they are on themselves. 'Course, we must

always make the distinction of separating the gentry and the
peasantry from the middle stations of life. The Scotch have
the finest peasantry in the world—and far and away the best
educated. Your gentry, with many notable exceptions, are
snobs and boors—believe me, for I've witnessed often enough
the spectacle they cut: pathetic and ridiculous figures in
English society. And they remain so bloody obtuse and arro-
gant and ape every damned silly foppery the English are up to
—and God knows the English gentry can be foppish enough.
On the whole I'd say your people in the middle station of
life are more solid and more virtuous than their English
counterparts—much though they are lacking in the graces of
life."

"They're poorer than the English."

"Ah, it's not merely a question of material poverty. There's
a poverty of deep-down self-respect. You're a defeated nation,
Robert. You all know this in your bones if you don't know it
in your heads. The English have beaten you and tamed you
as the English will beat and tame half the world before they're
done."

"They haven't beaten and tamed George Washington!"

"No. . . But they may do so yet."

"Never! But the Americans may beat and tame the
English."

"Too long a word, that 'never,' Robert. A lot can happen
in a hundred years. In five hundred years. . .? No: I think
the English will dominate the world yet—especially the
coloured races. And damn me if they won't get the Scotch to
do all their dirty work for them and fight all their bloodiest
battles for them—they've done that already. If you only heard
and saw your Scotch representatives in Parliament. . . That's
why the Scotch are so damned touchy, Robert: they're taking
second and third prize all the time. Huh? Often enough the
English take all the prizes and fob you off with some consolation
prize that would be degrading to any other people."

"Is there no good thing comes out of Nazareth?"

"Ho! as fighting material there's nothing to touch you. You have first-class philosophers and theologians: in landscape gardening you are supreme. Nothing can excel the quality of your beef or your mutton . . . but for all that you're a subject race and your bellies are turned sour with defeat— and the inevitability of defeat. . . Mind you, Robert, I talk with a fairly balanced judgment here. Remember that my father was Swiss: I have no English tradition behind me, though I think myself as English as the best Englishman living. Fortunately I share none of the English or Scotch national prejudices. . ."

"In that sense, Francis, I've none either. I belong to another category of Scot."

"You're of the category of poet! Huh?"

"Leave the poet aside for a moment. I'm a peasant or, if you will have it, a poor tenant-farmer—a modern peasant. And I'm a Scot. What do I want? I want freedom—freedom from all manner of lairds of whatever nationality. I believe in the essential brotherhood of man. Maybe, indeed, of all living creatures, since they share so much of our earth-bound fate. I'm no theologian. I leave Heaven and Hell to answer for themselves in the Hereafter—assuming that there is a Heaven and a Hell and a Hereafter. But I passionately desire freedom—freedom to write and to speak and to act. Freedom from poverty and want. Freedom from war and from man-made famine. Above all, maybe, freedom from morality, since all morality is man-made and essentially a snare and a delusion. I want men and women and children to be free in a free world. So I find myself opposed to the Scots who are for tyranny and the English who are for tyranny. That's why I've supported the American colonists' fight for freedom since that fight first began. But for all that, I'm a Scot. This is my homeland, the land of my fathers. So in fighting Scotland's battle for freedom, I fight for the principle of freedom. And I support the fight for freedom wherever that fight may be engaged—whether in France or Poland or Italy or Ireland. But I've got to wage my fight for Scottish freedom on Scottish soil, shoulder to shoulder with my fellow-Scots joined in this fight for freedom. And in this fight I ask for the support of all fighters for freedom wherever they may be—and by no means least of all the fighters for English freedom."

"And you fight for this freedom with a sword, huh? Or is the battle one of words and ideals?"

"Words for preference. But finally if freedom can only be won with the sword, then the sword will have to be unsheathed."

"A dangerous business, Robert! The sword doesn't really settle any argument—or injustice: it merely kills a lot of good men on either side."

"Aye; but the sword used to free is a very different weapon from the sword used to enslave. There's a Heaven and a Hell of difference here."

"Mostly Hell, Robert."

"There's no Hell so insufferable as thraldom."

"When your sword-arm is hacked off at the elbow, it matters little whether you're free or in thrall."

"To the individual it *may* matter little: to the cause of freedom it matters everything. You're a gentleman, Francis, and enjoy much freedom: I'm a peasant and must husband my poor stony acres—or starve."

"Or write poetry—huh?"

"When you're really starving you don't write anything: you perish. An odd exceptional individual may die with a song on his lips; but it's more likely to be with a curse in his throat—a death-rattle curse."

"We've got hellish serious—haven't we? And morbid too. Oh, I'm with you, Robert. At least my mind and my heart are with you. But no unsheathing of swords for me. And I must confess that I'm a bit dubious of the word freedom. Could not freedom be a snare and a delusion—like morality?"

"Yes and no. True, freedom is only a word and like all words can be abused. But the kind of freedom I want annihilates all bondage, all tyranny—especially the tyranny of morality. And my conception of freedom spells responsibility. For only when man is fully free can he be fully responsible—in so far as he can be reckoned responsible—for his own destiny."

"And just how far can a man be responsible for his own destiny?"

"How far we can only find out when we have achieved freedom. Do you think I'd have slaved all my life at the plough if I'd had freedom to do otherwise? Do you think my father would have died an out-worked, broken man if he'd known freedom? Do you think the slaves all around you would remain slaves if they knew freedom? Money alone does not give freedom, else the rich would be free, and we know them to be the miserable slaves of their fashions and prejudices. But once all men are free they will be responsible for their freedom. Then, Francis, and only then will we see what kind of race we become."

"By God, sir, you are eloquent—and damned convincing. But I feel that your conviction is that of the poet—of the genius."

"Damn my eloquence, Francis. All it reminds you of is my poetry. Oh, you're not the first to wave a hand and dismiss me as a poet. Poets are expected to have mad impractical ideas —poets are supposed to rave and tear their hair and mope and be melancholy——"

"But you aren't that kind of poet!"

"Then what kind of poet am I?"

"Huh! Then maybe you aren't a poet: for you're too much of a man and too much of a farmer and too much of a politician —and a philosopher—and too much of a bloody Scot—huh? And you don't drink enough. Drink prevents a man from too much action, too much philosophising. Drink warms your guts and makes you enjoy the world—without too much questioning. You question too much, Robert. And you want too much. You want perfection. You'll never get it, Robert. Perfection just isn't in man. And perfect men—and women—

would be ill beggars to live with. We'd have to shoot them."

"Which is just what we've done with all our great leaders: shot them, murdered them, crucified them, tortured them to death——"

"Precisely! Mankind will ever recognise perfectibility as a menace to their happiness."

"And mankind's so happy just now we're all laughing our guts sore. Francis: you're a bloody jesting rogue and I'm a stupid fool to sit here arguing with you."

"Thank God you've found that out at last. No, Robert: there's nothing I enjoy more. But you mustn't ask me to have convictions, for with convictions I might well become a miserable lanthorn-jawed reformer. You are different. You are a poet. The divine fire of unrest consumes you. You like all the things I like and you hate all the things I hate. But there's nothing half-hearted in either your liking or your hating. You are a man of intense vision! A man of blazing white-hot ideals! You are the modern Scotch Messiah—but with a devastating sense of humour. You're a bundle of contradictions, of opposites. You're half-a-dozen kinds and degrees of genius. But it's just as well you can make your fellows laugh, for otherwise, by God, they'd hang you. And if you ever lose your humour they will—and quickly and without mercy."

"No: I'm not important enough for hanging—or not dangerous enough. Maybe not brave enough. But to hell wi' it, Francis! I too maun live and laugh and enjoy myself. . . Fill up my glass at your elbow and we'll drink a toast."

"That's the beauty of toasts: they're always an excuse for more drinking."

The news from France gathered in volume and significance. The flashes of lightning, the low rumblings of muttered thunder at long last gave way to the storm of revolution. King Louis defied the National Assembly and, depending on his foreign mercenaries, sought to seize undisputed power.

But the people of Paris struck back. They stormed and captured the Bastille.

The world felt the after-effects of the storm and everywhere mankind was inspired, filled with hope and thrilled with the prospect of events. The world was freeing itself from the shackles of age-long tyranny and oppression. The dawn of liberty had broken for the peoples of the world.

The Bard discussed events eagerly with Grose.

"It's not just the Bastille, Francis. You see that Charlie Fox says it's the greatest event that has ever happened in the world and how much the best—Charles James Fox no less."

"Huh! Those damned politicians, Robert, always make me feel suspicious of anything they praise. But I've the feeling that here Fox speaks no less than truth. You were waxing eloquent about freedom the other night. Well, the people of Paris have not only drawn the sword of liberty—they've used big guns as reinforcement."

"And the French army has joined with the French people and beaten the foreign mercenaries. . . Things will move now, Francis. The fall of the Bastille, the hated symbol of all tyranny and oppression, will rouse the whole of humanity to fight for freedom here and now and not in some dim and distant future: King Louis had better look to his throne or the people may turn their wrath against it; and then not a crowned head will know ease or security; and then every slave and every peasant will cast off his chains and stand proudly erect in his manhood—despite his rags."

"Huh? But then we've had *our* revolution, Robert—the Glorious Revolution of 1688!"

"A flea-bite, Francis—and well you know it. What *was* our glorious Revolution but a tinklers' cloutin' o' the pots and pans o' the constitution——"

"When you turn Exciseman, Robert, you'll have to swear by that same constitution!"

"If a French soldier can give his King a lessson in the true meaning of loyalty, maybe a Scotch gauger could do likewise.

And damn me, but we'll drink a bumper to the French and Freedom before we say another word."

But Jean wasn't to be so easily swept off her feet by the news from France.

"What difference will it mak' for you and me, Rab?"

"But the world hasn't been the same since the Bastille fell!"

"I see nae difference except that the Captain and you got gey fu' about it. But maybe you'd hae got fu' onyway."

"Ah, Jean, lass: you don't know what you say. But you'll ken a difference for a' that."

"If it mak's things ony easier for you and me I'll hae nae fau't to find wi' it. Till then I'll just haud my wheest for it's something I ken nocht about."

"Damnit, I've talked plenty about it."

"Aye—you've talked o' nocht else. But dinna fash wi' me, Rab. I've enough to think about the now."

"I was forgetting, lass. But gin it's a boy he'll aey mind he was born the summer the Bastille prison fell. . ."

The Bard and Grose enjoyed many a night at the Ellisland fire-side, and sometimes they took a canny stroll in the summer evening by the banks of the Nith. They had each of them stated the fundamentals of their beliefs and now they roamed over every conceivable topic.

It was remarkable just at how many points their interests merged. On immediate politics they were agreed, on the monarchy they had everything in common and they had a brilliant and broad human interest in bawdry and in sex. In a sense, Grose wasn't joking when he declared that the Bard's collection of old bawdy songs—*The Crochallan Song Book*— was the most important work he'd done. And Grose was quick to note that in erotic symbolism the old Scots were unique.

But mostly it was their common humour that bound them

together. And Jean was never again to hear such hearty spontaneous laughter at her fire-side.

They parted on a bargain:

"If I find your Alloway Kirk all that you say it is—and if it were only for your worthy father's bones resting there I'll pay it a reverential visit. . . If I include a print of Alloway Kirk, Robert, then you must promise me to write a ballad to set up in my letterpress to enhance it."

"Well: that might not be so easy, Francis."

"Balderdash! You'll find nothing could be easier. Put your prose tale o' the witches and Auld Nick into rhyme and you have it."

"Just like that?"

"Just like that! And you'll have plenty of time. I won't be doing a great deal in Ayrshire until early next summer. But I'll see. . . I'll winter in Edinburgh, get my plates engraved and see my first Scotch volume through the press. . . You won't be in Town this winter? I wish I'd known you *before* I published my Dictionary: we could have made a rare work in collaboration. . ."

The summer's night hung hushed and reverent above the Dalswinton holms and the knowes of Ellisland. Yet the last swallows of the day were twittering as they flashed through the midge-dancing and the first bats of the evening zig-zagged in their erratic courses.

"I'll miss you, Francis. God, but you've been a rare tonic to me this summer! I think I'll do an odd satiric verse or twa on you, you beggar-lugged antiquarian! I'll send them on to you gin I think they'll be worth your postage."

"I insist on that as a promise—and put plenty o' bite in your lines, Robert—my girth can stand it. And you'll not forget my ballad on Alloway Kirk . . . and you'll write to Mrs. Dunlop and Professor Dugald Stewart at Catrine?"

"I'll forget nothing, Francis. If Jean presents me wi' a boy in August he'll be named after twa good friends, Mrs.

Frances Dunlop and yourself. If it's a boy, Francis: if a girl, Frances——"

"Don't name your boy after a sack of iniquity like me, Robert; but—huh—I appreciate the gesture. Mind you: more for Jean's sake than yours. A finer lady I haven't met in all my travels, Robert; and you know Francis Grose is no flatterer. And when she sings your songs. . .! God! what a fulfilment of life to be a poet living in this lovely rural vale and married to such a wife. Confound you, Robert Burns, but I envy you your colossal good fortune!"

Grose put his heavy arm on the Bard's shoulder.

"But you deserve it, my boy. Bless your pen and long may you fill the quarto sheets with your immortal verses. And long may you enjoy your Jean. . ."

GIVE YOU JOY

In the middle of August Jean was delivered of a fine boy who was soon afterwards christened Francis Wallace to the satisfaction of the Bard and the joy of Mrs. Frances Wallace Dunlop of Dunlop.

The Bard's mother, who had come down from Mossgiel for the lying-in, wasn't so pleased. She was of the opinion that children should be given family names. But Robert wouldn't hear of this.

"Juist let me name my ain bairns in my ain way, Mither."

"You should think o' honouring your family. You needna think about mine—but there's still the names o' your father's family and your ain brithers."

"Maybe I should hae christened the bairn Gilbert?"

"You could hae done waur——"

"Noo, Mither," broke in Nancy, " Robin kens best what he's doing. Mrs. Dunlop o' Dunlop has done a lot for Robin

—and the Dunlop family are no' likely to forget that Robin ca'd a son after their mither."

"Juist as ye say . . . but I'll no' change my opinion."

"A'right then; but we're no' goin' to argue; for you ken Robin'll no' change his opinion either."

But apart from her objection to the Christian names, the Bard's mother was proud of her grandson—just as she was proud of her first grandson Robert, whom she was now handing over to the charge and care of his parents after nearly four years.

His mother was as quiet as ever, just as bowed and as toil-worn as she had been since the death of her husband. Not that Agnes was really hard-worked now. And it wasn't that she didn't enjoy reasonable health; but the ingrained habits of her toil-laden years in Mount Oliphant and Lochlea couldn't be cast aside. Her heart had once been light and song had ever been on her lips; but the song of life had died in her heart long ago.

And always she feared for success. Robin had a grand farm here at Ellisland and a grand house well furnished. And he had a good wife and what appeared would turn out two fine boys, as like the world as could be wished. . . But still she feared, though she kept her fears hidden. It was the Burns' fate she feared. All this was costing money and money had to be won in hard toil. Well she knew that factors didn't wait long for their money. And if anything came to prevent Robin from working his farm. . .

And there was always this talk about the Excise—as if the Excise could make crops ripen in a cold wet summer.

But Robin was overjoyed about his immediate prospects of becoming a riding officer. His latest news from Graham of Fintry was, at last, positive.

He rode into Dumfries and had a word with Collector John Mitchell.

John Mitchell was a staid but sterling officer of great experience. He liked the Bard.

"There'll be an official posting any day noo, Burns—you'll get your appointment, I think. I've had a word wi' Leonard Smith. . ."

"This means everything to me, Mr. Mitchell. I mean to make the Excise my life work now that I'm as good as appointed; and as soon as I can see my way to quit myself of Ellisland—without loss—I'll do so: and willingly. You can depend on me to do everything I'm told. I've been giving my instructions a brush——"

"You'll be appointed to the Dumfries First Itinerancy—as I hinted in my letter to you. It's nae sinecure, Burns. In fact, it's one o' the toughest in the Division. . . Not that the work's so desperate: you'll manage the book-keeping side o' it wi' a bit o' application. But you've ten muirland parishes to ride ower—and in a' weathers. You'll need a good pownie . . . and you'll need a good constitution. Liquor and tobacco will be your main interest. But there'll be auctions, bricks, candles, hides and skins, malt, salt. . . No: I'm no' worried about the impost side o' your duties—it's the attention your duties demand that'll give you bother. . . Of course I'll give you a day or twa in the office going over the papers; and I'll send an experienced officer with you on your first round—that at least.

"And I'll help you in any way I can, Burns—as long as I'm assured that you're doing your work in a proper and conscientious manner. It's a strict service and the Excise doesna tak' ony excuse for laxity or carelessness or ony irregularity.

"And let me warn you against drink. Naebody minds you drinking. But not on duty. You can drink your fill when you've got your duties by for the day—and that can be a lang enough day at times."

"You need have no fear on the score of drink, Mr. Mitchell."

"Watch it though, Burns. I've seen drink ruin mair potentially good officers than bad ones. There'll be plenty of temptation put your way—deliberately put your way. You're nae man's friend as an Exciseman—you'll find that out before you're long on your rounds. Everybody likes to avoid an impost. And remember it's never for an officer to question the right or wrong of ony impost. We're here to collect and to see nobody evades what they are lawfully due. You know there's smuggling as well as I do. It's no' what it was of coorse—and the Excise has ways o' dealing wi' smugglers that you'll ken nothing about. The Excise has its agents that even I ken nothing about. . .

"It's an efficient and an honourable service, Burns; and I hope you'll be a credit to it. . .

". . . and now let's hae a drink for the merit of this meeting. We're no' Excisemen a' the time and we have our social hours and graces. . . I've read your poetry, Mr. Burns; and I must confess I'm your admirer here. You'll understand we're conversing as private citizens now. As your superior I'll treat you as an officer should and must be treated; and I'll aey have that respect from you that my rank and office is due. But as a private citizen or a public citizen I hope that at least I'll meet you on level terms, Mr. Burns."

"I understand, Mr. Mitchell; and I'll be as punctilious about this as you could wish. But I must say you give me a lift in wanting to meet me socially."

"Or maybe intellectually."

"That too, I hope."

"Weel then—— What are you doing with your poetic pen thae days? Can we hope for another volume o' poetry from you?"

"That I doubt. Certainly not in the immediate future. No' that my pen's idle altogether. And I have plans and schemes in the poetic way to keep me busy—had I nothing else to do."

"I've often wondered that you've written as much as you have. Does it come easy to you—you read that way?"

"Oh, the ideas come easy enough. And the verses too. But I've got to revise and polish: that's where the hard work comes in."

"I see. . . And you're weel acquaint wi' Mr. Graham?"

"He's my first patron: I can't recollect meeting with a worthier man. I did some lines on him—would you care to see them?"

"I would, Mr. Burns. Onything in that line would interest me."

"I'll see then that you get a perusal of my poems that I think worthy of your attention."

John Mitchell raised his glass.

"Weel: here's to our meeting and I hope to enjoy your company from time to time—and I hope I won't have occasion to be ower sair on you in my official capacity——"

"And here's to your health, sir—and to the health and happiness of your wife and family——"

The Bard parted from Collector Mitchell in high spirits. He was as good as settled in the Excise: his long wished-for ambition was at least realised. There was nothing that Mitchell had said by way of warning that troubled him. As for drink! Well, he could take another whisky now before he rode home with the good news to Jean.

He turned into the Globe Tavern Close. . .

MALIGNANT SQUINANCY

He commenced his duties on the 7th of September, though he wasn't sworn in till the Quarter Sessions of the Peace met on the 27th October.

By then his harvest was in—and a fair harvest it was—and everything was settling down for the long winter ahead.

His young cousin Willie had gone home with his mother to be apprenticed to Jean's father as a mason. John, his elder brother, had come to assist with the harvest and was now settled in as a farm servant. Fanny and Nancy still worked as conscientiously as ever; and Robert and Frank thrived. . .

A General Election was in full swing and he could not restrain his pen. There were times when his friends could not follow him in party politics. Sometimes they thought he dissembled.

But then the Bard had early learned of the dire need to dissemble and to confound his enemies by astute doubling on his tracks. But he was seldom able to dissemble at the cost of bottling himself up completely.

The truth was that he had long seen through the play-acting of party politicians. Neither party would ever do the country any real good, and though an honest man—as honest men in politics went—might attach himself to a party and proclaim his party's cause, the effect at Saint Stephen's Hall was negligible—if, indeed, there was any effect.

But now that he was a Government servant, there was no harm, in his public declarations, in *leaning* towards the ministerial side—or at least *seeming* to lean that way.

On the question of the election he expressed himself to Mrs. Dunlop with less dissembling than was his wont. On political grounds there was no reason why he should distrust her or deceive her—and he had to express something of his true sentiments to somebody.

So by the second day of October he headed a sheet "Ellisland," and commenced:

I beg your pardon, dear Madam, for this coarse paper, but I have no other large enough for a letter to you. I have often wished, when in fact, it was only the procrastinating, enfeebling tyranny of Indolence: now that excuse is literally true. Five days in the week, or four at least, I must be on horseback, and very frequently ride thirty or forty miles ere I return; besides four different kinds of book-keeping to post every day. Still, Madam, be not afraid, as you are pleased to express so much satisfaction in my correspondence, that this additional hurry will in the least detach my heart from that friendship with which you have honoured me, or even abridge my letters; though it must at times prevent the regularity of my answers to yours. I hold the epistles of a Friend to be the Sacraments of Friendship. To deface or destroy the shortest Billet of yours would shock my feelings as glaring Sacrilege.

In this country we are just now Election-mad. Sir Jas. Johnston, the present member for the Boroughs, has now opposite interests to the Great Man of this place, Queensberry. His Grace is keenly attached to the Buff and Blue Party: renegades and Apostates are, you know, always keen. My landlord's son, a young officer of twenty, is his Grace's creature, and is supported by the Foxites; Sir James, on the other hand, is backed by Ministerial influence. The Boroughs are much divided, and veer about with much uncertainty: the *weight* of the arguments of the several candidates will determine their success. I tell you all this insignificant stuff to enable you to understand the following Ballad which I have just composed on the occasion. The Boroughs are Dumfries; Lochmaben a small old town once the private residence of Robert Bruce and romantically situated among six or seven little lakes; Annan, Kirkcudbright and Sanquhar near which is the old castle of the Crightons:

THE FIVE CARLINS

Tune: Chevy Chase

There was five carlins in the South:
    They fell upon a scheme
To send a lad to London town
    To bring them tidings hame:

Nor only bring them tidings hame,
    But do their errands there:
And aiblins gowd and honour baith
    Might be that laddie's share.

There was Maggie by the banks o' Nith,
   A dame wi' pride eneugh;
And Marjorie o' the mony Lochs,
   A carlin auld and teugh;

And Blinkin Bess of Annandale,
   That dwelt near Solway-side;
And Brandy Jean, that took her gill
   In Galloway sae wide;

And Black Joán, frae Crichton Peel,
   O' gipsy kith an' kin:
Five wighter carlins were na found
   The South countrie within.

To send a lad to London town
   They met upon a day;
And mony a knight and mony a laird
   This errand fain wad gae.

O, mony a knight and mony a laird
   This errand fain wad gae;
But nae ane could their fancy please,
   O, ne'er ane but twae!

The first ane was a belted Knight,
   Bred of a Border band;
And he wad gae to London Town,
   Might nae man him withstand;

And he wad do their errands weel,
   And meikle he wad say;
And ilka ane at London court
   Wad bid to him guid-day.

The neist cam' in, a Soger boy,
   And spak' wi' modest grace;

And he wad gae to London Town,
 If sae their pleasure was.

He wad na hecht them courtly gifts,
 Nor meikle speech pretend;
But he wad hecht an honest heart
 Wad ne'er desert his friend.

Now what to chuse and what refuse
 At strife thae carlins fell;
For some had gentle folk to please,
 And some wad please themsel'.

Then out spak' mim-mou'd Meg o' Nith,
 And she spak' up wi' pride,
And she wad send the Soger lad,
 Whatever might betide.

For the auld Guidman o' London court
 She didna care a pin;
But she wad send the Soger lad
 To greet his eldest son.

Then up sprang Bess o' Annandale,
 And swore a deadly aith,
Says:—' I will send the belted Knight,
 Spite of you carlins baith!

' For far-aff fowls hae feathers fair,
 And fools o' change are fain;
But I hae tried this Border Knight:
 I'll try him yet again.'

Then Brandy Jean spak' owre her drink:—
 ' Ye weel ken, kimmers a'
The auld Guidman o' London court,
 His back's been at the wa';

'And mony a friend that kissed his caup
    Is now a fremit wight;
But it's ne'er be sae wi' Brandy Jean—
    I'll send the Border Knight.'

Says Black Joán frae Crichton Peel,
    A carlin stoor and grim:—
'The auld Guidman or the young Guidman
    For me may sink or swim!

'For fools will prate o' right or wrang,
    While knaves laugh in their sleeve;
But wha blaws best the horn shall win—
    I'll spier nae courtier's leave!'

Then slow raise Marjorie o' the Lochs,
    And wrinkled was her brow,
Her ancient weed was russet grey,
    Her auld Scots heart was true:—

'There's some great folk set light by me,
    I set as light by them;
But I will send to London town
    Wham I lo'e best at hame.'

Sae how this sturt and strife may end,
    There's naebody can tell.
God grant the King and ilka man
    May look weel to themsel'!

I dare say, Madam, you are by this, completely sick of
Ballads; else I might send you a new edition, much enlarged
and improved, of Doctor MacGill's ballad. That, with some
verses I made on Captain Grose, may be the subject of such
another Scots-mile Epistle.

Your little squalling Godson goes on, "improving in grace

C.B.W.   K and in favour with God and with man." Parental partiality apart he is in fact and very deed almost the finest boy I ever saw; and seems to say, by the vigorous tossings of his little limbs and the open manliness of his infant brow, that he will one day stand on the legs of *Independence* and hold up the face of *An Honest Man*. . .

Adieu! Le bon Dieu vous soulage et soutient!!!

Though he treated his Election Ballad with some diffidence, he was rather proud of it; for apart from the accuracy of his points, there were some subtle stabs at the essential buffoonery of the whole silly business.

As the long dark winter nights drew in, and the wind and rain lashed out of the south-west, a gloominess began to pervade Ellisland. Maybe the forebodings of disaster were felt only by the Bard. . . The strain of riding some two hundred miles a week in bad weather and over execrable roads began to affect his already-flawed heart. Certainly the continual soakings did not help his incipient rheumatism.

The truth was he had not the constitution to stand up to prolonged exposure to wind and rain—and to mental despair. His nerves were always taut and it was seldom he could relax. Now he realised, though he kept this realisation strictly to himself, that he couldn't go on as Exciseman *and* farmer. His money was almost gone, and poverty was beginning to bite into his economy. . .

There was no one who could or would take the farm off him even by way of management and control. When decisions had to be made, he had to make them; and if he didn't plan the day's work, nobody seemed to be able to plan it for him.

Most of all it was poverty that he feared. If he failed in his farm he would fail in the eyes of all Scotland—and in the eyes of his family. Such a failure might even jeopardise his Excise job or at least his prospects of promotion.

Sometimes he lingered a little longer than he should over a pint of ale in Hyslop's Globe Tavern. But then he liked

Willie Hyslop and his wife, Bess, and it was a comfort to get a heat at the fire and enjoy a friendly crack before he faced the darkness and the rain for six dreary miles to Ellisland.

Sometimes, coming home in the opposite direction, he lingered overlong at Bacon's Inn at Brownhill: especially if Willie Stewart or John MacMurdo were present.

Sometimes he felt that there were too many women about Ellisland. Always Jean and Nancy and Fanny. Often, too often, it was only in bed that he and Jean got a word with each other such as man and wife should.

And sometimes he was glad of a free evening to call on Glenriddell and discuss with him the matter of his manuscript volumes. For Riddell had obtained two stout volumes so that the Bard might enter his manuscript poems and transcribe copies of such of his correspondence that would be of a more permanent interest.

Riddell was talking of having Johnson's *Museum* rebound with blank interleaves that the Bard and he might annotate the songs. For Riddell thought himself something of a musician and wished to compose for the *Museum*. He had begun to interest himself with all the enthusiasm of the idle but opinionated amateur in everything that pertained to his work for Johnson.

And though the Bard paid little or no attention to Riddell's enthusiastic strictures on Scottish song, nevertheless he was glad of his interest in the work; and glad of a seat by his fire-side as a relief from the worry and drudgery of his days.

Maybe there was too much time for brooding on his long muirland rides on a horse that began to jade and tire too easily.

Slipping and sliding in the saddle, he couldn't always be crooning over a melody and essaying words to fit it.

Only too often now was he becoming morbid in his fears. He was beginning to look in front of him and behind him and to forget the present.

Too often now the women he had known came back to

haunt him. Mary Campbell was often in his thoughts—why, he couldn't tell. But rather than dismiss the thought of her, he brooded on her memory—re-lived the scenes with her.

God! but the fates had been unkind to Mary; and he had been too short-sighted, maybe too selfish to have done what he had. Time and again he reviewed the then situation. He could argue that he had done no wrong. And they had been married at a time when he considered his marriage to Jean null and void. It wasn't his fault that Mary had contracted the fever that had laid her in the dust. . .

But if she had never met him; if he had never persuaded her—aye, stormed her with his love-making; if he'd never evolved that marriage ritual, never given her the Bibles in troth and never pledged her to go to the Indies with him, she might well have been living yet. . .

The old rounds of "ifs" and the endless possibilities of what-might-have-been came back to him now a thousandfold.

Jean and Nancy could see that there was something wrong; but he would not allow them to approach him.

His temper got brittle. Why wouldn't they leave him alone? There was nothing wrong with him. Damnit, hadn't he enough to do with his Excise papers when he came home at night without cat-worrying him about his health and his appetite? Hadn't they enough work to keep them busy without pestering him?

But by November he was only too glad to allow them to pester.

There came a cold raw November morning when Jean took the situation in hand.

"You're no' getting up the day, Rab, and that's an end o' it. You're in a high fever. You've tossed and groaned and turned a' nicht."

"Right, Jean: I'll hae the day in my bed."

"You'll stay in your bed till you're better."

"You ken there's too—much—to do. You ken I canna absent myself frae the—Excise."

"Wheesht noo: dinna worry about the Excise or onything. A gauger can tak' no' weel the same as ither folk."

"Right, Jean. . . I'll need to send a note into Dumfries. Maybe John——"

"We'll see aboot that the morn. The Excise'll no' gang to ruin for ae day. . . I'll mak' you some thin hot gruel."

"Whatever you say, Jean."

Jean hurried into her clothes and bustled through to the kitchen.

"Put the bellows to the fire, Nancy! That's Rab in a high fever and hardly able to lift his head. I'll gie the bairn his feed noo and maybe Fanny could tak' him into your bed for an hour——"

"Aye: surely, Jean. I kent fine he was working for something. Oor Robin canna dae wi' wettings; and y'ken thae damned wa's are no' dry yet."

Jean set her teeth as the infant Francis bit into her inflamed teat. His lips had broken out as a result of a cold and this had infected her nipples. . .

Nancy plied the bellows to the fire in some agitation.

"And get ready a hot gruel, Nancy. We'll strain the oatmeal. . . It's aboot the only thing he'll tak'."

"It'll aey help to sweat him. D'you think he's richt bad? Will I go through and speir him?"

"No . . . no' the noo. You can come ben when he's at his gruel. But dinna say too much."

"Aye . . . I ken."

"Rab doesna lie doon to an illness. I should hae forced him to his bed a week ago."

"He's been affa restless this wee while—and snappy. It's no' like him to be snappy. Even Fanny noticed it."

"A blin' man could see it. Aye: that'll be enough meal— and a guid twa measures o' water. Is Fanny in the dairy? Weel—gie her a shout."

"I'll run oot for her."

Fanny came in looking worried.

"Aye, Auntie?"

"Listen, Fanny: I dinna want the wean to get the cauld and I dinna want him to be annoyin' your uncle. Slip into Nancy's bed and I'll hand you in the wean when you're warmed."

"I'll keep him warm and quiet, Auntie. Is my Uncle gey bad?"

"Bad enough, lassie! It's a raging fever he's gotten."

Fanny's eyes shone with sympathy. "I hope it isna too bad, Auntie. I dinna think my Uncle's been weel for a while back. Aye: I'll get to bed——"

For days the Bard lay sick and ill and fevered. Often he raved and often, but unintelligibly, he raved about Mary Campbell. . .

Jean knew about Mary Campbell—or thought she did. At his request she had brought him pen and paper to write to the Excise office in Dumfries. And she had read a draft of a song to "the dear departed shade" of Mary. . . She had no more than glanced at it; but an impression of its contents and of its general mood affected her. She said nothing. Someday, if it ever suited him, he would say what he wanted to say about Mary Campbell the Stairaird dairymaid; and if it never suited him to say anything—well, Jean wouldn't worry. There was nothing Mary Campbell could do for him now.

But the Bard was desperately ill. Dr. Mundell called from Dumfries. But there was nothing Mundell could do. He told Jean to keep him in bed . . . and he could have a dose of mercury and port wine . . . and a little laudanum now and then. A malignant squinancy and low fever . . . the disease would need to run its course. Yes: a hot gruel as he could take it would help to keep up his strength.

The truth was that Mundell knew nothing about the illness beyond the obvious fact that the Bard was fevered. His nostrums only made bad worse.

In his conscious moments he thought of impending death. The thought distressed him. For himself he didn't much mind.

He didn't want to die—ill and wretched and pain-racked as he was. But he didn't fear death. He feared its consequences for Jean and his two boys. . . How would they survive— and in what wretched poverty?

Collector Mitchell rode out to tell Jean not to worry—and to satisfy himself about the extent of the illness. Mitchell formed a high opinion of Jean.

"I'm no' worrying about the Excise, Mr. Mitchell, and I'm no' worrying about Mr. Miller's farm either. Mr. Burns is a' my worry. Gin he was hale and weel again he would aey manage to work for his food and his shelter—somewhere."

"That's the right attitude, Mrs. Burns. Get your husband well again. It's a bad fever he's gotten."

"And how could he escape, Mr. Mitchell? He comes hame on a wat day drenched through to the skin and blae wi' cauld."

"I'm no' responsible for the weather, Mistress——"

"Your pardon, sir; but I'm no' saying you are and I'm no' blaming Providence; but it's easy seen how he's gotten the fever."

"Aye. . . But he's worrying and I've told him there's nothing to worry about. Do your best to reassure him too and I've nae fear that you'll have him on his feet by the end o' the week. I'll hae a word with Doctor Mundell."

When he was getting better and the fever was subsiding, he insisted on seeing any letters that had come for him.

"You maun be feeling a lot better?"

"I'm a lot better, Jean. Noo bring me what letters there are and no' keep me waiting."

"You're no' to get impatient. You've a' day to read letters."

"Damnit, Jean, I'll no' be treated like a bairn."

"Aye: you'll be treated like a bairn—and a gey ill bairn you've been."

"Aye. . . You've been guid to me and I've been gey ill to thole——"

"Na, na, Rab: you gave us little bother——"

"Is everything all right? There's nane o' the beasts ill?"

But Jean reassured him on every point—and then she fetched him his letters.

There was one from Allan Masterton thanking him for *Willie Brewed a Peck o' Maut and Rob and Allan cam' to prie*—a decent wee fellow Allan Masterton. . . And here was a letter from Willie. Ha! Nicol was wanting him to inspect the farm and estate of Laggan—so Willie was determined on being a country laird. . . He'd forgotten to ask Jean how that damned mare o' his, Peg Nicholson, was doing. . . Well, he couldn't inspect Laggan at the moment. Who could he send? Better to send a stranger. . .

And here was a long letter from Gilbert. Gibby was in a black bitch of a depressed mood too. Aye: Gibby was in no position to help him out in the management of Ellisland. Gibby was a sinking soul too, was he. . .? Why the hell didn't he marry Jean Breckenridge and be done with it? What the hell was the good in shivering on the brink of the sea of matrimony—let him plunge in! It would be a shock; but it would be the life o' him.

He re-read his letters. . . He would need to get up. He would sit at the table with his back to the fire. . .

And then he knew he was too ill to rise—too weak. His legs seemed to be without strength and without supporting muscles. . .

The effort of reading the letters in the uncertain light, the mere effort of concentrating exhausted him. His head fell over on the pillow and he slept.

But it was a sleep that his exhausted frame needed; and his strained, over-burdened heart, fighting against Mundell's violent poisons, was thankful. Jean happed him up and let him sleep.

"He's sleeping, Nancy—the first natural sleep he's fa'n into since he took ill."

"I pray to God he's by the turn now."

"He'll mend now. And the fever's left him. God, he's

thin. . . We'll need to build up his strength what we can. You'll need to save him what cream there is, Nancy."

"There's gey little—but I'll dae what I can. And what aboot a bowl o' hen-bree—though there's hardly a pick o' fat on the birds the noo."

"Och, I've seen them worse. But we'll need to nurse him, Nancy. And we'll need to humour him too; for he doesna like to be pampered."

In a couple of days, with a good fire roaring in the chimney, he was at his study desk writing away in fits and starts.

He wrote to Mrs. Dunlop:

Many thanks, dear Madam for your sheet-full of rhymes. Tho' at present I am below the veriest Prose, yet from you everything pleases. I am groaning under the miseries of a diseased nervous System; a System of all others the most essential to our happiness—or the most productive of our Misery. For now near three weeks I have been so ill with a nervous head-ache, that I have been obliged to give up for a time my excise books, being scarce able to lift my head, much less to ride once a week over ten muir Parishes. Lord, what is Man! To-day, in the luxuriance of health, exulting in the enjoyment of existence; in a few days, perhaps in a few hours, loaded with conscious painful being, counting the tardy pace of the lingering moments by the repercussions of anguish, and refusing or denied a Comforter. Day follows night, and night comes after day, only to curse him with life which gives him no pleasure; and yet the awful, dark termination of that life, is a something—perhaps a Nothing—at which he recoils with still more horror.

> "Tell us, ye Dead; will none of you in pity
> Disclose the Secret—
> *What 'tis you are, and we must shortly be !*
> —'tis no matter:
> A little time will make us learn'd as you are."

Can it be possible, that when I resign this frail, feverish being, I shall still find myself in conscious existence! When the last gasp of agony has announced that I am no more to those that knew me, and the few who loved me; when the cold, stiffened, unconscious, ghastly corpse is resigned into the earth, to be the prey of unsightly reptiles, and to become in time a trodden clod, shall I be yet warm in life, seeing and seen, enjoying and enjoyed? Ye venerable Sages and holy Flamens, is there probability in your many conjectures, any truth in your many stories, of another world beyond death; or are they all alike baseless visions and fabricated fables? If there is another life, it must be only for the just, the benevolent, the amiable, and the humane; what a flattering idea, then, is a World to come! Would to God I as firmly believed it, as I ardently wish it! There I shall meet an aged Parent, now at rest from the many buffetings of an evil world against which he so long and bravely struggled. There should I meet the friend, the disinterested friend, of my early life; the man who rejoiced to see me, because he loved me and could serve me— Muir, thy weaknesses were the aberrations of Human-nature, but thy heart glowed with everything generous, manly and noble; and if ever emanation from the All-Good Being animated a human form, it was thine! There should I, with speechless agony of rapture, again recognise my lost, my ever dear Mary, whose bosom was fraught with Truth, Honour, Constancy and Love—

> Thou ling'ring star with less'ning ray,
>   Thou lov'st to greet the early morn,
> Again thou usher'st in the day
>   My Mary from my soul was torn.
> O Mary, dear departed shade!
>   Where is thy place of blissful rest?
> See'st thou thy lover lowly laid?
>   Hear'st thou the groans that rend his breast?

That sacred hour can I forget,
　Can I forget the hallow'd grove,
Where, by the winding Ayr, we met
　To live one day of parting love?
Eternity cannot efface
　Those records dear of transports past,
Thy image at our last embrace—
　Ah! little thought we 'twas our last!

Ayr, gurgling, kiss'd his pebbled shore,
　O'erhung with wild woods thickening green;
The fragrant birch and hawthorn hoar
　'Twin'd amorous round the raptur'd scene;
The flowers sprang wanton to be prest,
　The birds sang love on every spray,
Till too, too soon, the glowing west
　Proclaim'd the speed of wingèd day.

Still o'er these scenes my mem'ry wakes,
　And fondly broods with miser-care.
Time but th'impression stronger makes,
　As streams their channels deeper wear.
O Mary, dear departed shade!
　Where is thy place of blissful rest?
See'st thou thy lover lowly laid?
Hear'st thou the groans that rend his breast?

Jesus Christ, thou amiablest of characters, I trust thou art
no Impostor, and that thy revelation of blissful scenes of
existence beyond death and the grave, is not one of the many
impositions which time after time have been palmed on
credulous mankind. I trust that in Thee "shall all the Families
of the earth be blessed" by being yet connected together in a
better world, where every tie that bound heart to heart in
this state of existence shall be, far beyond our present concep-
tions, more endearing.

I am a good deal inclined to think with those who maintain that what are called nervous affections are in fact diseases of the mind. I cannot reason, I cannot think; and but to You, I would not venture to write anything above an order to a Cobbler. You have felt too much of the ills of life not to sympathise with a diseased wretch, who is impaired more than half of any faculties he possessed. Your goodness will excuse this distracted scrawl which the Writer dare scarcely read, and which he would throw into the fire, were he able to write anything better, or indeed anything at all. . .

If you have a minute's leisure, take up your pen in pity to le pauvre Miserable. . .

A week later he was out and trying Nicol's mare with two others in the plough. The poor beast tried her best; but it was a poor best. So he wrote to Willie Nicol accordingly, and added the information that his intelligence concerning Laggan was on the whole favourable.

A week later he was back on his Excise rounds and, of an evening, drafting a letter to Provost Robert Maxwell of Lochmaben, who had thanked him in verse—though it was but poor rhyming—for his Election Ballad *The Five Carlins*.

Dear Provost,—As my friend Mr. Graham goes for your good old town to-morrow, I cannot resist the temptation to send you a few lines; and as I have nothing to say, I have chosen this sheet of foolscap, and begun, as you see, at the top of the first page, because I have ever observed that when once people who have nothing to say have fairly set out, they know not when to stop. Now that my first sentence is concluded, I have nothing to do but to pray Heaven to help me to another. Shall I write you on Politics or Religion, two master-subjects for your Sayers of nothing? Of the first, by this time you are, I dare say, nearly surfeited; and for the last, whatever they may talk of it who make it a kind of Company concern, I never could endure it beyond a Soliloquy. I might write you on farming, on building, on marketing, on planning, etc., but my poor distracted mind is so torn, so jaded, so racked and bedevil'd with the task of the superlatively Damn'd—*Making one Guinea do the Business of Three*—that I detest, abhor and swoon at the very word, Business, though no less than four letters of my very short Sirname are in it.

Well, to make the matter short, I shall betake myself to a subject ever fertile of themes, a Subject, the turtle-feast of the Sons of Satan, and the delicious, secret Sugar-plumb of the Babes of Grace; a Subject, sparkling with all the jewels that Wit can find in the mines of Genius, and pregnant with all the stores of Learning, from Moses and Confucius to Franklin and Priestly—in short, may it please Your Lordship, I intend to write BAWDY!

Song—Tune—Auld Sir Symon:

> I'll tell you a tale of a Wife
> And she was a Whig and a Saunt. . .

You see, Sir, I have fulfilled my promise: I wish you would think of fulfilling yours, and come and see the rest of my Collection.

If at any time you expect a Field-day in your town, a Day when Dukes, Earls and Knights pay their court to Weavers, Taylors, and Cobblers, I should like to know of it two or three days beforehand. It is not that I care three skips of a cur-dog for the Politics, but I should like to see such an exhibition of Human Nature. . .

Part   Three

THE TAVERN IN THE TOWN

PLAYERS AND PROLOGUES

Though the Bard was physically fit enough to carry on with his Excise duties and to continue to overhaul his ten parishes, he did not fully recover from his November illness.

Melancholy assailed him by day and night; his nerves were frayed and his mind unable to cope, without irritation, with the problems that beset him. He could not see his way out of his manifold difficulties.

Ellisland remained the main problem. Now he hated the sight of it and revolted at its mean sour unproductive acres. He had little heart to labour on it and there was no joy, since there was no certainty in its prospects.

Certainly the gloom of winter did not help him. His house continued damp and all the firing did not seem to drive the moisture from the sweating walls. Even the books and papers in his study became limp with dampness. In the far corner, some of his books began to show a greyish scad of mildew.

And outside the earth was an ankle depth of mud and glaur. He set his labourers, when they had time, to paving the court with boulders—and God knows! there was no lack of boulders—but they were inexpert and the work progressed slowly. It wasn't a job for a wet day and on a dry one there were more urgent tasks to perform.

Even the Nith, usually his greatest natural solace at Ellisland, often failed to charm. There were times when it flooded and came tearing down from bank to brae an acre broad; and it was then he was thankful he had chosen the scaur-head for the site of his biggins. And often enough it gave him no satisfaction to see so much flooding of the Dalswinton holms across the muddy-brown water.

C.B.W. 161 L

Even on good days when the sun was shining and the air was pure and clean and the distant hills stood washed in dark blue and shimmering grey, the dampness was always underfoot. In such weather it was as much a necessity as a pleasure to linger in a howff in Thornhill or Dunscore. . . And always an added pleasure to linger in Dumfries.

There were many howffs in Dumfries. He liked to linger on an odd occasion with Henry Clint in the King's Arms—next door almost to the Globe Tavern. Sometimes he accompanied a brother-Exciseman to the George Inn or sometimes to Nancy Welsh's retreat . . . or the Jerusalem Tavern.

But most often he preferred the company of the Hyslops at the Globe. It was here that he stabled his horse and here that he directed any message to his care.

The Globe was easy of access. He could approach it from English Street—a dozen steps from the Excise office; or he could approach it from the High Street. It was here that the High Street broadened to such dimensions as to give it the air of a Square.

And indeed it served this function. It was here, where the road bottle-necked at the Mid-Steeple, that the casual citizens gathered, where important news was proclaimed, and about which the Town revolved. . .

The Dumfries Theatre was not the most elaborate or comfortable of the few provincial theatres in Scotland; but it was popular and the best touring companies visited it. In any case, a new one was a-building.

In December the Bard made the acquaintanceship of the actor-manager, George Sutherland, through an introductory letter from an old Ayrshire friend. He liked Sutherland and his company of players; and Sutherland was not slow to realise the potential value to his theatre of Scotland's greatest poet. He suggested that the Bard might care to consider the writing of a prologue since he had already written a prologue for William Woods in Edinburgh.

The Bard admitted he was no stranger to the theatre—or to prologues. He was grateful to Mr. Sutherland and he would see what he could do for him. He confessed that it had ever been his darling wish to write for the theatre. . .

Towards the end of December he sent him a short prologue for the New-Year's Day performance. Though slight, the prologue was well received and folks began to remark on what they considered was a new departure for him. . .

Sutherland presented the Bard with a complimentary ticket which allowed him entry to the pit any time it was presented —provided the house was not already filled to capacity.

His nights at the theatre and his talks with Sutherland and his wife renewed his urge to write plays—Scottish plays, historical, pastoral, tragic. But he didn't know where to begin. There was more to writing a stage piece than met the eye. A prologue was easy—indeed there was nothing easier, to him. But drama required a story and characters to depict the story.

Yet others had succeeded and why shouldn't he? None of the dramatic pieces he saw in Dumfries awed him either in the quality of their inspiration or the quality of their writing. But they had what he hadn't—a familiarity with the mechanics of the stage.

He determined to read all the dramatic authors he could lay hands on. He would commission Peter Hill to see what could be procured in Edinburgh.

Though his visits to the theatre helped to enliven his winter, they failed to banish his deep-seated melancholy. He could brighten in company. Sutherland and the players found no trace of melancholy in his presence, nor did his few intimate friends about Dumfries. The players indeed thought him a man of terrific verve and mental audacity.

But when he rode home at nights (and he found the six long miles to Ellisland dreary in the extreme) his melancholy would often come uppermost.

He felt his whole existence was somehow pointless and

fruitless. In every direction he seemed to be wasting his time, dissipating his energy.

He tried to dismiss Ellisland from his calculations. He had written Gilbert telling him outright that "it could go to hell." But for all that, Ellisland was all the home he had and it could no more be sent to hell than it could be transported across the Nith.

His Excise work was proving onerous and fatiguing: the ceaseless book-keeping was like a complicated treadmill. And yet he thirled himself to the Excise for the security of £50 a year. Yes: he'd come to this; that £50 constituted his security. And he'd cursed the Edinburgh gentry for allowing Fergusson to die of neglect and starvation!

If nothing came of his influence with Graham of Fintry he would have to wait nine years before his name would come up for the consideration of promotion. The thought was enough to blast anyone with melancholy.

Not that he despaired too much about that nine-year prospect. He just wouldn't be able to do his present rounds for very much longer: he would need to get a foot-walk somewhere or else it would be farewell to the Excise.

And he was beginning in his despair to spend too many evenings in Dumfries and to linger too long in the Globe. But the truth was that he had failed to confine himself to the concept and duties of a Nithsdale tenant-farmer; and he was failing to confine himself to the concept and duties of a riding gauger. He had failed to suppress the real Robert Burns—the Burns who was first and last a poet, the Burns who was ever thirsty for the experience of life that lay beyond the unimaginative drudgery of mere duty and the veriest existence.

In his desperation to assure Graham of Fintry, and his wife Jean, that he was first an Exciseman, and only on occasional off-moments a poet, he had almost convinced himself.

Almost! But again and again the real man in him kicked over the traces and spurned the idea of day-book duty.

The conflict was endless and both victory and defeat were

profitless. In the evening he would sit in the theatre and relax and be himself, the poet at his ease. But he rode home at nights as farmer-cum-Exciseman and rose in the morning to fulfil their interpenetrating roles. And not only was he farmer-Exciseman: he was very much husband and parent too: the days of bachelor-freedom were far behind him.

Sometimes he battered himself into the conviction that all this was but a temporary phase; that he would quite suddenly be promoted as an Examiner or Supervisor to some profitable port where his emoluments would at least equal his salary if not exceed it; where he could lead a pleasant comfortable life with all the time at his command to read and write and enjoy good conversation, rejoice in Jean and bring up a family in decency and order!

But even were he to be appointed Supervisor, or even Collector, in Port Glasgow to-morrow, Patrick Miller would still hold him to his lease of Ellisland. He couldn't quit his farm as and when he liked—and there was no sentiment in Patrick Miller.

There wasn't even common humanity in Miller. Once the Bard had been invited to Dalswinton—to be shown off, as he suspected, to his wife and friends. Not once had Patrick Miller visited Ellisland. Anything he wanted to know he got from David Newall.

And when the Bard spoke to the factor, Newall shrugged his shoulders: "Mr. Miller is a verra busy man, Robert, as you ken. But if he thocht there was much wrong wi' your conduct o' the place you would soon hear from him—no' from me."

Yes: indeed. Patrick Miller was a busy man. But he had plenty of money to throw away experimenting with a steam-paddled boat; and he could even go to the unheard-of folly of draining Dalswinton Loch for that purpose.

But for the farms that comprised Dalswinton estate, Patrick Miller had no interest. The whole of the estate had been exhausted and lay in bad heart. The very thought of it soured Miller's stomach. When he thought of Robert Burns, which was seldom, Miller was uncertain. His Election Ballad for his son hadn't come out in the straight-forward manner he would have liked. Burns the poet wasn't bowing his neck to the yoke of farming as he would have liked. True, he worked hard enough and Newall's reports were more than favourable. But he was dubious of this Excise venture—damned dubious. What was the countryside thinking about his tenant galloping in his bloody gauging over a dozen parishes? Not that he cared a damn what anybody thought; but there might be a reflection on his lairdship; and he didn't like that.

'Course there was little doubt—Burns had gotten a wheen doubtful acres across the Nith there. If all Newall said were true, Ellisland was about the poorest of the Dalswinton farms. And no doubt Burns knew this and maybe he was rueing his bargain. Well, maybe he was rueing the bargain himself. Dalswinton had been no gold mine for him—not that Burns would ever think of that.

Well, to hell with Burns! If poets couldn't support themselves without running into debt and whining about their misfortunes, they shouldn't craw so crouse in their poetry. . . Aye; and maybe Burns was hoping to slip out of his obligations. Well . . . he would see about that. He'd give him another year at this damned gauging. He could always cut his career there damned short.

More than this Patrick Miller refused to consider. He brushed Burns from his thoughts—or tried to. Somehow the poet remained lurking in the shadow of his thoughts; and his image often came back to annoy him at odd uncomfortable times.

Even his wife's attitude annoyed him.

"I'm often being asked about your poet, Peter?"

"He's nae poet o' mine: he's a tenant."

"And that's the rub, Peter: it mak's it verra awkward having him to dinner."

"Then dinna hae him to dinner. We've had dinners lang afore there was ony Robert Burns."

"May I remind you that it was you, not I, who used to boast that the celebrated Burns was your special pet?"

"Weel, ye ken I've nae special pets."

"I know——"

"Then what are you bothering me for wi' your damned yitter and yap about Burns? D'you think I havena enough to worry me——?"

"For all you've done for him he hasn't sung your praises, has he?"

"I need nae bluidy begging poets to sing my praises——"

"I understand that he praises and flatters the Riddells?"

"And wha's the Riddells when they're at hame?"

"They move wi' much acceptance in the county—the Craigdarroch and Maxwelton families think highly enough of them. You should think a little more of your county standing—if only for your wife and family's sake."

"I could buy and sell the lot o' them—and dinna fret yoursel': I'm mair highly thocht of and my company's mair socht after than ony ither man in the south o' Scotland. You and your country squires! Drinking themselves stupid for a bluidy auld whistle! And Robert Burns sitting snug in the corner celebrating their damned useless nonsense in a damned useless ballad! Wha the hell wants tae read a wheen tedious verses celebrating a Bacchanalian debauch amang a wheen ignorant country squires that hae damn a' else to dae wi' their time? You dinna see ony o' them sailing steam-boats on *their* lochs . . . Captain Riddell forsooth! And a wheen cairts o' auld stanes to build him a Druid's temple nae less: it wad gar you vomit! Huh! Your Riddells and Fergussons and Maxwells: I could buy and sell the whole damned lot."

"Money isn't everything——"

"See: awa' doon to the ford at Sandbed yonder: kilt your coats and wade across and tell that to your poet Burns. Noo:

let me get on wi' my work—hae you ony idea what your alterations are costing me here. . .?"

But, though he didn't tell her, his experiments with his steam-driven boat were costing him near on ten thousand pounds—so that he had little time to think about the affairs of a needy poet and some acres of impoverished ground. . .

When Mrs. Sutherland's Benefit Night at the Dumfries Theatre came round he wrote her a prologue that was different. It said something he felt needed saying and he felt he had said it well.

He had arranged to meet Sutherland at the Globe. They went through to the Room—a small private den on the right of the stairway.

"I've got a prologue here, George, for your good lady's benefit night. I think it's good—but I'm anxious about it too. There's a dark stroke of politics in the belly o' the piece—and it might be detected . . . and it might displease some of our gentry——"

"Ah—dangerous ground, Robert! Politics and the theatre are a kittle mixture. Besides, you ken how we depend on the patronage of the gentry. Without them——"

Sutherland made a large gesture. But he was a large man and liked to make large gestures and vent large exclamatory "aaahs!"

"However . . . let me read it over to you."

Sutherland composed himself to listen, which he did by crossing his legs, folding his arms across his chest and giving his head an elegant tilt to the side.

The Bard, head bowed and elbows on knees, read quietly but effectively from his much-corrected manuscript.

What needs this din about the town o' Lon'on,
How this new play an' that new song is comin'?
Why is outlandish stuff sae meikle courted?
Does Nonsense mend like brandy—when imported?

Is there nae poet, burning keen for fame,
Will bauldly try to gie us plays at hame?
For Comedy abroad he need na toil:
A knave and fool are plants of every soil.
Nor need he stray as far as Rome or Greece
To gather matter for a serious piece:
There's themes enow in Caledonian story
Would show the tragic Muse in a' her glory.

Is there no daring Bard will rise and tell
How glorious Wallace stood, how hapless fell?
Where are the Muses fled that could produce
A drama worthy o' the name o' Bruce?
How here; even here, he first unsheath'd the sword
'Gainst mighty England and her guilty lord,
And after mony a bloody, deathless doing,
Wrench'd his dear country from the jaws of Ruin!
O, for a Shakespeare, or an Otway scene
To paint the lovely, hapless Scottish Queen!
Vain all th' omnipotence of female charms
'Gainst headlong, ruthless, mad Rebellion's arms!
She fell, but fell with spirit truly Roman,
To glut the vengeance of a rival woman:
A woman (tho' the phrase may seem uncivil)
As able—and as cruel—as the Devil!
One Douglas lives in Home's immortal page,
But Douglasses were heroes every age;
And tho' your fathers, prodigal of life,
A Douglas followed to the martial strife,
Perhaps, if bowls row right, and Right succeeds,
Ye yet may follow where a Douglas leads!

As ye hae generous done, if a' the land
Would take the Muses' servants by the hand;
Not only hear, but patronise, befriend them,
And where ye justly can commend, commend them;

And aiblins, when they winna stand the test,
Wink hard, and say: "The folks hae done their best!"
Would a' the land do this, then I'll be caition
Ye'll soon hae Poets o' the Scottish nation
Will gar fame blaw until her trumpet crack,
And warsle Time, an' lay him on his back!
For us and for our stage, should ony spier:—
"Whase aught thae chiels maks a' this bustle here?"
My best leg foremost, I'll set up my brow:
"We have the honour to belong to you!"
We're your ain bairns, e'en guide us as ye like,
But like good mithers, shore before ye strike;
And gratefu' still, I trust ye'll ever find us
For gen'rous patronage and meikle kindness
We've got frae a' professions, setts an' ranks:
God help us! we're but poor—ye'se get but thanks!

Sutherland jumped to his feet. "By God, Robert: that *is* a prologue. A thundering performance! Mrs. Sutherland will be enthusiastic—I'm enthusiastic! Ah! but the politics!"

"Too strong?"

"To be quite frank, I don't know. The reference to England's Queen Elizabeth could give offence. I wonder? And the reference to Mary Stewart—too Jacobitical . . . maybe? But who am I to judge? *Who* am I to judge? *Were* I judge I wouldn't blot a line—not a word, not a syllable, not a comma. But—politics—dangerous—nothing more dangerous, my friend."

"Well . . . I could submit the prologue to the Provost as the first magistrate in the Town, and ask him to approve—or disapprove. We could easily put the onus on him. If we got his support, Mrs. Sutherland could say as much when she came forward——"

"Ah! Provost Staig! A stratagem, Robert. A most excellent stratagem. Ah! you've a head for more than poetry, Robert—you are very wise. Provost Staig then must be the bar of appeal. A worthy man, Mr. Staig—a worthy patron of our company——"

"Between you and me and the wa' here, David Staig's by far the most astute man in Dumfriesshire. My landlord, Patrick Miller, whom you know is an astute and able man—there are plenty would say he is the most successful man in Scotland—but if the fox is a fool to Patrick Miller, Miller's a puir skinned fox compared to David Staig—though for heaven's sake don't quote me on that."

"Ah—there's too much at stake to do anything so foolish. But, of course, I see your point. I've no illusions about Provost Staig—and I've been assiduous in courting his favour. But to our prologue: you will interview the provost at once?"

"Damn the fear—I'll *write* the provost—and even if he doesna *write* his reply, at least we'll have evidence that we wrote him."

"And you'll keep a copy o' the letter?"

"There would be little point in writing him otherwise——"

"If ever I'm in a difficulty I'll come and consult with you, Robert. Where have you acquired all your—wisdom, caution——"

"Cunning?"

"I didn't say——"

"No; but it's just what it is. A poor poet canna live otherwise than by using all the cunning he can acquire for the struggle with life. Don't imagine I have any illusions either about myself or the place I occupy in this damned dirty gossip-mongering hole."

"So you don't really like Dumfries?"

"Sometimes I loathe it so much that I could go back to Ayrshire and take a hired ploughman's job. But then I don't let the Great Folks hereabouts know anything of my real feelings—they think I'm enjoying myself and that I respect baith them and their midden o' a place."

"Oh, it isn't bad as places go, Robert—and it's got a theatre

—and an audience to flock to it. We've turned away money every night we've been here——"

"Oh, I'll grant you all that, George—but it's a damned clannish place for a stranger to bide about. I know I shouldna complain. Damn it: they made me a burgher o' the Toon the first time I visited it—just after my Edinburgh edition was launched—Clarke was the provost then. What I mean, George, is that it's a damned smug, through-ither, cleishmaclaver kind o' a place—rotten wi' inter-marriage and intrigue. And gossip—evil gossip—that's the stock-in-trade o' the place. And what company is there here for a poet—or for any man of lively intelligence? Damn little! You see my prologue? How many in Dumfries will or could appreciate it? D'you think Provost Staig will appreciate it?"

"In that respect, Robert, the bloody Town's lousy. There's no conversation in the taverns—nothing you'd call wit. And yet some remarkable folks do visit my company at the theatre."

"Yes—and they come frae far and wide. Gin you could tak' your pick in Dumfriesshire and place them in the King's or the George, you'd have a goodly company. But the ordinary work-a-day week-day Dumfries—dead! And a place run for the profit and convenience o' shopkeepers and merchants! Thank God for your Players, George—they break the grave-yard deadness o' the place: they bring folks out-of-doors: they make them laugh and make them appreciate—however little—that life can mean more than totting up the right side o' a sales ledger and finding fau't wi' their neighbours."

"Well . . . as Players, Robert, maybe we see a different side to the places we visit. We never stay long enough to become over-familiar with the inhabitants. Maybe in this we're fortunate—on the other hand we never have our roots anywhere. There *are* times when Mrs. Sutherland and I long to have a real home of our own where we could settle down and raise a family. Ah—but then—our life is the theatre; and as players we mustn't think of that. Though I do see your point, Robert— We couldn't settle down in Dumfries even if it is one of the best provincial towns we know of. What is there to do but drink—and gossip? Not that you'll ever stop people from gossiping. . ."

"Maybe no'—and maybe I'm not quite recovered from that damned bout o' fever I had in November. I get damnably melancholy at times."

"Ah—then let's have another drink. And you must promise to think about writing for us Players—a good broad comedy— it can't be too broad. Or a real thundering tragedy: that's what the public like. But nothing too subtle. The one thing the theatre-loving audiences will not use is their brains. Everything must be broad and large—and heavily underscored. We've got to beef into our roles—with everything we've got. Then they applaud to the echo."

But the Bard thought: Broad and large—as much as you like; but try to be natural too. No need for rhetoric and bombast. If he got round to writing a play, it would be as natural and inevitable as the characters in his poems. Suppose he put a character like John Rankine of Adamhill on the stage? But then it would take a John Rankine to act a John Rankine: whereas Sutherland here might well act Wallace or Bruce with dramatic acceptance. . . No: it wasn't going to be so easy to write for the theatre.

Meantime he'd better get away out to Ellisland and write his letter to Provost Staig.

SONGS

Early in February, when the year was at its dowiest, the third volume of the *Scots Musical Museum* arrived at Ellisland. As he turned the pages, the Bard thought that the printed volume was well worth all the tremendous effort he had bestowed on it.

He showed it with pride to Jean and Nancy.

"There's my third volume frae Johnson. What d'you think o' it?"

"It's nice, Rab. . . My, Nancy, does it no' mak' you proud. . .?"

"Aye . . . it mak's me proud, Jean. But I'd be prouder for Robin's sake gin I saw his name on the front o' it."

"Now, now: I've tellt you afore: this is a labour o' love and maist o' the credit maun go to Johnson—and there's Stephen Clarke's work. It's a labour o' love for a' concerned. You needna worry about my name, Nancy. I pride myself wi' a' a modesty that it'll no' be forgotten in a hurry. But I fear for Johnson. I fear he'll never get the credit he's due. But gin the generations to come dinna build a monument to James Johnson as high as the Castle Rock in Edinburgh— then they'll be a hantle sicht mair ill-gotten than I'm prepared to think. And maybe they'll mind o' me as a song-writer and as a collector and mender o' mony o' our auld sangs."

"And will they mind hoo Jean sang them for you?"

"Weel, Nancy: I'll dae what I can to see that Jean's no' forgotten——"

"Tuts! dinna haver, the pair o' you. I think it's a grand book, Rab—and a grand reward for a' your wark on it. And as lang as folk dinna forget the sangs, does it matter what else they remember?"

"There, Jean: you've got the sense o' the matter."

Jean was turning over the pages.

"Oh, I see you've got my sang in. You ken it, Nancy? Of a' the Airts the Wind can blaw, I dearly like the West? Aye —and O were I on Parnassus Hill—and The Rantin Dog, the Daddie o't."

"Hoo mony sangs hae you gotten in it?"

"A guid forty, Nancy—forbye some bits o' mended things."

"What's your favourite, Jean?"

"Favourite, Nancy. . .? Coorse, I'm fondest o' my ain sangs—the sangs that Rab made for me. But I like—let me see—I like Ay Waukin O . . . and Jamie come try me . . . and

Ca' the Yowes to the Knowes . . . and John Anderson my Jo
—aye, I'm fond o' John Anderson."

"A guid choice, Jean—I couldna hae bettered it."

"And what about you, Robin?"

"It's hard to tell wi' a guid sang. You can hae a prime
favourite for weeks—and then alang comes another tune and
displaces it—till alang comes anither. But I like a' the sangs
Jean's mentioned. Though I hae a fancy whiles for The Tailor
fell through the Bed, Thimble and a'. And there's The Braes
o' Ballochmyle. Allan Masterton composed a grand tune for
that—as he did for Willie Brewed a Peck o' Maut— But damned,
I'm real proud o' my efforts here. It's a volume will gie Jean
and me meikle pleasure doon the years and ane we'll aey gae
back to—will we no', Jean?"

"Oh—I'll gae back to it often enough—at least as lang as
you find pleasure in my singing, Rab. And when you dinna,
I'll juist croon them ower to mysel'."

"God! You're like a pair o' cooin' doves—there maun be
mair in a sang than I can see. Well, coo awa', the pair o' ye—
but I'll need to hash on wi' the wark."

"There's naebody keeping you back, Nancy—only you'll
find a sang can lichten the wark for you."

"Aye? I've yet to hear the sang that'll milk the coo and
kirn the butter—while I stand looking on wi' folded airms."

"Then I'll need to see what I can dae for you—some night
when my Muse is in fettle."

"Ca' your Muse oot to the byre in the mornin'—and then
she'll ken a' about it. But nae doubt she'll be like her master
and like her bed in the mornin'!"

When Nancy had gone, Jean closed the book and smiled.

"You ken Nancy doesna mean a word she says—but mind
you: she's an able one."

"Och, I ken our Nancy of old. She's got wit and a droll
sense o' humour. But I doubt gin she were married she'd fley
the back o' her man."

"Aye—she should be married."

"Nancy's had her chance, Jean. And she preferred to let it slip by. She'll fa' in wi' somebody yet. It'll maybe no' juist be an affair o' passion—though Nancy's got the Burns blood in her—but at her age she'll maybe be a' the better o' a steady fellow that's a bit gathered and settled like."

"I hope sae, Rab. I wouldna like to see her throwing hersel' awa' to the first pair o' breeks that shaped up to her."

"Na, na: had that been the way, Nancy would hae been ruined long gin now. But sometimes I think my mither held the lassies doon ower sair—at least when I was at hame."

"Aye: your mither has a big say wi' them. There was nane o' them got stravaigin' aboot Machlin when I was there. We often talked about it. Mind you: Isa'll no' be held in the same. She'll marry early or I'm mistaken."

"Aye: Isa's got plenty o' life about her. She'll be het o' the dowp whiles. . . What about Bell?"

"I dinna see Bell marrying—she's gotten sour as far as the lads are concerned."

"She hasna been at hersel' this wee while back. She's no' juist as weel as she should be."

"I wouldna say—she's got a touch o' Gilbert's nature."

"Weel, weel. . . This'll no' get on wi' the wark as Nancy says—and a' this talk aboot my sisters and us talking aboot my sangs."

"You dinna mind what I say, Rab——"

"No, Jean: I dinna mind what you say for you never say ocht but the truth; and your truths are aey kindly. At least you aey see the kindly side."

"Weel . . . I was gey hauden doon mysel', Rab. My faither—but come on! I'll see if Fanny greased your buits. . ."

The Bard picked up the volume and walked down to the parlour with it. He was happy and strangely satisfied. Later on he would write a thankful note to honest James Johnson. . .

JOHN SYME

John Syme was a pleasant fellow of some thirty-odd years who occupied the small Galloway estate of Barncailzie.

He had been an apprentice to his lawyer father in Edinburgh but had failed to make much of the dry musty arts of that profession. He had tried the army; but the army had appealed to him no more than the law. At the moment he was hoping for the appointment of Stamp Collector in Dumfries—at least he was hoping to assist Maxwell, the holding official, as he was near the point of retiral if not of dissolution.

Some time before this he had met the Bard at Tinwald Downs; and there they had got a bit drunk.

They had a common friend and correspondent in Edinburgh in the person of Alexander Cunningham, who, unlike Syme, had become a Writer to the Signet—though Cunningham hadn't any real use of his election to that privileged body.

The Bard hadn't written as often to Cunningham as he might—and as the strength of their mutual friendship warranted. Cunningham had written Syme for news of the Bard.

And now the pair of them sat in the King's Arms discussing Cunningham and life in general.

Syme was a cheery uncomplaining man, but nevertheless could complain in a mild deprecating manner. He liked good food, good wine and good conversation. He didn't like work —or even the thought of working—and he didn't like bores. Syme would have been quite content in his role of modest country laird, shooting and fishing and entertaining a few friends. And he liked books and a good story; and he had ideas about music and poetry and politics.

Syme liked to have ideas about things—provided his ideas didn't lead him into any kind of activity. He marvelled at the

Bard's energy as he laid aside the copy of the *Musical Museum*.

"I dinna understand, Burns, where you get all your terrific energy? Do you never relax and tak' things easy?"

"Certainly I relax—at times. In fact there are times when I can be marrow-bone lazy."

"I canna imagine you. When d'you get time to do a' this?" He tapped Johnson's volume.

"Find time—tak' it out o' my sleep when necessary; but that's seldom. There's aey a song running in my thoughts— sometimes half-a-dozen. And when I'm riding on my Excise duties I hae plenty time to sooth them over."

"And the words?"

"After I have the melody right, the words come. Sometimes easily. Sometimes wi' a bit o' spurring when the Muse is jaded. But eventually they come. But don't judge me as a poet by my song-writing. Sometimes I have to cobble a set of verses for a song—cobble them out of the poor remnants of an upper. But I'd rather mend the upper than throw it away. Even the bare title of an auld sang can be evocative. . . Of course, there're times when I can tak' an old bawdy sang and completely transform it—as I did wi' John Anderson. You ken the old indecent words?"

"No; but I'd like to hear them."

"I'll jot them down for you some day. Well now: I'm as fond o' a bawdy sang as onybody. In fact I've a theory about bawdry and I confess I'm addicted to bawdry."

"Good! I confess wi' you."

"But the fact is, my dear Syme, though you and I may relish a ripe bawdy old song or ballad, you'll admit we canna sing them in the presence o' the ladies."

"No, no: never before the ladies."

"So, for the sake of the ladies and mixed company, I've purified quite a number of our old songs—but mainly, I confess, for the beauty of the melody."

"Cunningham never told me you'd such a passion for songs —or were so gifted in that direction?"

"Ah well: many a good song I've given to Sandy Cunnin-ham; and many a guid bawdy song I've heard him render at the Crochallan Club at Dawney Douglas's yonder in the Anchor Close."

"I know it fine—though I was never a member of Crochallan. Yes: our friend Cunningham has a very sweet tenor voice."

"Most expressive when handling the tender and the pathetic. I've heard him sing Oonagh's Waterfall as sweetly as ever he did Fergusson's Lea-rig."

"Will you share a bottle of port wi' me, Burns? I must have a bottle beside me. It annoys me and interrupts the flow of our discourse to have the lass replenishing our glasses."

"Yes: I'll join you—but I've got to ride back to Ellisland to-night: so I mauna get fu'."

"Certainly, Burns: I'll undertake to see that you don't. It would indeed be unforgivable if anything should happen to you on your homeward ride where I had any responsibility for you drinking. It's just that good wine and good company are to me inseparable."

"Well, I canna say that I'm ower particular about wine, though I ken a good port and enjoy a good port. But I've seen me as happy as the night was long on a pint or two of guid ale—aye, and on a glass of twopenny."

"I can well believe you. I can even believe you being content on a glass of water. And why not?"

"Exactly. You know, Syme: I've drunk more spirit since I came to Nithsdale than ever I drank before."

"How d'you account for that?"

"Oh—just loneliness—melancholy——"

"What! You melancholy?"

"Yes, me. I've had a damned melancholy, low-spirited winter."

"You're deceiving. And how d'you account for the melancholy?"

"By the Lord God, when I came down to farm Ellisland—

or rather to my putting it to rights for farming, I thought
I'd come to the very elbow of existence."

"The elbow of existence? Excellent!"

"For a poet, it was like burying myself up to the chin in a
peat bog. There wasn't even a soul to talk to——"

"Ah, I can sympathise with you. I'll need to come and
shut myself up here in Dumfries—and what the hell is there
in Dumfries for you or me? I loathe towns—loathe the stink
and the filth of them. And by God, Dumfries can stink."

"It can—more ways than one."

"Exactly. Have you found many people to hold converse
with in Dumfries?"

"They're damn few and far between. Damnit, there's even
a lack o' characters about the Town. Or at least I havena fa'n
in wi' them yet."

"What kind of characters have you in mind?"

"But damnit, Syme, that's just the point. You can't have
a character *in mind*. A character is an oddity, an original—
someone who, for some trait or other, stands apart from—if
not above—the run-o'-mill humanity. Impossible to have a
genuine character in mind——"

"Shrewd, Burns! And true, of course. Yes: I see what you
mean. I must say I too like a man with an original bent to
him—even if it's only in conversation."

"And it mainly is in conversation. You know there's not
even a character in the Excise. Collector Mitchell is an excellent
and worthy man: I can't imagine a worthier superior. But
Mitchell is no character. As for my fellow-officers—well, for
the most part, they are good honest fellows, and having said
that, I've said all."

"I fear I'm going to find Dumfries fearfully dull—that's
why I'm so happy our friend Cunningham has managed to
bring us together—I hope you'll join me on occasion and, once
I get settled in a house, maybe you'll honour my fireside?"

"I'll be equally glad of your company, my friend. I enjoin
you now most heartily to come out to my farm and—such as it

is, share the comforts of my table. My Jean will make you welcome, and if you don't object to plain hamely fare—but excellently cooked——"

"Don't apologise for honest faring. I'll be charmed to meet your Jean. The first time I'm that way I'm due to call on Captain Riddell at Friars Carse——"

"You know the Captain?"

"Not too well—but we have common friends both in the South here and in Edinburgh——"

"And you're for Edinburgh to-morrow?"

"Well, I'll get half-way there with any luck—the days are still damnably short—and I won't forget to deliver your letter to Cunningham. At least I'll be able to tell him that we shared a bottle of port in Dumfries and that I found you well."

"Well enough anyway. But hardly in old use and wont. This damned damp weather fills my carcase with aches and pains. But maybe when the good weather comes in. . . We must meet oftener, my friend, and enjoy some civilised talk."

Syme was not a character. Yet there was something distinctive about him—once you got to know. His was a soothing presence free from any sense of urgency. Whatever he had to do, it seemed that Syme had at least a life-time in which to do it; and even his life-time seemed to stretch away into eternity . . . or at least far into the unseen future.

The Bard reckoned that John Syme would live ripely into a ripe old age: that he would mellow into the grave and not die in any sudden or decisive way.

A man of culture and a man of great personal charm; and a true fellow doubtless, and true to his word. . . The Bard was well pleased with their second meeting. He looked forward to having a quiet pleasant evening with John Syme, the rather impecunious laird of Barncailzie, who was angling for the sinecure of the Dumfries Stamp Office. That was several cuts above the Excise—but then impecunious John Syme was of the lower rung of the gentry—and his father had been a Writer to the Signet.

On the long dreary road to Ellisland, the wind blew cold and raw; but the rain held off and there was light enough for Pegasus to go at a modest jog-trot. And a half-bottle of good port knocked at least a mile off the journey.

Damned! if he'd only thought sooner. Syme was the very man who might have been coaxed into subscribing for Davie Sillar's book of Poems.

Still . . . maybe better not. Dear old Davie Sillar. The ace of hearts had Davie been back in the Lochlea days. But in honest truth, Davie was no poet—though in the old days his rhyming had done well enough. Well . . . for the sake o' auld lang syne and Davie Sillar he would do his best for his subscription. But he was afraid that Davie would be out-of-pocket and have a wheen copies left on his hands. The trouble with Davie, as with so many other folks, was that he'd no sense of humour and no sense of the incongruous or the ridiculous. . .

What a strange creature was man indeed. It was but yesterday in time when Davie and he used to have their arguments and debates. And yet now as he rode towards Ellisland, Tarbolton and Spittleside seemed almost to belong to another age.

And yet his *Epistle to Davie* was one of his best. It would stand up to a lot of hard wear. Folk would maybe go on reading it in days to come, when poor Davie himself was lost to the records. And doubtless better men and better poets had so been lost.

THE GOLDEN LOCKS OF ANNA

The affinity that arcs across the poles of male and female sexuality was ever instantaneous in so far as the Bard was concerned. And mostly, where the affinity was avid, the female was acutely conscious of the contact.

Mrs. Hyslop's niece, Helen Anne Park, was native of the Port of Leith, as was her aunt; but she had come to Dumfries to help her aunt out; and also, perhaps, from a feeling of superfluity in her parental home. She was in her early twenties, and had arrived the previous month.

Anna knew the Bard by repute. When Edinburgh had toasted him, Leith had no-wise been lacking— She had heard of his name and of his verses. Indeed she had read much of his Edinburgh volume.

When she heard from her aunt that Robert Burns sometimes visited the Globe, she was conscious of a thrill of anticipation. She had also heard rumours in Leith: rumours concerning his great conquests with the ladies of the Town. Rumour had it that the Ploughman Poet was an expert and successful lover.

But, speaking to her aunt, Anna suppressed her excitement.

"Oh, I've heard o' the Ploughman Poet—what's he like, Auntie?"

"Nane o' your Ploughman Poet here, Anne. Mr. Robert Burns to you: mind that! Ploughman Poet indeed! Mr. Burns is a gentleman—in every sense o' the word. A fine-looking, weel-set-up man—and manners o' the finest."

"But he's no' a real gentleman: I mean——"

"He's a farmer up the Nith. A place called Ellisland—a tenant o' Mr. Miller o' Dalswinton. No: he's no' a gentleman in the sense o' being ane o' the gentry. He's what you'd ca' a nature's gentleman; and I wish the gentry were ocht like him."

"He's got the name o' being fond o' the lassies—aye, and the ladies o' Edinburgh."

"My lass! dinna let me hear you talkin' like that aboot Mr. Burns. Your uncle and me's gey proud to hae him come aboot the Globe."

"I ken it's a great honour. I'll never let dab to onybody what I ken aboot Mr. Burns."

"And as far as the lassies are concerned, that's nane o' our business. You learn that when you're in the trade: you see plenty and you hear mair—but you shut baith your een and your ears."

"I ken, Auntie: I'm no' glaikit."

"I ken fine you're no' glaikit; but you can aey learn! If Mr. Burns is nice to you, you be nice to him—it's guid for trade. He'll maybe slip you a bit coin—if he does, you'll ken he likes you. Be sure you gie him a bit curtsy and thank him kindly."

"Oh, I'll dae that. Will I tell him I've read his book and that I heard aboot him in Edinburgh?"

"No' sae fast noo. Plenty time to speak to Mr. Burns when he speaks to you. You never ken: he'll maybe never notice you."

But the Bard noticed her. He came in one morning when William Hyslop was out buying and his wife was busy preparing the mid-day food and not yet dressed for the public.

He was in the Room warming his back at the fire when Anna entered at the summons of the bell.

They eyed each other for a moment and the arc of mutual attraction flashed between them.

Anna was an attractive lass. She had a fine figure, fine hips and urgent breasts. She had full red lips and her hair was the reddish-brown that is best described as golden. And she was sexually vibrant.

In that pause of mutual attraction she knew that the stranger was Robert Burns. And she found words before he did.

"Mr. Burns, sir—if I'm no' mistaken?"

"No . . . you're no' mistaken. But I dinna recollect—Ah, you'll be Mrs. Hyslop's niece?"

"That's right, Mr. Burns. And what would your pleasure be, sir?"

"Well . . . I hadn't intended drinking. Mr. Hyslop's no' aboot? I see. . . Well, while I'm waiting I'll drink a bottle o' porter. . ."

While Anna was fetching the porter, the Bard drew a chair to the fire. So this was Anne Park. A glow of well-being suffused him.

"Thank you, my dear. Can you no' spare me a minute o' your company? You're no' busy this morning?"

"We're never verra thrang at this time, except on Wednesday's mart."

"And how d'you like Dumfries? Mrs. Hyslop tells me you're frae Leith?"

"That's richt, Mr. Burns. I heard a' aboot you when you were stopping in Edinburgh."

"You did, did you? And what did you hear?"

"That you were a wonderfu' poet, sir."

"That wasna much to hear."

"Oh, but I read your book, sir."

"Oho—so you ken just how wonderful I am?"

"*I* think you're wonderful, Mr. Burns."

"That's verra nice o' you, my dear, to say so. And how did you know I was Mr. Burns?"

"I couldna mistake you, sir. I've never seen another man like you."

"God! am I showing a cloven hoof—or is my tail visible? Dae I no' look human?"

"Oh, I dinna mean onything disrespectfu'. The ither way aboot, sir. It's juist . . . you'd ken you were a poet."

"Sit doon, lass, and tell me about yourself. What d'you mean, you darena? D'you want me to go ben and ask your auntie's permission? You'd rather stand? And you've the beds to mak' yet? Well, I hope gin I need to stay the nicht here that you'll be on the chaumers."

"Oh aye . . . if I'm still here."

" 'The lass that made the bed for me.' Aye: you'd sit for the portrait perfectly. . . Just me thinking out loud, my dear: a habit o' mine I trust you'll no' object to."

"I couldna object to onything you would say, Mr. Burns."

"I wonder noo?"

"Onything respectable like. And I ken you wouldna say onything I could object to."

"I micht say something in the poetic way, my dear, that micht be misunderstood gin it was put in blunter or coarser words."

"But then, sir, you'll understand that I've never fa'n in wi' onybody like you afore. . . I mean . . . and you being Scotland's greatest poet."

"You'll need to stop thinking aboot me as a poet. Think o' me as I am: a plain country farmer, married, and verra much in love wi' a young wife."

"It's affa nice to hear you say that, sir. I mean you being in love wi' your wife. . . Maist married men say the opposite. But you're onything but plain, sir."

"You're no fool, Anne."

"I hope no': I wouldna need to be in this job."

"And hae you gotten a Dumfries lad yet?"

"I've seen naebody about Dumfries I'd walk to the midden wi'."

"That would be a silly-like place to walk wi' ony lad."

"Och, you ken fine what I mean."

"Fine I ken. . ." He stood up and lifted his drink from the mantel-shelf.

As they talked they were both uneasily aware of the underlying affinity between them. Had the Bard taken her in his arms then and there she would have offered no resistance: rather she would have welcomed him.

As he drank off his porter, she half-turned her head and

listened. She made a movement towards the door and listened
again without seeming to listen. Yet she knew that he
apprehended the significance of her every movement. She came
back towards him slowly with a panther-like, suspended tread.
His eyes seemed almost hypnotic. Hers fused in his: the focus
wavered and then blurred. She heard the sound of her voice
coming from afar. . .

"Will I re-fill your glass——?"

Their embrace was spontaneous. It was long and ardent.
She clung to him in a near frenzy. The long kiss seared. . .

She broke away with a low heaving gasp.

"Steady, lass, for Godsake! Bring me another porter."

Anne grasped the measure and fled from the room.

The Bard clutched the mantel-shelf. God! he was trembling.
It was a while since anything like this had happened—or so
suddenly. And since when had he experienced such a devastating embrace? Hell! And what a time and what a place for
this to happen! There would be no rest for him—or for her—
until that kiss was consummated. And how and when was
that to happen?

But it happened sooner than he reckoned. Later in the
afternoon, his business done, he was saddling Pegasus for the
homeward journey when Anne came to him.

"My auntie sent me to say you were to mind aboot the
cheeses from your brother."

"Are you sure *she* sent you?"

Anne nodded urgently, understandingly.

"D'you think we're safe?"

"Aye: for a wee while."

He took her to the stall where the fodder had been forked
down from the loft.

There was no need for any dalliance. She was almost
frantic.

"What have you done to me?" Her words were husky and
vibrant. "I've never felt like this before."

"If there was a reason for you being born, lass; this is the reason. Maybe I was born for this moment myself."

In all his long experience, the Bard had never known a lass whose need was so desperate, or who was so desperate in her need.

He had thought that nothing could happen to him in the way of a man with a maid that could shock or surprise him. Now he was both shocked and surprised. This morning he had entered the Globe Tavern with no thought of meeting Anna Park. Had he anticipated meeting her, his anticipation would have been rationalised by his experience. Nor, for that matter, had he any intention of allowing himself to be involved in any affair with a woman. Jean was a be-all and an end-all to him.

And yet, without any real forewarning, he had been swept into Anna's arms and she into his as if an outside force had motivated them—and ruthlessly. It wasn't possible to comprehend the devastation of what had taken place. . .

He wanted the strength of muscle and will to mount his horse. He led the beast out of the narrow court almost without knowing.

Then he found himself handing the bridle to an ostler-lad outside the Jerusalem Tavern and, entering, almost mechanically ordering a gill of spirits.

He gulped half of the raw drink down his parched throat and shuddered at the burning impact. The spirit violated his stomach. He ordered a glass of ale to counteract the effect. He drained the ale in one long convulsive gulp.

God damnit! When had he ever emptied drink into his wame like this? And yet the lowing drouth would not be quenched. He ordered more ale.

The wife who served him noted how he trembled.

"Are ye feeling the caul', sir?"

"Caul'? Yes . . maybe I've gotten a chill."

"Aye: or a foun'erin'. Naething like guid reekin' toddy, sir."

"No: nothing warm. Maybe I'm a bit fevered."

"Whatever you say, sir."

There were others drinking and conversing. He was oblivious to them. He sat in a corner table with his head in his hands trying to compose himself, trying to think. The mixture of ale and spirit began to quell the jumping nerves and quieten the pounding heart. He drank off the remainder of the spirit and never felt it going down.

The drink crept into his veins and the easing effect was infinitely soothing.

God, but that was better! What an experience. . . He took out his kerchief and dabbed the sweat from his brow. But his thoughts reacted in a series of exclamations, a series of overpowering images.

Of course he should still have been relaxing in Anna's arms. Couldn't he have stayed longer? Aye; but the risk! What if Hyslop had caught them? But there hadn't been a minute to think or plan. It had come like a clap of thunder from a cloudless sky. He'd known quick conquests. Aye; but always he'd *wanted* to conquer. This had just damn well happened without as much as a by-your-leave on either side. Had just happened! Suddenly from zero—damn near from the Greenland Bay of indifference. Smack into a maelstrom of passion. . .

Hell! The drink was having no effect on him. He caught the wife's eye: "Another gill, wife—the strongest proof you've got. That was like milk."

"That's the strongest i' the hoose, sir: costs anither tippence; but there's naething stronger in Dumfriesshire."

He swallowed a mouthful. Aye: that was better. "Keep the change, guidwife."

What was wrong when the drink was having so little effect on him? He must be needing it.

And then the sear of Anna's kisses burned across his lips.

Should he risk going back again? Hell! his appetite was only whetted. His curiosity hardly roused—or roused but unsatisfied. They should have had a night together—a week of nights.

And yet he was puzzled. This had never happened to him before. Never! There was an unknown quality about this Anna Park—and an unknown quantity too. But, either way, devastating.

He'd experienced all that was to experience. No woman could love like Jean. Jean had all other women weighed in the balance—and that included Mary Campbell and Annie Rankine. And Jean Glover and Clarinda. But, by God, this Anna Park had something that not one of them had. But what was it —and what was the mystery of this devastating effect on him?

Desire writhed in his guts like a frenzied snake: it knotted and unknotted and reknotted. Sweat ran down his face in tiny rivulets. He mopped himself dry.

Almighty God: he was insanely in love. That was it. Furiously in love: like a brainstorm; like delirium. A love, new, fresh, instantaneous—and completely overwhelming. Oh no: this was no buttered-up simulated passion.

And something he hadn't wanted, hadn't longed for, hadn't anticipated—couldn't even yet comprehend its significance.

And never a thought yet of possible consequences.

But why blame Anna? Maybe there was a quality in himself he hadn't realised before. There was something in this. Why were his hands shaking so that he had difficulty in raising his drink—and why was the drink so slow to affect him? It was easing, soothing—but it wasn't acting as drink invariably acted on him.

His reactions must be changing—maybe he was in a species of climacteric. . .

And Anna had to be a virgin. Not a stubborn or difficult virgin; but still a virgin—almost self-deflowering in her passion. . .

He ordered another drink and felt his body slowly sinking into a happily-relaxed state.

He was tired, exhausted: beyond caring now; beyond mental exclamations; beyond wondering at himself; beyond seeking explanations for the inexplicable. Content in a strange impersonal way to feel the ebb and flow of sensation. To taste her kissing, to hear her breathing, her convulsive gasps as if the soul were taking leave of her body. And the body itself: the cool firm smoothly-moulded hips; the curve of her thighs—throbbing thumping thighs. The maddening delicious unbearable faculty of seeming to embrace with the whole body. The insane suggestion that he too was a virgin: that this was the first experience—the shattering convulsive explosion of the first orgasmic spasm, causing every nerve to tremble and tauten, to tauten and tremble. . .

At last the fumes of alcohol began to reach the brain and dull and deaden sensation; make recollection bearable; make the jaw slacken and sag and cause the eyelids to droop in a tire of grateful drowsiness; to release languor to lap softly against the sentient boundary walls of being and awareness; to withdraw the image of Anna into a haze of dim remembrance.

The fever abated, the clamour died away, the blood resumed its accustomed flow along its accustomed channels —and seemingly, but gently, assisted by drink.

Walter Auld, the saddler, came in and sat down at his table.

"I thocht that was your mount outby! How're ye, Robert?"

"Oh . . . it's you, Wattie. Me? And how are *you*, my good friend?"

"Doin' awa': what're ye drinkin'? What's the matter: no' feelin' weel?"

"God kens how I'm feeling. How? Am I looking bad?"

"You've either had a hell o' a fricht—or come intil a fortune."

"A bit o' baith, Wattie . . . aye, a guid bit o' baith."

He signalled the guidwife. "You'll hae an ale along wi' your spirits, Wattie—rum or gin?"

"Ye still think the Dumfries whisky's bad?"

"Rank! It micht pass in a sweet toddy—but it wad nae mair nor pass."

"I'll hae the rum then: I'm nae fond o' the gin."

"Nor me . . . only it doesna stink your breath like the rum."

"Maybe my breath stinks onyway. And how's things wi' ye? Ony word o' your brother William?"

"No' recently. He's aboot Newcastle—thinking o' making for London."

"Lunnon, eh? He's travellin', the lad. I suppose a wheen o' folk look to Lunnon as a likely place to mak' a quick fortune?"

"Let them go to hell, Wattie, and save themselves the trouble. To hell wi' folk that want to mak' fortunes—and to hell wi' them that hae fortunes. Hell's for a' fortune-makers."

"What's ta'en you the night?"

"Drink, you suppose! What's a fortune in the bank? Or in your pouch? Can you eat a fortune? Can you sleep in twa-three beds at once—or lie wi' twa-three women at once? A' a man needs, Wattie, is just enough to do him—and his dependants. Man *needs* nothing more. And yet damned greed will make men beasts so that they may bank their wealth and become rich and powerful. But for what? Can you tell me?"

"Ah, folk need a bawbee or twa past them for a rainy day."

"Ah, prudence! Very nice fault, prudence: a bawbee i' the bank against a rainy day! Damn you, Wattie! I'm talking about fortune-gathering, the lust for lucre, the greed for gold. A bawbee or twa i' the bank! Aye, and to hell wi' your canny cheese-paring prudence too. . ."

"It looks like to hell wi' everything the nicht, Robert?"

"Every day and every nicht! Greed and canny prudence:

they baith land you in hell—in the end. A bawbee i' the bank!
Man, for some folks it rains every day o' their lives—it micht
as well rain bawbees."

"Were you at the whisky afore the gin?"

"Drink again—I know! Burns is drunk! The Bard's as
drunk as Bacchus, as fu' as Bartie! Aha! But you're wrong,
Walter, my bonnie saddler, you ugly sinner! Oh aye: I should
be fu'—blin' fu'. But I'm wealthier, richer than ony India
Company nabob! To-day I had a fortune o' the richest and
purest gold poured in my lap—and I've spent every penny of
it. And why? Because the fortune will still be there the morn
and it'll still be mine."

"A queer kind o' fortune, Robert. I could dae wi' the like
mysel'."

"You! Na, na, Wattie... Twa-three bags o' bawbees'll
do you by way o' fortune. D'you understand?"

"There're some things no' worth trying to understand——"

"Mony a true word, Wattie... That's richt: you don't
bother your fat backside trying to understand me. I'd hate to
see you wasting your time and your energies. You're a guid
fellow, Wattie, and ken what side your bap's buttered. But
dinna mistake me! You befriended me, Wattie; and ony man
that befriends Robert Burns, or ony belongin' him, is a friend
for life. And if I hang a sermon on you—that's just because
you're sitting here wi' me the nicht: a convenient peg for a
sermon to be hung on——"

"Right then, Robert! Are you for another drink?"

"Certainly I'm for another drink——"

"Weel, damn you! I'm asking you: it's my round!"

"Doesn't matter a curse whose round it is. That's more
prudence—and caution. But thank you, Wattie—a drap o' gin;
and a tankard o' ale to ease it doon. Now: where were we?
Ah! Talking about wealth——"

"Bletherin', you mean. Damned, Robert, you can gabble
awa' as much skite as you like; but you canna get awa' frae
cauld prudence—nor can you talk debt oot o' existence."

C.B.W.   N

"Cauld Prudence—and she *is* a cauld bitch: as cauld as Death. As for debt! What debt? Whose debt?"

"The debt the debtors' gaol provides for."

"Whose gaol? Whose debt? The apparatus o' morality—the bankers' and merchants' thumbscrews and leg irons. To hell wi' them too, Wattie. ... I'm a wealthy man to-night—this day hae I been in Paradise——"

"You've been somewhaur ye shouldna hae been onyway!"

"Exactly! Somewhere I shouldna hae been. Exactly! Who says so? Who has a right to say where I'll go and where I'll not go? What I'll do and what I mauna? Walter Auld says so. And why does Walter Auld say so? Because the Kirk and the State says so: therefore so says Walter Auld, staunch upholder o' State and Kirk. So to hell wi' Kirk and State——"

"Canny, Robert, canny! Damnit, man, you're an Exciseman noo. You're nae longer an independent irresponsible poet. Folk hae ears."

"So I've bartered my independence for the £50 o' the Excise? I'm no longer an irresponsible poet——"

"You're a Government servant noo, sae you've got to bridle your tongue in public. There's folk sitting here the nicht wad gae oot o' their way to report you to Collector Mitchell."

"So I've got to mutter under my breath to a friend in a tavern over a social drink because o' a wheen creepin' crawlin' black-nebbed bastards that should hae been strangled at birth? Because they are luggin' to my conversation? That's what it's come to, is it? Well, I can send the Excise to hell too!"

"Go ahead, you daft beggar! I suppose you can go hame and send your wife and weans to hell—since nae doubt they're in the road o' your displeasure too?"

"Ah—you chirt me there, Wattie—that's where you've gotten my cods in a cleft stick! Aye: wife and weans. Thank you, my friend, for bringing me down off my perch wi' a weel-aimed shot."

"Naebody's trying to shoot ye doon—only ye maun be reasonable."

"Reasonable—aye. Her other name's Cauld Prudence. Ah, you kent you'd win in the long run, Wattie. The ace o' the pack, nae less—and played wi' skill and caution just at the bit. Right then: the only body that goes to Hell is Robert Burns, Poet. Stand forward Robert Burns: Excise Officer, Common Gauger, Searcher of Auld Wives' clarty Ale-barrels: Impounder o' the Widows' bit stock o' tea and roll o' tobacco! Stand forward Robert Burns: servant o' the Excise Board and enemy o' a' mankind: the terror o' smugglers and a' manner o' sly, sleekit, under-hand tax-dodgers. Step forward, sir, and salute Cauld Prudence and Cauld Caution and Cauld Duty; that you may know who is who and what is what and that Royal George is King of all and the State's weel-shored wi' the stout timbers of morality; bound wi' the iron legislation o' Saint Stephen's Hall. . . Step forward, sir, even if it means that when you do you'll fall on your arse. . ."

Wattie Auld raised his drink slowly; but his grey eyes were meditative and maybe there was a shot of sadness in his expression.

"And that's juist what you'll do, Robert: so tak' it easy. I've nae notion to see you carried out."

"Dinna fash yoursel', Wattie. I'm no' drunk . . . nor next door to it. Maybe a bit delirious. . . Poets are allowed to get that way whiles. . ."

"Maybe aye and maybe no'! But you're no' that kind o' poet."

"You are well acquainted with poets, Walter?"

"No: I ken nocht about poets—but I ken something aboot men; and I've a notion what kind o' a man you are; and sae whatever kind o' a man you are, you maun be the same kind o' poet."

"I wonder, Walter—I wonder if you dae ken what kind of man I am?"

"Weel to hell then: I'm nae spae-wife!"

"'The gossip keekit in his loof. . .' Uhuh! 'But twenty fau'ts he may hae waur. . .'"

"Talking to yoursel' noo?"

"I could be daein' that. . ."

"Then gie me a ca' in some time you're passing—and you're no' delirious. Guid-nicht, Robert."

"Guid-nicht, Wattie—and joy be wi' you."

As he went out, Walter Auld spoke to Meg Halliday.

"Dinna gie Mr. Burns ony mair to drink, Meg—if you dae, and it gets to Collector Mitchell's lugs, it'll dae the hoose nae guid."

"Dinna worry, Mr. Auld: I watered his last two gless. I'll watch him. You ken I got a fair start when he cam' in: he was fair chittering and shaking. Burns—ye said his name was —an Exciseman?"

"Aye: damn Meg! That's Robert Burns the poet!"

"Ah weel . . . that's nae loss to me, for I never kent a line in my life and I'm ower auld to start."

"So you never heard o' the poet Burns? Weel, weel. . . In some ways that's maybe the maist famous man in Scotland."

"I doubt he canna be much o' a famous poet or he wouldna be a common gauger!"

"Weel, guid-nicht to you—but watch oot that he doesna put you in a poem."

"Guid-nicht, Mr. Auld. . ."

Meg Halliday looked at him with some curiosity. A poet, was he? Certes, he didna behave like an ordinary mortal.

She shook him gently by the shoulder.

"Wake up, Mr. Burns, sir. It's getting late! Come on noo, sir: there's a guid wise-like man. . . That's richt. Easy noo . . . ane o' the laddies has your beast at the door. Och, you're fine, sir. . . Get to your bed when ye get hame and ye'll be as richt as rain i' the morning."

He had come into the kitchen where Jean and Nancy and Fanny were sitting round the fire.

He had looked strange, far away, terribly remote and impersonal. He had refused food and refused a seat by the fire. He had stood irresolute for a moment and then, bidding them an abrupt good-night, had gone to bed.

Nancy looked at Jean. But Jean shook her head almost imperceptibly.

"Bed then, Fanny, my lass! You were just aboot fa'in' ower there."

Fanny admitted she was feeling sleepy and went to bed. When she had gone, Nancy said:

"What d'you think's wrong the nicht?"

"I dinna ken, Nancy. But something's gone wrong somewhaur."

"I dinna think it's drink."

"No, no. You've got an affa fear o' drink, Nancy."

"I've a fear, Jean, that if Robin tak's to the drink there'll be nae stoppin' him. He never did onything by halves."

"I wouldna worry aboot Rab and drink. Noo my faither took spells o' drinkin' whiles——"

"My faither never knew the taste o' it."

"But then your faither was nae ordinary man, frae a' accounts."

"It's maybe that I was never used seeing drink aboot the hoose, and it's maybe that I was aey feared o' a drunk man."

"Oh, a drunk man's no' a bonnie sicht: I ken that fine. But I think whiles a man's the better o' a drink—it seems to kind o' ease them."

"D'you think sae?"

"Aye: I dae, Nancy. And I ken Rab's whiles the better o' a dram. But I've never seen him what you ca' drunk. But I'll better awa' ben and see what's what. I aey ken when Rab's in trouble."

Jean stripped quickly and got into bed without lighting the candle.

She could feel he was cold—on the point of shivering.

"You're no' sleeping, are you?"

"No. . ."

"You're cauld!"

"A wee bit."

"Did you get your business done at Dumfries?"

"Aye."

"What's wrong, Rab?"

"There's nothing wrong."

"Are you sure?"

"Aye. . ."

"You're dry. . . Maybe you dinna want to talk?"

"I'm tired, Jean."

"I ken you're tired. Well, lie round and I'll cuddle into you."

He turned round heavily. Jean snuggled into his back.

"That better?"

"Fine!"

"Guid-nicht then, Rab."

"Guid-nicht, Jean."

He didn't want to take her in his arms and kiss her good-night. The kissing of Anna Park still seared his lips.

NEWS FROM FRANCE

John Syme preferred the comparative luxury of Henry Clint's King's Arms to the homely comfort of William Hyslop's Globe Tavern. The King's and the George were the rendezvous of the élite of Dumfries and district.

Besides, Anna was at the Globe; and it was impossible to think of anything but her when he was there.

So Syme and he took their ease in a back room of the King's and enjoyed themselves. The Bard had much to ask concerning Syme's Edinburgh visit.

"Alexander Cunningham's doing nicely. But you'll have

heard from him? Aye: he knew my father too—we were inseparable when I was in Edinburgh in the old days. No: not so old either, Robert, when you mention it—but those days seem far away now. Golden days they were. And I saw your friend Peter Hill—an excellent fellow and doing excellently well. I suspect your auld friend Creech is feeling the draught. A cunning customer, William Creech! Ah, but I've news for you. All Edinburgh is enjoying its best laugh in years at Creech's expense.

"You would know of your namesake, the pretty bawd, Miss Burns. Aye, I ken she adopted that name and not out of any compliment to you. She was up before Creech as magistrate. Oh, and Creech was very much on his magisterial high-horse——"

"Aye: he's gelded . . . either that or he's a jenny-willock —neither man nor woman. I ken a' aboot the affair o' her and the Sanderson bawd up afore Creech. I rated him soundly for the part he played in my last letter to Hill. I was never a whore-monger, John. This is nae holier-than-thou attitude! I've enjoyed mony a drink wi' an Edinburgh bawd. Some o' them are intelligent beyond the ordinary—and they've a damned deep, if peculiar, experience o' human nature which, when they can draw on it, makes them interesting companions across a tavern table. But I was never tempted to trade with them. Never *tempted*—note the word! But many excellent fellows carried on a habitual commerce wi' them and *seemed* nane the waur . . . though whiles I wondered. . .

"But for a lousy magistrate to sit on the bench and judge them—I just canna thole the idea o' it! Aye: or for *ony* man to sit judgment on a whore. If ony o' our sisters need—and merit—the kindness and charity o' brither-men, then it's your bawd. It's men that make them bawds; men that degrade them; men that support them: so man should be the last to condemn them."

"I never looked at the matter in that light, Robert. I thought women didna become bawds until, through drink or lack o' character, they first became abandoned—in themselves. After all, it's only a small percentage o' women take to that trade."

"There were thousands in the Toon when I was there. No, John: look at it squarely and you'll find there's a deal o' the bawd in maist women."

"Not married women—surely?"

"And what difference does marriage make—*essential* difference?"

"I canna follow you there——"

"What's the essence o' a bawd? She trades her body for the wherewithal to live. Weel, your marriage-line is nae mair than a licence to do the same in a fashion that meets wi' the approval o' Kirk and State. There's nae essential difference.

"Admittedly there's a hell o' a difference between a happily married wife and mother and a common whore; but it's a difference o' degree only. And mony a bawd marries and makes baith a good wife and a good mother. And this is saying nothing aboot the vast majority o' women that play the bawd as inclination and opportunity—and desirability—offers. When you get down to it, John, I doubt gin ony woman, married or single, but at least has the inclination——"

"Ah! Inclination and performance! Women at least successfully resist temptation much more so than men."

"Well, women hae more to lose, John. But considering how much they hae to lose, does it no' indicate to you the strength o' their desires?"

"I suppose it does. Damn it, Robert, we shouldn't think too deeply about such things. They make the mind uneasy. It's a mistake, surely to be over-suspicious, over-doubting——"

"For myself, John, I've neither doubts nor suspicions—and I hope I've nae illusions."

"Ah, but we maun hae illusions, Robert. We maun hae our ideals."

"Ideals . . . certainly. . . And the ideal must never be

absent from our thoughts. Love is the greatest ideal a man can have. The perfect love betwixt man and woman is the greatest ideal on earth. That's why we continually seek it even though we seldom find it—or, having found it, are unable to keep it so for long. . . Make no mistake: as far as I'm concerned, whether as man or poet, you'll meet wi' nae greater votary of love. . . And dinna forget that in marrying my Jean I got the finest woman that ever blessed a man wi' generous love."

"I insist that we drink a bumper to that, Robert."

And so they drank a hearty bumper to Jean.

"And now a bumper to your newly-wedded wife, John—Jane, isn't it?"

"Aye—Jane Millar that lately was."

"And now having drunk to the ladies, our conjugal yoke-fellows in loving and the Lord—what's the latest news frae France?"

"Weel, there's great speculation about the French going into three days' mourning in commemoration of Benjamin Franklin—I suppose for his work as American minister in Paris just before the Revolution——"

"Damned, the news frae France gets better and better every time I hear it! Franklin was an outstanding man and a grand negotiator. But don't you see, John, that in honouring Benjamin Franklin, France honours the independence of America?"

"Of course . . . there's that aspect."

"But that is the vital aspect. The French are a truly glorious race . . . there's been nothing like them since the dawn o' history!"

"I confess I hope for much from that nation, Robert. I trust their example will lead to many much-needed reforms here."

"Things will never be the same here . . . things are bound to change. Now that the Tree o' Liberty has been planted in France, what's to prevent the seeds blowing across the sea to us? What's to ail the French sending us a wheen shoots to hasten on a good growth?"

"I see you're a keen votary, Robert."

"None keener! And how could it be otherwise? No man can espouse a greater cause than Liberty. No man can have a greater ideal. Believe me, the vision of Liberty has beckoned to me from my earliest days. . . For Liberty, for Freedom, for Independence, I would shed my dearest blood."

"But we mauna hae bloodshed, Robert. Mony worthy folk—and judicious observers—are fearing that's just the road the French may be travelling."

"No blood will be shed but the blood of tyrants—of those who would lay an axe to the Tree o' Liberty. That's sacred: let any man touch it at his peril."

"I can see what you mean. Put *that* way, of course——"

"And what other way would you have it put? Only aristocrats—and the flunkeys o' the aristocracy—would have it put any other way."

"Weel, y'ken: I'm nae aristocrat, Robert—nor friendly to them, and as I say I hae great hopes arising here from the French example; but maybe I've a sort o' horror o' bloodshed —ony kind o' bloodshed. That's one o' my main reasons for quitting the 72nd Regiment: I've no stomach for armed slaughter."

"Nor has any man wi' an atom o' sense or an ounce o' sensibility. . . As I see things, the French will put an end— ultimately—to all wars—the wars of armies—the senseless slaughters engineered by kings and politicians—aye, and priests——"

"Which reminds me that when the King o' Sweden took Karmankoffsky the ither day, twa thousand Russians were killed in the counter-attack."

"Twa thousand! That means maybe twa thousand Russian mithers grieving; or twa thousand widows mourning and God kens how many thousands o' bairns fatherless. An' a' to suit the bloody Swedes!"

"Of course the Russians are gey blood-thirsty too!"

"Are they? The Swedes hae been battering awa' at them for long enough . . . but the Russians will swallow them up! Charles the Twelfth'll ken that afore he's through. Great Catherine o' Russia'll see to that. By the Lord! Gin Russian Kate gets her claws well dug into Swedish Chairlie——"

"You take a byornar interest in foreign affairs, Robert——"

"Is there ocht wrong in that?"

"No, no: naething wrang. Only I'd never have imagined that a poet——"

"You think that a poet should write nothing but love-songs?"

"Weel, rather love-songs than war-songs."

"Humanity's songs: that's what a true poet maun ever sing. And mind you, John, you and me are sitting here in a back room in a tavern in Dumfries and, God knows, Russia and Sweden and France and America may seem a lang road off and of little consequence to us—you a gentleman o' misfortune and me a puir bluidy gauger. But no: neither Russia nor America are *that* far off. And France is just at our door. Nothing o' ony consequence can happen in the world now without it affecting the rest of the world. The world's becoming one again. Divided and re-divided and torn apart by every kind o' fell tyrant and bluidy monster; yet despite a' the man-made differences atween race and creed, mankind's coming thegither again. The Tree o' Liberty's the symbol— and beneath that tree the human race will dance and sing and rejoice in new-won, re-won affection and brotherhood. It's bound to come; it canna be stopped. Mankind is moving as it hasna moved for mony a century. . . D'you think Liberty's a new-fangled invention o' the French? To hell! William Wallace fought for Liberty here in Scotland. . .

" . . . Blind Harry's Life o' Wallace was my Bible as a boy; and I knew the call o' Liberty lang afore I ever heard o' the French. Liberty is no' something that you pull down from the sky or dig out o' the earth. The need for Liberty is para-

mount to every human being that hasna been corrupted by
the lust o' power. Liberty's the very spirit of the human Ark
o' the Covenant—and its tabernacle is erected in every human
breast. . . It's just that in France, as was once in Scotland,
that there is a general, a popular resurgence o' the spirit o'
Liberty and that in France they have been able to put their
feelings into practice: give their ideals practical effect. . .
You see now that in France the fact that a man doesna belong
to the Roman Church doesna debar him from holding ony
kind of official position. . . And you saw that in February
there, they managed to get Trial by Jury made a fundamental
part o' the Constitution. . .

"Yes, John . . . now that the Tree o' Liberty has been well
and truly planted, the French are seeing to it that the roots
are well nourished so that it will grow and bear fruit—aye,
in abundance."

"It must be wonderful to have such enthusiasm. Damnit,
you make me positively glow wi' the mere reflection, so to
speak, o' your infernal eloquence. And Guid kens I hae a gey
calm and placid nature. It takes a gey lot to get me wrocht up
about onything."

"But you are on the side o' the French?"

"Have no fear on that score, Robert. I'd have your Tree of
Liberty planted in every kail-yard and every village green.
I'm all for Liberty—only I canna get so fired up aboot it. But
sincerely, Robert, and wi' every drop of my blood, for what it
may be worth—and that it matters at all is what I gravely
doubt—then let me propose the Toast: To France—and
Liberty!"

They drank off a good bumper to that. Syme was excited.
And he had never known such excitement before. But in the
Bard's company it was impossible to be otherwise. What the
Bard said was sensible in all truth; but how he said it was
more remarkable still. His eloquence was peculiar, but it was
poetic and overpowering. Sometimes he reinforced the sense
of a phrase by the use of his hands, by the clenching of a fist

or by the use of an upturned open palm. But also he seemed to speak with his entire features. The eyes were predominating: they flashed and smouldered, burned and glowed and occasionally Syme thought that an illuminating beam literally sprang from them. Then his lips were manipulated expressively: sometimes taut, sometimes opened; sometimes they spat out a word or a phrase; again they caressed a word and rolled along an entire sentence. The risible muscles were seldom inactive—or when they were so, the inaction seemed deliberate and effective. The head assumed a characteristic cant according to the sentiment or the force behind the sentiment; sometimes cast back or forwards or to the side. . .

Syme was fascinated; though when he tried to analyse exactly what it was that fascinated him he could only list a number of meaningless poses.

Maybe the spell lay in the unusual quality of the rich baritone voice that could register every expression from the mere breathing of a word to a torrent of words that rumbled like not too-distant thunder. And yet, somehow, whether the Bard spoke in a whisper or a roar, audibility remained perfect. He was no mumbler and no incoherent blaster.

To-night Syme felt that Robert Burns was a being infinitely greater than a great poet. He had something too of the quality of a great prophet, and a great leader and inspirer of men. And in this mood Syme felt that men would readily, almost enthusiastically, follow him.

But though Syme was elated he was also disturbed. The Bard made him want to do things and John Syme didn't want to do anything but drink and eat and talk and read a book— and then go to bed with his new-wed wife, who was quiet and plump and comfortably twenty-five and without any more desire than to do a modicum of housework and receive the not over-ardent embrace of her easy-going uncomplaining husband.

John Syme wondered what kind of woman the Bard's Bonnie Jean was like. He always spoke of her with an embarrassing enthusiasm altogether unusual in a married man.

No doubt a man with the figure, the presence and the personal magnetism of the Bard could have had whatever wife he chose. And it seemed that Bonnie Jean had been very much his choice. Syme considered that she must be a most fortunate woman.

But then everything about Robert Burns was so much bigger and so much more dazzling than anything else in life. How he could tolerate his role of common gauger in Dumfries —an outrageous anomaly. Surely some of the Great and some of the Great and the Influential about Edinburgh could have done more for him. But then he had wanted to be a farmer. . . Or was it that he was too independent?

When the Bard had ridden off home, John Syme took out his notebook, for he was an inveterate note-taker, and copied down the witty lines the Bard had written with his diamond pencil on a window pane. The lines were not only witty in themselves. They expressed a something that he could only term pure Burns. He read the lines over before he closed his leather-bound pocket-book.

Ye men of wit and wealth, why all this sneering
'Gainst poor Excisemen? Give the cause a hearing.
What are your Landlord's rent-rolls? Taxing ledgers!
What Premiers? What ev'n Monarchs? Mighty Gaugers!
Nay what are Priests (those seemingly godly wise-men)?
What are they, pray, but Spiritual Excisemen!

It was certainly, reflected Syme, an exceedingly Mighty Gauger who had not only written these lines but written them where all the élite of the town and county might read them.

John Syme resolved that he would seek the Bard's company as opportunity presented. He had never met anyone like him— or remotely like him. He was indeed even as Alexander Cunningham had described him: "Not one man but a dozen men—and all of them remarkable." And Cunningham had never heard him enthuse about the Tree of Liberty. He must write Cunningham about this night's glorious meeting.

A PINT OF WINE

The first meeting with Anna Park had been devastating. The result had been an emotional fever that had interrupted his thoughts and his habits. The family realised that something had upset him; but as yet they had no idea what it was. Jean had her suspicions; but she kept them to herself. If anything she became more solicitous of his comfort and welfare.

As he began to see more of Anna he became more infatuated with her. The mere presence of her sent the blood drumming to his temples. By the month of June he became quite reckless in his actions. He didn't care who knew how he felt about Anna or how Anna felt about him.

He explained part of his position to Collector Mitchell.

"I think you'll admit, Mr. Mitchell, that my rounds have hitherto been damned carelessly surveyed."

"At least you've been more thorough than your predecessor, Burns."

"I havena spared myself. True, I've made myself a bit o' money from my share o' the fines—but just a flea-bite to what's accrued to the Revenue. But—I would like a transfer."

"What kind o' transfer?"

"I would like a port division somewhere—but I ken I'm maybe no' ready for a big move yet. I've told you how my Ayrshire patron, Mrs. Dunlop of Dunlop, is trying to get the Supervisor-General, Mr. William Corbett, interested in my promotion?"

"I hope she succeeds. Mr. Corbett could do a lot for you, Burns—gin he was interested. My report on your work and your character will be, as always, honest—so that won't be against you."

"I'll ever be indebted to you for that, Mr. Mitchell. Now

. . . could you, in the meantime, recommend me for a foot-walk in the town here? I understand William Johnston is expecting a change and I think I could manage the Tobacco Division. . . I'm no' complaining—but ten parishes take a lot o' damned hard riding; and in the dead o' winter——"

"Somebody's got to ride them, Burns—and you're no' a year on the Itinerancy yet. Still, by the time the transfer came through— You'd want it afore the winter sets in? I'll see what I can do, Burns. But understand: I can give no promises——"

He explained his position to Mr. and Mrs. Hyslop.

"It would save me a lot o' expense, a lot o' labour, and a' the damned bad drookin's——"

"Aye: ye got mony a sair drookin'. Nae wonder you bided overnicht whiles."

"But for the hospitality o' the Globe, guidwife, I canna think what I wad hae done. The thocht of it sustained me on mony a lang hameward mile. But if John Mitchell can work a transfer to a foot-walk here, it'll part answer my prayers—and I'll hae mair time for my farm."

"Are you still i' the mind to gie it up?"

"Just as soon as I can see my way——"

"And what aboot that transfer to Greenock or Port Glasgow that you aey talked aboot?"

"One thing at a time. A wee bit experience o' the port work here will do me no harm. But mind you: there's only one thing would hold me to Dumfries—and that's the Globe."

"It's nice o' you to say that, Robert. We'd miss you. Man, the wife fair lichts up when she hears your voice oot in the Close."

"You see, Robert, I ken you aey manage to put William in a guid mood. And look what you've done to Anne!"

The Bard started: "What have I done to Anne?"

"You've gone to her head. The lass is fair daft aboot you. Noo, dinna blush, man—I'm glad to see the pair o' you gettin' on—and the lass hasna much company here——"

"Oh, I confess I'm gey fond o' Anne—but I didna ettle to turn her head."

"I tellt her she needna bother fa'in' in love wi' you. Though I dinna blame her. I suppose a' the lassies fa' in love wi' you?"

"You seem to forget, Bess, that I'm a respectable married man starting on a young family and that I hae neither the time nor the inclination to canter aboot the countraside turning the lassies' heads—gin they were as easy turned as you think."

"Awa' wi' you! A bit daffin' wi' the lassies never did ony harm. I've tellt William that mony a time. But William's no' interested in the lassies. I see you winkin'—but I ken you're no' interested: otherwise I wouldna be sae keen on your jaunts to Edinburgh. He's goin' through for twa-three days next week, Robert."

"Business, man—just damned business. But we're aey slack at this time o' year. Sae if you can gie the place a look-in to mak' sure there's naebody runs aff wi' the wife——"

"You never ken, William. I'll be around sometime——"

"Gin you can spend the nicht, see that the doors are barred——"

"Aye: what's to hinder you? And Tam, the groom, can keep his een on the attics."

"I doobt Tam wad be a bit o' a broken reed to lean on."

"Oh weel, he's aey a man-body."

"Onything I can dae for you when I'm in Edinburgh, Robert?"

"Let me see. . . Maybe you could hand in twa-three letters to Williamson's penny post——?"

"Certainly . . . just let me ken. Hae you much writin' the day?"

"I've a wheen damned returns to mak'——"

"Weel, awa' up to your room—it's the only place you'll get ony quiet the day. I drew some wine the ither day—it's in grand order—and no' ower strong. Will I send Anne up wi' a pint?"

"Aye . . . and can I hae a bite in aboot twa hours' time. . .?"

The Bard's room was on the first floor and to the right of the landing. It contained a large mahogany bed and a table set convenient to the light from the window. He set his Excise pocket-book and some sheets of Excise paper on the table and drew in his chair.

The Hyslops were good to him. Already they had come to treat him as something between a privileged guest and a member of the family. But he was in two minds about their attitude to Anna and him. How much did they suspect? How much did they know? And if they knew everything would they still approve? He was certain William Hyslop wouldn't mind. But he wasn't so sure of his wife. After all, Anna was her niece, and to this extent she was responsible for her. And yet Mrs. Hyslop was a gay enough lass herself, even if she was in her uncertain forties.

And then, as he was ruminating, Anna came in with the wine. They embraced immediately.

"I've missed you, Robert—are you staying long?"

"An hour or twa— It's been hell for me too, Anna. Every hour I'm away from you is hell. It's getting that I canna live without you."

"Nor me. . . What was my auntie saying to you?"

"Come and sit doon on the bed here till I talk to you?"

"Will I no' slip the bolt?"

"Right! Slip the bolt and we'll talk after. . ."

He rolled the wine round his parched gums. "God, lass, you'll be the death o' me. . . D'you want a sup?"

Anna took a good pull at the wine, sighed and set it down.

"I never thocht it would be like this, Robert. My auntie'll ken whenever I gang doon."

"Bide as lang as you can. Slip back the bolt and leave the door ajee."

"Oh, she never ca's me when she kens I'm wi' you. But she aey spiers me."

"What does she say?"

"Oh, she just says, 'Watch your step, my lass: you can never trust a married man.'"

"So! And what does she spier you?"

"She asks if you ever kiss me."

"And you say?"

"Whiles—but just a wee bit."

"D'you think she suspects?"

"I wonder whiles. I used to think it was only for the trade you brocht aboot the place; but she's fond o' you—and so's my uncle."

"That's one consolation—though it doesna mak' things ony easier for me."

"I'm no' carin'. I'm auld enough to ken my ain mind. I'm no' for being tied to my auntie's strings a' the time."

"Are you sure you ken your mind?"

"Maybe it's silly; but I just canna live without you. You've nae idea what it's like when you're awa'. I feel I could drink if it wad mak' me forget."

"Na, na: drink's nae solace. Drink would only make you worse. Weel . . . I dinna richt ken mysel', Anna, how things are for turning out. We're in a hell o' a fix, you and me. . . I thocht maybe that after a time things would cool doon a wee——"

"D'you want them to cool doon?"

"What I want or dinna want doesna matter, my dear. Once we're thegither nothing matters, nothing counts; and God! how sweet and precious is every minute I spend wi' you —how lang and lonely the hours without you. . ."

"But I've guid news. I saw Collector Mitchell the day and he has hopes o' a transfer to Dumfries——"

"That means you'll be here a' the time?"

"Weel, I'll hae *mair* time."

"I've news for you. My uncle's takin' a jaunt to Edinburgh——"

"Early next week! They were telling me. . . I've been invited to stay ower-nicht."

"And are you?"

"By God, I'm staying: we can hae the nicht thegither. You'd like that, wouldn't you?"

"Aye: the nicht and every nicht."

"The pity that it canna be every nicht."

"Surely we can aey be thegither—some day?"

"You ken, Anna, just how much I love you and just how much you mean to me?"

"Nae mair nor you mean to me."

"There's this difference, lass. . . If I ever had to mak' a decision between you and Mrs. Burns——"

"You'd stick to Mrs. Burns?"

"That's how it would be, lass. I micht eat my heart out—but I'd need to stand by Jean and the bairns——"

"Are you saying it's wrang for you and me to be like this?"

"No, my dear, I'm no' saying it's wrang. The richtness or the wrangness o' the business is no' for me to decide. I can only tell you how I'd act if ever I had to mak' a choice."

"I aey kent that. But there's aey a chance you micht change your mind."

"It's possible—since a' things are possible—that I micht change as far as Mrs. Burns is concerned—but I could never change in respect o' the children—not at least until they were grown up and married. And you'll be married lang afore that."

"D'you want me married?"

"Hell, lass, I just want you the way you are. I didna ask to fa' in love wi' you. Nor did you. It happened! Juist bluidy well happened like a flash o' lightning—and we havena got ower the shock yet——"

"Och, weel: I dinna care what happens as lang as we can

be thegither." She ran her fingers through his hair. "You're a hell o' a man to talk, Robert; but God! I love you: I'd dae onything for you. I could hae bairns too—if you wanted me. . ."

He rose and took her in his arms. "Dinna talk aboot bairns, lass. . . I'm a beggar for paternity. . . I could bairn the half o' Dumfries in a fortnight if it cam' to a test!"

"Och, never mind the half o' Dumfries. Tak' me noo, for Godsake; for I canna thole this ony langer."

By the beginning of the week William Hyslop was gone to Edinburgh and for two nights the Bard stayed at the Globe and for two love-drunken nights Anna was with him.

There were to be many other nights; but these June nights carried an ecstasy he was never to know again. Maybe the Bard was never to experience again such sheer physical rapture.

Anna was gifted; and he swore he had never before known such an altar of love, such a perfection of passion. Never before in his life had he been so drunk and delirious with love. There was a day when he had been crazed about Jean Armour—but he had wanted to be crazed about Jean and he had married Jean under the green thorn tree by the banks of the Ayr—long ago that seemed. He had experienced all the shades and degrees of love he had thought possible. He did not reckon that any surprises awaited him. He'd known many women, many a sweet and passion-tossed lass since Jean Glover in the dim Irvine days. . . He had thought he'd had his day of love and love-making and that he'd settled down with Jean in the certainty of an undying affection and love that would last him to the grave. He had not intended that it should be otherwise. There was nothing that Jean denied him; there was nothing deficient in their married love, which indeed was just beginning to bloom into maturity. Jean had every quality he desired in a wife and without her he might as well turn his face to the wall.

And then, in the midst of this conjugal happiness and deep

contentment, Anna had appeared. And Anna had disturbed him with such a violent instantaneousness that even now he couldn't grasp its full significance. Something had happened to his whole being, some strange maddening fever had entered his blood and altered his judgment and character.

It wasn't that Jean no longer mattered. She affected him now more than ever; his passion for Jean was in no wise abated. But Anna Park was on top of them both. Anna was dominant, all-devouring.

Nor could this be regarded as some sort of Indian Summer. He reminded himself that he had a lifetime of physical love ahead of him to be consumed in his own way, in his own rhythm at his own time.

Here was the puzzle. Everything was being determined for him without the slightest consideration for his desires or wishes. Nor was it Anna who dictated. Anna was as helpless —maybe more helpless—than he was. It was the inexplicable something that had flashed between them at their first unsought-for coming together. Both of them were caught up in a passion they could neither direct nor control nor comprehend.

As he said to her in one of his more rational interludes: "Lying here wi' you in the heat and stillness of this summer nicht in this inn that micht be dead—there's a devilish paradox somewhere. To hell: we hardly ken each other!"

"There's no' much aboot each other we dinna ken—noo!"

"No' that kind o' kennin', lass. We ken, at this minute, nothing about ourselves. In a damned queer sense I'm no' even sure that I'm Robert Burns and I dinna care whether I am or no'. As for you—you micht be the blackest bitch oot o' hell for a' I really know."

"I'm a bitch noo. Is there ony name you havena ca'ed me?"

"Of course you're nae bitch—here and now. And I canna think of you as a bitch at ony time. But for a' I *know*—know with ony certainty—you could be."

"You could be a black beggar yoursel'."

"I could. For a' you ken maybe I am'"

"Sometimes I think I could lie a' nicht juist listening to you talking. But dinna let's talk the noo: the mornin'll come ower soon . . . and we'll never hae closed an e'e."

"Are you tired?"

She kissed his flesh caressingly.

"Just let me lie in your oxter for a wee while—I dinna want to sleep. I wonder: does everybody love as happy as we dae? Oh God, Robert! I'm feared this is ower guid to last."

He snuggled her in the crook of his arm.

"Nothing lasts, my dear. Sae let us treasure the minutes we hae thegither. . . Fate brocht us thegither and Fate will decide our future wi' nae reference to our wishes. Life is all a variorum: we regard not how it goes—as I made one o' my beggars say in a cantata I wrote long ago. It's no' every day that Fate hands out a pint o' the rich red wine o' life and we'd be fools to refuse it. And maybe there's a draught o' gall in it—and maybe no'. We've had a guid quaff at the measure so far—and we'll juist need to hope that the lees are as sweet. . .

". . . never be taken away. Nae matter what happens we'll aey hae our memories o' this glorious nicht. . . Aye; and we're no' richt started yet! We'll chaw the *Gods* the nicht, Anna, gin they were never chawed by mortals afore. . ."

Twice the next day Mrs. Hyslop looked into his room but each time he was in such a sound sleep that she shook her head and retired carefully. And when a man would ask if Mr. Burns was about her invariable reply was that "he went out a while ago."

When she visited him for the third time he was busy at the table writing. He was naked as he had risen from the bed.

"For Godsake, guidwife— A minute till I pu' on my breeks. . . Richt, come in noo. I'm sorry. . . You see, I was thinking aboot a sang and I juist louped oot o' bed till I got the draft o' it doon on paper. . . What time o' day is it?"

Mrs. Hyslop stood shaking her head. Then she smiled.

"God! but you're a comical sicht standing there haudin' up your breeks! But dinna fash aboot me—I've seen a naked man afore noo."

The Bard reached for his shirt and struggled into it.

"It's nearly three o'clock, Mr. Robert Burns, if you please! Hae you nae wark to dae?"

"Three o'clock! God! I maun hae slept in!"

"Slept in? When did you fa' asleep?"

"Dinna ask . . . I whiles hae turns like this: then I sleep the clock round."

"I put Anne to her bed for an hour. It seems she didna sleep either!"

"The heat's terrible: there's no' a breath o' wind——"

"Just so! Are you feeling like eating?"

"Eating. . . Weel, now that you mention it, I believe I could dae wi' a bite."

"Are you dressing and coming doon? Or will I bring it up to you?"

"I was busy wi' my sang."

"On you go then: I'll bring you up a bite. If you've nae business to tak' you outby and you canna be fashed wi' ony callers——"

"Aye—nae callers, Bess—no' the day. You see the Muse doesna visit me as often as she once did—sae I've got to bone the hizzie whenever she comes ower me. Am I a nuisance to you?"

"Aye: you're a nuisance and a byornar nuisance at that! But in mony ways, Robert, you're juist a laddie—sae I'll juist tak' the privilege o' mithering you a wee bit. Did you like the wine?"

"I never lipped better."

"I'll fetch you a pint then—or hae you a fancy for ocht else?"

"Just whatever you think."

Mrs. Hyslop turned towards the door. Then she closed it and stood with her back to it.

"Robert! Tell me ae thing—and tell me nae mair. Was Anne here last nicht?"

"Weel . . . she was. . ."

"I kent she was; but I juist wanted to hear it frae your ain lips."

"D'you want me to leave?"

"Leave? No, I dinna want you to leave. Another thing. The first time you met Anne—something happened then?"

"Believe me, wife, I didna plot or plan to seduce Anna. It happened! And I canna tell you *how* it happened yet. I . . . I dinna ken richt what to say to you for, to be honest, I dinna richt ken what to say to mysel'. . . Are you annoyed wi' Anna?"

"No' now— I was upset at first. Though she denied it, I kent fine what had happened. She hasna the guile to hide a thing like that—and you were the first. No, I'm no' angry, Robert. I only wish *I'd* been young enough. . . You see, there was a man that loved me once—but I thocht I could mak' a better match. . . And yet I was in love wi' him— Ah weel . . . I've nae fau't to find wi' William Hyslop. . . But if I'd my life to live ower again I'd risk everything for the man I loved and for the man that loved me. There's a love that comes to a lass, Robert; but it only comes once if it comes at a'. . . Mind you: I've said nocht to William aboot Anne and you and I've nae intention o' saying ocht——"

"Damnit, Bess, the whole thing's beyond me! I'll never be able to thank you for what you've done—for your uncanny understandin'——"

"Oh, I dinna profess to understand much, Robert. I juist kent there was a something atween Anne and you—a something I could dae nocht aboot. Suppose I had banned the pair o' you? You'd still hae found another road to come thegither. And I'm glad in a way it was you, Robert, and no' some of thae blackguard beggars aboot the toon here."

After she had gone, the Bard stood for a long moment in contemplation. Mrs. Hyslop should have reacted differently —especially since she'd known from the beginning what was happening. There was little doubt now but that she had deliberately planned for them to be in bed together for the two nights. And yet he should have known her better. She had never had any morals, at least she had never set any store by them. There was a deep unconventional streak in her, beneath the greedy landlady. And, from the first, she had waived aside all rules and customs—made him a complete exception to whatever rules she ever had. He was certain that, had she appealed to him as a woman, he could have had her for the asking. She could hardly be hoping that one day he might ask her. . .! Or was she experiencing a vicarious thrill through Anna?

The Bard came out of his mood, sat down to the table and read over his song. He hummed the tune *The Banks o' the Banna*, as he conned the lines:

> Yestreen I had a pint o' wine,
>   A place where body saw na;
> Yestreen lay on this breast o' mine
>   The gowden locks of Anna.
>
> The huggry Jew in wilderness
>   Rejoicing o'er his manna
> Was naething to my hiney bliss
>   Upon the lips of Anna.
>
> Ye monarchs take the East and West
>   Frae Indus to Savannah:
> Gie me within my straining grasp
>   The melting form of Anna!
>
> There I'll despise Imperial charms,
>   An Empress or Sultana,

While dying raptures in her arms
I give and take wi' Anna!

Awa', thou flaunting God of Day!
Awa', thou pale Diana!
Ilk star, gae hide thy twinkling ray,
When I'm to meet my Anna!

Come, in thy raven plumage, Night
(Sun, Moon and Stars, withdrawn a'),
And bring an Angel-pen to write
My transports with my Anna!

And then he took his quill and added quickly by way of postscript:

She is the sunshine o' my e'e,
To live but her I canna:
Had I on earth but wishes three,
The first should be my Anna.

The Kirk an' State may join, and tell
To do sic things I mauna:
The Kirk an' State may gae to Hell,
And I'll gae to my Anna.

Damned but this was a good song—as fine a love song as ever he'd written. And written white-hot, too—not a cobbled line in the whole production.

Lord, what a night it had been. Fate had never been kinder to him. Never had she lavished on him such two-handed bounty. Hell! he was just coming into his prime—into the zenith of his love-making. And to think that here in Dumfries, dirty dozing Dumfries, dovering away quietly through the long summer days, and in dear dirty Dumfries, up a narrow close and in a gey nondescript tavern he should meet a beauty and know a love such as he had never known. . . .

If only the guidwife would come with the wine now—and Anna follow not long behind her!

He filled the basin with water from the jug and washed himself, singing of Anna's golden locks as he slunged the tepid water about him.

The following afternoon he rode into Ellisland under a baking sun. As he turned in by the Isle and came down to the waterside he found Jean walking in the shade of the trees with Francis in her arms and Robert toddling at her side.

He dismounted and came to her eagerly and kissed her with a passion that went through her like a shock.

"For Godsake, Rab! Mind the bairn. You'd think you'd been awa' a month."

"I've been awa' for a thousand years, Jean—awa' in the hanging gardens o' Babylon. God! it's grand to be back! Dumfries is stinkin' like rotten fish—damned near as bad as Auld Reekie. Thank God for the Nith here. . .

"Onything fresh? And how's my wee Bobbie? Come here, you randy, and tell me the names o' the flo'ers you've been gatherin'. . . Sit doon on the bank here, Jean—damnit, there's nae hurry. . . You came out to meet me?"

"I kent you'd be coming aboot noo."

"Jean lass—you mind when you used to walk out o' Machlin and doon the Cumnock road to meet me? And you aey kent where to stop for me!"

"You ken I'd aey come to meet you, Rab—whaurever you were."

"I ken, lass . . . and there's naebody I'd rather meet. . . And if it werena for the bairns you ken what would happen richt now!"

"Fine! I kent what was coming as soon as you dismounted. I can aey tell when you're feeling like that——"

"And juist how can you tell?"

"Because the feeling comes ower me too . . . and then I wad ken it was you a mile awa'."

"God! what a woman! But you're richt, lass. There was aey that understanding atween us that needed nae words. Damnit, is Nancy or Fanny no' aboot to tak' the weans. . ."

Later Jean said to Nancy: "Twa nichts awa' in Dumfries and he's a different man."

"And I'm glad to see it. He hasna been at himsel' this twa months back—aye, since April. I thocht he was gaun demented whiles."

"He's his auld sel' noo, then. When you hear him singing like that and hear the crack o' his heels. . . But when you hear him dragging his feet and see that his brows are doon——"

"Then you ken to keep oot o' his gate and say nocht till he comes round."

"That's the poet in him, Nancy. His head's fu' o' the maist wonderfu' thochts and when he canna get them doon the way he wants. . . Wait till you see: he'll be at the writing for days noo—aye, and half into the nicht."

"You're a changed woman yoursel', Jean."

"When he's happy, Nancy, I dinna care what happens and I could live on muslin kale and a dry tattie."

"Huh! You folk in love beat a': you're never twice the same way. I hope when I get married—if I ever see a man worth marrying—I'll act mair sensible-like."

"You'll dae just as things'll dae wi' you: like the rest o' folk. . . I wonder what we'll gie Rab for his supper?"

"Weel: you ken the auld sang—'Gie my love brose, lassie. . .'"

Mrs. Hyslop brought a cup of tea to Anna's bedside.

"Come on, Anne: I canna let you lie a' day."

"I'll get up richt away, Auntie."

"Drink this cup o' tea—it'll help to freshen you up."

Anna yawned deeply; but it was a yawn of contentment and not of tiredness. Her eyes had a remote look in them.

"Weel, Anne—and was it worth it?"

"Oh, Auntie—I just never thocht it could be sae—wonderful. Och—it was like another world."

"You've nae regrets?"

"That's the last thing I could hae . . . and if onything's happened I dinna care either."

"But I don't suppose you ever gave that a thocht?"

"I didna . . . and I'm no' going to think aboot it noo. I tellt Robert no' to worry aboot it either."

"Weel . . . maybe I've done wrang, lassie. Maybe I should never hae allowed this to happen. But, as I've told you— you're old enough to ken your ain mind. And you ken as weel as me that lying wi' a man's the quickest way to get wi' bairn."

"Are *you* going to worry noo?"

"No . . . I'll no' worry. But mind: never a word to your uncle! I'm no' sure about him yet—I mean as far as you and Robert are concerned."

"Noo, Auntie, you're no' going back on what you said to me?"

"And what did I say to you? I've said plenty."

"You said if you were me you wad dae what I've done."

"Aye: so I did—but noo that it's done. . . Och, I dinna ken, lassie. I'm getting a' muddled up mysel'—maybe I should never hae interfered."

"I'm glad you did—and I'll aey be gratefu' to you. But it gi'es me a queer feeling to think he's awa' hame——"

"'Deed aye, lassie: maybe we're no fair to his wife—I've heard frae ithers as weel as him that he's gey fond o' her."

"But d'you think that's richt?"

"Listen, Anne: there's nothing richt in this warld and never has been. A' you can do is grab whatever happiness comes your way. You pay dearly in the end, whether you dae or dinna. Preaching folk may say what they like—but that's what life's taught me. . . And maybe I canna help being happy to ken you and him's sae happy. And if Bess Hyslop's daft, that's gey sma' odds to onybody—exceptin' mysel'. . .

Noo, come on; for we've a feck o' reddin' up to dae afore
William Hyslop comes hame."

That night Jean was deeply happy. She had her lover
again: the lover who was her husband. He was as abandoned
and joyous and ardent as ever he had been—and ten times
more so than he had been since his winter illness. The lion-
strength was back in his loving and all his daft tempestuous
poet's ardour.

"I doubt it's twins the nicht, Rab."

"Weel, lass—whether is it you or me doing our best?"

"I think we're baith daeing gey weel."

"But you're happy?"

"Happiness is no' the word, Rab: it gangs a lot deeper
than that."

"You're richt, Jean. God knows what I'd hae done had I
no' married you."

NEWS FROM LONDON

The days were hot with sunshine, work, love and news.
All Europe seemed to be heading for wars and revolutions.
Nothing remained constant; nothing seemed permanent in
the affairs of state any longer.

The Bard, as always, consumed what news he could get
with avidity. He was fully conscious that he was living in a
time of great stress and that unpredictable changes were
inevitable. His one regret was that he was so far removed
from any centre of activity; that he was unable to influence
events in any way; that he was politically impotent. Yet
he felt that the day might not be so very far away when even
Dumfries would be mightily involved in world events.

In the beginning of July the Russian fleet had celebrated

a great victory over the Swedes at Viborg and a week later the Swedes had revenged themselves to good purpose over a fleet of Russian galleys. . .

But the news from France was the most exciting and the Bard felt by far the most important. The National Assembly had lately deprived the King of the power of making war and early in June the Dundee Whig Club had sent a congratulatory address to the Assembly signed in the name of the Club's President by George Dempster of Dunichen.

By the end of July the Assembly had replied over the signature of President Trielhard of the National Assembly.

All this gave great heart to the friends of France in Scotland. In Dundee the Whig Club sporting the national cockade, the symbolic red cap of Liberty, were jubilant. The toast of liberty was everywhere in the air and men of goodwill were everywhere rejoicing.

Glenriddell rejoiced ; MacMurdo rejoiced ; Willie Stewart of Closeburn rejoiced—and these were Whigs of some consequence among the Bard's Nithsdale friends.

And if Patrick Miller of Dalswinton was too busy to rejoice about events abroad, the opening of the Forth and Clyde Canal, in which he was deeply involved, was no doubt reason enough for his silence about French affairs.

Not that Patrick Miller had completely forgotten about the Bard across the Nith. He had commanded him on the morning of the Election Day in Dumfries to assemble at Dalswinton with as many of his servants as could mount horse and help to swell the bodyguard gathered to conduct his candidate son into Dumfries.

The Bard had done so with great reluctance and had made himself scarce as soon as the party reached Dumfries. He had no wish to be engaged in any election brawl either on behalf of Captain William Miller or his gallant rival. He might write election ballads; but he'd be damned before he'd break crowns or have his own broken in senseless brawling.

And it irked him almost beyond measure to think that

Patrick Miller thought so little of his Bardship as to demand his presence on such an occasion. Miller had now made it clear beyond any doubt that he considered Robert Burns a tenant of his and no more. And had not Miller been such a power in the land the Bard would have seen him in hell—tenant or no tenant.

And then Jean wanted to go home to Machlin to see her mother and her sisters and some of her old friends. The Bard could not deny her.

"Yes, Jean: there's no reason why you shouldna tak' a jaunt the length o' Machlin. It'll do you good and set you up for the winter. I agree that you havena had much change o' scenery doon here."

"It's juist that I long whiles for my mither—and my sisters."

"I ken, lass. . . Weel, I could get a loan o' John Carson's gig—he's promised it often enough. And maybe if Adam was going hame—maybe at the end o' the month?"

"That would dae fine. . . There's anither thing, Rab: I'll no' be certain till I get back but I doubt I'm awa' again."

"You're no'?"

"I dinna think there's ony doubt——"

"Glory be then, Jean! Was it yon nicht I cam' back frae Dumfries?"

"Aye: fine you ken!"

"As long as it's no' triplets."

"Wheest, wheest! Even twins wad be ower mony."

"Ah! damn the fear. You're . . . no' . . . regretting onything?"

"No, I'm quite happy. . . I'll be carrying through the winter and it'll gie the bairn a chance gin the spring. I expect it'll be aboot the end o' March——"

"Ah—things have a way o' working oot, lass. And you've no' to worry aboot onything."

"You'll be looking for a lassie?"

C.B.W.   P

"There's a ratio about such things. . . They say it tak's a guid man to mak' a lassie——"

"That's juist auld wives' clishmaclavers!"

"Just! Lad or lass, Jean—as lang as they're at themselves and like the world. But no: I wouldna turn up my nose at a lass—just something like yoursel'."

"But if it's a lass I'm no' ca'ing her Jean. I dinna like repeating names in a family. My mither had three Jameses before one lived——"

"I've a notion for Elizabeth mysel'."

"After wha?"

"Naebody, Jean: just I like the name. She'd be ca'ed Betty or Betsy or Bet . . . Betty Burns would be nice."

"Aye . . . maybe. But come and sleep—it'll no' be this in the morning."

By the end of the month Jean was all set for Machlin. Adam Armour came over early and helped to strap a box for Jean's and the bairns' bits of things.

And while Jean was getting ready and the house was in a stir, the mail was brought in from Dumfries. The Bard was busy in his room writing out a letter and some verses for Mrs. Dunlop. The letter would be carried on from Machlin and so save Mrs. Dunlop the postage.

The Bard noted the London frank on the cover of the letter; but the handwriting was not brother William's.

He broke the seal. It was a letter from his old Alloway tutor, John Murdoch, informing him of the death of William from a putrid fever.

For a while the Bard sat numbed at his desk. Poor William! Ill and then dead in a foreign town like London. And never a kent face to comfort him in his last extremities. . . He went numb inside himself: the news was curiously unreal.

Whenever he entered the kitchen Jean said: "What's wrang, Rab?"

"God help us a'—William's dead! Died in London o' the fever—on the 24th o' the month."

"Oh, no, Rab: no, no. . ."

Nancy tore her apron.

"Is it true, Robin?"

"Aye . . . it's true, Nancy."

Nancy ran out into the court-yard. Adam Armour said: "God, I'm affa sorry, Robert."

"Thanks, Adam. Damned, he was only a boy—twenty-three years old. Naebody there he kent. My auld tutor in Alloway, John Murdoch—you've heard me speak o' him mony a time— he went to see him; but it was ower late——"

"Puir William: I canna believe it, Rab. Adam! you can tak' the trap back to the Carse Mill: I'm no' gaun noo."

"Aye, Jean, you'll have to go. You'll need to break the news at Mossgiel. Better you than getting a letter."

"But Rab——"

"No, no, lass. There's nothing we can dae here aboot it— mair's the pity. Damnit, I should hae kept him here wi' me. He'd hae gotten nae fever here. William was never made for the rough ca-through o' life. Awa' and hae a bit word wi' Nancy, Jean! Dinna you greet, Fanny. Death comes to us a' —and the why and the wherefore will aey be beyond us. . . John Murdoch too—it's a funny world! Whiles I think we were blasted at our birth, the whole family o' us. John got a sudden ca'—noo William—that leaves Gilbert and me. Come ben a minute, Adam, and I'll tell you what you're to do."

By evening the Bard was restless. Ellisland couldn't hold him. Not now that Jean and the bairns were away.

He called Nancy aside.

"Are you a bit calmer noo, Nancy?"

"I'm no' bad, Robin. This is going to be an affa blow to my mither."

"Aye: it's a blow. . . You'll be all right if I go into Dumfries?"

"I'll be all right."

"I'll maybe stay the nicht."

"If you need to, Robin."

"It's no' that I need to, Nancy—but the hoose canna haud me—'specially noo that Jean's awa'."

"I ken, Robin . . . and I ken you were maybe fonder o' William than ony o' us. Though God forgie me—that's hardly possible."

"It's the waste o' a young life, Nancy—and he was a sensitive boy, William: ower sensitive. But there's nae point in grieving ower sair. A' the grievin' we can dae'll no' bring him back."

"I ken a' that, Robin; but it doesna mak' it ony easier. . . But—on you go: you'll be back in the morning?"

"I'll be back, Nancy . . . and . . . there's nae need to say ocht to onybody . . . you understand?"

That night Anna said: "Dinna drink sae much, Robert."

"D'you think I'm getting drunk?"

"No: I've never seen you drunk and I wadna like to see you. Men are . . . no' nice . . . drunk."

"You couldna carry enough drink to mak' me drunk this night, Anna. But I never held wi' drunkenness and never will. A drunk man's no' a bonnie sicht."

"You maun hae been gey fond o' your brither?"

"Fond? It's no' that either. The strange thing is I'm fond o' none o' my family. Leastways no' the same way some families are fond. But there was a something atween William and me. Oh, I got angry wi' him at times—but then he was too fine i' the fibre: too sensitive—no' near ruthless enough for the outside world. You see, Anna, you've got to be ruthless and cunning and a' sorts o' damned unpleasant things in order to make your way in this world—aye, even just to hold your own."

"And d'you think you're ruthless?"

"Me? But then I havena got on, Anna. I'm Scotland's Bard. Look at me! I've hardly the money to send to London to pay the expense o' my brither's funeral. I'm stuck wi' a damned bad bargain o' a bluidy farm on my hands and I work like a drainer on the Excise work—me, the Caledonian Bard, the first poet o' my native land. Oh, a big honour, Anna, and one that only a better poet will ever tak' away from me—and my blessing on the first man to do that. No: I'm no' ruthless. But I've got cunning—so I keep what I have, such as it is—and employ my cunning to plot and plan for more."

"So being a poet's no' everything?"

"It's a high honour and one to be treated wi' grave respect. Aye, and I've earned more money as a poet than ever I would have done as a farmer. My Edinburgh edition didna sit on the shelves till it was blue-moulded. . . On one side o' the ledger I've nae complaints. And I'm a man doubly blessed in my Jean —and doubly blessed in my Anna. Forgive me the nicht, lass: the shock I got this morning's only beginning to tell on me. . ."

"You'll no' be wanting me in the bed the nicht?"

"Aye, certes, I'm wanting you. God, Anna, I'm tired; but I'll no' sleep without you beside me."

"I'm ready when you are, Robert. Just come to bed—and dinna drink ony mair the nicht. Come on: I'll pu' aff your boots. . ."

He was almost immobilised. Anna did all but undress him completely and assisted him to bed. It seemed that he needed to be nursed and it gave her a deep satisfaction to nurse him.

She undressed quickly and got in beside him. She took him in her arms.

"There noo—just lie quiet and dinna worry aboot a thing —and dinna tire yoursel' talking. I'll dae the talking for a change. Dinna mind me: make *yoursel'* comfortable. Roun' this way a wee bit. . . Lift your head a wee till I sort your pillow. That better?"

"Ah! You're an angel. . ."

"No: I'm nae angel—but I'm nae gawkie either. And you canna say but that I'd mak' you a guid wife. Maybe no' as guid's your Jean—but I wouldna be far ahint her. Noo . . .

just keep your hand where it was—you've come to bed to sleep. . ."

Anna did the talking; but after a few words the Bard didn't hear her. He fell into a soft gentle slumber.

And Anna thought: here I am holding the poet o' Scotland in my arms. . . And who would believe me if I were to tell? I canna richt believe it mysel'. Four months ago he was just a name to me—a weel-kent, a famous name; but just a name. And now. . .

And she remembered how when her aunt had first talked about him coming to the Globe she had trembled with curious anticipation. Maybe he was right: this had been planned for them, arranged by fate. . . Aye, there must be something of that kind about it. . . The day she'd first met him and brought him his jug of porter. . . How they'd just fallen into one another's arms—as if she'd been brought into the world to live for that day. And every subsequent meeting had added a new wonder, a new delight, and stoked-up the terrible fever of desire.

And now, to crown all, she was bairned—and bairned beyond any possibility of mishap or miscarriage. Before she had met him she would have dreaded the thought. Her fear of being bairned had indeed kept her from any ultimate yield-ing to any other man (and many had sought her). But she had never worried about the possibility of conception from that first afternoon in the stable. Now she knew that deep down she had wanted to be bairned by him; that if she hadn't been bairned by him the gnawing want would have troubled her all her life. Only now that she was fully conscious that his seed had held in her was the fever of her desire somewhat abated. The temperature of her passion had subsided. She felt at ease now and deeply unspeakably fulfilled. Oh yes: he could still rouse her—he'd only to look at her to do that. But her plexus quivering was gone and the abdominal craving was gone. She realised if but dimly on the floor of her conscious mind that her whole being had craved that it should become fecund to

Robert Burns and to no other man: that there had been no possibility of peace or physical contentment until she had conceived.

She would have to worry now of course; and she would need to start worrying to some practical purpose in six or seven months' time. But she would postpone the worry—the worry of the ways and means. She wouldn't be the first lass to have a bastard bairn: she wouldn't worry about that too much and she certainly wouldn't worry about what folk said. She would be proud of the fact that she'd borne a baby to Robert Burns—triumphantly proud. But she wouldn't tell anyone yet—not even her aunt, though she would know soon enough. Between them they would think up something. The only trouble was that she would need to work for herself and the child—and it wouldn't be easy to work when she was bearing and nursing—this was a real worry.

But there was no pressing hurry for the moment: time to face everything in the days that lay ahead.

But she would tell Robert in the morning. She was certain what his reaction would be—but she was anxious to tell him herself.

The morning came warm and hazy in a muffled crowing of many cocks.

They wakened simultaneously and opened their eyes on one another. The Bard took her gently in his arms and kissed her tenderly.

"Blessings on you, my love, for a night's refreshing sleep."

"If we could aey waken like this!"

They embraced long and affectionately with only a slumbering murmur of passion and the contact of their naked bodies was deeply satisfying.

They sat up in bed.

"Wi' a lot o' useless bluidy work, Anna, the human race has made a hell for itself. There's thousands o' puir folk up and working already."

"I'll need to get up mysel' and start working—but you tak' a long lie when you get the chance—I'll bring you up a bowl o' brose."

"You're determined to kill me wi' kindness."

"If kindness would kill you, you wouldna live long wi' me."

"That could be a truer word than you think, lass."

"I ken it could—that's why I said it. Maybe I'd be far ower saft wi' you for your ain good."

"You could . . . but maybe I'd be that good to you that we'd end up wi' being the death o' one anither."

"You've been good to me in the only way I wanted—and if it'll be the death o' me then I'll hae nae regrets."

The Bard turned sharply towards her. She looked calmly into his wide anxious eyes.

"You're fa'en wi' bairn?"

She nodded.

They embraced.

"Oh, my dear, my dear! I shouldna be happy—but I am. . . Now you're no' to worry. That's the first and most important thing. I'll see you right: you hae my sacred solemn promise on that. You'll no' be ticht for money ower the birth. I'll provide for a' that—and provide handsomely and willingly. And—somehow—I'll bind mysel' responsible for the bairn's upbringing. Hae you ony fears?"

"I never had ony fears, Robert, but I've less than ony noo, if you understand me. I kent you wouldna deny me or my bairn."

"Deny you! But bide a wee—*our* bairn: no' just yours."

"Richt: oor bairn."

"Hae you ony idea when you held?"

"Aye, fine: yon first nicht we were thegither."

"Then, certes, it'll be a braw bairn—gin it's no' twins. . .

"Mind you: there'll be a wheen bad corners in the road ahead—but we'll get round them. For a start: my transfer to a Dumfries Walk has been granted——"

"Oh, I'm glad of that too. . . You ken: I felt somehow that my news wad please you. If I'd thocht it wouldna I'd never hae tellt you. And if you hadna taken my news the way you have——"

Suddenly she was in his arms and sobbing. But there was no pain and no agony in her sobbing.

And the Bard's eyes softened and filled as he stroked her golden hair and soothed and calmed her with his assurance.

VISITORS TO ELLISLAND

Nature had designed the young laird of Barncailzie for a country gentleman of leisure. His ambition had been to "improve" his estate since all intelligent country lairds who liked to be in the fashion had taken to the craze for planting and draining and enclosing. Syme would have supervised all the improvements he had money for and when he was not thus improving he would be busy with the gun and the fishing rod.

But the failure of the Douglas and Heron Bank had put an end to all his ambitions and had brought about the death of his Edinburgh-lawyer father.

As the estate was being wound up Syme had his eyes on a sinecure; and, being a gentleman with influential friends, that sinecure seemed in the offing. He would assist the aged and ailing Maxwell, Distributor of Stamps in Dumfries, and when death came to Mr. Maxwell (and he had already overstayed his official welcome) that plum of office and preferment would fall naturally and inevitably into John Syme's waiting lap.

But the laird of Barncailzie didn't like Dumfries. He disliked all towns. He could thole Edinburgh, for Edinburgh was a town of important business and he had many good and influential friends there. But in Dumfries itself Syme had few friends. To him it was petty and provincial; its social circles were narrow and back-biting—and it stank.

To make matters worse, the Stamp Office was on the ground floor at the Nith-end of the Stinking Vennel—so called from the open sewer that ran down the middle of the causeway; a sewer that was mostly choked and overflowed into the gutters and in dry weather gave off what Syme described to his friends as a "most shocking effluvium." Only when it rained heavily and the downpour washed the ordure into the Nith was there any relief.

On the whole, town dwellers didn't mind. Sewage had to be disposed of somehow and one finally became inured to the smell. Nevertheless the Dumfriesians hadn't labelled the vennel stinking from any ironic sense of understatement.

But so far as social company was concerned there was one bright spot. There was Robert Burns. And, for the Bard, Barncailzie had quickly developed an admiration that bordered on gentlemanly hero-worship. Barncailzie was a shrewd judge of human character though his sense of social values sometimes led him astray. He had a wide circle of friends for he cultivated friendship even as he had improved his estate. But he reckoned that in Robert Burns he had an unique and invaluable friend.

He admired the Bard's poetry; he warmed to his presence as a man and he was vastly stimulated by his conversation. Besides, the Bard had a devilish wit at times and Syme was partial to wit—especially if there was some devilry about it. He was likewise partial to bawdry especially if it was leavened with wit. He was mildly agnostic and vaguely anarchistic— but always mildly and always gentlemanly so.

Withal a kindly man, John Syme, overfond maybe of ease and comfort and an idle self-sufficiency. If there was any malice in him it was directed only to those manifestations of un-gentlemanly conduct which gentlemen must ever abhor.

The Bard liked John Syme. Syme was cultured—he could converse on books and poetry and politics and manners. And he was a good listener. There was no one quite like him about

Dumfries and he needed someone with whom he could have a change of conversation and a keen and intelligent change at that.

At the beginning of September Syme turned his mount in at the Isle and directed his long aquiline nose towards Ellisland. He had an appointment for breakfast there. He had accepted the Bard's invitation for he was anxious to see him in his domestic surroundings and he was looking forward to meeting with the Bonnie Jean whose virtues the Bard never ceased to extol.

Of course he had other business. Later he had an appointment with his friend Robert Riddell at Friars Carse. There he would meet with Captain Francis Grose and the pair would go sketching old ruins together—probably Lincluden College among them. John Syme was partial to the daubing of landscapes—after a gentlemanly fashion. And he shared the Bard's enthusiasm for Francis Grose's outsize in character. . .

It was a different Robert Burns Syme met that morning. Here was the Bard in the role of farmer and head-of-the-farmhouse. And somehow, as fitted the role, the Bard seemed rougher but heartier and more jocund. It was immediately obvious that he was essentially farmer and undisputed master of his own household. And he did the honours in a hearty and generous fashion.

But gentleman though he was, Syme blinked twice at Bonnie Jean. He did not forget his politeness nor his elaborate courtesy. But Jean was a shock to him.

Somehow he had expected to find a slim lithesome lass in the first bloom of youth and endowed with the dazzling beauty of a poet's fancy.

Instead he encountered a strong robust woman with an ample bosom, sturdy hips, legs both trim and tight though hardly genteel, and a thickish waist and innocent of cosseting corsetry. Her face was honest and frank, her hair was abundantly black and her large black eyes were not unexpressive. But she had a more than usually firm mouth, a strong chin and a decided nose. True, she was surprisingly light on her feet; but he could not rid himself of the sense of dourness, strong will and an almost masculine muscularity. An excellent farmer's wife, no doubt; but hardly a poet's fancy.

Syme liked women to be dumb, slightly wilting, capable of a sigh of sensibility as well as a sweet smile—and, of course, feminine in the gentlewomanly sense of the word.

The truth was that the Jean Armours of this world, whether gentle or simple, were altogether too healthy and robust for the John Symes.

As for Jean: any friend of her husband was welcome. But she didn't warm to John Syme. She distrusted people who were over-polite—and she was instinctively on guard against anyone who was so obviously gentry.

It was Nancy who summed him up after he had left with the Bard to call at Friars Carse. "An important wee body to himsel'—but a fushionless cratur alongside o' oor Robin. I dinna ken how he can fash himsel' wi' some o' thae oddities."

"But you can see he has a great admiration for Rab."

"And well he may. And Robin would be set up gin that was a' he could get to admire him."

"Well: I wonder what Captain Grose thinks aboot him."

"Noo yon was a man! A droll ane, Captain Grose, but nae nonsense aboot him—and he thocht plenty o' Robin."

"Aye: they were pack and thick thegither. I was aey glad to see the fat Captain. God knows: he maun be an affa burden to himself. I ken what it's like to carry twins—but the Captain's carrying twins a' the time."

"Aye: front *and* back."

"The fattest woman ever I saw hadna a hin-end like the Captain's! And he wad crack a joke aboot it."

"Captain Grose wad crack a joke aboot onything. I'll bet Robin and him had mony a hearty crack when they were their lane."

"You should hae seen the book he wrote. On the vulgar

tongue, as he ca'ed it. And yet, a decent man: you couldna tak' ony offence: he was aey that hearty and genuine."

"Ah weel: I just hope Mr. Syme o' Barncailzie enjoyed his breakfast. We'll better redd aff the table. If the weather hauds, Robin was thinking o' startin' shearin'—Stookhill I heard him say. . ."

"This is Wednesday? Aye, and we'll need anither bed made up in the attic—Fanny's brither will be here come Saturday for the shearing—my sister Nelly is coming doon wi' them. . ."

Syme said to Grose: "The Bard's a noble fellow, Captain."

"None nobler, Syme. . . I must observe that Auld Scotia hasn't been overgenerous in her treatment of him."

"You mean his being in the Excise?"

"Aye . . . or a farmer either. Who the hell does Mr. Miller in Dalswinton think he is?"

"'Course, Miller is truly a great man. A trifle mad perhaps. But a man of many manifold capabilities."

"Huh! He could have made Robert a present of Ellisland."

"Not much of a present. Though I must say the Bard's making a heroic show as farmer."

"He *is* a farmer and a good one from all that I can gather —and I learn that he's a bloody fine Exciseman too. I must see what I can do by way of promotion for him through some of my friends who have influence with the Treasury."

"That would be generous of you. . . By the by, Captain, I met Mrs. Burns for the first time to-day—I ratherly think the Bard must have been exercising his poetic faculties when he sang of her."

"Mrs. Burns, sir! Ha! A most excellent woman. I admire her tremendously. An exceptional downright honest woman: a veritable mountain of strength to our friend. And a woman of wit and sense and taste—huh! We are the best of friends. I spent many an hour in their company last summer. Gad, sir: I can hear her merry laughter yet. And kindly, as only the Scots peasant women can be kindly——"

"I understood her father to be a pretty considerable architect in Ayrshire."

"And why not? He's providing me with some elevations. . . But Mistress Burns is a peasant for all that——"

"Hardly a woman of culture, I should imagine, as would befit a poet's wife."

"Women of culture, my dear Syme? Huh! And a bloody lot of good I've found them. No: the Bard made an excellent choice of a wife—and a mother. Can you see our Bard *married* to some of the ladies of fashion and culture we know? Can you imagine it?"

But John Syme could not imagine it. Nor could he see in Jean any of the qualities that aroused the admiration of Francis Grose. He shrugged his shoulders and applied himself to his sketch. No doubt where women were concerned it was every man to his own choice; but he'd always considered that a man's choice of a wife was an index to his true character.

The Bard was throng with his harvest for the month of September: indeed it was well into the beginning of October before his fields were gleaned and every thrave was secured in the barn.

On the Friday, the 15th of October, he celebrated his harvest home with the usual kirn dance. It had been a successful harvest: by far the best that had ever been garnered from the stony acres of Ellisland since man had first attempted to crop its dour unyielding soil.

The Bard was proud and rightly proud of his success as a farmer. He was proud that he had won from Ellisland crops such as no other man had won.

David Newall was also proud, as was John Cunningham the land-steward from Sandbed; but Patrick Miller was too busy with more important matters to listen to the reports concerning his tenants.

As things would have it, Robert Ainslie—now Writer to

the Signet—had business in the south-west; and he had accepted the Bard's offer of hospitality.

Ainslie had grown since the Edinburgh days when the Bard had found him young and gay and carefree.

When he had accompanied the Bard on his Border tour he had been something of a young buck anxious to sow as many wild oats as opportunity afforded.

Now in business for himself and at the age of twenty-four years he was an old man. Only a year older than William Burns and six years younger than the Bard he was, in spirit, at least twenty years older.

At heart Robert Ainslie was at once a snob, a cad and an ass. Maybe he was something of a fool too; for he had grown respectable as lawyers like to think they are respectable.

Still, he had come under the Bard's influence and he thrilled to the prospect of meeting him again.

But he had another reason for seeking the Bard out at Ellisland. Ainslie had to some little extent taken the Bard's place in Clarinda's affections. True enough, Robert Ainslie wasn't even the shadow of Robert Burns in any respect. But if Ainslie was but the invoice of a lover yet he was a man and Clarinda needed a man who loved her and with whom she could be intimate. Besides, she could twist Ainslie round her little finger.

But maybe Clarinda, desperate though she was and terribly lonely, would not have seduced Ainslie had he not been one of the Bard's most intimate Edinburgh friends. She held to Ainslie as the one vital link that connected her with the Sylvander that had been.

When she had heard that Ainslie was to visit him at Ellisland she was all a-dither. And she made Ainslie promise that he would report to her, and that by letter, every circumstance of his visit. She wanted a first-hand description of Bonnie Jean and what the Bard now thought of her; she wanted to be acquainted of every tittle-tattle of gossip that concerned them; she wanted to know what Ellisland was like and how

Sylvander shaped as farmer and how he and his Jean fitted into whatever Nithsdale social life afforded.

It was true that Ainslie had sown his wild oats and had paid for the crop: it was true that he still haunted his favourite brothel; but it was equally true that he was in thrall to Clarinda.

Clarinda gave him an assurance and a satisfaction that no other woman could. Clarinda had charm and she exercised that charm on Robert Ainslie with devastating effect.

The Bard, for his part, spared no effort to make Robert Ainslie comfortable. He had had a bed set up for him in his own room; and he had arranged that there he would eat with Jean and him as was his habit when he had important visitors. He explained matters to Jean:

"Bob Ainslie is a good friend of mine, Jean: you must have heard me speak o' him mony a time. I admit that he could hae come at a more convenient time; but what the hell! We can put him up and we can feed him. Oh, I'll tak' him out as much as I can. If he gets his bed and his breakfast that'll be about a' you need see o' him. He's a writer now—a Writer to His Majesty's Signet no less—and shaping to be one o' Edinburgh's important and influential citizens. I started on my Border tour wi' Bob Ainslie and his parents did me the honours o' their fine house at Berrywell near Dunse; and very proud they did me. Besides since then I hae been indebted to Ainslie for many kindnesses . . . and a wheen intimate favours.

"So I welcome the opportunity to repay past favours, Jean. Of course we canna interrupt our kirn dance—Ainslie'll just need to mak' the best o' that he can. . . But I dinna want you to worry, lass, or put yoursel' about. I ken how to deal wi' Bob Ainslie and we've nothing to be ashamed o'. Of course he'll meet Nancy and Nelly and Fanny and Mr. and Mrs. Hyslop—and why shouldn't he? Listen, Jean: he's just a young lawyer frae Edinburgh whose father is a weel-doing Border farmer; and, but for his friendship wi' me, of no great importance."

"Whatever you say, Rab—only you ken how thrang we are the noo—there's hardly room to move. The place is needing redd frae top to bottom—but we canna start on that till the kirn's a' by. . ."

Ainslie arrived on the Friday afternoon and in the evening everybody assembled for the kirn dance. There were lashings of drink and lashings of food—and the Bard was in his happiest farmer-mood.

But for once in his life Robert Ainslie found himself completely out of the picture. The Bard was more than friendly to him and more than gracious; and Jean did what she could to make him comfortable and to feel at ease. The others ignored him.

He elected not to dance. The Bard coaxed him but the others were glad that he withdrew to the ingle-neuk and drank his whisky in silence and in his own company.

It was a merry evening. Dance followed dance; Jean sang; drinks were passed round; there was much kissing and hugging at the end of every dance. . . Ainslie noted that the Bard kissed freely and hugged with abandon. And when his wife was his partner he embraced in an embarrassingly intimate manner.

Ainslie elected to find the scene disgusting. Bonnie Jean was fat and sweated and talked in the broadest Ayrshire; the Bard's sister Nancy and his good-sister Nelly were plain country girls without either grace or charm. William Hyslop and his wife—tavern-keepers from Dumfries—were inexpressibly common and vulgar. . . As for the Bard's cousins Fanny and John and William. . . Ainslie sniffed in disdain. . .

But he writhed in chagrin too. Here was a family; here were happy, even boisterous, human beings enjoying themselves fully and freely under the roof-tree of Robert Burns. And he, Robert Ainslie, could not join in the wholesome fun and merriment because there was neither fun nor merriment left in his soul; for he had sold his soul to the devil of Edin-

Q

burgh respectability and decorum. How he envied them! And yet for a respected Writer to His Majesty's Signet they did not give a snap of their thumbs nor a hooch of their warm breaths.

They had tilled the earth and the earth had brought forth food; and if not in abundance yet abundantly enough to feed them. What did it concern them that Geordie sat on his throne, that Pitt plotted and planned in parliament, that be-wigged lawyers thronged the Court of Session or that learned counsel harangued an idiot judge as deaf to pleading as he was to sound? What did those happy carefree peasants care for the world of learning and pomp and fashion and pride and arrogance and wealth and power. . .?

Ainslie envied them even as his soul shrivelled within him. He became melancholy and morbid and utterly miserable. Outwardly his nose twitched and he elected to appear cold and indifferent and superciliously superior to all around him.

The fiddler played, the dancers linked and the lassies laughed and skirled and the autumn night drove on heedless of an alien jaundiced eye. . .

The following evening the Bard rode with Ainslie to Brownhill Inn. As the company in the public room was not to Ainslie's liking the Bard took him to a private room.

"Well, Bob—at last we have a place to ourselves and a bottle between us. That's how it used to be and that's how it is again. What ails you, man?"

"I'm fine, Robert. Perhaps the effects of the journey. . . A damned melancholy has got me by the throat these months past——"

"Melancholy? I sympathise wi' you. She's a bad bitch to thole. But there! your cure's in the bottle: for to-night. . .

"Now about Mrs. Mac: what's the latest?"

"She's partly forgiven you——"

"Partly forgiven me! God forgive her: the shoe's on the other foot!"

"You won't convince Mrs. Mac of that."

"Well, well: I can follow you. So now that she's forgiven me?"

"But you wanted that, didn't you? I mean: you wanted to be on friendly terms again?"

"There's no point in keeping a wound open by poking your finger into it every now and again. How are *you* getting on wi' her?"

"Mrs. Mac and I have become very dear friends—but our relationship is entirely respectable and utterly platonic."

"I ken a lass that said she'd never believe in platonic love again—that was when she found herself wi' bairn."

"You will have your joke, Robert—as always."

"As you say, Bob—as always. Where would we be gin we couldna crack a joke back and forward—and especially atween friends."

"I dinna seem to savour a joke nowadays."

"Drink up, damn you, and dinna sit there wi' a face like Harley's ghost. Hell, man! you've aged twenty years since I saw you last. Damnit, you're no' twenty-five yet! You shouldna hae missed a dance last nicht—no' at your age."

"No, Robert: you maun forgive me—but really my dancing days are past."

"Hae you got a lass yet?"

"It's too early to contemplate marriage."

"Oh, if you're for *contemplating* marriage! You mean you're looking for a wife wi' a good tocher?"

"I'm not looking for a wife at all."

"No . . . just contemplating. Weel: you micht *never* marry. So you still chap Lucky Dow's door?"

"Certainly not: I've given all that up."

"I see! Maybe you're courting Pale Religion?"

"You well know, Robert, that I never liked your sallies at the expense of religion."

"Certes, you've turned a gey solemn beggar, Bob. It maun be the way you're feeling: it's maybe your liver . . . or your kidneys. . . Maybe a guid country shite would help you.

There's nothing like a guid squat-doon on your hunkers. Aye: keep your bowels open and your mind free——"

Ainslie smiled wanly. He had elected that his smile should be wan.

"You'll want me to take a message back to Mistress MacLehose?"

"Why should I want to give her a message? We've nothing to communicate about."

"She doesn't mean anything to you any more?"

"She never did."

The Bard watched the effect of this lie on Ainslie.

"You can hardly ask me to believe that, Robert. I know to some extent what she meant to you—and it was a pretty considerable something."

"That was only my Old Hawk's way wi' Clarinda. You see, Bob: it was entirely a platonic affair. Pastorally platonic you micht even say—even though the scene was yon poverty-struck stinking hole in General's Entry in the Potter-row——"

"She's more to be pitied than mocked for her tragic poverty."

"Agreed! So you see I was Sylvander and she was Clarinda——"

"But I always understood that these Arcadian titles originated with you!"

"Mind me when I get hame and I'll show you the very letter she sets out the plan."

"You keep some of her letters?"

"Every line she ever wrote me I keep preserved. I understand she's got all mine?"

"That's a woman's privilege, surely. But d'you think you're wise keeping hers? I mean: they could fall into other less-understanding hands . . . besides, there's your wife."

"Tuts! Jean kens a' aboot Mrs. Mac—she read the letters and laughed her sides sore. No, no: Jean has nae objections to a platonic friendship."

The Bard lied recklessly; but Ainslie elected not to notice the irony.

"The point is, Robert, that you have no message for Mistress Mac by my hands—I had in mind the saving of her the prohibitive cost of postage."

"Well, you could mention to her that the next message I hae for her will be delivered in person."

"Excellent! That means you're coming through to Edinburgh soon?"

"Oh, like enough some day I'll mak' the jaunt through to the Toon. Maybe next year or the next again."

"You wouldn't be joking with me, Robert——"

"Joke wi' you! Damnit, you wouldna ken a joke if you saw it in letters ten feet high. You're beyond a' manner o' jokes noo, Bob. You dinna go near Lucky's noo—and your friendship wi' Mistress Mac is not only platonic—it's the very height of respectability into the bargain. Certes, Bob, it wad be a waste o' time for me to joke wi' you. But drink up and get that melancholy off your mind."

Ainslie flushed and took a long pull at the wine. The Bard refilled his glass. Ainslie quaffed that too.

"At least I can still drink."

"Grand! Maybe we'll talk to some purpose when we get round to the second bottle. . ."

But by the time they got to the second bottle Ainslie was finished. The Bard did everything he could to cheer his friend; but he failed to realise that there was no friendship left in Robert Ainslie. The natural youth of the boy had run out of him and had left him empty. And now he was filling up the empty shell of himself with respectability and decorum —and cant and humbug and hypocrisy and an intolerable smugness.

Yet even in his drink Ainslie deferred to the Bard and hid from him the worst aspects of his newly-acquired snobbery.

The Bard had lashed him and mocked him and castigated him and Ainslie had not fought back because he knew that the

Bard was right and that he was no match for him in any respect.

And then the Bard had softened towards him and had encouraged him.

"You're fu', Bob—blin' fu'. But keep on drinking till you fa': the landlord and me are friends. John Bacon's got a bed for you and there you'll be able to snore awa' your distemper and your melancholy. You're changing, Bob—changing from a beardless youth into a beardless man and skipping a decade as you go. The strain's been ower meikle for you. Your ambition has owergrown your strength. You'll need to lie fallow for a while in order to get back into good heart. You see: it's a fell responsibility being a Writer to the Signet and the burden o' the law weighing heavy on you.

". . . if I'd time to go another Border tour wi' you—or accompany you into Ayrshire I'd blast the melancholy out o' you.

". . . of course I've changed too. I'm glad you noted that. I hae my worries *and* my melancholy. The bluidy farm's a failure despite the crops I've gathered this year. Oh, I could mak' a bare living if I devoted every ounce o' my energy to it. But to hell wi' that— So I got me a ride in the Excise and now I've gotten a foot-walk in Dumfries. . . And I've other plans maturing. Oho! I'm a devoted servant to His Majesty's Excise. I haud the offenders' noses to the grindstane. I gar them skirl and see that they're weel fined afore the magistrates. I'm Law and Order as far as the Excise is concerned. I ken that as a lawyer you'll be proud o' me in this. So I'm planning greater things. I expect I'll transfer out o' Dumfries to a port Supervisorship—and then I'll go on to a Collectorship. Oho! I'll maybe end up on the Board yet. Certainly I hae the best o' friends in the district. Sir Robert Laurie of Maxwelton, Alexander Fergusson of Craigdarroch, Captain Riddell of Glenriddell now of Friars Carse—and a wheen mair o' the gentry are the Bard's firm friends hereabouts. And Robert Graham of Fintry presides over my interest with the Excise

Commissioners. . . Mony a guid bottle Queensberry's chamberlain John MacMurdo and Closeburn factor William Stewart
drink wi' me in this verra room. . .

". . . there's nae reason either for you or for Clarinda to
think that the Bard's forgotten and neglected aboot Nithsdale
or Dumfries. Nor does the Muse neglect me. I turn out my
songs for James Johnson's Museum and verses for my friends
in an orderly and regular fashion. . ."

Robert Ainslie bleared at him with bloodshot drunken eyes.

"Yes, Robert . . . you are still as wonderful as ever and
. . . you can still . . . slay the Philistines . . . but you still
love Clarinda. . ."

"Ah! you canna get awa' frae Clarinda. Sensibility how
charming, Dearest Nancy canst thou tell. . . Chords that thrill
wi' sweetest pleasure vibrate deepest notes of woe . . . or
words to that effect. . . Clarinda that's now mistress o' your
soul, Bob. Weel . . . I canna wish the puir unfortunate wife
ony ill: her and her bits o' bairns and her husband awa' in the
Indies. . . Just as well your friendship's platonic or you'd be
in danger o' adultery, Bob. A fell sin to cuckold a husband——"

"But . . . your friendship wi' Clarinda wasna . . . platonic.
But . . . Robert . . . dinna let us say . . . hard things. Let
us drink a bumper to your good friend Nancy."

"Fill your glass then. And now: Fairest Nancy——"

Ainslie managed to stagger to his feet and drink off his
bumper—the wine spilling at the corners of his mouth and
running down into his cravat.

"Robert. . . You . . . 're the great . . . est poet, the great . . .
est man, the great . . . est lover in the world . . . Mis . . . tress
Mac . . . says . . . so—Robert Burns. . ."

The effort was too much for him. The Bard caught him
by the lapels before he fell—then he let him sink gently to the
floor. He loosened his cravat.

Ainslie closed his eyes and muttered some unintelligible
words. . .

Far from drunk but by no means sober, the Bard went out

unsteadily to find John Bacon. They would need to carry Ainslie to bed.

"Aye: I've had a drink, Jean, but I'm far frae drunk. Ainslie's safe wi' John Bacon at Brownhill."

"Ower drunk to ride back to Ellisland! A nice way to behave himsel'."

"Now, now, lass——"

"Dinna lass me, Rab. Are you wantin' a bite?"

"Nothing."

"Are we gaun to bed then? I waited up for your frien'."

"I know, Jean . . . but I thocht it was better to leave him where he was. You see, Bob Ainslie was a good friend to me."

"Once upon a time—mebbe. But you were best to leave him wi' the Bacons. Come on, noo, get to your bed: we'd a late nicht last nicht and noo it's the Sabbath morning."

"Richt then, Jean—just whatever you say——"

"Och, sit doon there and I'll pu' aff your buits."

"I'll manage——"

"Sit doon when you're tellt—you'll only end up wi' fa'in' in the fire—or waukenin' the bairns."

"Aye . . . that's true."

"Did you unsaddle the horse?"

"Certainly—the beast maun be made comfortable."

"Aye, weel . . . I'll dae the same for you."

"You ken, Jean: mony a man wad get a curtain lecture coming in at this time—and the smell o' drink on him. . . But no: Jean never raises her voice. Never complains. Never an angry word crosses her lips. I could crawl hame blin' fu', drunk as a coot, and be received like the prodigal son—and if I felt like eating the fatted calf I'd get the whole bluidy carcase served up to me in my bed. . ."

"Come on, you daft beggar—you'd provoke a saint. Gie me that can'le: you'll set the hoose on fire. . ."

Robert Ainslie sat in the King's Arms and, still feeling the effects of Bacon's wine, wrote to Mrs. MacLehose:

DUMFRIES, 18th Oct., 1790

I promised to write my Dear Friend and for that end now seat myself at Dumfries—I have been with Burns since Friday —and as his duty as Exciseman engaged him this day, I have taken the Opportunity of coming here to Visit this Town— You desired that I should let you hear everything regarding him and his family and how I was pleased— This is a difficult question as my short room here will not permit me to be so full as I might—and part of the Question admits of Double Answers— I was pleased with Burns' hearty welcome of me— and it was an addition to his pleasure, that my arrival was upon his *Kirn* night, when he Expected some of his friends to help make merry, but much displeased with the Company when they arrived— They consisted of a Vulgar looking Tavern keeper from Dumfries; and his wife more Vulgar— Mr. Miller of Dalswinton's gardener and his wife—and said wife's sister—and a little fellow from Dumfries, who had been a Clerk— These were the Strangers, and the rest of the Company who are inmates of the home were Burns' Sister, and Mrs. Burns' Sister, who are Two common looking Girls who act as their Servants—and 3 Male and female cousins who had been shearing for him— We spent the evening in the common way of Such occasions of Dancing, and Kissing the Lasses at the End of every dance—with regard to the helpmate She seems Vulgar and Common-place in a considerable degree—and pretty round and fat— She is however a kind Body in her Own way, and the husband Tolerably attentive to her— As to the house, it is ill contrived—and pretty Dirty, and *Hugry Mugry*— Tho last, not least Our Friend himself is as ingenious as ever, and seemed very happy with the great mixture of the poet and the Excise man— One day he sits down and writes a Beautiful poem—and the next he Seizes a cargo of Tobacco from some unfortunate Smuggler—or Roups out some poor wretch for Selling liquors without a License. From his conversation he Seems to be frequently among the Great—but no attention is paid by people of any rank to his wife— Having found that his farm does not answer he is about to Give it up, and depend wholly on the Excise—

Now, having given you such a description of those you wished to hear of, As to myself, that Cursed Melancholy, which I was complaining of, has been daily increasing—and all Burns' Jokes cannot dispel it. I sit silent and frail even amidst mirth—and instead of that joyous laugh which I used to have so frequently discover the Tear start into my Eyes, and Sigh most piteously— I know of no Sufficient reason for Such Misery, but the Effect of constitution, and am sorry now to be Obliged to go among absolute Strangers— Nothing under the Sun would be so agreeable as Seeing you, and a letter from you would be the next Best— If you write to me, address to me to be left till called for at the post office of *Ayr*, where I shall be in a few days—and for fear of accidents in that country, you may use the letter A or any such, if you speak of B—

Burns and I drunk your health on Saturday at an inn and to Settle the matter Got both Exceedingly drunk—you need say nothing of this letter to any Body

Yours most affectionately

R. AINSLIE

TAM O' SHANTER

November came with customary blasts and long days of driving rain turning the roads into quagmires.

The Bard was doubly glad that his transfer to Dumfries had now taken practical effect and that his weekly riding was reduced from some two hundred miles to a mere sixty.

These two hundred odd miles every week had worn out his favourite young horse Pegasus. On his last moorland round Pegasus had fallen at least twenty times and had nearly broken the Bard's neck. . .

But not every day was wind and rain and a swollen Nith drumming to the Solway. There were days of sunshine and warmth when it was possible to sit on a stone by the river and catch the rhythm of the water's play.

It was about the beginning of the month when he had been thinking of his promise to Francis Grose to write him a poem on the Alloway witches' dance (and now time was running short) that he began to grow heavy with inspiration.

He had been sitting at his desk among a litter of Excise papers cudgelling his brains and trying, it seemed in vain, to get a form for his tale, when suddenly he was seized with the vision of a Carrick farmer returning late from Ayr market. He even got his name—Tam. But Tam who or what? And then he remembered burly Dugal Graham of Shanter Farm —recalled him vividly from his days at Kirkoswald and the riotous nights at Kirkton Jean's. . .

He rose from his desk, grabbed his gilt-knobbed wangee stick and was out of the house and on the banks of the Nith almost before he realised where he was.

He'd got it! Tam, o' Shanter Farm—just Tam o' Shanter. There was his main character and his title too! Tam would be drinking in Ayr; there would be a sonsie landlady and a cunning jovial landlord. And a friend of Tam's to keep the conversational pot boiling. No: not another farmer. An Ayr crony—somebody Tam would leave behind when he set out for Alloway. Grand, grand! And what a night! Inside social mirth and glee and Tam's friend—a souter. Aye, a souter johnnie—Souter Johnnie—his ancient trusty drouthy crony. His-ancient-trusty-drouthy-crony—hell, there was his metre right to hand!

The wangee stick sliced the air and smacked against the leg of his boot. He strode up and down and up on the level stretch of road beyond the house.

Start in Auld Ayr, too—Auld Ayr wham ne'er a toon surpasses for honest men and bonnie lassies. God! it was coming! Flowing naturally—a fine, easy-going metre; line running into line; naturally; inevitably. . .

Start just as the market was finishing—as market day was wearing late. And just carry on. . .

Jean said to her sister Nelly:

"I wonder whaur that daft beggar's awa' to noo?"

"It's gey near twa hours since he tore out o' the hoose. He said never a word either."

"Oh, he's like that whiles. There'll be something on his mind."

"You've a time o' it wi' him."

"Och no: Rab's no' hard to get on wi' aince you understand his moods and his ways."

"He's been gey nice to me, Jean."

"I told you, didn't I?"

"Adam said the same. But my mither wasna sae sure. He's guid to you!"

"He's guid to me and I'm guid to him. I've never rued an hour since I first met him."

"Noo, Jean!"

"Aye . . . weel: there were times when he was awa' in Edinburgh. . . But . . . I never lost faith. . . I aey kent he'd come back. But even gin he hadna, Nell, I wadna hae regretted having the bairns to him."

"You wadna?"

"No: I wad not. Of coorse, that's what naebody could understand. That's what made my faither sae angry."

"God, and he was angry——"

"It's me kens that: he near killed me; and what was worse I near-han' lost Rab. . . Throw on a bit mair fire, Nell, and I'll awa' oot and see if there's ony word o' him. If it's a sang that's worrying him he'll be aboot the water somewhaur."

"He's gey keen on the sangs gotten: I suppose there's money in them."

"Damn the penny—but you daurna say a word."

He was still pacing up and down when Jean came on him. But as soon as he saw her he stopped and hailed her.

"I've struck it, Jean: I've struck it! My verses for Captain Grose about the witches' dance at Alloway: I've got the whole thing complete—just needs polishing up. Listen to this. This is where Tam gets the length o' Alloway and sees the auld ruined kirk in a bleeze."

There and then he gave Jean a swatch of Tam that rooted her to the spot. When he halted she gasped for breath.

"Oh, Rab! You've never done onything as guid as that afore."

"I kent you'd like it. This is my masterpiece, Jean. And you havena heard the half o' it—no' the half o' it. Tam's guid, isn't he? Aye, Tam's guid—and the auld grey mare! Come on and I'll get it committed to paper—and then I'll read it to the family."

Jean stood looking at him in admiration and wonder. He took her in his arms and kissed her.

"There now! That's for liking my poem."

"I'm sae glad, Rab. You've worried about this for a lang time. And I ken the Captain'll like it."

"Aye . . . Francis'll get a gey surprise when he opens the packet and Tam jumps oot on him."

At supper time that night the Bard came through from his room with a great sheaf of papers—the first draft of *Tam o' Shanter*.

The family were expectant, for Jean had warned them that a new poem was to be read to them concerning a witches' tale: beyond this she had been warned to say nothing.

He stood with his back to the fire so that he could get the light from the candles on the mantel-shelf. He was in great spirit. He looked round his audience. His wife with young Robert on her lap, Nelly, Fanny, Adam Armour and Nancy. Francis was sound asleep in his cradle. All eyes were on him and their eyes shone where their faces, cast slightly upwards, caught the light. Nobody spoke.

"Noo dinna be sae solemn. This is just a simple tale I'm going to read to you—a tale so simple that even a child might understand—aye, even wee Frankie there gin he was wauken. It'll maybe even wauken Robbie a bit more, for I see he's near sleeping."

"It's by his bed-time, Rab."

"Ah weel: I hope you'll think I've given you good reason for that. It's a guid thing the Nith's low, Adam, or you wouldna mak' Dalswinton the nicht."

"I'll manage—if I hae to swim her."

"Mak' a note o' that, Fanny! But to our tale. Ready then:

"When chapman billies leave the street, and drouthy neebors neebors meet: as market days are wearing late, an' folk begin to tak' the gate; while we sit bousing at the nappy an' getting fu' and unco happy, we think na on the lang Scots miles, the mosses, waters, slaps, and styles, that lie between us and our hame, where sits our sulky, sullen dame, gathering her brows like gathering storm, nursing her wrath to keep it warm.

"This truth fand honest Tam o' Shanter, as he frae Ayr ae night did canter: (Auld Ayr, wham ne'er a town surpasses, for honest men and bonnie lassies).

"O Tam, had'st thou but been sae wise, as ta'en thy ain wife Kate's advice! She tauld thee weel thou was a skellum, a blethering, blustering, drunken blellum; that frae November till October, ae market day thou wasnae sober; that ilka melder wi' the miller, thou sat as lang as thou had siller; that every naig was ca'd a shoe on, the smith and thee gat roaring fu' on; that at the Lord's house, even on Sunday, thou drank wi' Kirkton Jean till Monday. She prophesied, that, late or soon, thou would be found deep drowned in Doon, or catched wi' warlocks in the mirk by Alloway's auld, haunted kirk.

"Ah! gentle dames, it gars me greet, to think how mony

counsels sweet, how mony lengthened, sage advices the husband frae the wife despises!

"But to our tale:— Ae market night, Tam had got planted unco right, fast by an ingle, bleezing finely, wi' reaming swats, that drank divinely; and at his elbow, Souter Johnnie, his ancient, trusty, drouthy crony; Tam lo'ed him like a very brither; they had been fu' for weeks thegither. The night drave on wi' sangs and clatter; and aey the ale was growing better; the landlady and Tam grew gracious wi' secret favours, sweet and precious; the Souter tauld his queerest stories; the landlord's laugh was ready chorus; the crickets joined the chirping cry, the kittlin chased her tail for joy: the storm without might rair and rustle, Tam didna mind the storm a whistle.

"Care, mad to see a man sae happy, e'en drowned himsel' amang the nappy. As bees flee hame wi' lades o' treasure, the minutes winged their way wi' pleasure: kings may be blest but Tam was glorious, o'er a' the ills o' life victorious!

"But pleasures are like poppies spread: you seize the flower, its bloom is shed; or like the snow falls in the river, a moment white—then melts for ever; or like the Borealis' race, that flit ere you can point their place; or like the rainbow's lovely form evanishing amid the storm. Nae man can tether time or tide; the hour approaches Tam maun ride: that hour, o' night's black arch the key-stane, that dreary hour Tam mounts his beast in; and sic a night he tak's the road in, as ne'er poor sinner was abroad in.

"The wind blew as 'twad blawn its last; the rattling showers rose on the blast; the speedy gleams the darkness swallowed; loud, deep, and lang the thunder bellowed: that night, a child might understand, the Deil had business on his hand.

"Weel mounted on his grey meare Meg, a better never lifted leg, Tam skelpit on through dub and mire, despising wind, and rain, and fire; whiles holding fast his guid blue bonnet, whiles crooning o'er some auld Scots sonnet, whiles glow'ring round wi' prudent cares, lest bogles catch him unawares:

Kirk-Alloway was drawing nigh, where ghaists and houlets nightly cry.

"By this time he was cross the ford, where in the snaw the chapman smoored; and past the birks and meikle stane, where drunken Charlie brak's neck-bane; and through the whins, and by the cairn, where hunters fand the murdered bairn; and near the thorn, aboon the well, where Mungo's mither hanged hersel'. Before him Doon pours all his floods; the doubling storm roars through the woods; the lightnings flash from pole to pole; near and more near the thunders roll: when, glimmering through the groaning trees, Kirk-Alloway seemed in a bleeze, through ilka bore the beams were glancing, and loud resounded mirth and dancing.

"Inspiring, bold John Barleycorn! what dangers thou canst make us scorn! Wi' tippenny, we fear nae evil; wi' usquabae, we'll face the Devil! The swats sae reamed in Tammie's noddle, fair play, he cared na deils a boddle. But Maggie stood, right sair astonished, till, by the heel and hand admonished, she ventured forward on the light; and wow! Tam saw an unco sight!

"Warlocks and witches in a dance: nae cotillion, brent new frae France, but hornpipes, jigs, strathspeys, and reels, put life and mettle in their heels. A winnock-bunker in the east, there sat Auld Nick, in shape o' beast; a tousy tyke, black, grim, and large, to gi'e them music was his charge: he screwed the pipes and gart them skirl, till roof and rafters a' did dirl. Coffins stood round, like open presses, that shawed the dead in their last dresses; and, by some devilish cantraip sleight, each in its cauld hand held a light: by which heroic Tam was able to note upon the haly table, a murderer's banes, in gibbet-airns; twa span-lang, wee, unchristened bairns; a thief new-cutted frae a rape—wi' his last gasp his gab did gape; five tomahawks wi' bluid red-rusted; five scymitars wi' murder crusted; seven gallows pins; three hangman's whittles; a raw o' weel-sealed Doctor's bottles; a garter which a babe had strangled; a knife a father's throat had mangled—whom his ain son o' life bereft—the grey hairs yet stack to the heft; wi' mair of horrible and awfu', which even to name wad be unlawfu'.

"Three Lawyers' tongues, turned inside out, wi' lies seamed like a beggar's clout; three Priests' hearts, rotten, black as muck, lay stinking, vile, in every neuk.

"As Tammie glowred, amazed, and curious, the mirth and fun grew fast and furious; the piper loud and louder blew, the dancers quick and quicker flew, they reeled, they set, they crossed, they cleekit, till ilka carlin swat and reekit, and coost her duddies to the wark, and linket at it in her sark!

"Now Tam, O Tam! had thae been queans, a' plump and strapping in their teens! Their sarks, instead o' creeshie flannen, been snaw-white seventeen hunder linen!— Thir breeks o' mine, my only pair, that ance were plush, o' guid blue hair, I wad hae gi'en them off my hurdies for ae blink o' the bonnie burdies!

"But withered beldams, auld and droll, rigwoodie hags wad spean a foal, louping and flinging on a crummock, I wonder did na turn thy stomach!

"But Tam kend what was what fu' brawly: there was ae winsome wench and wawly, that night enlisted in the core, lang after kend on Carrick shore (for mony a beast to dead she shot, an' perished mony a bonnie boat, and shook baith meikle corn and bear, and kept the country-side in fear). Her cutty sark, o' Paisley harn, that while a lassie she had worn, in longitude though sorely scanty, it was her best, and she was vauntie. . . Ah! little thought thy reverend grannie, that sark she coft for her wee Nannie, wi' twa pund Scots ('twas a' her riches), wad ever graced a dance of witches!

"But here my Muse her wing maun cour, sic flights are far beyond her power: to sing how Nannie lap and flang (a souple jad she was and strang), and how Tam stood like ane bewitched, and thought his very een enriched; even Satan glowred, and fidged fu' fain, and hotched and blew wi' might and main; till first ae caper, syne anither, Tam tint his reason

C.B.W.   R

a'thegither, and roars out: ' Weel done, Cutty-sark!' And in an instant all was dark; and scarcely had he Maggie rallied, when out the hellish legion sallied.

"As bees bizz out wi' angry fyke, when plundering herds assail their byke; as open pussie's mortal foes, when, pop! she starts before their nose; as eager runs the market crowd, when ' Catch the thief!' resounds aloud: so Maggie runs, the witches follow, wi' mony an eldritch skriech and holow.

"Ah, Tam! Ah Tam! thou'll get thy fairin'! in hell they'll roast thee like a herrin'! In vain thy Kate awaits thy comin'! Kate soon will be a woefu' woman! Now, do thy speedy utmost, Meg, and win the key-stane of the brig; there, at them thou thy tail may toss, a running stream they darena cross! But ere the key-stane she could make, the fient a tail she had to shake; for Nannie, far before the rest, hard upon noble Maggie pressed, and flew at Tam wi' furious ettle; but little wist she Maggie's mettle! Ae spring brought off her master hale, but left behind her ain grey tail: the carlin claught her by the rump, and left poor Maggie scarce a stump.

"Now, wha this tale o' truth shall read, ilk man, and, mother's son, take heed: whene'er to drink you are inclined or cutty sarks run in your mind, think! ye may buy the joys o'er dear: remember Tam o' Shanter's meare."

The reading had generated terrific excitement. Two or three times Fanny had skirled and both Nelly and Nancy had made queer strangled noises. Young Robert had not comprehended anything—but he had caught the dramatic impact of his father's voice and had stared at him in a wide fixed-eyed wonderment.

And now it was over and Adam Armour was on his feet shaking the Bard's hand.

"By God, sir: that's the greatest thing I ever heard. I was on Maggie's back a' the time——"

"So was I!"

"So was I!"

It seemed they'd all been on Maggie's back. . . But the

Bard had got from them all the reaction he wanted, all the reaction he could absorb. He thanked them in good-humoured banter and chased them off to bed. He was exhausted. He sank into his elbow chair and wiped the sweat from his face. He had never doubted the success of his tale; but he knew now from this fireside reception that it was even more successful than he had first thought.

Jean beamed at him across the fireside.

"If I havena said ocht till noo, Rab, it's because I'm just owercam . . . my heart—almost like a pain. I'm mair nor proud o' you. It's just beyond me how you do it. And it's a' doon sae easy and naturally——"

"Weel, I'm proud that you liked it, Jean. . . Aye, and I think they a' liked it."

"Aye, they liked it: they'll be dreaming aboot it a' nicht. Even Robbie kent there was something byornar in the air."

"I believe the wee deil did, for his een never left me the whole time. . . What aboot pouring me a dram, lass? I'm tired and I'm dry."

"Aye, fegs, I'll pour you a drink the nicht, Rab, for you richly deserve it. My, I only wish the Captain had been here to hear you. You'd hae heard the roars o' him up at the Isle. . . There you are noo—that'll help you—that's some o' the guid stuff Mr. Tennant sent you."

They sat by the dying fire and talked away quietly, the Bard well satisfied with his day's work and Jean warm with pride in his greatness—the greatness of his poetry and the greatness of his personality. And she felt again how blessed she was to be the wife of such a man.

And indeed a happier and more contented man and wife seldom went to bed as they did that night.

The barn owls from Dalswinton ruin hooted softly from his steading roof and the Nith from her boulder-bed crooned softly to the stars.

THE PRISON WITH GOLDEN BARS

Copies of *Tam* were sent far and near and were everywhere received with acclamation. *Tam* was definitely rated as the Bard's masterpiece, and as something unique in poetic literature. True, Mrs. Dunlop was offended at the picture of the too-scantily-clad Nannie; but he had never paid much attention to his Ayrshire patroness's peculiar puritanical strictures.

The general acceptance of *Tam* gratified the delighted Bard; but he began to resent the implication that he had never written anything memorable before *Tam*. So he began, in an instinctive self-defence, to refer to his tale as "my standard performance in that manner."

But the crest of the creative urge that produced *Tam* did not exhaust itself: it surged into the fourth volume for Johnson's *Museum* and other pieces, so that his literary output was strong and continuous.

And all this though he was busy with his Excise work and spent an odd night in Dumfries with Anna. . .

Mrs. Hyslop came to him one night for what she called a "private word" with him.

"Weel," she began, "I dinna think there can be ony doubt noo, Robert. A'body'll soon ken what condition Anne's in."

"I suppose so. . . Still, she's no' what you'd ca' showing yet."

"Whaur's thae big een o' yours? Of course she's showing —she's damn near six months on the road."

"Hardly that, Bess, surely——"

"We'll no' argue for a day or twa. Hae the pair o' you ony plans made?"

"I havena spoken to Jean yet. Naturally I'm no' looking forward to that! I could think o' a more pleasant topic to discuss wi' a wife. It looks as if they're to be lying-in about the same date. . . But I think the upshot'll be that Anna's bairn will come to Ellisland."

"You're asking mair frae Jean than ony woman has a right to be asked."

"Aye; but Jean's no' just ony woman: Jean's a woman in ten thousand—indeed, she's no' unlike yoursel' in that respect. . . I think Anna's made up her mind to go through to her sister in Leith to have the bairn."

"That'll be a'richt if her sister agrees."

"D'you think she will?"

"I'll put in a word for Anne, of coorse—and if Jean decides to tak' the bairn——"

"It's understood that I'll stand a' the expense o' the affair—and I hope to see Anna richt for a twelvemonth. At least I'll be able to keep her frae begging aff onybody for that time. By then something will maybe turn up for her."

"I canna understand you, Robert. You maun love Anne."

"Did you ever doubt that?"

"But you love Jean?"

"I love Jean mair than I've ever loved a lass and I love her mair than Anna; but I still love Anna."

"So you can love mair than one lass at a time?"

"And since when has that become remarkable? Listen, guidwife: even your Old Testament is filled wi' examples. But because the Lord allowed the Jews mair than one wife you think nothing about it. That was a long time ago and doubtless an auld wives' tale at that—maybe! But because the British constitution says a man can only hae one wife, then twa's a cardinal sin and an abomination in the eyes o' the Lord—though what cam' ower the eyes o' the Lord since the Old Testament, history, along wi' religion, is silent. Oh, a man can hae a wife and a mistress—twa or three or a dozen mistresses. But he canna love twa women at the same time— Oh no! Damn it, wife, I'm no' to be catechised in this matter. I'll fulfil my obligations to Jean and the bairns and I'll fulfil the only obligation I hae to Anna: I'll provide for and bring up her bairn—somehow. Mair I canna dae. Anna's nae sweet innocent lass seduced by a blackguard. Anna's a' the woman she'll ever be. Life threw us thegither—no' on ony houghma-gandie ploy but wi' a ruthlessness I hae never before ex-perienced. Neither o' us had ony chance to escape. I blame naebody—and I'm far frae blaming mysel'. But Anna'll get ower it—and sae will I—in time! It's the bairn that matters."

"You'd think you really wanted this bairn!"

"Of course I want it—noo that it's on the way! I'm its father. D'you expect me to turn my back on it? Is it ony the waur o' being love-begotten? It wasna begotten in a ditch to be delivered in a ditch and to die in a ditch——"

"You wouldna get angry wi' me, Robert?"

"No: I couldna get angry wi' you, Bess. You were more than understanding . . . and you've been kindness itsel' to Anna and me——"

"Aye . . . I've aided and abetted you—that's what I've done. But I'm like you, Robert: I canna see ony real sin in it. I ken how much Anne loves you—and I ken how you've doted on her."

"I tell you we'd nae choice in the matter——"

"Maybe that was it. It just had to be. . . William says he's taking nothing to dae wi' it one way or the other—and he says it'll mak' nae difference atween you and him. But he says he's sorry for Jean's sake. And we baith think a lot o' Jean. . . I was thinking, Robert—are you listening? I was thinking that if Anne gaed awa' afore the end o' the year there's naebody need ken what's happened—and there'll be nae talk aboot the Toon. The less scandal the better—d'you agree?"

"Yes: I agree. Though I could see the Toon and a' its scandal in hell. . . I'm damned scant o' cash the noo. But I've ten yellow Geordies here—d'you think that would see Anna through the birth?"

"Ten would be ample, Robert. She's no' leaving the Globe penniless."

"There'll be more when I can get more—but that's a'
I can scrape thegither now. And, by God, wife, but I loathe
this damned haggling huxtering side o' things. Maybe poets
and puir folk should be gelded——"

"Noo, noo, Robert: I ken you're bitter and I ken how
hard things are wi' you. But William and me hae a gey
struggle oursel's. . . But I've upset you and you writing. . .
D'you want to see Anne?"

"Later, wife. I've wark to dae."

So the night came in gloomy December when the Bard
and Anna said good-bye.

Anna wept a little; but she was wonderfully composed.

"I'm only sorry I'll need to part wi' my bairn——"

"You'll be parting wi' him to the father."

"It'll maybe no' be a boy."

"The sex'll no' matter."

"I wouldna part wi' my bairn to onybody but you; and
I'll need to be sure that your wife'll be guid to it—and mak'
nae difference atween it and her ain."

"I'll be the guarantee o' that: you can surely trust me?"

"Aye . . . I can trust you. I don't suppose we'll see much
o' ane anither again?"

"That we canna tell. God kens where I'll end up wi' the
Excise. The Port o' Leith's no' an impossibility."

"I'll aey want to ken how my bairn's doing——"

"You're going wi' a heavy heart, lass——"

"Wad you want me licht-hearted, Robert? What d'you
expect? But I've tellt you ower and ower again I've nae
regrets. To hell wi' my folks and everybody but you and me
and the bairn: I'll see this through if I've to dee in the daeing
o' it." She smiled wanly. "And you never ken—maybe I'll
be back for another ane!"

"God! you've a great spirit, lass."

"I dinna think we'll ever forget ane anither. It's been

wonderful . . . in this room. Promise me you'll no' bring anither lass to this bed!"

"For Godsake, Anna——"

"No: I tak' that back. But if you dae meet in wi' onybody to tak' my place——"

He silenced her with a kiss.

"Robert . . . I want to remember this our last nicht——"

Suddenly Anna abandoned herself on him and kissed him with such a pent-up emotional and physical intensity that the blood went drumming in his ears and the darkness of the room was prisoned with gold bars and flecked with crimson and the night swayed among the stars.

Part Four

THE END OF THE DREAM

LETTERS

THE YEAR of 1791 began badly for the Bard. His first patron, James Cunningham, Earl of Glencairn, died. Pegasus stumbled and, in falling, the Bard's arm broke.

He got home in agony to find Mrs. Dunlop's "poetical dairymaid" Jenny Little calling on him.

He bit down his pain, sent a boy to Dumfries for Dr. James Mundell and received Jenny politely.

But by nightfall the pain was so excruciating that Mundell prescribed a stiff dosage of laudanum and suggested that he take whatever rest he could in his chair.

The Bard cursed and fretted and fumed at his bad luck; but there was nothing for it: he had to rest his arm the best way he could and content himself by the fire-side.

By the end of February his arm was well enough to wield the pen; and he had gotten himself a canny black mare and walked her out and in to Dumfries and sometimes attempted an even cannier canter. Fortunately Collector Mitchell sympathised with him, as the accident had occurred in the course of his duties.

He found his greatest relief in writing to his friends; and he had much to write about.

To his London correspondent Dr. Moore, the Anglo-Scots author and friend of Mrs. Dunlop, he wrote:

28th FEBRUARY, 1791

I do not know, Sir, whether you are a Subscriber to Grose's *Antiquities of Scotland*. If you are, the inclosed poem will not be altogether new to you. Captain Grose did me the favour to send me a dozen copies of the Proof-sheet, of which this is one. Should you have read the piece before, still this will answer the principal end I have in view: it will give me another opportunity of thanking you for all your goodness to the rustic Bard; and also of shewing you, that the abilities you have been pleased to commend and patronise are still employed in the way you wish.

The Elegy on Captain Henderson, is a tribute to the memory of a Man I loved much. Poets have in this the same advantage as Roman Catholics; they can be of service to their Friends after thay have passed that bourne where all other kindness ceases to be of any avail. Whether after all, either the one or the other be of any real service to the Dead is, I fear, very problematical; but I am sure they are highly gratifying to the Living: and as a very orthodox text, I forget where, in Scripture, says "Whatsoever is not of faith, is sin;"— so, say I, Whatsoever is not detrimental to Society and is of positive Enjoyment, is of God the Giver of all good things, and ought to be received and enjoyed by His creatures with thankful delight. As almost all my Religious tenets originate from my heart, I am wonderfully pleased with the idea that I can still keep up a tender intercourse with the dearly beloved Friend, or still more dearly beloved Mistress, who is gone to the world of Spirits.

The Ballad on Queen Mary, was begun while I was busy with Percy's *Reliques of English Poetry*. . . What a rocky-hearted, perfidious Succubus was that Queen Elizabeth! Judas Iscariot was a sad dog to be sure, but still his demerits shrink to insignificance, compared with the doings of the infernal Bess Tudor. Judas did not know, at least was by no means sure, what or who that Master was; his turpitude was simply, betraying a worthy man who had ever been a good Master to him: a degree of turpitude which has ever been outdone by many of his kind since. Iscariot, poor wretch, was a man of nothing at all per Annum, and by consequence, thirty pieces of silver was a very serious temptation to *him,* but, to give but one instance, the Duke of Queensberry, the other day, just played the same trick to *his* kind Master, tho' His Grace is a man of thirty thousand a year, and come to that imbecile period of life when no temptation but Avarice can be supposed to affect him.

I have just read over, once more of many times, your *Zelucco*. I marked with my pencil, as I went along every passage that pleased me particularly above the rest, and one or two I think, which with humble deference I am disposed to think unequal to the merit of the Book. I have sometimes thought to transcribe these marked passages, or at least so much of them as to point where they are, and send them to you. Original strokes, that strongly depict the human heart is your and Fielding's province beyond any other Novelist, I have ever perused. Richardson indeed might perhaps be excepted; but unhappily, his Dramatis personae are beings of some other world; and however they may captivate the unexperienced, romantic fancy of a boy or a girl, they will ever, in proportion as we have made human nature our study, disgust our riper minds.

As to my private concerns, I am going on, a mighty Tax-gatherer before the lord, and have lately had the interest to get myself ranked on the list of Excise as a Supervisor. I am not yet employed as such, but in a few years I will fall into the file of Supervisorship by seniority. I have had an immense loss in the death of the Earl of Glencairn; the Patron from whom all my fame and good fortune took its rise. Independent of my grateful attachment to him, which was indeed so strong that it pervaded my very soul, and was entwined with the thread of my existence; so soon as the Prince's friends had got in, (and every dog you know has his day) my getting forward in the Excise would have been an easier business than otherwise it will be. Though this was a consummation devoutly to be wished, yet, thank Heaven, I can live and rhyme, as I am; and as to my boys, poor, little fellows! if I cannot place them on as high an elevation in life, as I could wish; I shall, if I am favoured so much of the Disposer of events as to see that period, fix them on as broad and independent basis as possible. Among the many wise adages which have been treasured by our Scottish Ancestors, this is one of the best —"Better be the head o' the Commonalty, as the tail o' the Gentry."

To Alexander Dalziel, the Glencairn factor, he wrote:

I have taken the liberty to frank this letter to you, as it incloses an idle Poem of mine, which I send you; and God knows you may perhaps pay dear enough for it if you read it through. Not that this is my own opinion; but an Author, by the time he has composed and corrected his work, has quite poured away all his powers of critical discrimination.

I can easily guess from my own heart what you have felt on a late most melancholy event. God knows what I have suffered, at the loss of my best Friend, my first, my dearest Patron and Benefactor; the man to whom I owe all that I am and have! I am gone into mourning for him, and with more sincerity of grief than I fear some will, who by Nature's ties ought to feel on the occasion.

I will be exceedingly obliged to you indeed, to let me know the news of the Noble Family, how the poor Mother and the two sisters support their loss. I had a packet of Poetic bagatelles ready to send to Lady Betty, when I saw the fatal tidings in the Newspaper. I see by the same channel that the honoured Remains of my noble Patron are designed to be brought to the Family's Burial place. Dare I trouble you to let me know privately before the day of interment, that I may cross the country and steal among the crowd, to pay a tear to the last sight of my ever-revered Benefactor? It will oblige me beyond expression. . .

LAMENT for JAMES EARL OF GLENCAIRN

The wind blew hollow frae the hills;
    By fits the sun's departing beam
Looked on the fading yellow woods,
    That waved o'er Lugar's winding stream.

Beneath a craigy steep a Bard,
 Laden with years and meikle pain,
In loud lament bewailed his lord,
 Whom Death had all untimely ta'en.

He leaned him to an ancient aik,
 Whose trunk was mouldering down with years;
His locks were bleachèd white with time,
 His hoary cheek was wet wi' tears;
And as he touched his trembling harp,
 And as he tuned his doleful sang,
The winds, lamenting through their caves,
 To echo bore the notes alang:—

' Ye scattered birds that faintly sing,
 The reliques of the vernal quire!
Ye woods that shed on a' the winds
 The honours of the agèd year!
A few short months, and, glad and gay,
 Again ye'll charm the ear and e'e;
But nocht in all revolving time
 Can gladness bring again to me.

' I am a bending agèd tree
 That long has stood the wind and rain;
But now has come a cruel blast,
 And my last hold of earth is gane;
Nae leaf o' mine shall greet the spring,
 Nae simmer sun exalt my bloom;
But I maun lie before the storm,
 And ithers plant them in my room.

' I've seen sae mony changefu' years,
 On earth I am a stranger grown:
I wander in the ways of men,
 Alike unknowing and unknown:

Unheard, unpitied, unrelieved,
  I bear alane my lade o' care;
For silent, low, on beds of dust,
  Lie a' that would my sorrows share.

' And last (the sum of a' my griefs!)
  My noble master lies in clay;
The flower amang our barons bold,
  His country's pride, his country's stay:
In weary being now I pine,
  For a' the life of life is dead,
And hope has left my agèd ken,
  On forward wing for ever fled.

' Awake thy last sad voice, my harp!
  The voice of woe and wild despair!
Awake, resound thy latest lay,
  Then sleep in silence evermair!
And thou, my last, best, only friend,
  That fillest an untimely tomb,
Accept this tribute from the Bard
  Thou brought from Fortune's mirkest gloom.

' In poverty's low barren vale
  Thick mists obscure involved me round;
Though oft I turned the wistful eye,
  Nae ray of fame was to be found;
Thou found'st me, like the morning sun
  That melts the fogs in limpid air:
The friendless Bard and rustic song
  Became alike thy fostering care.

' O, why has Worth so short a date,
  While villains ripen grey with time!
Must thou, the noble, gen'rous, great,
  Fall in bold manhood's hardy prime?

Why did I live to see that day,
    A day to me so full of woe?
O, had I met the mortal shaft
    Which laid my benefactor low!

' The bridegroom may forget the bride
    Was made his wedded wife yestreen;
The monarch may forget the crown
    That on his head an hour has been;
The mother may forget the child
    That smiles sae sweetly on her knee;
But I'll remember thee, Glencairn,
    And a' that thou hast done for me! '

To his old friend Peter Hill, the Edinburgh bookseller, he wrote:

I shall say nothing at all to your mad present. You have long and often been of important service to me, and I suppose you mean to go on conferring obligations until I shall not be able to lift up my face before you. In the meantime, as Sir Roger de Coverley, because it happened to be a cold day in which he made his will, ordered his servants, Great Coats, for mourning, so because I have been this week plagued with an indigestion, I have sent you by the Carrier a fine old ewe-milk Cheese.

Indigestion is the devil: nay, 'tis the devil and all. It besets a man in every one of his senses. I lose my appetite at the sight of successful Knavery; sicken to loathing at the noise and nonsense of self-important Folly. When the hollow-hearted wretch takes me by the hand, the feeling spoils my dinner; the proud man's wine so offends my palate that it chokes me in the gullet; and the *pulvilis'd*, feathered, pert coxcomb is so horrible in my nostril that my stomach turns.

If ever you have any of these disagreeable sensations, let me prescribe for you, Patience, and a bit of my Cheese. I know that you are no niggard of your good things among your friends, and some of them are in much need of a slice. There in my eye is our friend Smellie; a man positively of the first abilities and greatest strength of mind, as well as one of the best hearts and keenest wits that I have ever met with; when you see him, as, alas! he too often is, smarting at the pinch of distressful circumstance aggravated by the sneer of contumelious greatness—a bit of my cheese alone will not cure him, but if you add a tankard of Brown Stout and superadd a magnum of right Oporto, you will see his sorrows vanish like the morning mist before the summer sun.

Candlish, the earliest friend except my only brother that I have on earth, and one of the worthiest fellows that ever any man called by the name of Friend, if a luncheon of my cheese would help to rid him of some of his superabundant Modesty, you would do well to give it him.

David Ramsay with his *Courant* comes, too, across my recollection, and I beg you will help him largely from the said ewe-milk cheese, to enable him to digest those damned bedaubing paragraphs with which he is eternally larding the lean characters of certain Great Men in a certain Great Town. I grant you the periods are very well turned; so, a fresh egg is a very good thing, but when thrown at a man in a pillory it does not at all improve his figure, not to mention the irreparable loss of the egg.

My facetious little friend, Colonel Dunbar, I would wish also to be a partaker; not to digest his spleen for that he laughs off, but to digest his last night's wine at the last field-day of the Crochallan corps.

Among our common friends, I must not forget one of the dearest of them, Cunningham. The brutality, insolence, and selfishness of a world unworthy of having such a fellow as he in it, I know sticks in his stomach, and if you can help him to any thing that will make him a little easier on that score, it will be very obliging.

As to honest John Sommerville, he is such a contented happy man that I know not what can annoy him, except perhaps he may not have got the better of a parcel of modest anecdotes which a certain Poet gave him one night at supper, the last time the said Poet was in town.

Though I have mentioned so many men of Law, I shall have nothing to do with them professedly—the Faculty are beyond my prescription— As to their *Clients*, that is another thing; God knows they have much to Digest!!!

The Clergy, I pass by—their profundity of erudition, and the liberality of sentiment; their total want of Pride, and their Detestation of Hypocrisy, are so proverbally notorious, as to place them far, far above either my Praise or Censure.

I was going to mention a man of worth whom I have the honour to call Friend, the Laird of Craigdarroch; but I have spoken to the landlord of the King's Arms Inn here, to have at the next County Meeting, a large ewe-milk cheese on the table, for the benefit of the Dumfriesshire Whigs, to enable them to digest the Duke of Queenberry's late political conduct.

I have just this moment an opportunity of a private hand to Edinburgh, as perhaps you would not Digest double Postage. So, God bless you. . .

And finally to Mrs. Dunlop he wrote, two days after Jean had given birth to his third son, William Nicol Burns:

ELLISLAND, 11th April, 1791

I am once more able, my honoured friend, to return you with my own hand, thanks for the many instances of your friendship and particularly for your kind anxiety in this last disaster that my evil genius had in store for me. However, life is chequered, joy and sorrow, for on Saturday morning last Mrs. Burns made me a present of a fine boy, rather stouter but not so handsome as your God-son at his time of life was. Indeed I look on your little Namesake to be my chef d'oeuvre in that species of manufacture, as I look on *Tam o' Shanter* to be my standard performance in the Poetical line. 'Tis true, both the one and the other discover a spice of roguish waggery that might perhaps be as well spared; but then they also shew in my opinion a force of genius and a finishing polish that I despair of ever excelling. Mrs. Burns is getting stout again, and laid as lustily about her today at Breakfast as a Reaper from the corn-ridge. That is the peculiar privilege and blessing of our hale, sprightly damsels, that are bred among the Hay and Heather. We cannot hope for that highly polished mind, that charming delicacy of soul, which is found among the Female world in the more elevated stations of life, which is certainly by far the most bewitching charm in the famous cestus of Venus. It is indeed such an inestimable treasure, that, where it can be had in its native heavenly purity, unstained by some one or other of the many shades of affection, and unalloyed by some one or other of the many species of caprice, I declare to Heaven I would think it cheaply purchased at the expense of every other earthly good! But as this angelic creature is I am afraid extremely rare in any station and rank of life, and totally denied to such a humble one as mine; we meaner mortals must put up with the next rank of female excellence— as fine a figure and face we can produce as any rank of life whatever; rustic, native grace; unaffected modesty, and unsullied purity; Nature's mother-wit and the rudiments of Taste; a simplicity of soul, unsuspicious of, because unacquainted with, the crooked ways of a selfish, interested, disingenuous world; and the dearest charm of all the rest, a yielding sweetness of disposition and a generous warmth of heart, grateful for love on our part, and ardently glowing with a more than equal return; these, with a healthy frame, sound, vigorous constitution, which your higher ranks can scarcely ever hope to enjoy, are the charms of lovely woman in my humble walk of life. . .

THE GREATNESS OF BONNIE JEAN

Jean had made an unusually quick recovery and her recoveries had never been slow. She was very happy.

But Anna had given birth to a daughter, Elizabeth, eight days before Jean, and she too was doing well.

The Bard waited till he was certain Jean had made a complete recovery and then one night he broke the news. Jean saw that there was something worrying him.

"What's worrying you, Rab?"

"Plenty, Jean. I've news for you, lass; news no' o' the best for you. I've hid it from you till I was sure you could bear up to it. You ken Bess Hyslop's niece that was at the Globe——?"

Jean knew what was coming and she turned away her gaze from him, for his eyes were tortured.

"—weel, eight days afore William was born she had a lass to me. . . I confess I'm at a loss to account to you how it happened. Only I hae a high regard for the mither and I hae nae wish to deny her bairn is mine. . . I'm no' for begging your forgiveness, Jean—the only begging there was to dae should hae been done long afore this. There's nae excuse, Jean, but this: I didna seek the lass nor did the lass seek me: it just happened! There was a while I was damn-near crazed—I certainly wasna responsible for my actions or anywhaur near responsible.

"But the lass was never left in ony doubt as to where my love and affection and responsibility lay. . . I riskèd the soul and she ventured the body.

"Now she's tholed her assize and that's that chapter finished. But—the bairn remains. I want to plead for her, Jean: beg on my bended knees if necessary——"

Jean turned her head and raised her eyes.

"The bairn can come here—I'll nurse it what I can——"

"Jean——"

"But first—before I mak' up my mind finally I want to see the mither and her bairn. I want to see the mither and I want a word wi' her. . . As for you, Rab—maybe you should hae had twa wives—or half-a-dizzen. I jaloused as much. I kent there was something gaun on last spring. But I didna juist think you were running frae one to the other o' us. . . What dae the Hyslops think o' you noo? What am I to tell Nancy?"

"The Hyslops hae made nae difference; and I'll tell Nancy mysel'——"

"No . . . I'll tell her. How much o' the truth dae you want her to ken?"

"Nae mair than that I'm the faither."

"And that Bess Hyslop's niece is the mither?"

"I suppose sae."

"As far as the others are concerned, it's just a neebor's bairn whase mither died. There's nae need for any other body to ken. Or does the whole o' Dumfries ken?"

"Naebody but the Hyslops."

"No' that it matters, I suppose—except for the bairn *and* your ain bairns."

"Jean: if the mither had been some sort o' a whore or I'd been whoring after her, I'd never hae mentioned this to you—far less would I hae asked you to let the bairn come into our hoose——"

"Weel . . . I'll see what the mither's like—only you'll better tell her to come through wi' the bairn as soon as she can—I've ower much milk on me the now. There's plenty for baith."

"I was never verra guid at makin' promises, Jean; and maybe I was never verra guid at keeping such promises as I did mak'. But you'll never be asked to dae the like again. You've humbled me inside—deep, deep inside me wi' gratitude to you and I ken now as I've had mony an occasion to ken that I never was fit to be your husband."

"I'm no' excusing you in ony way, Rab. But I canna bear to hear you talk like that. And I ken fine—naebody better—that I hae nae richt to feel hurt and heart-sair. I've kent frae the beginning that I had nae mair than a richt to a share in you—and I dinna doubt that I've had the lion's share. Now we're baith gey sick and sorry for oursel's. . . Sae you'll better come to your bed and we'll say nae mair about it."

Mrs. Hyslop arranged for Anna and her daughter to see Jean.

Nancy made them a cup of tea and they talked for some time without ever talking about anything in particular. Everybody except Jean was very ill-at-ease; and Jean was in consummate command of the situation.

Then she took Anna aside into the bedroom.

"Weel, my lassie: you ken what it's like to be a mither' without a husband. . . I hope you hadna too sair a time? Sit doon. Mr. Burns said you were nae kind o' a whore and I can see you're no'. Weel, dinna think I'm here to catechise you. I married Mr. Burns on his word and his written declaration. But even though he hadna done that, I'd hae been proud o' his bairns for a' that—and I had twins. Now, there's only one condition I hae to mak' to you. I want you to tell me why you want quit o' your bairn."

"But I dinna want quit o' my bairn, Mistress Burns. It's me that'll pey a' my days for letting her go. Only—what kind o' life can I offer her? I want to dae my best for her—and I wadna let her come to onybody but you. I've done you a big wrong, Mistress Burns—I ken that noo. But I dinna want you to think noo or ever that your man was to blame——"

"And were you to blame?"

"Were you, Mistress—when you first kent him? Could you hae helped yoursel'—gin even you had wanted to help yoursel'? Did you ken what was for happening to you *before* it happened? And when it had happened had you ony regrets? I ken I should feel a gey sma' woman in your presence and maybe I dae. But I dinna want you to think that what happened between your man and me could hae happened wi' ony ither man—or could happen again wi' ony ither man."

"You've nae regrets then?"

"Aye, I've regrets. I can never be Mistress Burns—and I can never be the mither o' his bairn—and it'll only be me that'll ken I was the mither. But I'm nae slut and never was; and before I leave you my dochter I want a promise frae you, Mistress."

"If it's the kind o' promise I should mak' then I'll mak' it."

"I want you to promise that my lassie'll never be made to feel like ony step-bairn. That's a' I really ask, Mistress: that you'll treat her as you would your ain. Ony fau't there is is mine: no' hers."

"I'll gie you that promise richt willingly, my lass—and I'm richt glad and relieved that you've asked me. In fact that's the main reason I sent for you. I told mysel' that if I couldna bring mysel' to do just what you're asking, I wadna bind mysel' to mither it at a'. Now: you mauna break your heart aboot this—and you'll need to forget that you ever had a bairn—and you ken that if I'm to bring up the lass you canna come back afterhand—you canna even think o' such a thing. And your lass'll never ken I'm no' her mither—at least frae me. . . You maun hae been gey fond o' Mr. Burns too."

"He was the only man I ever kent and I canna see how I'll ever thole to ken anither. And mind you I couldna bear to see him again—I'm feared I'd break doon."

"Weel, weel . . . life's a gey queer mixty-maxty. But you'll get ower a' this. And I'm sure you'll fa' in wi' a decent-like man that'll mak' a guid husband to you yet. . . Will you hae bother getting rid o' your milk?"

"I havena that much—for a' I was aey big breasted."

"Try some glauber salts—and bind your breasts ticht wi' a broad length o' linen——"

With great tact and much success Jean led the talk into a different channel. The sweetness of her nature and the depth of her humanity won Anna completely, and when she came to place her daughter into Jean's arms at parting she was able to smile above her tears.

When they were gone Nancy said: "She's affa like our Robin, Jean—but she's a sweet wee lass. But God'll hae a special blessing for you, Jean Armour: there'll be a blessing on you a' your days. That's mair nor I can hope for *him*."

"Now, Nancy, you promised me! Never let me hear you say an ill word aboot Rab."

"I—I just canna help it, Jean. I'll try and no' show him what I think o' him. Twa or three times I've felt I'd like to tak' my hands to him. Wha he tak's it aff I dinna ken—he's the only one like that in the family."

"I wouldna like you and me to fa' out aboot this, Nancy. But I'm telling you I'll no' stand for ony talk about Rab. There'll be nae mair mention o' this in this hoose as lang as I'm aboot the floor-head. I'm sorry, Nancy; but I maun insist."

"Oh weel: I suppose I'm in the wrang as usual. But why he should get aff Scot-free——"

Jean was unbuttoning her bodice.

"Hand me ower the bairn: the puir wee lamb's bound to be hungry."

Nancy did so without another word. She sat opposite Jean and watched how Elizabeth took to her new mother; but Jean was too experienced and too natural a mother to have any difficulty; and Elizabeth liked the flavour of her new feed. And as she watched, Nancy was conscious of a strange maternal pain in her own breasts and a strange longing in her heart.

And yet she marvelled too at Jean's strange magnanimity —nursing so kindly and contentedly the child another woman had borne to her husband. There wasn't another woman who would have acted so generously. Her love for Robin must be a terrible love when she could do that for him. . .

There was a subtle and profound change in the relationship between the Bard and his wife. Though she did not want it so, Jean was morally ascendant. But what Jean could not explain to anyone in words, not even to her husband, was her deep feeling that he must have had a great faith in her to come to her so downrightly in his trouble and to hide nothing. And there was a something about Anna Park too: there was character and dignity and courage about the lass forbye her fresh golden beauty—and yet her bairn was as black as Rab and more like him in feature and expression than any child she had borne him (though she hoped no other body would notice that).

The trouble was that the Bard—though he resolutely refused to blame himself for what had happened—had nothing but a boundless admiration for Jean. It was an admiration that was born of deep respect and, for the moment at least, the quality of this respect erected itself as a disturbing barrier between him and her. He was self-conscious in her presence and constrainedly deferential in his manners.

Apart from this relationship with Jean, he was secretly proud of Anna's child. He knew she was like him and he was certain that she would grow up dark and comely. But in conversation with everyone his remarks were formal and, for him, unnaturally colourless.

The problem of Anna's child had been solved; but it was going to take some time to solve the problems the child brought with her to Ellisland.

THE LASS WITH THE LINT-WHITE LOCKS

Spring came to Nithsdale, in sun and rain, even as it had come across the Ayrshire years; but now the Nith was at his door with the broom golden on its banks and the mavis's song close by the windows so that its singing fell across the supper table with the lengthening shadows.

And there were lambs, calves, laying hens, the mare heavy with foal and a brown and golden rooster crowing defiance on the midden heap. And ducks, in a busy conversational clamour, waddling down to the Nith while the amorous drake, drilling their ranks, cursed them roundly for a lazy corps of gossip-mongers.

It was spring again. A spring that had seemed long in coming. The Bard rejoiced in it. For now everything was awakened out of the static melancholy of the dank drab unfortunate winter. And the corn was brairded and the grass was coming green.

As the days lengthened and the air grew warmer he felt invigorated. There was a new jauntiness to his step and a healthier glow in his eyes and his appetite was mightily improved. The strain and worry attending the coming of William Nicol and Anna's Elizabeth had passed over. Everything seemed to be accepted.

It was a fine day and he decided to pay a professional and personal visit to Kemys Hall, in the parish of Kirkmahoe, and see the Lorimers.

The Nith was low; so he directed his horse downstream to the Sandbed ford, passed the time of day with John Cunningham who farmed there, and then moved across the mile and a

bit to the farm that lay handy half-way between the villages
of Dunscore and Kirkmahoe on the Dumfries road.

William Lorimer was taking things easy too, for the back
of the spring's work was broken and it was a natural time to
relax. And Mr. and Mrs. Lorimer liked to relax—within easy
reach of the bottle.

The Bard rode into the court at the back of the house and
found them in good fettle. The farmer was enjoying a pipe
in the warm sun and his wife was busy plucking a hen.

"Well, you randy!" cried Lorimer, "are you here official?"

"That, as well, Willie."

"Remount then and get to hell frae Kemys Ha': we dinna
want you."

"Oh, it's nae pleasure to check your stock—though it's
aey a comfort to hae a bit crack wi' the guidwife."

"Thank you, Rab. . . I've a drap of decent stuff—wad you
fancy a gill?"

"For Godsake, wife! No: it's ower early i' the day for
gills——"

"On you go, wife, and gie the puir bluidy gauger a gill:
he'll maybe no' be sae sharp wi' his quill later on. I'd gie a lot
to see you fu', Burns."

"Ah, but Rab's no' like some gaugers we've kent."

"I was forgettin'. Weel: bring me a gill and I'll see if I
canna chaw him into mair social habits. Sit doon, damn you,
and dinna haud the sun aff me. Hell: we get little enough.
How's Jean?"

"Doing fine—*and* the bairns."

"That's grand."

"And you?"

"Oh, we're fine for the time o' year—a' things considered.
Jeannie's ben the hoose somewhaur. I suppose you'll be wanting to see her?"

"Aye . . . I'm workin' on a sang the noo."

"Anither one?"

"She makes a perfect model, Willie—and I maun hae a model for my sangs."

"Weel: since you think Jeannie's your model. . . D'you aey need a model?"

"That's the way I compose. I put myself on the regimen of admiring a fine lass and—gin I've a fine tune needing words —the song's damn-near finished before I right begin."

"Easy wark being a poet."

"Easy enough—when you've the woman and the tune."

"God, there's plenty women—I canna say for the tunes."

"Aye—but what kind o' women?"

"Noo look here, Robert: you dinna mean to sit there on this fine May morning and tell me that walking doon by the Duncow burn yonder wi' our Jeannie mak's you write a sang ony better?"

"You don't believe in inspiration?"

"No' that kind o' inspiration. You're maybe a poet—but you're a man, aren't you?"

"Jean micht say I was."

"Then what the hell's a' this walking about the burnside for? Inspiration my foot! You like walking oot wi' Jeannie— and you'd be as weel to own up to it."

"If I thocht you meant that, Lorimer, I'd never set foot in Kemys Hall except on official duty. Damnit, man: what age is your lass?"

"About sixteen. . . Ah, but she'll grow a year or twa yet; and she looks twenty."

"She'll grow into a splendid woman—and still remember the sangs in which I celebrated—to the best of my ability—her remarkable beauty. I can only pray that if I'm ever blessed wi' lassies that they'll grow up like your Jean—both in their looks and in their natures—and their characters."

The Bard uttered the words with such force of quiet dignity that Lorimer took another look at him.

William Lorimer did not for a moment fear that the Bard would seduce his daughter. But he reckoned he was familiar

enough with human nature to know that the Bard's attraction
was a sexual one. Nor did he consider that his daughter was
any sexless faggot. . . A lot of men were at her wooing, and
Burns's fellow-gaugers John Lewars and Archibald Thomson
were as persistent as any. Lorimer was glad enough to have the
Excise so interested in his daughter: it tended to shut their
eyes to his smuggling and re-setting deals. Jean knew what
she was doing—so let the Excisemen wench away.

Walking down by the thorn hedge to the burn-path, he
discussed this aspect with Lorimer's Chloris—as he had
poetically christened her.

"I was speaking to your father before you cam' oot. . .
He's entirely sceptical of our partnership in song——"

"In what way?"

"He just doesn't believe in the fact that you inspire me,
Chloris."

"Och, him! I wouldna worry about my faither—he kens
nocht about poetry or songs or inspiration. But sometimes
—och, just sometimes—I wonder that I dae inspire you."

"But you can never, never doubt that, my dear?"

"Och, just whiles! But I like to think it's me you write
about— And Chloris is a bonnie name: no' like Jean or
Jeannie."

"Jean's a fine name. It's a hamely comfortable name and
I'm proud that my own Jean bears it——"

"I didna mean ony slight on Mrs. Burns—and when *you*
say Jean it sounds different than when my faither or mither
cry at me. But then I couldna share it wi' Mrs. Burns in a
sang, could I?"

"No: that's another reason. But the name Chloris takes
you clean away from Kemys Hall—transports you into a
different world—an ideal, poetical world."

"Aye. . . You dinna like Kemys Hall and neither dae I.
Someday I'll get married and run awa'."

"Get married—yes; but why run away? You're no' happy at hame?"

"No. . . My faither and mither are aey drinking—I've never seen Mrs. Burns and you drinking at Ellisland——"

"No: and you never will, my dear. Oh, I can tak' a drink and I'm as fond o' it as the next man—when the occasion demands or when I need it. But I couldna dae wi' sooking at the bottle morning and nicht."

"I dinna mind my faither sae much—it's my mither! She gets affa drunk. I've had to trail her through to the bed—her lying on the floor— It's no' nice."

"No: it's far frae nice and I juist canna bear to think about you in sic a connection. . . Now listen to me: ony time you'd like to come across to Ellisland you ken the road and you ken how pleased Mrs. Burns will be to see you——"

"Aye, I like Mrs. Burns."

"Well: the lang simmer's afore us. So ony time you feel like a change o' scenery. . . And I'll take you along the banks o' the Nith yonder—up by Friars Carse—I've Captain Riddell's permission to go there maist onytime I tak' the fancy——"

"Aye . . . I wad like that. . . You're fond o' me—aside frae writing about me?"

"Fond o' you? Sit doon here and let me look at you. . . There! Of course I'm fond o' you, lassie. In my ain daft poet's way I'm head ower heels in love with you!"

"But just in a poet's way?"

"There's nae ither way, lass."

"But you dinna love me enough to kiss me?"

"My dear, my dear! I could kiss—and I will kiss you."

She put her arms round his neck. He kissed her—but there was no passion in his kiss.

"Ah, Chloris, my dear. . . That's a poet's kiss and that's a' the kiss I can ever gie you."

"Wad it be wrong for us to kiss ony other way?"

"No . . . no . . . it wouldna be wrang. . . But then the

dream would vanish . . . melt away like the morning mists. . .
You see, Chloris, I just love you as a poet——"

"What way would you love me if you werena a poet?"

"There you have me, Chloris! Maybe I'm no' fair to you
talking this way about being a poet and of loving you as a
poet. I don't think I'll write you ony mair sangs. . ."

"You dinna like me noo. . .? Are you angry that I wanted
you to kiss me? You've kissed dizzens o' lassies, hae you no'?"

"Aye . . . dozens; but. . ."

"And aey as a poet?"

"Damned, you're laughing at me! Aye, and I deserve it—
You're nae mair deceived by this play-acting o' mine than
your faither is."

"But you're no' play-acting——"

"I'm not— But how d'you ken I'm no' play-acting?"

"Juist because I ken. There's plenty lads been in love wi'
me and still are. I could hae my pick ony day——"

"You could?"

"Ach, lads are easy—and silly. Ach, and men as weel. A'
men are silly—excepting you."

"You've been kissed afore. . . Lewars and Thomson?"

"Aye . . . mony a time. There's nae harm in kissing, is
there?"

"No . . . no harm at all, providing——"

"What? I'm sure you ken mair about love than ony ither
man. Is that no' why you're a poet?"

"Chloris! I just meant to admire you. To worship your
flaxen hair and your blue eyes—and your youth. . . And yet
I never stopped to consider what *you* were thinking—and that
was wrong o' me. I was too busy writing what effect you made
on me without considering what effect I had on you. . .
Man's a silly, selfish, feckless creature—and more so when he's
a poet. See! I get a fine tune in my head, and it keeps running
through my head until I can get words to fit it. And I canna
just conjure images out o' the air—though, God forgive me,
I whiles do just that. . . No: I tingle to a personal living

attachment. . . Then I *see* things, I make comparisons, I enlarge on life. . . Damnit, lass, I physically tremble wi' a poetic awareness. . . And then I try to bring it a' into the compass o' a few verses, a few words, two-three images. . . D'you understand? This is much better because it's more real than just imagining a fair charmer. And then there's a something about you, Chloris . . . something fresh, something different. . . Maybe no' so different either as a variation—a delightful variation—of the Eternal Charmer that the poet maun aey be singing. God, I could drink too—and lie sodden on the floor in an effort to escape from the damned treadmill of our daily life. . . And that's what life mainly is—a treadmill o' drudgery.

"That's why your mither drinks as she does. Your mither has a keen, keen sense o' life, Chloris. She kens how the savour o' life should be and sae seldom is. Here's me trying to give the wit o' age to youth. . . And sae your puir mither tak's to the bottle whiles . . . as I tak' to a sang. Do you understand —a wee bit?"

"I think I ken what you mean. . . But then what about Mrs. Burns? Since she doesna drink . . . I mean. . ."

"You mean has Mrs. Burns no' a keen sense o' the pleasure and purpose o' life? Aye: naebody more so. But then, Chloris, Mrs. Burns has a strong, terribly strong sense o' the inevitability o' life. By this I mean that she's nae illusions to be destroyed. Mrs. Burns kens the worst that life can bring and she's happy when things dinna turn out as bad as experience tells her they should. Your mither, I'm afeared, kens that there's nocht in life but the dreary round and kens that nocht but the bottle tak's the edge off dull care and lightens the load o' worry and toil . . . and disappointment. . ."

She reached out and took his hand.

"You're ower kind to me—but I'll never forget what you mean to me. I'd like to marry a poet—but he wad need to be like you—and I ken there can only be one Robert Burns——"

"Promise me but one thing!"

"What?"

"Never be tempted to marry onybody till you're certain beyond ony doubt that you're marrying for love."

"And how can you be certain—beyond ony doubt?"

"If you feel there's ony doubt then ye'll ken it's no' certain. Whatever the way it is you'll ken. . . There's so much life in you, so much joyful awareness o' the very gift o' life, that it wad be a terrible tragedy gin you were to throw it away on some smooth-tongued blackguard that had nae real appreciation o' life at a'. . . Ah, but I'm sure you'll fa' in wi' the richt lad yet, Chloris. . . And noo the sang I was thinking on is farther away than the back o' beyond——"

"Hae I spoiled your day?"

"No, no: dinna get that idea into your head—I'll get a sang oot o' this, dinna worry—and sang or no sang I've enjoyed this talk wi' you mair than making a sang."

"I'm glad it's no' just for the sang——"

"My dear: I've travelled a lang lang road through this life. I've been travelling for hundreds o' years. Sometimes I hae the notion I've been travelling since the dawn o' history— and I'm no' twice your age yet. It's no' the years that matter and it canna be what the years bring sae much as that we are touched by experience. Maybe I've talked to you this spring day like the ancient of days; as if I'd as white a pow as Methuselum. . ."

"I could listen to you talking for ever. You talk as nae ither body talks. I ken I'm only sixteen . . . but I ken I'm nae gawkie. I read a lot besides your poems. I whiles get a row for reading. My mither says that reading only stuffs your head fu' o' ideas that mak' you discontented wi' life. She says a lassie doesna need book education as lang as she can cook and mend and keep a hoose. She says gin I ken what it's like to hae a bairn every year I'll hae nae time for books or poetry or sangs. . . She says: 'Dinna think because Mr. Burns mak's a sang on you that you're ony better than ony ither farmer's lass. . .' and then when she's been a while at the bottle, and my

faither's doon in Dumfries, she blubbers and greets and says
naebody ever made a sang on her. . . And whiles I greet wi'
her for it's a gey pity for my mither. . . And she says I'll
no' aey be young and guid-lookin' and that gin I was married
and bairned a wheen times no' even you wad write a sang about
me . . . that I wad get fat and my breists would fa' and the
bloom wad gae oot o' my cheeks. No . . . I ken mair than
folk gie me credit for. But *you* ken I'm nae gawkie."

"God! you're nae gawkie—as you word it. My dear: your
mither's coarse, nae doubt: she states things gey bluntly—but
she's richt for a' that."

"Then I shouldna think o' getting married——?"

"Weel, there's nae reason why marriage should prove a
disaster and a trial and a heartbreak. Guid kens there's ower
mony marriages turn out that way. But damnit, there are
decent happy marriages. And bairns shouldna prove a trachle
and a heartbreak. Bairns that are the fruit o' a happy mutual
union, bless that union. That's the meaning o' marriage—
or it has nae meaning."

"I dinna see that there's meaning in onything—except
that folks put their ain meaning to things."

"D'you ken what you're saying?"

"Fine I ken."

"Then a lass like you in the dewy morn o' her existence
shouldna be thinking—and talking—like a grey-bearded
philosopher. But gin you feel about things as you do, then
you maun get a lover and go courting while the days are lang
and the sun's warm. You'll no' aey be young—as you've been
told often enough. Listen to naebody, lass, and think o'
naebody."

"Are you no' changing your tune?"

"I am that. I was ettling to give you guid sound cautious
advice—the kind o' advice a father micht give a daughter
that was as full o' life and as well favoured as you. But the
advice I'm giving you now, Chloris, is, by the world's standards,
bad advice. It's just this. Gang your ain gate—let your heart

dictate the course of your actions. You've a kind heart and a wise heart and it canna lead you far astray. Let the canting preaching humbugs gae to hell. Even if you do land in the midden ultimately, it's sma' odds—we're a' couped in the midden they ca' the grave at the hinderend. But enjoy your youth, lassie—what you can and every minute that you can——"

"But why are you getting wrocht up? I'm sure that's juist what I dae!"

"Weel . . . forget that I ever spoke to you, for I've a damned bad failing o' putting things into words—thoughts that shouldna be spoken. Noo: let's get back hame and put a finish to this philosophising."

"My! I've never seen you change sae sudden. If I didna ken you I'd say you were angry."

"Ah—but no' wi' you, Chloris. Juist angry at myself for being sae downricht stupid—and maybe a wee bit annoyed that life orders things in sic a haphazard, throw-o'-the-dice fashion. And maybe angriest of a' that I'm no' sixteen and without a thocht for tomorrow."

"Maist folk dinna think enough—but maybe poets think ower much. I'm sure I'm no' worrying aboot the difference in our ages."

But the Bard had jumped to his feet and would hear no more.

And then he relented.

"Listen, lass: I baith like you and love you—baith the poet in me and the man in me. The poet willingly lays his tribute o' sang at your feet or pins it in your breast for a posie. But the man in me, the man that would take you quicker than John Lewars or Baldy Thomson or John Gillespie—that man you maun just take for granted, for he'll never offer himself to you ony other way. Sae that way, Jeannie lass, you can expect nothing."

"Oh, but tell me you dinna think ony the less o' me—I should hae kept my mouth shut and never minded how I felt."

" Far frae thinking the less of you I think the mair o' you—
and if you tak' my advice you'll think kindly aboot John
Lewars—he's far and away the cleverest young officer in
Dumfries. A bit o' the poet in John Lewars."

"He doesna kiss as weel as Archie Thomson."

"Does he no'? Well, I don't expect you'll be seeing much
more of Thomson. Dinna say I told you, but I think his
discharge will be announced ony day—but I'm saying no more
than that. And dinna think I'm trying to throw you into
Lewars's arms—I'm merely suggesting that you think kindly
on him. And if his kissing's no' up to your high standard,
it could be for want of practice and want of experience. A
young lad's got to learn——"

"I never needed to learn and I'm sure you didna—you're
either born that way or you're no'. If I cam' over this afternoon
to see Mrs. Burns would you convoy me hame?"

"I'll see you hame in broad daylicht else Adam and Fanny
can see you hame. Noo, dinna toss your flaxen ringlets—
you're bewitching enough as you are. Noo. . . I think I've
given your father and mother enough warning that I hae
some official business wi' them."

"There's nothing you dinna ken——"

"Aye, plenty—and plenty I dinna want to ken."

THE WEDDING OF GILBERT BURNS

On the nineteenth of June the Bard set out for Machlin
to witness Gilbert's marriage to Jean Breckenridge of Kilmarnock. He had time only to ride there, attend the wedding
the following day and the next day ride home: the Excise
did not believe in holidays.

On the wedding eve, in the long June night, Gilbert and
his brother strode the ridge of Mossgiel and talked. It was a
perfect June night and the great rolling acres of Kyle fell away

from them on every hand and the sun went down in a paean of red and gold and muted purple.

The Bard drank in the familiar scene. On such a night there wasn't a fairer in all Scotland.

"I've said it before, Gilbert, and maybe I'll never tire saying it. But if we could hae lived on a view we'd hae been the richest farmers in Ayrshire—or Scotland."

"Aye . . . it's a bonnie bit here. And you've a bonnie bit at Ellisland. But we're as puir as kirk mice for a' that."

"And likely to be puirer. You're doing the wise thing to marry. Jean Breckenridge is a guid lass."

"I'm glad you like her."

"I aey wondered what kind o' lass you'd marry."

"Maybe you thocht I'd marry somebody as useless as mysel'?"

"You useless! I wish I'd half your sober sense."

"You didna aey see things that way."

"I'm no' saying I see them that way yet. But what's the prospects wi' you?"

"Well: I canna pay you back yet. I canna even see ony immediate prospect o' paying you back onything. I suppose you could be doing wi' some?"

"I could be doing wi' every bluidy penny—and a wheen mair. But I'm no' pressing you the now. What about your prospects?"

"My wife will bring me a pound or twa—oh, nothing much; but at least the wedding'll no' set me back ocht. . . I'm taking ower the spence and I've bocht a new bed and some bits o' things."

"Damnit, man, that's naebody's business but your ain—you havena to account to me for every penny."

"Well . . . since I owe you and canna pay——"

"As far as the immediate future's concerned I dinna look for repayment. If you were drinkin' or whorin' awa' the money it *micht* be a different story. But fine I ken you're spending nothing but what canna, in decency, be avoided. I've

brocht you a present o' a five pound note! You can put Jean
and me—and Nancy—doon for your new bed."

"Five pounds is ower much, Robin——"

"No' anither word. Are you haudin' on to Mossgiel?"

"I canna see where I can better mysel' at the minute. My
mither isna fit for ony heavy work and Bell doesna keep too
weel. This leaves the heavy end to Isa and me—and John
Begg; and he eats up a man's wages. My Jean'll dae what she
can. But you ken better nor me how it is should there be
weans."

"Aye. . . But dinna deny yoursel' weans whatever you do:
you'll aey manage to provide for *them*, and damnit, man,
they're a' we hae in life. . . The only real joy we ever hae.
Oh, they're a fell responsibility and a constant worry—but a
constant joy too, Gilbert."

"I hope we'll be blessed wi' them, Robin. . . I've waited a
lang time for marriage though I'm nae better gathered now
than I was ten years ago."

"You've gathered ten years' mair experience—and that's
something money canna buy. Weel . . . I'm about finished
wi' Ellisland. You ken Miller wouldna let me sub-lease. I
think I've forced his hand now. I'll be having a talk wi' him
when I get back and gin he can spare me the time. Patrick
Miller's a busy man and deals in tens o' thousands where you
and I canna venture wi' the like number o' bawbees. David
Newall was telling me that he thinks Miller would rather sell
than be humbugged wi' anither tenant—and besides Ellisland's
on the wrong side o' the Nith for Dalswinton——"

"If he sells does that mean you'll get a clean break?"

"Damn near it. I'll sell my crops at valuation—growing—
if the incoming buyer doesna want them. Then I'll quit on
the November term: that's my lease. I canna get a house in
Dumfries afore November. Damn it, houses are just no' to be
got for a reasonable rent onywhaur. Say what you like; but
folk are crowding into the toons."

"And can the Excise support you?"

"It'll have to. I need a horse for the Tobacco Division the now; but if I was getting into the first or second footwalk I'd then be a port officer proper and I'd be saved the expense o' a beast; and my salary would go up to seventy-five pounds a year. I could manage on that. Besides, you ken I was put on the list o' Supervisors and Examiners at the beginning o' the year——?"

"And what exactly does that mean?"

"It means the certainty o' promotion sooner or later. Later by waiting my term o' years—sooner by influence and a touch o' luck and expediency. At worst it means that I can look for £150 per annum in six or seven years—sooner if my friends in high places can help me. Mrs. Dunlop's working on Corbett and I'm working on Graham o' Fintry."

"You're wise to haud by the Excise. You had your head screwed on there from the beginning. I confess I couldna see the sense o' your turning gauger at the time you did. But then you aey saw further than ever I did."

"I dinna ken about that, Gilbert; but there's nae man living able to convince me that there's ony kind o' life in hashing out your guts on unrewarding soil. And to rent guid land has aey been beyond your means or mine."

"True enough. . . If you go in November you'll no' be needin' Nancy?"

"No. . . Jean and me'll be sorry to part wi' her. She's a grand worker and a great comfort to the wife. Oh, Nancy can be nebby enough: her damned tongue would clip clouts whiles—but she's got a heart o' gold. I wish I saw her decently married."

"Weel, we could dae wi' her here—gin the spring. But she'll aey hae a hame wi' me."

"Or me—gin I got promotion and a bigger house. I've got the half-promise the now o' twa rooms and bit. But it'll be a ticht enough squeeze for us. I'll take Fanny wi' us. But I think that gin Adam Armour had his time out and prospects o' settled work Fanny and him'll get married."

"They're a likely pair. I hear Fanny's brither William is settling doon fine wi' auld Armour. There's waur nor Armour, Robin——"

"Oh, he's come roun'—and there was meikle need. Will ye want Fanny's younger brither John? He's a guid lad and will mair nor earn his bite onywhaur."

"I could aey dae wi' a guid boy that wasna looking for too much. There's just nae spare money for wages."

"If you gie the lad a guid bite and a guid bed and a penny or twa for his fairin' back and forward, he'll be grateful enough. The lad needs some kind o' a hame. . . Well, it looks like you'll hae a grand day the morn and I maun say your crops are shaping bravely for the time o' year. . ."

The Bard inadvertently put his hand in his coat pocket.

"Oh—and by the way, Gilbert! Here's a new pamphlet frae London. I'll throw it in wi' your wedding present. The title's got no domestic significance. But the contents'll dae you a lot o' good."

"And what is it, Robin?"

"It's by Commonsense Paine—Thomas Paine. It settles Mr. Burke's hash about the French Revolution. It's entitled The Rights of Man. You'll be hearing plenty about both the author and his subject before long. Read it at your leisure; but dinna let it interrupt your honeymoon!"

As was inevitable where Gilbert was concerned, the wedding was a quiet, decorous and purely private affair. There was neither joy nor rejoicing.

The Reverend William Auld married them in the manse and blessed their union. Daddy Auld was a frail man, white of hair and feeble of voice, and he peered at the Book through his horn-rimmed spectacles as if his sight was almost gone. But his intellect and his authority seemed unimpaired.

It was evident that he strongly approved of Gilbert and equally of his choice of a wife. But he was glad to see the Bard. After the ceremony was over he shook hands again with him.

"Weel, Robert, I'm verra glad you managed through to your brother's marriage. How is your wife Jean?"

"Never better, Mr. Auld, thank you. She sends you her respects by me."

"Aye. . . I mind when she was just a wee bit lass skippin' bare-fit ower the green: the flower o' my parish I thocht then. Tell her, Robert, that I remember her kindly and that I'll mind her in my prayers afore the Lord. . . Aye: my health's no' what it was twenty years ago; but I'm wonderful weel, a' things considered. The Lord has been verra guid to me. . . Grand weather for you farmer folk. . . Ah, but at my age we grumble at the heat and grumble at the cauld. . ."

The Bard gazed round the heavy musty room where he had often had a sermon from Daddy Auld delivered for his sole benefit.

The sun burned at the window but could not be said to enter the room. Decay was there and death did not seem very far away. Clearly Father Auld, at the end of a long ministry, was gathering himself for the grave. The Bard was touched by his frail friendliness. In all their bitter differences they had always had a mutual respect for each other.

Driving back to Mossgiel, to a slightly more elaborate dinner than usual, Jean Breckenridge looked at him quizzically and said: "I suppose I may ca' you Robert noo?"

"Certainly, Jean, and I hope you never hae occasion to ca' me onything waur."

"I hope no'. You see it's a gey privilege to hae you as a guid-brither."

But Gilbert's new-wed wife was thinking: So that's the great Robert Burns! No wonder he's a poet and no wonder he's made so much of—a big handsome man wi' a pair of eyes and a gift of tongue would turn ony lassie's head.

On the surface Gilbert did not compare favourably with him. Gilbert was slightly taller, slimmer and more pinched of feature; and he had a sad aquiline nose. But they were unmistakably brothers. But everything about Gilbert was canny and cautious—at times almost sly and secretive. And in the Bard's presence he played a very one-stringed second fiddle.

But Jean Breckenridge, though she couldn't help comparing the Bard to her husband's disadvantage, loved Gilbert. Of the men she might have married, he was by far the best. And in any case the Bard was a man who contrasted boldly in the front rank with his fellow-men. Jean Breckenridge would have given a lot to have known him longer: maybe as his good-sister she would have the opportunity of getting to know him more intimately in the days ahead. And maybe their ways wouldn't always lie as far apart as Kyle and Nithsdale. . .

Chatting with his first child Betty—the dear-bought Bess that Betty Paton had borne him—he could not help but think of his daughter by Anna Park. Both were named Elizabeth! And yet he had no daughter living by Jean Armour. There was plenty of time to remedy this of course. But Mossgiel Betty was coming six—in fact she'd just had her sixth birthday—and a fine chubby lass she was—and growing more like himself than the mother.

Six years ago! He'd packed a lot of experience into those six years. Six momentous, varied years. Since Betty was born Jean had borne him six children: three—all girls—were dead. Mary Campbell had taken hers to her grave. Peggy Cameron had been delivered of still-born triplets and Jenny Clow still had his son. Anna Park had presented him with the latest— as sweet a wee lass as had ever been born. Aye: his record of paternity was imposing. And he couldn't help reflecting on it with some pride. But it was a pity that necessity had compelled his to allow his own mother to assume the motherhood of Lizzie Paton's lass and that, as a consequence, he was no more than uncle to her. No doubt she would learn the truth of things—and when that day came he hoped he wouldn't be too far away for her to learn his way of the truth. For there was no doubt that there were two sides to every truth—and maybe a wheen more.

He spoke to Bell in the dairy.

"Weel, Bell: I'm sorry to hear that you havena been keeping as fit as you micht?"

"Och—it's nothing. You're a' weel doon by? I had aey hoped to get doon to see your farm, Robin."

"I'm hoping to quit my farm by the November term, Bell. If you could manage doon after harvest, the change would dae you guid."

"God! I could dae wi' a change, Robin. I'm bluidy sick and tired o' Mossgiel."

The Bard raised his dark eyebrows. He hadn't heard Bell swear before. Bell noted his surprise.

"Aye, you may look, Robin, and wonder at me swearin'. But it wad gar a body sin their soul every day they rose."

"Swear awa', lass. It does you guid when you feel like it. But what like's the trouble? Surely something can be done about it?"

"There's nothing onybody can dae. There's never ony money but the wark's aey to be done. And there's naebody ever cam' courtin' a tocherless lass."

"You've had your lads, Bell?"

"Me? Whaur? And when did I hae the chance or the time? If I'd had a fraction o' the lads that you've had lassies——"

"Damnit, I've tellt you mony a time that you're too conscientious. The world wags nae matter what happens."

"It's different for a man."

"Not a bit, lass. We're a' the same at the heart o' us. But is this your bother?"

"It's no' my bother—and it's no' bothering me. It's just part and parcel o' how things are here. Canna you see, Robin: I'll never get out o' the bit here— It'll aey be the same. Pinchin' and scrapin': daeing without this and daeing without that. And aey the cows to milk nicht and morn, the butter to kirn and the cheese to mak'. And never a decent-like man-body about the place. . . I'm telling you this. But I'd cut my tongue out afore I'd tell ony ither body."

"And, of course, you couldna say a word to Gilbert?"

"Ah, what can Gilbert dae? His head's in the noose too. Jean Breckenridge'll soon find that out. She'll no' have her sorrows to seek——"

"So things are just as gloomy as ever? Yet Isa seems happy enough. How does she manage?"

"Isa's just coming nineteen: I'm twenty-six. Besides, Isa's no' bothered much wi' her conscience. She kens how to enjoy hersel'. She's mair like you, Robin, than ony o' the rest o' us."

"I'm glad to hear somebody kens how to enjoy themselves!"

"She'll no' be lang till she's married!"

"Well, I'll awa' and hae a word wi' her. But listen, Bell, you canna go on like this. Tak' things in your own hands and to hell wi' what onybody thinks! If I get promotion in the Excise I'll can afford a bigger place and you can come and bide wi' me for a while. . ."

"It's guid o' you, Robin. Oh, I've been angry wi' you whiles. But if it hadna been for you the family would hae been broken up and scattered lang afore noo. And I can understand now how it was that you just had to get awa' on your ain. . . But dinna worry about me: I'll try and get doon to your place about the back-en'. Tell Jean I was speirin' for her. . ."

Isa was certainly the brightest member of the family. She seemed to have escaped the gloom that had gathered about Lochlea—and she'd never known Mount Oliphant.

She came into the stable as he was saddling his black mare, Nell.

"Are you for awa', Robin?"

"It's you, Isa— You're looking weel! And how're you getting on wi' the lads?"

"Fine. I aey get on well wi' them!"

"Good for you. And wha's your favourite the now?"

"I'm no' telling. . . Wha's your favourite?"

"You ken I'm a married man— What kind o' talk is that to gie your big brother?"

"Juist joking."

"Well, for Godsake joke: for there's gey little about Mossgiel thae days."

"Uch . . . I never fash wi' them. D'you like Gilbert's wife?"

"Do you?"

"Oh aye: she'll dae."

"She'll be pleased to ken that."

"As long as she doesna start to boss me."

"I see. You dinna like to be bossed?"

"Do you?"

"You're coming out o' your shell ower quick, my lassie. Aye: you're getting a fully-bold jad!"

"You never asked me doon to Nithsdale, Robin."

"Oh, there's nae guid-looking lads doon yonder."

"I could soon find them—if you hae ony dancing."

"There's nae time for dancing."

"I could aey come doon to your kirn dance. I hear you hae a grand new hoose. You're lucky!"

"Aye . . . I'm lucky. I think you hae a notion o' John Begg here?"

"He's a' richt—when he's no' feared o' Gibby."

"Weel . . . watch you dinna get couped."

"Naebody'll coup me till I'm ready."

"And you're no' ready yet?"

"When the ring's on!"

"Ah, you're a Jezebel, Isa—that's what you are! But you'll dae wi' standin' a year or twa."

"Just till it suits me! You'll tell Jean I was asking kindly for her—and gie a' the bairns a hug frae me—especially Robbie —he's a wee deil——"

As the Bard rode through Machlin in the heat of the late afternoon after paying calls on the Armours, John MacKenzie and Johnnie Dow, he had no regrets that he was away from it. Mossgiel and Machlin belonged to the past and never in any circumstances could he see them playing any part in his future. His future, wherever it might lie, was elsewhere in Scotland: of this he felt certain.

There was no warmth for him anywhere in Machlin now—like Daddy Auld it had grown old and death and decay seemed everywhere about it.

But it was the Bard who had changed, not Machlin. There was no living contact there to hold him for more than an hour or two's pleasant conversation.

But he was sorry about Mossgiel. For all the brightness of the June days, there was a heavy oppressive gloom about the place and not all the youth of his sister Isa or the fun of his daughter Betty could dispel it. Nor even the fact of Gilbert's wedding.

He could only hope for Jean Breckenridge's sake that Gilbert didn't carry his stodgy sensible matter-of-factness to bed with him.

Apart from the lack of room at Mossgiel he could not have spent the wedding night under Gilbert's roof: he wouldn't have been able to look either Jean or Gilbert in the face in the morning.

And so he quietly cantered on down into New Cumnock and put up with John Merry and Annie Rankine for the night. At least he could have a drink there and a good inhibition-free crack with two old friends.

THE DRAGON OF DALSWINTON

There was still plenty of building and reconstruction going on about Dalswinton House, but Patrick Miller had a fine office with windows overlooking a fine lawn. There he received the Bard with a certain limited show of politeness.

"So I understand you're determined on quitting Ellisland, Burns?"

"I can't quit until Mr. Miller agrees to release me."

"You're not just a prisoner, Burns."

"In a sense that's just what I am, Mr. Miller; and I canna see that you're insensible to my meaning."

"A lease is a lease, Burns—not a prison sentence. And I'm nae gaoler. But you want your lease broke. . . Well: I cam' to your assistance when you were desperate for a farm, so maybe I'll come to your assistance now that you're desperate to be rid o' one. Are you quite satisfied that you did your best to mak', a success o' Ellisland?"

"More than satisfied, Mr. Miller. I think my crops will testify to my application in that direction."

"Uhuh—imphm! And riding aboot ten parishes in the interests o' the Excise wad doubtless help your crops! No, Burns: I canna think you've done your best to mak' Ellisland a success. And I'm disappointed in you."

"I couldna have done more had I laboured with my own hands night and day in Ellisland— And Mr. Miller knows how impossible that would have been. I have my disappointments too, Mr. Miller."

"I've nae doubt. But I suppose you find the Excise a congenial occupation for a poet?"

"The Excise doesna pay me for being a poet but for carrying out the duties of an officer of the Excise."

"And I help to pay the Government! But I didna send for

you to banter words and I see you're in nae better mood nor I am mysel'. Weel . . . a John Morine in Laggan, on your side o' the water, is interested in *buying* Ellisland; and when a man offers to *buy* a farm he maistly kens what he's aboot. Frae what I gather Mr. John Morine is nae fool as a farmer."

"There's mair than one opinion about Morine in Nithsdale, Mr. Miller—but that's no reason why he might want to buy Ellisland. I'm sorry, Mr. Miller, that you and me seem to have come to loggerheads over this matter. I'm aware I'm asking a favour from you—but I think the favour is in your interests too."

"I've nae doubt about that point. Weel . . . there are a wheen points outstanding, but I'll deal wi' them through my factor, Mr. Newall, and my land-steward, Mr. Cunningham. But the important thing as far as you are concerned is that Mr. Morine, should I decide to sell, will want a valuation. And whatever agreement is come to, it will hae to be adhered to— to the verra letter."

"I see no difficulty there—there's nothing about Ellisland I want to take with me into Dumfries but my personal goods, and even they dinna amount to verra much. But I thought maybe you would give me your answer to-day, Mr. Miller. This hanging-on is a big worry to me and unsettles all my plans. Small enough plans and of no great consequence to a gentleman; but I canna be blamed for looking to the happiness of my wife and children."

"Oh, I'll give you a decision. You can go at the November term and for a' I'm really concerned Ellisland can grow nocht but thrissles for cadgers' cuddies— But your terms o' outgaun maun be drawn up and adhered to. Meantime I'll hae Mr. Morine instructed that he can view the place—crops and biggins."

"He's done that already."

"Aye—but no' officially. He needs *my* permission when it comes to acting officially. I tak' it you dinna haud wi' Mr. Morine?"

"That is so."

"Aye. . . And does your gauging wark gie you mair time for your verses, Burns?"

"Well . . . it'll give me more leisure and more *independence* to write certain kinds o' verses."

"Oh weel: I see you're in nae mood either to be advised or guided. But I rescued you frae a garret in Edinburgh—sae I hope you'll never need rescuing frae the Excise."

"Dinna think I'm insensible to your by-gone good offices to me, Mr. Miller. But we did have a bargain and up till now I've kept my part of it as you have yours. Apart from this question of a break, is there any point on which I have legitimately incurred your displeasure?"

"I'm no' that interested in Ellisland to hae incurred ony displeasure. I'm ower busy for that sort o' nonsense. I'm just disappointed in you, Burns—you're no' the man I thocht you were. But we'll let that flea stick to the wa'. Nae doubt you're disappointed in me. Weel, we can let twa fleas stick to the wa'. I wish you nae ill luck, Burns, and if it does lie in my power to dae you ony guid turn in the future I'll dae what I can for you."

"I'm duly grateful to you, Mr. Miller. There's one good turn you could do for me. Should onybody be interested enough to ask you why I quit Ellisland, you can say that it wasn't on account of being an indifferent farmer—however indifferent a business man I might have been. And the fact that Mr. Miller hasn't turned out to be the man I thocht he was doesna make me the less sensible to Mr. Miller's many private and public merits——"

"D'you ken what's wrang wi' you, Burns? You hae too big an opinion o' yoursel'—baith as poet and farmer. The country needs farmers—hardy industrious farmers wi' the intelligence to apply new ideas to their farming. But the nation can do without poets. And it's my opinion that far ower meikle's made o' the whole damned fraternity o' scribblers and poets. Richt enough maybe for the women-folk in the drawing-room o' an evening and them round the piano. But compared wi' agriculture, Burns, poetry's o' sma' consequence. Of course, I dinna mean to offend you—but these are my views."

"Mr. Miller is entitled to his views. . . But equally so is Mr. Burns."

"And I suppose you hae a sma' opinion o' my views?"

"There's this vital difference atween us, Mr. Miller. You can afford to insult me because I happen to be your unfortunate tenant and I canna afford to answer you back. You have me here at a sore disadvantage and only consideration for my wife and children holds me back. But for them I'd answer you were it the last thing I ever did; and by the Lord God you'd be a gey sma' man gin I'd finished wi' you——"

"Steady, Burns, steady. Damnit, man, I'm sorry if I've hurt you. . . Maybe I hae abused my position. It's juist, it's juist. . . Oh, let's hae a drink thegither for Godsake——"

"I may have to swallow your insults; but I'm damned if I'll swallow your drink."

"Aye, you'll swallow my drink and without ony mair damnation atween us. We're baith headstrong and we're baith fools. But damnit! I'm coming mair than half-roads to meet you! D'you expect me to gae down on my knees? And this is my best Ferintosh: stuff I dinna jaw out to a' and sundry. A byornar occasion like this calls for a byornar drap o' the verra best."

It was the first time the Bard had seen behind the bold and ruthless exterior of Patrick Miller. He took the proffered drink. Yet, though he had now the advantage of the laird, he hadn't the heart to press it. In the end, he had less interest in Patrick Miller than Miller had in him.

But the Bard left Dalswinton in a cold anger. Damn Miller and all his kind to all eternity! He'd farmed his damned acres that had consisted of little more than the riddlings of creation. He'd put the land in heart, had improved it out of all recognition. That was why Morine of Laggan wanted to buy it—he would reap the benefit of his labour. But Morine was of the Miller breed. Hard, emotionless and incurably selfish and self-opinionated. Morine and Miller cared only for the making of money. Every human activity to them had to have a practical money-relationship: otherwise nothing was of value. . .

But at least he could now arrange to move into Dumfries and to dispose of his crops and plenishments.

THE BRAVE FRONT

James Armour looked long at the baby girl.

"Weel, Jean: you say she's a neighbour's bairn—but, damn me, if she hasna the black looks o' Rab Burns about her."

"How can you say that, Faither?"

"Ah weel: never mind what I say—you're no' gaun to be short o' bairns onyway."

"That's aey a blessing."

"I'm glad you feel that way about it. And how was he when you left?"

"Fine. . . The sale o' the crops'll be on now; and like as no' there'll be a lot o' drinking."

"So he wanted you and the bairns out o' the road—is that it?"

"Weel . . . we canna be o' much use noo and I wanted hame to see you a' afore I gaed doon into Dumfries."

"Tell me this, Jean—oh, and dinna think we're no' glad to see you, lass—tell me this. Had he to part wi' the farm?"

"You see, it wasna paying and Rab couldna dae baith the farm *and* the Excise."

"Aye, but could he no' hae stuck into the farm and left the Excise alane?"

"And what would we hae done for ready money if it hadna been for the Excise? Folk canna live on the wind."

"Then the farm was a failure or he was a failure as a farmer?"

"Rab was nae failure as a farmer! Rab was never a failure at onything. But the money was a' sunk in the farm."

"Weel, then: he hadna enough money to commence farmer?"

"Maybe no'; but that's no' Rab's fau't."

"No. . . I maun say I'm disappointed, Jean. The pair o' you had big hopes for this Ellisland—and I had hopes for you."

"Listen, Faither: we had plenty o' hope. We a' worked hard and nane harder than Rab. If we could hae stuck out for a year or twa mair there would hae been a gey different story to tell. We were a' happy enough at Ellisland and we'll a' be sorry to leave it. Ask Adam: he'll tell you!"

"Fine I ken Adam thinks there's naebody like Rab Burns——"

"Neither there is."

"Aye, weel. . . It was a respectable-like thing being a farmer's wife. But a gauger's wife's a sow wi' anither snout."

"Oh, Rab'll be a Supervisor afore lang: he'll be a big man in the Excise. He could rise to five hundred pounds in the year yet."

"Oh, he could?"

"Without much bother."

"Oh weel then: the quicker the better. I'd nae idea his prospects were that guid. Certes, five hundred pounds is no' to be sneezed at."

"I would think no'!"

"I hope the pair o' you prosper then: I can wish you nae mair than that."

To her mother, Jean said:

"Now, you've no' to be worrying, Mither. Rab and me'll aey be the same."

"Aye: Nell said that the pair o' you get on gey weel. But your faither was annoyed at the idea o' him giein' up the farm for the Excise."

"I've had a gey sair heart about it mysel', Mither. I've had a greet mony a time when naebody kent. And I'm no' much looking forward to biding up a stair in a Dumfries vennel. But you dinna ken Rab as I ken him. I hae faith in him. We'll a' be proud o' him in the Excise yet: I'm no' a bit feared o' that. . . I couldna live without him, Mither. So I'll gang into Dumfries wi' him and haud into his back the way I've aey done at Ellisland. . . But it's a gey pity things hae turned out like this and I ken Rab feels sair about it."

"It's beyond me, Jean. A' I ken is that you're as fond o' Rab Burns noo as you ever were and you'll just need to dae as things will dae wi' you. And what about this cousin o' his that Adam's ettling to marry?"

"Fanny? She'll mak' Adam a grand wife: he couldna dae better, Mither. And you'll like her."

"Oh, it doesna matter about me, Jean: I was only thinking about Adam."

"Weel, I'll miss her when she goes. And I'll miss Adam too; and I'll miss Rab's sister Nancy——"

"You'll hae naebody about Dumfries you ken then?"

"There's a Mrs. Hyslop that keeps an inn—but that's about a'. Ach—but I've the bairns and I'll hae nae time to weary."

John Rankine of Adamhill hailed her in the street. He dismounted heavily: he was ageing.

"Damn, Jean, you're looking better than ever! How mony weans hae you now?"

"Three boys . . . and a lassie."

"Ah. Rab's keeping his end up! What's a' this I hear about him quitting his farm?"

"Och, he's gotten a fine job wi' the Excise in Dumfries—
he'll be a Supervisor afore you ken, Mr. Rankine."

"The hell he will! Damned, the randy beggar was to hae
looked me up the time he was at Gilbert's weddin'. Sae he's
doing weel in the Excise, is he?"

"Oh aye: he's weel gotten with the Big Folk in the Excise.
Gin a year, mebbe, he'll be takin' charge o' Greenock or Port
Glasgow—or he may gae awa' North. . . How're you keeping,
Mr. Rankine?"

"Oh fine, fine! Only I'm getting a wee stiff i' my joints.
Auld age creeping on, Jean. Oh, but I'm real glad to see you
and to hear Rab's daein' sae weel. Meg Muir o' the Mill was
telling me a' about the grand new hoose he got bigged. Seems
you'd a grand place on the Nith."

"Oh, we've a grand place and we were daein' weel. But, of
course, naething to what the Excise'll be. Rab said if I saw
you I was to say that he'd a packet o' verses for you—just as
soon as he gets settled into Dumfries."

"Tell him I'll be mair nor glad to see them. Ah, damned,
the countraside's no' the same since Rab gaed awa'. Mony a
grand nicht we had in Johnnie Dow's there. Noo, damned,
there's naebody about it worth a caup o' yill. . . Weel . . .
you'll mind me to Rab, Jean? And tell him no' to forget thae
verses for me."

"You can be sure I'll no' forget, Mr. Rankine. Rab often
talks about you. I've heard him say often enough that he
wished Adamhill farm marched wi' Ellisland."

John Rankine's eyes lit and he half-turned back.

"Adamhill marching wi' Ellisland! By God, Jean, we'd
hae had mony a grand nicht. . . And tell him that gin he
comes this airt again and doesna ca' in by Adamhill that I'll
be damned annoyed wi' him. Guid luck to you, Jean, and your
bairns. . ."

And as he rode home John Rankine felt proud that Robert
Burns still had a kindly thought for him away down in Dumfriesshire. Rab was a great man now, one of the greatest in

Scotland; and John Rankine felt that he had given him as much encouragement as anyone when he had first started to take his poetry seriously. And many a good piece of advice had he given the young Bard then—yes, and when other folk didn't look the road he was on.

Damnit, it warmed the heart to think he was not forgotten about. But Lord God! what would he not give to have him round the ingle-neuk again and to hear his crack—and maybe the first reading of a new poem. . .

Jean lied to her Machlin friends about the giving up of Ellisland; and she could not resist painting Rab's Excise prospects in rosy colours. She didn't want it thought by anyone that in any way he had been a failure in Ellisland or that poverty had driven him out of it.

And Jean was convinced that her lies were only temporary ones. In the end, Rab would more than justify his new move. Not even the mighty Excise could keep a man of Rab's genius working as a common gauger: promotion was bound to come to him.

And though nobody apart from her father had made any direct reference to Rab in connection with wee Bess, it was obvious to Jean that neither at the Cowgate nor at Mossgiel was there anyone in doubt as to who her father was. She began to be sorry that Bess had been born of Anna Park and not of herself.

As Mary Smith said to her husband:

"That wee lass is maybe no' our Jean's; but she's fonder o' her than she is o' the boy— And there's nae doubt wha the faither is."

To which James Armour replied:

"There's damn the doubt about that, Mary; but then our Jean was never natural whaur Rab Burns was concerned. Besides: as lang as there's nae scandal it's nane o' our business."

And when, on the homeward journey, Jean stopped at John Merry's Inn at New Cumnock for refreshment, and

Annie Rankine said: "My God! Twins again, Jean! And the wee lass the spit and image o' Rab. . ." she didn't bother to contradict her, but smiled so happily that Annie took her smile as a token of maternal pride.

NEVER TO DESPAIR

The sale day came on Thursday the 25th of August. And it was a day of some note. The Bard and his friends had advertised the sale widely. Few folks in the district had any love for John Morine, though he had his staunch adherents. But the Bard had determined that Morine would have to bid for every acre and for every article he wanted and some of his friends were prepared, for his sake, to see that Morine paid dearly. . .

But Morine was no fool and he had agents posted among the crowd of bidders, and those agents appeared to be bidding against him. Morine's spies had told him what was afoot.

Notwithstanding, the day went decisively to the Bard. As was custom, he had laid in a stock of drink—and plenty of John Carson's wretched whisky. What good drink there was he kept for his friends.

But there were few connoisseurs of whisky about Nithsdale and free whisky was not to be despised. The crowd drank freely and the Bard, keeping himself rigidly sober, went among them with a grim-humoured countenance.

Damn them: let them drink themselves silly! It was his labour they were buying up; his dream of being an independent farmer; his dream of a pleasant rural economy wedded to a blissful pastoral life, gradually taking his ease as the labour of it passed to his growing family of sons and daughters . . . of grandsons and granddaughters. . . It was his vision that was being hammered into pieces under the auctioneer's mallet. Let them drink and squabble over a poet's dear-bought dream of self-sufficiency and modest prosperity. They didn't know, they couldn't know—nor could they be expected to care. It was only a sale of crops like any other—only it was the poet Burns's crops. This gave the event the little added importance; gave it a gossip value. So that this one could say he bought the poet's hens or his cow or his harrows or his mattocks. . .

Let them drink and be damned to them. . . By November he'd be settled in Dumfries and he'd be finished with farming for ever. Let them drink; for he was finished with farming here and now. There would never be any dreams again of rural ease and patriarchal fulfilment. . .

Aye; but never again would he waken in the morning to listen to the thrush on the bough and the lark in the heavens and know how the green fields enfolded his habitation. Never again would he stride forth of a fine morning and scatter the seed and watch it braird and grow and ripen; bind with his sheavers and rejoice at his harvest home and revel in his kirn dance.

And no longer would he stroll in solitary meditation the banks of the Nith catching a rhythm from the waters. . .

Henceforth he would be incarcerated in two small rooms up a winding stair with no more soil in his possession than he carried in the seams of his boots. . .

Let them drink then. Let everybody drink till they didn't know the hour or the day or the century they lived in. Aye, and he could well afford to open another jar of whisky—he was averaging a pound an acre above current prices as it was. Miller and Morine could put that in their pipes and smoke themselves sick. . .

And drink they did. Drank till they fell down and vomited up their guts and staggered up and drank more.

Indeed the sale ended in something of a riot. Morine's men, vicious at their defeat, attacked innocent buyers and soon a fight arose involving some thirty to forty men. They fought with fists and sticks and feet. . . They bellowed and roared and cursed at each other. They fought in the court and out of the court and into the fields and some waded into the Nith. . . Even the dogs howled and yelled and snarled and fell to worrying each other.

Willie Stewart, the Closeburn factor, said: "We'll need to stop this somehow, Robert—they'll wreck the place—or set it on fire."

"Damn them, Willie—let them wreck the place—and set it on fire and themselves wi' it. But no: they're too damned drunk even to kill themselves, which would be the best thing that could happen. And by the Lord God! it's a fitting end to all my plans and all my dreams."

"Aye—and you planned and you toiled, Robert—I'll say that for you. I mind when you first cam' and John MacMurdo and me were talking about you—ye ken how it is? And MacMurdo said to me: 'I wonder what kind o' a farmer a poet'll mak'?' And I said: 'John, it's no' a case o' poet turned farmer but a damned hard-working farmer turned aside frae verse-makin'—and by God, he's shapin' weel!' You were cairtin' lime at the time frae the Closeburn kiln. . . It's a gey pity it had to come to this after a' your work. And it's a damneder pity that John Morine's for stepping in."

"My feelings are mixed, Willie—a' mixed and tangled up. I could get drunk too—oh, as drunk as ony man the day. But that wad spoil my appreciation of this memorable scene o' human dignity and human worth. But—I'm mighty glad too. That's a chapter finished, Willie: the last chapter o' a stout volume—a treatise on the folly o' farming without sufficient capital—o' making one guinea do the work o' five—and, over all, a landlord wi' nae mair bowels o' compassion in him than a smiddy anvil. . . .

"But come in and hae a drink, Willie. The brawl's dying away. . . Damnit, I'll need the byreman in to muck out this kitchen afore Jean comes back. . . Aye, 'you'll find mankind an unco squad and meikle they may grieve you'—as I wrote to a young friend once. . . Well, here's your health, Willie: I reckon you the best friend I hae in Nithsdale—you befriended me even before I set foot here as farmer——"

"Here's to your future, Robert—and may a' guid things attend you and yours. No . . . I did nae mair, Robert, than should be done to a stranger coming into our midst. And ony bit thing I ever did for you you paid for a hunder times ower wi' your verses and your company. . . But damned, man, you're only gaen the length o' Dumfries—and you ken I'm gey often there. And my howff's William Hyslop's Globe—same as yours. Mind you: gin you get ony quick-like promotion in the Excise, you're doing the richt thing, Robert. For you were only knocking your guts oot here."

"I've nae guts left to knock out, Willie. And maybe there's no' another man in Nithsdale I could tell this to. I should be happy enough: I'm getting quit o' Ellisland better than I'd ony reason to hope. I'm going to Dumfries and the certainty o' the Excise. . . I'm no' ruined and I'm no' disgraced—the prices I got the day proved that. But I'm sair defeated for a' that, Willie. Broken inside me: broken when I was on the crest o' the wave. Defeated and smashed. Oh, I'll put a face on things—and maybe I'll salvage something. But I didna come down to Nithsdale to be a bluidy gauger in a dirty vennel in Dumfries. I came to be a farmer and to win my independence as a farmer. Eventually I ettled to be my own master here and to die here in the ripeness and fullness o' time. That was the hope, Willie: that was the dream. But a poet's dream—and as such fit only to be shattered."

"You're takin' it ower sair, Robert."

"Dinna mistake me. I'm no' pitying mysel'. It's the way things had to be."

"But man, if you win through to be a Supervisor o' the Excise——"

"It'll still be the Excise. . . A man canna leave a supervisorship to his eldest son. But wi' a farm a man can work away wi' his family working wi' him and about him. There's a satisfaction about that. . . But to hell, Willie, what's the use o' regrets and what's the use o' mournin'. Come on: I'll ride back to John Bacon's wi' you. MacMurdo said he'd look in the nicht and hear how I got on wi' my sale—and I could dae wi' a change o' scene."

"You could dae waur, Robert. But mind you: you havena had a fair crack o' the whip—or ocht like it. I ken how you feel. It's a pity it had to end this way. Aye: a damned pity."

It was a long weary drag putting in the long weeks till the 11th of November, more wearisome for Jean and Nancy and Fanny. The Bard at least had the interest as well as the distraction of his work in Dumfries.

"Little did I think," said Nancy to Jean, " when I cam' here nearly three years ago that this wad be the upshot!"

"Nae mair nor me, Nancy. But truth to tell, Rab was never sure o' the place frae the day he took it. He kent it wad dae weel enough eventually; but he aey doubted that he'd hae enough money to weather him through the lean years. And yet, Nancy, there were mony happy days here too."

"Aye—that's true. There was mony a blink o' cheery sunshine. Mind you: I'll miss you a'."

"I'll miss you too, Nancy. We've aey got on weel enough."

"And I'll miss the company. There's damn few folk ever come about Mossgiel—but there was aey somebody ca'ing on Robin and I suppose it'll be the same in Dumfries—only you'll no' hae the same room there."

"No. . . I canna say I'm looking forward to biding up a stair in Dumfries. . . I'll miss the open door and it'll no' be handy wi' the bairns."

"I dinna like the sound o' the house Robin's gotten."

"It's a' he can get—and he's lucky to get it. But Rab thinks it'll only be for a wee while. If he gets this promotion he's set on, then he'll be transferred out o' Dumfries a'thegither. He seems to hae a notion o' Greenock or Port Glasgow—or somewhaur North."

"He'd be better awa' out o' Dumfries if you ask me. Frae a' I can hear it's a gey drunken hole!"

"And here's you and me and we've never been in it yet!"

"We're only women, Jean. You can say what you like but the men hae the best o' it."

"Whiles—and whiles no'. And for a' that I wouldna change places. And I never was the jaunting kind."

"And I never got time for jaunting. This is the biggest jaunt I've ever had. Ach weel: there's nae guid o' grumblin': it comes to the same in the hinderend. I dinna suppose you'll hae Fanny long wi' you?"

"No: they're thinking o' getting married gin the spring. Adam's going back to Machlin. I'll miss Fanny as weel. . ."

"Oh, a guid lass Fanny, and she'll mak' a guid wife to your Adam. Everything seems to be breaking up. It's like a death in a family—ane goes and then there's aey twa or three follow."

"Tuts, Nancy: you mauna talk like that. What's for us'll no' gae by us—but we mauna look for the worst to happen."

"Whaur the Burnses are concerned it's generally the worst that happens—you ken that as weel as me!"

"Fiddlesticks! A' families hae their ups and their doons."

"It's been a' doons as far as we're concerned——"

"You're an affa lassie, Nancy. If I didna ken you I'd get worried at times. Rab and you hae a lot in common."

"Ah weel: there's a gey lot we haena got in common—Lord be thankit. But did you ever see rain like that?"

Mossgiel was exposed to all the blasts and rains and storms that swept across Kyle or came roaring in from the Atlantic; but it seldom rained there as it did in Nithsdale. Gathering about the hills it came sweeping down the valley in long driving waves of thin grey water. And on the instant it did the burns rose in their wrath and the Nith changed colour and began to roar in its boulder bed and rise and swell and swirl; and down would come branches and logs and all manner of debris and decaying carcases of dogs and sheep and cattle. . .

Thus it would rain for days and the Nith would grow more sullen and swollen and muddy with brown earth and red earth and prove a constant menace to all low-lying ground including the Green and the White Sands in Dumfries itself. . . On such a flood Willie Nicol's guid grey mare had floated to her Solway grave. . .

And ever the dampness rose around Ellisland farm-house, seeped into its foundations and crept up its walls so that only at the chimney-lug was it dry and warm and comfortable.

Jean sat by the fire and listened to the drumming rain and the squalling wind and the dull anger of the Nith. And first she fed Willie and then she fed Betty and then she happed them in the twin cradle and, crooning softly to the bairns and herself, rocked the cradle with her foot till sleep claimed them.

The outside world could wag as was its wont: she had her work to do and her family to nurse. Nancy had no husband to worry about and no children to tie her to the kitchen and the fireside. So Nancy took a moment's leisure at the window and watched the rain and the gathering darkness—and fretted. She had no desire to go back home to Mossgiel. Jean Brecken-ridge might be all right but she could never be a Jean Armour.

It took three carts to remove them to Dumfries. Adam Armour came over from Dalswinton to help with the flitting —and to be beside Fanny.

It was a Friday and the day was dull but dry. The family occupied the first cart together with some personal belongings. A fat young quey that Jean had a fancy for followed the cart. Adam with the follower brought up the rear. . .

The Bard went through the empty house to see that nothing was left behind—he had already examined the out-buildings. It was the first house he had ever had and it had been built as much to his wishes as Boyd had found possible. And now it was empty and bare—and dead: as irrevocably dead as only death can be. His steps rang on the flag-stones and the doors came to with an empty clap. He raked out the dying fire in a shower of fine grey ash.

Then he turned to the window and remembered he had written lines on the glass with Glencairn's diamond pencil. John Morine would never show these lines to his friends and laugh and sneer at the poet who had been a farmer. He drew his riding crop from the leg of his boot and smashed out the panes with the butt.

He swallowed his bitterness and went out, took the horse's head and led it out of the court. He would need to set the pace for it would be early dark and it was six long miles to Dumfries.

Six long and dreary miles and every step taking him farther and farther away from the life he had known since boyhood, the life of a poor tenant-farmer and the never-ending struggle against hungry ruin.

Whatever the future held, that life was finished now and forever. True enough he was now but a common gauger heading for a stinking vennel in a county town. He had come to Ellisland, brave-hearted and full of hope, utterly alone and without a friend or the comfort of a kent face. He had friends enough now; and he was no longer alone. The cart he led carried a fair load of care and responsibility.

Again he swallowed on the sour distaste of bitterness and urged the horse to the long hard road.

THE END